W9-BRU-878

# Distant Echoes

## Judie Aitken

**B**

**BERKLEY SENSATION, NEW YORK**

This is a work of fiction. Names, characters, places, and incidents either are the product of the author's imagination or are used fictitiously, and any resemblance to actual persons, living or dead, business establishments, events, or locales is entirely coincidental.

## DISTANT ECHOES

A Berkley Sensation Book / published by arrangement with the author

PRINTING HISTORY
Berkley Sensation edition / September 2003

Copyright © 2003 by Judie Aitken
Cover design by Elaine Groh
Text design by Kristin del Rosario

ISBN: 0-425-19211-3

A BERKLEY SENSATION™ BOOK
Berkley Sensation Books are published by The Berkley Publishing Group,
a division of Penguin Group (USA) Inc.,
375 Hudson Street, New York, New York 10014.
BERKLEY SENSATION and the "B" design
are trademarks belonging to Penguin Group (USA) Inc.

PRINTED IN THE UNITED STATES OF AMERICA

10  9  8  7  6  5  4  3  2  1

For the thousands of American Indians, both in the United States and Canada, who as children and young men and women were part of the off-reservation Indian school experience.

For Evelyne Wahkinney Voelker, a proud and beautiful Comanche lady who survived her own years at Indian school. Living far from her Comanche home and people, she proudly kept the traditions and the language alive. When we see a red bird fly, when we hear her favorite songs, and when we think of someone who loved and honored her heritage, we will think of you, *Piah*.

# AUTHOR'S NOTE

DuBois Indian Industrial School is a figment of my imagination—a mixture of the best and the worst of the off-reservation Indian schools that did exist. This story is also a work of fiction, but some of the events told actually happened at many of the schools. My intent is not to sway anyone's opinion or lecture about the right or wrong of these institutions. My intent is to write a story that touches your heart.

Few tribes can be named that did not have someone at Carlisle, Hampton, Red Cloud, Riverside, Carcross, Spanish, Shingawauk, or any of the other institutions in both the United States and Canada. With the initiative for these schools beginning as a part of Manifest Destiny and lingering through to the twentieth century, not all were bad . . . not all were good . . . but all left their mark.

I am so very grateful to those individuals who graciously helped me glean information for this book: Barbara Landis, Carlisle Indian Industrial School, for sharing weekly newsletters from the archives; my beloved *Piah* for sharing her own experiences and who left us much too soon; and once again Earl C. Fenner, who lets me make withdrawals from his bank of knowledge and from his enticing bookshelves. Heartfelt thanks to Linda Kruger, who makes having an agent totally delicious. Many thanks also to Roxa, Faith, Peggy, Alicia, and Jenna, you all know why. *Oodah.*

I am delighted that I'm able to take you on a slide through time with Jesse and Kathleen. I hope you enjoy the journey.

Judie Aitken
http://www.judieaitken.com

# Chapter 1

"COME ON, HORSE. How long are you gonna sit and stare at it?" Norville "Tooter" Poolaw leaned forward in his chair and tapped his index finger on the desktop. "Open it. Hurry up, will ya?"

Jesse Spotted Horse ignored his friend's impatience and continued to stare at the white envelope that lay on the desk in front of him. The envelope had arrived in the morning mail stacked between a three-page invoice for film, a renewal for a magazine subscription, and a flyer with coupons for great deals on stuffed-crust pizzas from Papa Bopo's PizzaRama. He'd known that its arrival was imminent. It was the contents that held the mystery.

Jesse had sweated out the weeks and days since he'd submitted the grant application for his film project. He'd asked the foundation for a lot of money, and now that their answer lay before him, his nerves zinged with uncertainty. He drew a deep, yet ragged breath and placed both of his hands over the envelope, covering it from corner to corner. "Give me a minute."

"Bite the bullet, Horse. Just open the damned thing, will ya?" Tooter quickly rose from his chair, sending the wooden legs skidding loudly across the linoleum floor. "You're drivin' me crazy." He paced back and forth. "I've got a stake in this, too, you know. Come on. Open it."

Jesse closed his eyes and caressed the white paper. His stomach tightened into a hard knot, and dry cotton seemed to fill every corner of his mouth. Every hope, every dream, every promise he'd made rested on the contents. What if the grant hadn't been approved? What if it had?

He moved his fingers over the paper as though he were reading a page of Braille. He touched the edges of the stamp in the upper right corner then slid his fingers to the embossed return address in the upper left. The sharp raised outline of the letters and the logo were unmistakable—the Brookstone Foundation for the Arts.

"Well, Karnak the Magnificent, now that you've tuned into your karmic vibes, what does your swami soul tell you? Did we get the money?"

Jesse quickly looked up at Tooter. "Did you see me open it yet? Are all you Kiowas so damned impatient?"

Tooter drove his fisted hands into the pockets of his jeans and stopped pacing. "I swear, Horse, if you don't open that envelope right now, I'm gonna come over the top of the desk, rip it outta your hands, and do it myself."

No matter how long he waited, Jesse knew the answer from the Brookstone Foundation wouldn't change. There was no point prolonging the agony. He tried to ignore the knot in his stomach that twisted with a cruel jerk as he picked up the envelope. He tore off one end, tipped it, and watched the contents spill out onto his desk. A pale green piece of paper peeked out from under the edge of the folded pages.

A check?

He struggled to remain calm and forced himself to take a deep breath. He could make out a portion of the Brookstone Foundation's distinct watermark on the corner of the green piece of paper. It *was* a check. And a check meant only one thing: His grant application had been approved. But for how much?

Jesse reached for the foam cup on his desk. Coffee. He needed a boost of caffeine. He took a deep draught, but when he tried to swallow, it felt as though his rapidly beating heart had wedged in his throat. *Quit being a coward.*

*Turn the check over. Look at the damn numbers. It's what you've been waiting for all of your life.*

He stretched his fingers toward the green slip of paper and drew it closer.

"Sometime today would be good," Tooter goaded.

"Okay!" Jesse snatched the check up and quickly read the amount. Then, not believing what he'd seen, he read it again. In an instant he felt the knot in his stomach unwind like a loosened spring, pushing enough adrenaline throughout his body to leave a thrilling heat in its wake. In the rush of elation his voice was little more than an astounded whisper. "We got it."

Tooter bent over the desk. "How much? How much did they give us?"

Jesse scanned the printed numbers on the check one more time just in case he'd read it wrong the first two times. He hadn't. "They gave us the full amount." Nearly breathless, he fell back in his chair, the check clutched in his hand. "Damn. They gave us the full two million, five-hundred thousand."

Tooter punched the air with his fist, gave a wild whoop that would have made his Kiowa ancestors proud, and did a quick victory dance around Jesse's office. He suddenly stopped and held out his hand. "Give it here. Let me hold it." He gave a quick "come here" gesture with his fingers. "Come on, come on . . . just let me touch it."

Tooter plucked the check from Jesse's fingers and, wide-eyed, stared at the oblong piece of paper. "Man, oh, man . . . I've never seen so many numbers on one piece of paper in my life. It's as long as my Social Security number." He lifted the check to his nose and drew a deep breath. "Gawd . . . it even smells good." He grinned, then thrust the check back at Jesse. "Here, take a whiff, Horse. Next to a hot, sexy woman, it's the best damn thing I've ever smelled in my life!"

Tooter's expression sobered and he dropped back into his chair. He leaned forward, resting his forearms on his knees, and looked up at Jesse. "Holy crap, this is really gonna happen, isn't it, Horse? There's no dreaming about it anymore . . . no wishful thinking, no more beatin' on doors for financing and gettin' turned down. No more stayin' up all night long and talking about the *what-if*s." He paused for a moment, lowering his head. After a deep sigh he looked up at Jesse. "We've got the *what-if*s right there." He pointed at the check. "We're really gonna do it, Horse. We're really gonna do it." He shook his head. "I never thought I'd see the day." He slapped his knee with his palm. "Damn, there's a ton of stuff to do." He began counting items off on his fingers. "We gotta hire a crew, get all the equipment together, order film, rent a studio, get the permits, the site, the costumes, hotel rooms, a caterer, cast, editing equipment, and we gotta quit our jobs, get a . . ."

Jesse held up his hand. "Whoa. Slow down, *kola*. I'm way ahead of you." He pulled three thick folders from his file drawer and plopped them down on the desktop beside the letter from the foundation. He glanced at Tooter, touched by the sheen of unshed tears that filled his friend's dark eyes. "I've narrowed everything down, got the bids, and I've decided who I want to work with. I've even lined up a few of the actors for the live shots." He tapped the folders with the tips of his fingers. "I've got a tentative yes on the narration from Graham Green, and all it's going to take now are a few phone calls."

"Well, let's make 'em." Tooter pulled a red calico handkerchief from the pocket of his jeans, gave a loud sniffle, then wiped his nose. "You did it, man. Jesse Spotted Horse, you got your dream. You're gonna do your documentary . . . just like you promised Grandma Boo." Tooter blew his nose, the sound rivaling the air horn on an eighteen-wheeler. "I'm so darned proud of you, Horse." He raised the handkerchief to his nose, and the air horn blew again. "Man, they're gonna write about you in *Time* and *People*. I bet your film's gonna be seen on PBS, maybe even the History Channel." With a final sniffle, Tooter stuffed the handkerchief back into his pocket. "Know what? I bet that good-looking blonde on *Entertainment Tonight* is gonna want to interview you." Tooter pointed his index finger at Jesse. "And that documentary guru, that Ken Burns guy, he's gonna be real pissed that he didn't do this one first."

"This story isn't his to tell," Jesse said, looking at the photo of his grandmother on his desk. "It belongs to us . . . the ones whose people lived it."

"You are *Suŋgléska*, Spotted Horse, warrior for the people," Tooter proclaimed, striking his fisted hand over his heart. He then gave an apologetic shrug and lowered his head. "Sorry, I guess I kinda got carried away. There's nothin' worse than a Kiowa trying to talk Lakota." The room fell silent for a moment or two before Tooter took a quiet breath and spoke again, his voice filled with awe. "I bet you're gonna win another Emmy for this one, too." He looked up. "No . . . better'n that—you're gonna win the Academy Award." He slapped his knee with the flat of his hand. "Horse, you're gonna win a damned Oscar!" He left his chair and perched on the edge of Jesse's desk. Lifting his hands, he framed an imaginary movie screen with his fingers. "I can see it all now. Julia Roberts and Mel Gibson will read off the nominations, and then some busty babe named Megan or Cherie will carry out the envelope and one of the Oscars." Tooter barely stopped for a breath. "The place gets real quiet while Mel opens the envelope. He makes some smart-ass remark like he always does, then gives the envelope to Julia so she can read the winner's name. She'll say something like 'and the Oscar for Best Documentary of the Year goes to Jesse Spotted Horse for *Stolen Childhood, Stolen Culture: The Story of the Off-Reservation Indian Schools.*' " Tooter leaned over the desk and gave Jesse a playful punch on the shoulder. "Hell, man, you're gonna get to kiss Julia Roberts!"

Jesse shrugged but couldn't stop the good-feeling grin that broke wide on his mouth. Tooter sure could talk a blue streak. "Let's get the film done before you start having me pucker up for Julia or clearing shelves for awards. Okay?"

Jesse picked up the letter from the Brookstone Foundation, scanned the elegant letterhead, and silently thanked each board member for giving him his dream. He then carefully read every word of the letter congratulating him on being selected for a grant. On the second page he found the usual list of regulations that included instructions for him to file an annual report providing an accounting of how the funds were used. On the third page he was instructed to submit any changes he might make to the original grant application that he'd submitted . . . but there wasn't a damned chance of that ever happening.

He'd begun working on the idea for his film while still in high school and continued working on the plans, fine-tuning them, even doing a large portion of his research all through college. Most of his script was written, his overall cost figured out, his shooting sequence and storyboards were just about set, and now, thanks to Brookstone, he had the money to make it all happen. The truth about the off-reservation Indian schools of the late 1800s—Carlisle, Riverside, Haskell, Hampton, Spanish, DuBois, and all the others—would finally be told.

They wouldn't be the self-serving fabricated truths . . . the lies . . . told by the Bureau of Indian Affairs or the white man's history books. And they weren't going to be the stories of just the Lakota students. Almost every tribe had children who had been taken away to these schools, who had been subjected to the stripping away of their traditions. Those were the stories Jesse would tell.

Tooter glanced up at the clock. "Oops. Gotta go. I'm on late shift all this week, studio camera for the eleven o'clock news." He paused at the door. "Let me know when we're leaving so I can tell the boss to take my job and . . ." He gave the air an upward thrust with his fist.

After the door closed behind Tooter, Jesse sat quietly for a few minutes. His life had just drastically changed. For good or bad, he had no one to blame except himself. He'd set everything in motion from the time he was fifteen, and now, he had to confess, he was nervous. Nervous? Hell, he was *terrified*.

Did having your dream come true always feel like this?

He switched on his computer and, after waiting for it to boot up, clicked on the word processing program's icon and began to write his letter of resignation. He'd enjoyed working at KXBQ-TV for the past eight years. It had been a great ride. Two years ago he'd won an Emmy for his documentary on the inner-city gangs of Indian kids, and then he'd been promoted to chief film editor. That was quite a feat for a reservation-raised Indian kid. Tooter had even teased him for a week or two about finally becoming a chief.

Jesse glanced up and stared at the golden statuette on his bookcase and grinned. Who would have thought an orphaned Indian kid from Cold Creek Reservation could win an Emmy. That little winged lady holding the globe over her head had opened a lot of doors for him, and now she'd talked the Brookstone Foundation into opening their purse.

Yeah, no doubt about it, he'd miss the job and the people he worked with at the station. Being Indian in this city made it difficult enough under normal circumstances to get a job and keep it, but he'd made good friends and good professional contacts and he'd been accepted—not only for his expertise with film but also for himself. No one seemed to mind his long braids, beaded belt buckles, jeans, and cowboy boots. No one seemed to mind the tapes of powwow songs he liked to play on the small boom box in his studio while he worked. This was where he'd met Tooter. Yeah, he'd miss KXBQ, but he had the best reason for leaving.

JESSE PARKED HIS pickup next to the shabby two-bedroom government-built bungalow and cut the engine. Cold Creek Lakota Reserve had changed little since he was a child playing in the yard and riding his rusted-out, garbage-dump bicycle up and down the rutted dirt road. The kids he'd played with had now all gone their own ways. Some had moved away—Chicago, New York, wherever the jobs were, and others had stayed, married, and become part of life on the rez. Some had killed themselves with booze or drugs or bullets, and some had crossed the law and were scattered in federal prisons across the country. Few had been as lucky as he. Few had escaped to find success in the outside white world.

He gazed at the house and watched as two scruff-yellow dogs rose from their dirt dugouts beside the front stoop. With sullen glances in Jesse's direction, they trotted across the weed-riddled driveway to the side lot and disappeared in the tall grass behind the rusted remains of the blue Studebaker coupe.

Jesse couldn't remember when the Studebaker hadn't been there. It had belonged to his father, Carl. Jesse had been only a year old when his father's two-week leave after boot camp was over and he shipped out to Vietnam. Hell, the car had been old then. On that last day at home Carl had parked the Studebaker on the side lot, hung the keys on a nail in the kitchen, and told everyone that the car would stay there until he came home from Nam. The keys still hung in the kitchen. The Studebaker had never moved again.

Jesse rolled down his truck window and sat quietly for a minute or two. Down the street the laughter of children playing made Cold Creek sound like any urban community, but the fading light of late evening did little to disguise the poverty and despair of the reservation. This was where he grew up. This was where his mother had left him when she ran off to Rapid City and lost herself in drugs and alcohol and death. This is where Beulah Spotted Horse, his *uŋci,* his Grandma Boo, had raised him and sent him to school. And this is where he'd first heard the stories of the Indian schools. This is where he'd first heard about DuBois.

The old woman had told him about the years she had spent at an Indian school, had told him her parents' stories, and aunts' and uncles' stories. And then Grandma Boo had told him about *Tokalu Sapa,* Black Fox, her little uncle, who had been taken off to DuBois Indian School, somewhere in a place called Indiana, when he was nine years old. *Tokalu Sapa* had never come home.

Jesse had been no older than ten when he'd first promised his grandmother that he'd tell the truth about the schools to as many people as he could. He also promised the old woman that he would find out what had happened to *Tokalu Sapa.* Today, twenty-two years later, he was about to keep his promise . . . and it felt good, real good.

He slid from behind the steering wheel, grabbed the two bags of groceries from the pickup bed, and stepped up on the crumbling concrete stoop.

Damn the rules of the Brookstone grant. If he had to report it as monies spent for research, he would, but the first check written on that two million, five-hundred would be to fix some things around here for the old woman. He'd have the steps redone and fix the plumbing in the house. His grandmother deserved that and much, much more.

A pang of guilt gave his conscience a hard poke. She certainly deserved more than he'd offered in the last thirteen or so years since he'd left Cold Creek, gone off to college, and moved into his condo in Rapid City. Infrequent visits with a few sacks of groceries, Sunday phone calls, and cash sent in pretty greeting cards wasn't nearly enough. Certainly not enough for the woman who had raised him with love and encouragement, reassuring him that an orphaned Lakota boy raised on Cold Creek Lakota Reservation *was* allowed to have dreams.

Jesse paused at the door and noticed the cleverly woven red and blue thread that filled at least five or six holes in the worn screen. He could imagine the old woman dragging one of the ancient chrome kitchen chairs from the table to the door, settling herself down and patiently weaving her needle back and forth in the screen, determined to keep the flies and mosquitoes outside where they belonged.

Balancing one sack of groceries on top of the other, he pulled the door open and felt it list precariously on a loosened hinge. Grandma Boo was going to get a new storm door with glass for the winter and screens for the summer, too.

"'Bout time you showed your pretty face 'round here, boy."

Even as a kid he'd never been able to sneak up on her and catch her resting. If the old woman wasn't cooking or cleaning, she was fringing shawls for someone's giveaway at the next powwow or doing some pieces of beadwork for the tourist shops in town. Today was no exception. She stood at the kitchen table, wrist-deep in frybread dough, a dusting of flour stark white against the cherrywood tint of her arms.

After leaving the groceries on the countertop, Jesse wrapped his arms around her, hugged her, and placed a kiss on her age-creased forehead. "Don't you ever sit down and watch that TV?" He glanced at the new thirty-six-inch color set he'd bought her for Christmas.

The old woman snorted, gave her chin a quick lift, and pointed at the silent television with pursed lips. "Eee, that thing. Ain't nothin' on but wrestlin' and that Jerry guy from Chicago with them dumb folks on his show . . . them all sleepin' 'round and ruinin' their families." She wiped her dough-covered hands on her apron and gave a small harrumph. "All I gotta do is look out my window to see that kinda stuff going on 'round here." She glanced at the bubbling oil in the deep skillet on the stove. "It look hot enough to you?"

Without waiting for him to answer, she pinched off a pool ball–sized piece of dough, flattened it between the palms of her hands, poked a small hole in the middle, and dropped it into the hot fat. She cast a sidelong look at him, her dark eyes squinting behind the flour-dusted lenses of her glasses. "It ain't Saturday. Whatcha doing here in the middle of the week? You get fired?"

"Nope." He grinned, knowing the one-word answer that offered no explanation would aggravate her. He teased her further by prolonging his silence and reaching into the grease-stained paper sack on the countertop. He took out a golden piece of frybread.

As long as Jesse could remember, the kitchen smelled of frying grease, and there had always been a paper sack of frybread on the counter, its top rolled closed. Just about every home on the rez had a sack exactly like it in the kitchen. The old folks called them Indian bread boxes, and today Grandma Boo's bread box was almost filled with warm, freshly made frybread—enough for every meal for the next week.

"You keep taking this long to answer and I'm gonna be dead before I find out." Grandma Boo shook a long-handled pair of tongs at him, then turned and flipped over the piece of bread in the skillet.

Jesse bit into his piece of warm bread, enjoying the flavor that spread over his tongue. Around his mouthful, he finally gave his answer. "I quit my job."

• • •

"THE BOARD'S DECISION was unanimous, Kathleen."

As usual when he spoke to her, Richmond Brock's voice held a condescending tone. It always irritated Kathleen Prescott and set her nerves on edge. "Not quite, Richmond. *My* vote was a nay. I do not want this . . . this Jesse Spotted Horse and his cameras at DuBois."

Her gesture precise, expending no unnecessary movement, Kathleen tucked a loose strand of hair back into the tightly pinned twist at the nape of her neck. Her hand then traveled to the high collar of her blouse, where her fingers lightly grazed across the steep row of pearl buttons. Satisfied to find them all secure, she tipped her chin upward and defiantly met Richmond Brock's gaze.

Granted she stood alone with her vote, but how dare the board, and Richmond Brock, ignore it as though it didn't exist? They knew how much DuBois Indian School meant to her. Caring for the school museum and extensive archives wasn't just a job, it was her life, her inheritance. Kathleen's great-great-grandfather, the Reverend Providence Divine, had been the founder and first headmaster at DuBois. When he had died, her great-grandfather Elijah and then her grandfather Jacob had filled the office. Her father, Hamilton Prescott, had married Jacob Divine's only child, his daughter, Patience. When Jacob died, Hamilton had picked up the reins. And now she was the guardian.

In 1955, when the Indian school closed, Hamilton had seen the transition of some of the buildings from school to museum. The grounds and buildings were sold and became the very exclusive and very expensive DuBois Military Academy. An agreement added to the sale guaranteed the preservation of a small portion of the Indian school and the formation of a museum. Kathleen now served as the archivist and curator for the museum. It was a slim technicality, but she could boast that the line remained unbroken. A member of the Reverend Providence Divine's family still served DuBois.

"Kathleen, my dear," Richmond Brock said, easing back in the chair across from her desk. With his elbows resting on the chair arms, he opened his hands in counterfeit petition. "Forgive me. I should have said that the *majority* vote—"

"Yes, Richmond," Kathleen interrupted, "you should have." She drew a breath to further bolster her nerve, then continued. "I apologize that unlike the other board members, my position isn't due to social status or a large donation to the academy." Pausing, she tried to control her anger, and yet it flowed from her lips in another barrage of words. "Do you think I don't know that you all would like nothing better than to be rid of me? But since the academy's charter guarantees, in perpetuity, a seat for a descendant of Reverend Divine's . . . well, getting rid of me is quite impossible, isn't it?" Kathleen tightened her hand resting in her lap into a fist. Although she had every right to sit on the board, Richmond Brock always succeeded in making her feel like an intruder.

"Kathleen, I'm sorry you think we don't appreciate your services to DuBois Academy." Richmond Brock offered a toothy, insincere smile. "We all value your hard work and dedication, believe me."

Kathleen didn't believe Richmond Brock for a moment, and furthermore, she didn't like or trust the man. As a married man he stared too much and too long at women other than his wife, and Kathleen certainly didn't like the way he stared at her. Little Red Riding Hood's wolf could probably learn a thing or two from Richmond Brock.

She wished he would leave her office. In fact, she wished Richmond Brock would leave her life. He had made his point . . . her argument had failed. She'd been unable to sway the board. Perhaps if she looked too busy to talk with him further, he would go back to his own posh office in the academy's administration building. She reached for the stack of file folders on her desk and began to methodically position each one until they aligned perfectly with the edge of her desk. This job done, there was little else to do. She folded her hands in her lap and sat upright, her spine straight, her back not touching her chair.

Kathleen Divine Prescott preferred order and consistency in her life, and there wasn't the sliver of a doubt that her preference was about to be sorely challenged. Her family's legacy was going to be turned into a three-ring circus, and the Board of Directors of the DuBois Academy, all but one, approved of the fiasco. If it weren't impolite and thoroughly unladylike, she would have snorted with disgust. A movie production company . . . indeed.

Rising from behind the sanctuary of her desk, Kathleen moved to the window. She pushed the drapes aside and stood motionless except for the rise and fall of her breasts as she fought to steady each breath, fought for composure. Richmond Brock always made her feel uncomfortable, as though she were a meal and he a starving gourmand. Once more Kathleen involuntarily lifted her hand to her high-buttoned collar.

In the shaded corner of the windowpane she could see Brock's reflection. He now stood behind her, his expression eager as he waited for her surrender to the board's majority vote. The sigh that fled her lips spoke clearly of her resignation, but her heart and conscience were steadfast. She had little choice but to follow the board's decision, but nothing said she had to do it graciously.

Kathleen glanced away from Richmond Brock's reflection. She looked out over the well-manicured lawn that once had been the school's parade ground. The promenade, the original walkway that encircled the parade ground and led from building to building, still survived, as did its ash surface. But the original drive that led into the school from the main road and lay between the buildings and the promenade had been paved since 1956.

The bandstand, freshly painted, still stood at the south end of the parade ground, but little remained of the original structure. As old boards rotted, new boards took their place. Three of the school's original dormitories were gone as well. Fire had completely destroyed one in 1923. An outdoor basketball court now filled the space. Four years ago the other two dormitories had been torn down to make room for a new state-of-the-art gymnasium for the academy. The Jessop County Historical Society had not been pleased, but Richmond Brock's influence and a large donation had taken care of everything. The building that held her office had originally been the administration building, but now the school museum was housed on the first floor. Her apartment on the third floor was the same as when Providence Divine and his family lived there.

Kathleen's gaze swept across the rolling grassy slope to the tall stand of oaks and the large barn that stood in their shade. The original barn had burned in 1886, but the one that now stood in its stead was an accurate reproduction, right down to the hand-hammered wrought-iron latches and hinges. The bandstand, the barn, one of the dormitories, and the administration building which now held her office and apartment, made up the DuBois Indian School Museum and Library.

Gone were the Indian children for whom Providence Divine's plan was forged, the plan that would save them from their savage lives of filth and ignorance. In their place were the sons and daughters of very wealthy families who annually paid many thousands of dollars in tuition fees and donations to the DuBois Military Academy. Gone were the dark gray uniforms the Indian boys had worn. Gone were the high-collared white blouses and dark skirts that had been issued to the girls. Now students wore crisply tailored military-styled navy blue academy uniforms with their brightly polished rows of brass buttons.

Many changes had occurred over the years, some subtle, some drastic, but Kathleen didn't love the school and the grounds any less. In fact, she loved it more. Loved it not only because DuBois was part of who she was, but loved it because losing it inch by inch was the same as losing a loved one to a devastating, wasting disease.

"Is it all about money, Richmond?" Kathleen slowly turned away from the window and met Richmond Brock's eager gaze. "You keep shoving shrinking budgets under my nose, you demand that I lower operating expenses, surrender more space, increase admission charges and prices in the gift shop, and charge for information from our archives." She crossed her arms over her breasts as though the simple gesture offered her protection. "Is it about the money?"

Richmond Brock stepped closer. He reached out and

placed his hand on her arm. Kathleen allowed it to rest there for no more than a second before she stepped away.

"Kathleen, I can understand your reluctance to have this film company here. It's no secret that some believe, especially the Indians . . . the Native Americans . . . or whatever they're calling themselves now, that the Indian school system was . . . well . . . appalling." He raised his hand against her imminent protest. "Of course, I'm not saying that I agree."

He smiled his snake-oil-salesman smile again and moved his hand until it rested over his heart, as if the gesture would give sincerity and credence to his words. "But have you considered that this might be just what is needed to bring more tourists to your little museum, to help sway negative opinions . . . to create new interest in what's left of your wonderful school?" He paused again, the moment of silence adding cold authority to his next words. "The number of visitors *has* dropped off the past two summers." He turned, picked up his briefcase, and moved toward the door. "This year we had to supplement your budget with money from the academy." He glanced at her over his shoulder, his expression no longer patronizing but cold and cruel. "We can't keep doing that, Kathleen."

He stopped at the door, his hand resting on the antique brass knob. "Jesse Spotted Horse and his film crew will be arriving next week. I expect . . . uh . . . the board expects you to comply with the *majority* vote. Remember, this is a very important project for the academy as well." His gaze swept over her from head to toe and traveled slowly back up again. "And, yes, Kathleen, it *is* all about money."

# Chapter 2

Our views of the Indian's interests and not their own, ought to govern them.

—JOHN C. CALHOUN,
SECRETARY OF WAR, 1818

KATHLEEN HEARD THE light knock on her open office door and quickly finished adding the last column of her monthly financial report before looking up. Nothing prepared her for the vision that met her.

Tall, broad-shouldered, standing with his feet slightly apart, the silhouette of a man filled the open doorway. Startled, she drew a quick breath and dropped her pen.

"Miss Prescott?"

Two words, and yet the timbre of his voice was deep and rich like fine dark velvet. Her breath shallowed. Inadvertently her hand flew up to her collar. "Yes, I'm Kathleen Prescott."

He stepped farther into the room, stopping a few feet from her desk in a golden shaft of morning sunlight that shone through the window. The transition from dark to bright light was disconcerting. Kathleen quickly surmised that this man would be disconcerting in any light. She needed no introduction; she knew who her visitor was.

"I'm Jesse Spotted Horse. I expect Richmond Brock told you to expect me."

Tight, well-worn jeans clung to his hips and legs. A navy blue Henley shirt stretched over his broad shoulders and chest before disappearing behind an intricately beaded belt buckle and into his jeans. But it was the long, near-black braids that hung over his shoulders, the dark eyes, the high planes of his face, and the rich color of his skin that indicated his race and won Kathleen's reluctant admiration. Jesse Spotted Horse was the kind of man that would draw the attention of women of any age.

She slowly rose to her feet, thankful that her desk hid her trembling legs. Confrontations. She hated confrontations, but knew that this one was unavoidable. She'd bolstered herself for this moment ever since Richmond Brock had told her about the film. She just hoped she was ready.

"Mr. Spotted Horse, you're early. I didn't expect you until next week." He was much taller than she'd anticipated. Six feet and perhaps then some. He was also younger and more imposing than she'd imagined. More breathtaking than she'd expected. "We're not prepared for you yet."

Kathleen knew she certainly wasn't prepared for Jesse Spotted Horse. She held her hands behind her back, the fingers of her left nervously grasping and twisting the fingers of her right.

"My partner and our camera crew won't arrive until next Wednesday." A friendly smile moved his lips. "I came early to get some last-minute research done and hire a few extras for our crew and cast." He stepped closer. His smile broadened and he held out his hand. "It's very nice to meet you, Miss Prescott. How'd you like to be in my movie?"

She glanced down at his hand and hesitated a moment before taking it. She allowed the touch to be brief, just long enough to fulfill the terms of good etiquette. "No, Mr. Spotted Horse, I most certainly would not like to be in your movie. And, before you get too settled here, there is something else I think you should know." She straightened her shoulders and added a defiant upward tilt to her chin that caused her wire-rimmed glasses to slide lower on her nose. "I am strongly opposed to your film, and if it were up to me, you would not be here at DuBois."

Kathleen anticipated an angry response. None surfaced. What did appear was what she could only classify as another smile—neither full-blown nor smug. Indulgent, perhaps.

Jesse Spotted Horse casually hooked his thumb in the

pocket of his jeans. "Would you care to tell me what you have against my film?" Without being invited, he eased himself into one of the chairs in front of her desk.

Taken aback by how quickly he had made himself comfortable, Kathleen slowly sank to her chair. Resigned to the unpleasant conversation that lay ahead, she was thankful to be behind her desk, thankful for the safe distance and barrier that it offered. She soon discovered that Jesse Spotted Horse was just as imposing sitting in a chair as he was standing.

What did she have against his film? His question was fair and her answer came easy. Everything. Perhaps Jesse Spotted Horse needed to be reminded of the illustrious history of the DuBois Indian School, and be reminded of who her family was. Perhaps he needed to be reminded of the good works that were done for his people—all Indian people—at DuBois. Perhaps that would tell him exactly what she had against his film, his film of lies.

"Mr. Spotted Horse, my great-great-grandfather, the Reverend Providence Divine, founded DuBois." She placed her hands on the desktop and folded one over the other, hoping the simple act would stop their shaking. "He named the school after his mother, Lydia. DuBois was her maiden name. The land on which the school was built had been in her family for many years." Nervous tension tightened the muscles across her shoulders, and she felt the beginning of a headache. This was the same dialogue she used with the tourists. They always seemed to be interested, but there had been no change in the impassive expression of Jesse Spotted Horse's face. Maybe she should try to be a little more agreeable. "Forgive my levity, but it has been said that a *Divine* presence has been at the school ever since."

A sick, sinking feeling immediately hit her stomach. The well-practiced line usually received a polite laugh or at least a smile from the tourists. Jesse Spotted Horse obviously wasn't a tourist. There hadn't even been a slight twitch to his lips. Embarrassed, Kathleen promised herself two things: She would never use that ridiculous phrase again, and she wouldn't back down from Jesse Spotted Horse.

"Why is it so important that you make your film at DuBois?" she asked. "Surely there are other school sites that would serve your purpose just as well, if not better." She watched him give a slight shrug.

"I considered a couple of others, Carlisle, Hampton, even Red Cloud," he said. "Most people know about those, but I wanted them to know there were others, especially in the Midwest—the heartland of America." He glanced around the room, his gaze stopping momentarily at each of the old photos on the wall before returning to meet Kathleen. "Besides, Miss Prescott, I have a personal interest in DuBois."

A moment or two passed, an uncomfortable silence growing while she waited for him to explain his last statement. He didn't.

When she'd learned Jesse Spotted Horse was going to be making the film, she had checked the student enrollment records. It stood to reason that perhaps he had a relative who had been at DuBois. The name Spotted Horse wasn't on any of the enrollment lists. She wouldn't ask him outright what he'd meant, either. It wasn't, after all, polite to pry.

"I took a short walk around the grounds before I came to your office. I'm impressed with how well the buildings and grounds have been cared for," Jesse said. "It looks as though little has changed, except the Indian kids aren't here any longer to do the work."

She chose to ignore his jab while meeting his dark gaze. "The maintenance staff employed by the academy also takes care of the museum's buildings and grounds. It is part of the agreement my father made when the property was sold and became DuBois Military Academy." She took a quick breath, wondering why Jesse Spotted Horse unnerved her so much. She'd faced this kind of defiance before. It wasn't uncommon for families of former students to make unsubstantiated accusations about how poorly their relatives had been treated while at the Indian schools.

"I bet there's a real big difference between the teaching and guardianship of the two schools, too."

Another jab. Kathleen knew if she didn't set firm

ground rules now, there was no telling what kind of lies Jesse Spotted Horse's film would lead the public to believe about the school and her family. She collected her frayed nerves. "I've met people like you before, Mr. Spotted Horse."

"Are you referring to the fact that I'm a filmmaker or that I'm an Indian?" He casually crossed his legs, left over right, and appeared to settle in for the skirmish.

Was he insinuating that she was a bigot? The atrocious gall of the man! "Neither," she replied testily. "I only meant that I have met people like you who want to denigrate both the good works done by the Indian schools and the people who selflessly gave their lives over to the caring and education of the Indian students."

"Such as your ancestors did?"

"Exactly." The spark of sarcasm in his words didn't surprise her. The gauntlet had been thrown down. "I can understand your position. I also understand that many Indian people didn't appreciate the schools or the opportunities and education they offered."

"Miss Prescott, unless you were Indian and forced to attend one of these hellholes, you couldn't possibly *understand* anything."

She bristled. How dare this man walk in here and not only insult her, but everyone and everything she loved and believed in? "Well, Mr. Spotted Horse, I *fully understand* the hard work people such as my family did in improving the lives and the welfare of the Indians. And I believe your description of the schools as 'hellholes' is inaccurate and totally uncalled for."

Kathleen watched Jesse Spotted Horse quickly sit forward and she found herself just as quickly moving away, her retreat stopped by the back of her chair.

"What would you know about what DuBois and the other institutions did to their students?"

"Of course I would know. DuBois has been in my family since its inception. This school is my family's legacy. I was born and raised on these grounds. I have spent my entire life studying my great-great-grandfather's journals, and those of my great-grandfather and grandfather." She took a

quick breath before continuing. "The journals hold the accurate history of the school. I've read the account books
showing every penny that was spent, I've read all the corre-
spondence, the students' enrollment records—"

"All written by whites who were dependent on receiving
government funding."

"Are you inferring some impropriety existed, Mr. Spotted Horse?" she sniffed. "If so, I can assure you that my
great-great-grandfather was a man of God who . . ."

"Ah, yes. An upstanding, respected, and believable
source."

Indignant, Kathleen replied, "There were also the
newsletters that were written and published weekly by the
students and sent to the patrons of the school."

"The propaganda. I've read some of those pieces of fiction," Jesse said. "Heavily edited by the school officials, no
doubt."

How far would this man go to anger her? She fought
back the bitter words that formed in her mind and battled to
hold her tongue in check. "Of course the newsletters were
edited by staff members, but the articles reflected the students' thoughts and words and ideas." She knew her complexion had flushed. She could feel the heat on her neck
and cheeks. "The newsletters, journals, and school archives
hold the entire history of this school. I've read it from top
to bottom, studied the archives. I know everything about
DuBois."

"Really? Is that so?" Jesse Spotted Horse settled back in
his chair, rested his elbows on the armrests, and steepled
his fingers under his chin. He stared at her, his dark eyes
unrelenting. A moment or two slid by. "Well, good. Perhaps
you can tell me where my grandmother's uncle is?"

"Pardon me?" She leaned forward, startled by his question. "What did you say?"

"*Tokalu Sapa*, Black Fox, was brought here when he
was nine years old. He'd been yanked out of my great-
grandmother's arms by Albert McCrimmen, the Indian
agent at Cold Creek Reservation."

"I hardly think he was yanked from her arms, Mr. Spotted Horse. Besides, there was good reason that—"

"What possible good reason could there be to take a child from his home, from his mother? None. Absolutely none." He drew a ragged breath. "The boy was taken from our reservation and put on a train headed for DuBois with seventeen other boys and girls from Cold Creek." Jesse Spotted Horse turned and looked again at the photos on the wall. "The boy was stolen from his mother's arms, just like every one of those kids."

"Stolen? No. I sincerely doubt that," Kathleen countered, shaking her head, unnerved by the calm, quiet sound of his voice. "I know that the Indian agents occasionally met with some resistance when they went to collect the children, but they never stole them or used force to take them. Why would they have to?" A slight uplift of her hand punctuated her question. "It was a well-known fact that DuBois and the other schools offered endless opportunities for these children." She squared her shoulders. "They were taken away from squalor and poverty and were educated in skills that would benefit everyone in their tribes: reading, mathematics, home economics, skilled trades. Besides, it's a known fact that many of the tribes volunteered to have their children taken to the schools for an education."

"Really? Then your meaning of *volunteer* and mine are obviously quite different. The word *hostage* comes to my mind."

A very unladylike snort became part of Kathleen's response. "If that is so, then why did some of the tribal chiefs insist on sending their own older children to get an education?" She couldn't remember ever being this angry; even Richmond Brock had never riled her this much.

Jesse Spotted Horse glanced beyond Kathleen and out the office window. "It was called 'taking care of your own people.' Sometimes a spy in the enemy's camp is a good thing to have." He turned back to her. "I don't know how much of an education *Tokalu Sapa* had in the time he was here. My grandma's mother received only one note from him about a year after he'd been taken, but I don't think they believed he'd written it. What ten-year-old would use phrases such as 'I am absolutely delighted' and 'Worry not, Mother dear,' especially some wild little Indian kid?"

His sarcasm was not lost on her. "I'm sure a teacher would have helped him write his—"

"Oh, I'm sure, too, but where was this teacher's compassionate talent for writing notes to the family when the boy disappeared or died?"

An uncomfortable silence followed Jesse's claim, expanding and filling every corner of the room, before he continued. "Do your school records mention that his family never heard from him again?" He waited, but she didn't answer. "No, I didn't think so." He stood, and placing both hands flat on the edge of Kathleen's desk, leaned over her. "What happened to *Tokalu Sapa*? Why didn't he ever come home?"

Kathleen recoiled. With a nervous tremor, her hand flew to her throat and covered the high collar of her blouse. "*Tokalu Sapa* . . . he would have been given a Christian name, from the Bible, of course. If you know what it was, I'll gladly go through the archives and get that information for you."

Jesse watched Kathleen Prescott fidget with the buttons on her collar, and then he pushed back from her desk and turned away. "Don't bother."

Her obvious discomfort made him regret his anger, but he'd held on to it for too long. Making it go away wasn't going to be easy. "You won't find anything in your damn records, and you know it." He sat down again in the chair across from her, leaned back, and tried to find some hint of regret or remorse in Kathleen Prescott's face. He didn't see any. "Miss Prescott, how many headstones in the school's cemetery are marked 'Indian Child—Unknown'?"

Jesse already knew the answer to the question. He didn't need to hear the number from Kathleen Prescott. There were seven such grave markers at DuBois. Seven Indian kids had died in the jumble of the white man's bureaucracy. Seven kids had meant so little to the self-appointed guardians and do-gooders that they'd been buried without their own names.

He watched Kathleen Prescott glance away, her face flushed with what . . . unease? Shame? Finally. And shamed she should be, as should have been the whole damned lot of them, from Providence Divine on down.

Jesse knew he'd come down hard on her, perhaps harder than he should have, but the prim and uptight little lady needed to be jarred out of her blind-eyed, distorted view of the truth. Shoving his conscience aside, he pressed on. "Richmond Brock assured me that I would have your complete cooperation. Can I count on that?"

Her posture stiffened. "Mr. Spotted Horse, I assure you, Mr. Brock and I have already had this discussion." Looking up, she met his gaze. "I didn't enjoy it then, either."

Jesse wondered how much longer the dam that held her emotions would hold before it burst. He pushed against it again. "I'd like to begin my work today. I need to look through the archives, the photos and papers from 1880 through to the school's closing."

"Oh, is that all?" Ice coated each word.

"I'd also like to have access to some of the entries from your family's journals, if that can be arranged. It would help to show your family's and the school's opinions about Indian education. Of course I would pay for the opportunity."

She seemed to consider his suggestion, and he saw her shoulders relax a fraction. Money always helped to sway someone's decision.

"I think that would certainly add accurate information to your film. You will see for yourself the dedication my family had and the good they did." She took a moment to resettle a loose hairpin in the tight roll of hair at her nape.

Jesse realized that the word *prim* barely described Miss Kathleen Prescott. Her white high-necked, long-sleeved blouse, dark skirt, and scraped-back hair gave her a severe old-maid schoolmarm look. He would also bet every dollar in his pocket that her shoes were flat-heeled and clunky, and were what she would refer to as being "sensible." She even spoke prudishly, her choice of words professorial, as though common words and phrases were beneath her. Kathleen Prescott was pricklier than a patch of wild prairie cactus.

There were also things about Kathleen Prescott that he

hadn't expected. Younger than he'd anticipated, she appeared to be a delicate woman, small, her gray eyes almost too large for her face, her hands finely boned.

The clothes she wore seemed to have been chosen to deliberately mask every trace of her youth and her femininity. But a few tender morsels survived. The crisp white fabric of her blouse accentuated the pleasing slope of her breasts and the high collar defined a graceful neck and a determined yet charming jawline and chin. Sunlight from the window gave sheen to the bright highlights of burnished copper in her dark brown hair. Jesse tried to imagine what she would look like without it being harshly pulled back from her face and pinned into that tight coil at the back of her head.

Surely there had to be a warm human being, a soft, gentle woman somewhere beneath her bristly exterior. He needed to find that human being because he certainly didn't want to spend the next two months battling with Kathleen Prescott. Okay, he'd admit that maybe he'd started the clash, and if not, then he certainly was responsible for keeping it going. She'd given back as good as she'd received, but he still felt a twinge of guilt. After all, he was the intruder in her world, and although she perpetuated the Divine myth, it wasn't fair to hold her responsible for what her ancestors had done. She didn't deserve his attack. He offered an apologetic smile. "Look, I'm sorry. It seems we've gotten off to a bad start. I hope, well . . . I'd rather not start this venture at odds with you."

The tight-lipped, judgmental expression didn't leave her face. His apology had apparently done nothing to soften her opinion. Jesse gave a slight, regret-filled shake of his head. No doubt about it, he was in for a long two months.

"I am usually occupied in the mornings with my administrative duties." She pointed toward the file folders stacked at the corner of her desk. "Our tours for the visitors are held in the early afternoon. If you could limit your exploration of our files to an hour or so in the late afternoons, I suppose I could set time aside to accommodate you."

Her eyes were cold and stormy with anger, and Jesse couldn't help but wonder if they had ever been smoky and dark with passion. He doubted it. Her mouth . . . ah, now there was another story entirely. Definitely a surprise. Full and lush; and there was little that Miss Prim could do to change or hide that fact. She wore no lipstick, but her lips had a natural pink hue. They didn't need artificial coloring. On another woman that mouth would have been very enticing and have a man thinking all sorts of thoughts that would raise more than his libido. On Kathleen Prescott that mouth seemed . . . wasted.

Maybe if she made some attempts with makeup or a new hairdo, maybe she could be somewhat attractive. It was a big maybe, though. Of course, the formidable expression on her face would have to go as well.

He tugged his thoughts away from his critical assessment and back to the battle at hand. "The reason I came early was to get more than an hour or two a day of research time. I don't need your undivided attention. You can leave me alone in the archives. I'll find what I'm looking for."

She rose to her feet and clasped her hands together at her waist. The defiant tilt of her chin was back. "That would be quite impossible, Mr. Spotted Horse. No one other than a Divine, my father, or myself, has ever had unsupervised access to the records."

Jesse stood. "Then, Ms. Prescott, I guess you're going to have to supervise me."

# Chapter 3

... the Sioux were selected on the principle of taking the most pains with those who give the most trouble.

—RICHARD H. PRATT,
CARLISLE INDIAN INDUSTRIAL SCHOOL, 1878

KATHLEEN STRETCHED UPWARD. Standing tiptoe on the stepladder, she withdrew a green file box from the top shelf, then gingerly stepped down to the floor. "I hope this won't take much longer." She set the box on the table in front of Jesse. "I've already taken too much time away from my duties."

"I've appreciated all your help," Jesse replied, pulling his chair closer to the table. When she'd stepped up on the ladder, he'd noticed how the material of her blouse had stretched over her breasts, and he'd seen the trim ankles and calves that her rising skirt had shown. He'd been wrong. Somewhere under the cold exterior, whether Kathleen Prescott wanted it to show or not, there was an attractive woman. *Get a grip, Horse, get a grip.* "You've been a great help. I'm sure the film will be much better because of you."

Her arched left brow gave silent proof of her doubt. "Mr. Spotted Horse, I haven't changed my mind about your film. If my helping you runs the risk of improving your movie, then I'm sadly defeating my own purpose. Your film is nothing less than an attack on my family's honor and good name."

"No, my film is about telling the truth. The Brookstone Foundation appreciated that, I was hoping you could, too."

He immediately regretted the tone of his reply. Kathleen Prescott looked as though he'd just slapped her. Damn it, he couldn't find solid footing with this woman at all. One moment he wanted to strangle her, the next he was looking at her ankles and breasts, and then a second later he was back to thinking about throttling her again. He didn't want this debate to keep rearing up between them, over and over. Some common ground had to be found, and soon. "By the way, it's Jesse."

"Excuse me?"

"My name. Jesse. Please, call me Jesse." He casually shrugged, then added a smile. "Just think of all the time you'll save by not calling me Mr. Spotted Horse. That must take about a second or so to say. If you add up every time—"

"Our relationship is strictly professional," Kathleen interrupted. "Calling you Mr. Spotted Horse is proper."

"I suppose it is, but if we're going to keep spending time together, this is how it should work," he cajoled. "You call me Jesse and I'll call you Katie-girl."

"You most definitely will not call me Katie-girl." She stiffened and gave a very unladylike snort. "That is asinine."

"Okay, okay." Jesse lifted his hands, a smile quirking the corner of his mouth. "For now I'll call you Kathleen, but I warn you, somewhere in the middle of all this we'll become friends, and when we do, I'll probably call you Katie-girl . . . once in a while." Seeing the pinched expression on her face, he added, "We can be friends, can't we?"

"I am here *only* at Richmond Brock's directive. There is, Mr. Spotted Horse, absolutely nothing friendly about that."

"Ah, but there could be, Kathleen." His voice softened and he gave her a wink. "There certainly could be."

Her eyebrow took another quick climb and a bright shade of pink tinted her cheeks before she lowered her gaze.

*My god, I've made her blush.* Jesse's guilt factor jumped up a notch, but it didn't stop him from wondering how far down that blush went beneath her starched high-collared blouse.

Kathleen fussed with the lid of the file box. "I think *you* should get back to work and stop wasting my time."

"You do, do you? Well, then, I guess I'd better." Jesse chuckled then looked down at the box. There wasn't a speck of dust on the green lid. A quick glance told him there wasn't any dust on the other three file boxes on the table, either. Now that he thought about it, he hadn't seen dust anywhere in Kathleen Prescott's world. She kept her legacy pristine and void of any of life's intrusions. Nothing she had said or done in the past few days had made the true and sad essence of her life more obvious than the absence of that simple light coating of dust.

The remnants of DuBois Indian School—the museum, her office, the archives—were her home, her family, her lover. But more than that, he now realized that the remnants of DuBois Indian School were also her prison.

Jesse saw the proud lift of her chin, the tightly composed expression on her face, and the sad shadows in her eyes. How would she look if she stepped out of her prison and into the real world? Would she pull the pins out of her hair and let it blow wild and free in the wind? Would she laugh unrestrained and tip her face up to capture raindrops on her tongue? No, he'd bet a bundle that the pins would stay in her hair and an umbrella would keep the rain from her face. He shoved the thoughts aside. What Kathleen Prescott did with her life was no concern of his. "Okay," he said, determined to stay on track. "What's next?"

"These." Kathleen flipped open the lid on the box. "These photographs were taken in 1884 by a friend of my great-great-grandfather's—Matthew Brady. Perhaps you've heard of him?" She pulled a couple of manila envelopes from the box.

"Perhaps I've heard of him? *The* Matthew Brady?" Dammit, how had he missed that gem in his research? Matthew Brady, the renowned Civil War photographer, at DuBois?

"Mr. Spotted . . . Jesse, I don't fabricate information."

Jesse grinned. She'd used his first name. At least she'd made one concession and that was a beginning. "I wasn't inferring that you were . . . fabricating. It's just that, well, I was surprised, that's all."

Kathleen Prescott opened one of the envelopes and withdrew a stack of old photographs. "Mr. Brady and Providence became friends during the war. In the summer of 1885 he came to DuBois for a three-week visit." She pushed the file box aside. "It's such a shame; did you know he died eleven years later, a penniless slave to drink?"

"Your great-great-grandpa?" Jesse teased, hoping to coax a smile from her and ease some of the tension between them.

"No," she replied, obviously annoyed and not granting the desired upward curve to her lips. "Mr. Brady, of course."

Jesse gave a solemn nod. "Of course."

She shot him a quick icy glare, then spread the sepia-toned photographs out on the table, setting each precisely beside the next, corner-to-corner, edge-to-edge.

High-cheekboned faces with dark haunted eyes stared back at Jesse. In one photo a group of Indian kids dressed in stiff-collared, buttoned-up uniforms sat straight-backed and rigid in a classroom. In another at least a hundred children stood shoulder to shoulder in regimental style on the parade ground. In a third, five boys, their hair cut short above their ears, stood beside a printing press. And in a fourth, girls dressed in long skirts and white blouses, their thick black hair styled with curls and bangs and ringlets, worked at treadle sewing machines. There wasn't a smile among them.

Jesse's heart wrenched at the children's empty gazes. He recognized a few of the faces from other photos he'd seen. He even knew some of their families who still lived on Cold Creek. There were no surprises in the photographs, just in the photographer. "Matthew Brady," he said, astounded that there was a collection of priceless Brady photographs at his fingertips. "Have any of these ever been published?"

"No. Of course not. They are private family photographs, a gift to my great-great-grandfather." Her indignation clear, she began to gather up the photos.

"No. Wait. Please. Kathleen, will you give me permission to use some of these? They're magnificent."

She hesitated, a scowl creasing her brow as she considered his request. Then finally, her answer. "I suppose I could allow that."

Jesse almost let go with one of Tooter's infamous war whoops. *Just keep it cool, Horse. Don't scare the lady into changing her mind.* "Thanks. I really appreciate it. I'll take very good care of them."

He checked his notes and began to pick out a few of the prints, recording each one in his notebook. They were perfect for a few of the segments. He'd have Tooter pan the camera slowly from left to right, allowing the lens to capture each face for a few seconds before moving on. He placed the selected photos in a stack beside the others he'd chosen.

Two other piles of pictures sat on the table to his right, pictures taken by the school photographer. The date the picture had been taken along with the photographer's name, Randall Watson, was written on the back of each in India ink. The student's name was printed in block letters on the back as well. The first stack held the "before" shots of the students when they'd first arrived at DuBois, still wearing their Indian clothes. Although their wide eyes showed fear, there was a solemn dignity about the way they sat or stood, and their skin held a healthy bronze color. The second pile were the "after" shots of the same children after their clothes had been burned, after they'd had their hair cut, after they had suffered DuBois for at least a year. In the "after" photos, the children were stiffly posed and dressed in drab school uniforms. Their skin had paled from being kept inside too much, and their eyes held a sad and flat emptiness.

Although Watson's pictures were good, Brady's photographs were magnificent. Jesse couldn't help but wonder about one thing. "If you've never allowed them to be published before, why are you willing to let me use them now?"

"Because these pictures will help me prove that your film is wrong," Kathleen replied, the corners of her mouth finally giving in to a smile, although it appeared to be a smug one. "They all show well-fed, well-clothed, happy children who were learning their lessons. Look at these boys," she added, pointing to the photo taken in the print shop. "They were being taught an excellent trade that would earn them good jobs and good wages to support their families."

Instead of meeting her challenge or telling her that in the late 1800s there would have been very few print shops or newspapers that would hire an Indian, he merely nodded and picked up another photograph. "Do you know what just one of these photos is worth to a Brady collector?" His gaze swept the table from photo to photo. "There's a damned fortune in just these ten."

"They are my family's heirlooms." The tone was as cold as an Alaskan January. "Would you sell your family's heirlooms?"

"No, but then, we were never given the choice. Most of ours were stolen or taken by shysters," Jesse replied. "Almost every museum in the country has some." He paused, then quietly added, "Along, even, with some of my old ancestors."

"My family's possessions are not for sale, and the only museum that will display any of our belongings is this one." She dealt out another ten photographs.

"Is this your great-great-grandmother?" Jesse asked, singling out one image of an austere-appearing woman in a classroom with a trio of Indian girls.

"My real great-great-grandmother died quite young. Providence remarried during the period these photographs were taken. I don't know why, but there are no known photos of his second wife, Libby." Kathleen replied. "The woman in this picture is Margaret Lester. She taught mathematics and also worked a few hours a day in Providence's office as his assistant and bookkeeper. Margaret Lester was at DuBois from 1883 to about mid-1886."

Jesse wrote the name in his notebook and looked up. "What do you mean 'about?'" he teased. "Don't you know how long she was here—to the hour and the minute, and what she ate for lunch?"

Kathleen stiffened and angled a hot glare at him. She obviously didn't take teasing very well.

"There is little information in the school records about her, her leaving, or her lunch." She pushed a stray strand of hair back from her face and poked it into the tight roll at the back of her head. "If you're interested, these are photographs of some of the other teachers at DuBois."

Jesse ducked his head to hide his amusement. Kathleen Prescott had a raw nerve that wasn't too difficult to find. "I would be very interested."

"Throughout the 1880s the school had a full complement of teachers, nineteen in all; ten women and nine men. A few of the single teachers also served as housemothers and fathers, living in the dormitories with the children. The staff, of course, also included cooks and caretakers."

Jesse watched her rattle off the details of the school's history as though she were repeating her catechism. *You're not far off, Horse.* In a way it was Kathleen Prescott's catechism. He'd wager his grandmother's secret frybread recipe that Kathleen didn't know the words to any Pink Floyd songs, had never heard of the Dixie Chicks, David Letterman, or Szechuan cooking. And he knew with certainty that she had no idea how it felt to ride the wildest roller coaster and scream at the top of her lungs when the car took a rocket-fast deep plunge.

"What about the married teachers?" he asked. "Where did they live?"

Kathleen glanced up from the photos she had placed on the table. "There were a couple of cottages on the north side of the school grounds for married staff. They're gone now, but Providence preferred to hire single teachers— those who had never married or were widowed. According to his journal, they were more malleable to the school's rules."

Malleable. Now, there was a word he hadn't heard often. This lady tossed around a fifty-dollar vocabulary. Jesse guessed it was another brick in the protective wall she kept tightly sealed around herself.

He picked out another four photographs, older students,

boys and girls, standing in front of farm wagons with people who were white and looked like locals.

Kathleen glanced over his shoulder as he spread them out on the table. "Those were taken in 1889, the first year that DuBois began the outing program. Carlisle had a very successful outing program, so the Reverend decided to give it a try at DuBois." She pointed at two of the Indian boys in the photos. "Senior students were hired out for the summer to work for local families." She added another photo to the four. "That year DuBois went from a year-round school to a September-through-June school."

Jesse picked two prints and added them to his collection. "And I suppose the school got the money the kids earned."

Kathleen looked away. "Not all, one third. The rest was banked for the student. They received it all when they left."

"Tell me about the teachers, any interesting stories about them—you know, something that would add a human-interest aspect from the staff's viewpoint?"

"Hmm, let's see," she said, thoughtfully worrying at her bottom lip with her teeth. "Alma Briggs, the penmanship teacher, had a pet pig named Sam that she kept in a small pen by the harness shop. It was slaughtered by mistake. From that time forward, Easter dinner was always referred to as Sam, instead of ham. My mother even carried on the tradition." She paused, a furrow in her brow. "This isn't all that unique, but there was an interesting event in 1886," she replied. "Providence had hired a young widow from Ohio, a Mrs. Shore, to teach English. Although highly recommended by the minister of her church, Mrs. Shore never arrived."

Kathleen paused as if that were the end of the story.

"And?" Jesse prompted. "So far it's not that interesting."

Kathleen shrugged. "She ran off with a shoe salesman from Topeka. Another teacher arrived in her stead. The odd thing is that the records don't give the new teacher's complete name, just Katherine. Apparently she disappeared after being here only a short while."

"That's it? Nothing else?"

After an indignant harrumph Kathleen shook her head. "Providence's journal speaks of her arrival in mid-June,

and there are a few more entries where he speaks of his admiration for her and her teaching style, but there aren't any
clues about why she left or where she went."

"Were the police involved?"

"Police?" Kathleen quickly glanced at Jesse. "Why
would the police be involved?"

Jesse shrugged. "I just wondered if anyone considered
foul play."

"I don't know. That information might be in the lost
journal."

"The lost journal?"

"The journal from July fifteenth through the thirty-first
of December of 1886 is missing." She straightened a couple
of the photos on the desk. "It is a mystery, isn't it?" Kathleen quietly added.

"A mystery like the disappearance of a ten-year-old boy
named *Tokalu Sapa*." He had tossed the remark out at her
without thinking and immediately regretted it. It wasn't
fair. The boy's disappearance, after all, wasn't her doing.
He heard her exasperated sigh.

Obviously piqued, Kathleen firmly placed another three
pictures on the table. "These were also taken by *the* Mr.
Brady. They are photos of the original barn. It burned on
the afternoon of Wednesday, July seventh, 1886. The
Pritchart Fire Department's collection of old records gave
us that date, and it's also reported in a couple of newspaper
articles and the newsletter written by the students." She cast
a disapproving glance at Jesse. "I can only hope that you
and your film people won't burn it down a second time."
She placed another collection of photographs in front of
him. "And these Brady photos I think will once again prove
my argument about DuBois."

Jesse almost laughed. Prim Ms. Prescott was more than
capable of rising to the occasion and firing salvos at him.
His amusement ended as he looked at the new photos.

"It was a school theatrical production based on Longfel-
low's *Song of Hiawatha*," Kathleen offered. "According to
the students' weekly newsletter, *The Eagle,* it was one of
their favorite plays."

Jesse quickly glanced up at her and then back at the

photos. He couldn't believe she would really think what she'd said was true. The expression on her face proved she did, but the photos showed another point of view. Jesse studied the solemn faces of the kids, some too embarrassed to look at the camera, which told the truth.

The children were dressed in ridiculous costumes, fabric cut at the hem and ends of the sleeves to look like fringed buckskin—mockeries of their own tribal clothing. Paint streaked their faces and turkey feathers stuck out at odd angles from their hair. Couldn't Kathleen Prescott see the tragic irony?

He selected two pictures from this collection and placed them in his "keeper" pile. They would definitely have a place in his film; besides, he couldn't wait till Tooter got a look at them. They'd be the brunt of his Kiowa friend's jokes for at least six months.

"Oh, wait, I almost forgot." Kathleen turned away and took a file box from a lower shelf. "These are some of my personal favorites, portraits of my ancestors, my family." Her voice had lightened and she sounded eager. "I'm sure you'll want to use some of these, as well." She placed more photos in front of him, one by one, as the dealer in a poker game might set out the players' cards. "You should consider yourself to be very privileged. None of these have ever been seen before by anyone outside of my family." She placed her hand lightly on one photo, her gesture almost reverent. "This is my great-great-grandfather, Providence Divine."

Hearing the homage in her voice, Jesse looked at her. He hadn't been wrong. Her face shone with the adoration of a true believer. To Kathleen Prescott, Providence Divine was nothing less than a saint. With a slight, regret-filled shake of his head, he looked at the photo. The unforgiving camera of the 1880s gave the good reverend a forbidding expression. But then again, maybe it was the true look of the man.

She placed another photo on the table to the immediate right of the first. "And this is my great-grandfather, Elijah . . . an only child. He was about thirty-five when this photo was taken. After Providence retired, Elijah took over as headmaster." A third picture was set to the right of the second. "My grandfather, Jacob, and the child on his knee is my mother, Patience." She rifled through the collection still left in her hand and chose one more. "And this . . . this is my father, Hamilton, and my mother on their wedding day. My father called her his pretty Patience." She paused and breathed what could only be described as a wistful sigh. "You're welcome to use any of these, as well."

"You look like your mother."

The room fell quiet for a moment, and then she replied with a soft catch in her voice, "Do you really think so?"

Jesse heard the pleasure in her question and looked up at her as she leaned over and drew the picture of her parents closer. His gaze caressed her face. Peaches and cream. Isn't that what advertisements called a velvet soft, fair, and flawless complexion? Kathleen Prescott was definitely peaches and cream. Her fragrance was unusual. It took him a few moments before he recognized the faintest hint of Shalimar. The exotic aroma seemed to be a curious inconsistency for the overly modest Miss Prescott, but he supposed that every woman was allowed a secret or two.

The urge to reach up and lightly stroke his finger down the smooth turn of her cheek pushed at him. His eyes traveled to her mouth and to the faint smile on her lips. And then it hit him like a well-directed punch. Damned if he wasn't beginning to enjoy the time he was spending with Kathleen. And, as unbelievable as it was, she was beginning to enjoy helping him put his film together. She just didn't know it yet.

Kathleen tried to swallow the tightness in her throat, but it stayed to antagonize her, as it always did when she looked at these photographs. She placed her hand on the back of Jesse's chair and gazed down at the familiar faces before her. How many times had she opened this box, withdrawn these photos from their envelopes, spread them out on the table, and spent an afternoon or evening quietly sitting with her family?

Photos. That was all she had left.

Gone. They were all gone now, all gone except her.

Alone. She'd been alone since she was twenty, left to

fend off the likes of Richmond Brock and his puppet board of directors.

There had been too many Christmases spent alone, too many New Year's Eves toasting the last stroke of midnight by herself. There had been too many Thanksgivings made up of little more than a small roasted capon, just enough for one. There had been too many holidays spent remembering what it was like to be part of a family, imagining what it would be like to have those times again.

As painful as the past ten years had been, she'd dealt with each hardship and had, she thought, dealt with them very well. What burdens could Jesse Spotted Horse possibly load on her shoulders that she couldn't manage?

Kathleen watched his hands gently handle the photos. Jesse Spotted Horse had nice hands, strong hands, tanned to a warm copper shade with long tapered fingers and neatly trimmed nails. He wore a silver and turquoise ring on the ring finger of his right hand, the color of the metal and stone perfect against the tint of his skin. She'd also noticed that he had treated everything she'd shared with him with respect, and she appreciated that. She reluctantly confessed that it did raise her opinion of him.

There was a clean, crisp pine scent about him. Soap. Nothing artificial like cologne. Each day in the past week since she'd met him, his hair had been plaited in black braids that fell almost to his waist. Today the braids were gone and his hair, tied at the nape of his neck with a leather thong, fell loose down his back. It shifted in black lustrous strands each time he moved.

Jesse suddenly sat back and Kathleen found her fingers trapped against the hard wooden back of the chair. She drew a sharp breath, and quickly withdrew her hand, still feeling the hard, warm press of his body and the silken touch of his hair on her fingers. She drove her hand into her pocket, as if hiding it from view would stop the tingle that tormented her skin, and stop the eager rush of warmth throughout her body. She had never touched a man like that before in her life. Of course, she rationalized, she really hadn't touched him on purpose, it had happened accidentally. But it had happened.

She stepped back, afraid that if she stood too close she'd want to touch him again, and this time it wouldn't be accidental.

What had happened to her objectivity? At first she had hated the idea of helping Jesse Spotted Horse with his loathsome film and had only gone along with the idea to insure DuBois's pristine reputation. But sometime in the past four days, and she wasn't sure exactly when, she had begun to look forward to their time together. Yesterday morning she had been up and dressed before her alarm clock buzzed, eager to get her museum duties completed so she could spend more time with him, helping with his research. This morning wasn't too different from the day before except she had foregone her usual breakfast of hot oatmeal and coddled eggs, settling instead for a quick and portable peanut butter sandwich so she could be on her way.

When she'd arrived in the archive room and found him already there, pen in hand and bending over his notes, she had paused at the doorway and watched him. He seemed to fill the room with his presence. And just like now, reining in her quickening breath had proved next to impossible.

Kathleen pressed her hand just above her left breast. She could feel the hard thumping of her heart through her blouse. Common sense told her she was being ridiculous. She wasn't a schoolgirl in the throes of her first crush. But common sense didn't always tell the whole truth. And the truth was that working shoulder to shoulder and hand to hand with Jesse Spotted Horse caused rash and wonderful thoughts that crowded her mind long after she turned out the light each night.

Why would she even wonder what it would feel like to have him touch or hold her? And worse, what perversion existed in her mind to make her wonder what it would be like to feel his lips pressed to hers? And those beautiful hands touching . . . She gave a firm mental shake of her head. No! Well-mannered and proper ladies didn't allow those kind of impure thoughts to dwell in their heads.

"I think we're just about finished for the day, unless you have another box or two of photos," Jesse said.

Jolted from her thoughts, it took a moment for Kathleen

to focus and reply. "There may be a few in the files in my office, more current ones taken by the Indianapolis newspapers during a powwow that some of the local Indians held here on the grounds a year ago."

"That's great. If you've got the names and addresses of some of those people, I'd like to get a hold of them. We still need a few extras for some of the scenes."

Kathleen nodded as she gathered up the old photos from the table, put them in their envelopes, and then filed them away in the right boxes. Picking up one of the boxes, she moved to the storage shelves.

"I saw a nice restaurant in town yesterday, Loon Lake Lodge. Do you know it?" Jesse asked, waiting for her nod before he continued. "I'd like to thank you for all your help and hard work. I know it's last minute, but would you have dinner with me this evening? My treat."

Kathleen felt a warm flush spread throughout her body. She had never been asked out to dinner by a man before. What should she say? What should she do? "I . . . I don't . . ." She fumbled and dropped the file box onto the shelf. "I don't know if that would be appropriate." She turned and looked at Jesse. What difference did it make that today was actually her birthday? "We hardly know each other."

"Kathleen, I'm just talking about enjoying a good meal and conversation together, like friends do; not buying silk sheets and getting married."

"M . . . married?" she sputtered. "That's certainly *not* what I meant." The flush turned to a burn. Embarrassed, her hand flew to her face to cover the bright red blush she knew colored her cheeks. She turned away and, fighting to control the nervous shaking of her hands, grabbed the last file box off the table. Maybe if she kept busy she could quiet her hammering heart. She looked at the label on the box. It belonged on the top shelf. Without hesitating, she stepped up on the ladder.

"Here, let me get that for you," Jesse offered, moving close behind her.

"No, I can manage, thank you." Uncomfortable with him standing so close, she awkwardly stretched upward until she was finally able to set the back edge of the box on the lip of the shelf.

"Careful."

"I *am* being careful," she replied, teetering tiptoe on the ladder. "I'm just a little nervous with you standing so close and watching me." She stretched up and tried to push the box onto the shelf. In the next instant she lost her balance and began to fall. "Oh!"

Her downward plunge suddenly stopped. "What . . . ?" And then, more embarrassed than she had ever been in her life, she realized what had stopped her fall. Jesse's hands, strong and firm, cupped each cheek of her bottom and pressed her against the ladder. She couldn't move. She could barely breathe. Time seemed to stand still while her heart took off like a Roman candle.

"Horse, you know that ain't no way to treat a lady . . . coppin' a feel like that. You oughta be ashamed of yourself, *kola.*"

The stranger's voice startled Kathleen from her daze. At the same time she felt Jesse move his hands up over her buttocks to her waist, all the more humiliating. With apparent ease, he lifted her off the stepladder and set her gently on the floor.

"Hey, Tooter," Jesse said, turning toward the door. He casually draped his arm around Kathleen's shoulders and drew her close. "Meet Kathleen Prescott. We're either going out to dinner tonight or we're getting married."

# Chapter 4

The Indian is born a blank. Transfer the savage-born infant to the surroundings of civilization and he will grow to possess a civilized language and habit.

—RICHARD H. PRATT,
CARLISLE INDIAN INDUSTRIAL SCHOOL

"MAN, THIS IS perfect." Tooter looked around the inside of the barn. "I hope you're plannin' on shooting in here."

"We're doing the one scene," Jesse replied, slowly walking down the center aisle of the stable, glancing into the horse stalls on either side. "When *Haŋha'pi Waha' caŋka,* Night Shield, came to visit his children, this is where Providence and his wife met him." He glanced at the lights hanging from the rafters. "What can we do about those? They're too low. I don't want them in the shot."

Tooter looked up and shrugged. "No problem. My camera angles aren't going up that high."

Jesse checked the light meter in his hand. "How about the lighting?"

"You worry too much, Horse. I got everything covered. I'm using fast film and I brought some of those new light bars. They'll give me good clean light." Tooter's shoulders lifted with a nonchalant shrug. "I'm gonna try a couple of colored filters for an antique look." He bent over and laughed as he snatched a handful of straw off the floor. "We just have to make sure we don't set any of this on fire."

"I'd appreciate that," Jesse said. "We're already on Kathleen Prescott's bad side. Just think where burning

down her barn would put us." He looked up at the haylofts
that ran the length of the aisle on both sides of the barn. A
season's worth of loose hay filled each loft, ample food for
a hungry fire. Two wooden ladders, one on either side and
nailed to the wall, provided the only way up to the lofts.
"Kathleen told me this place has already burned down
once, July 1886, I think."

Suddenly uneasy, Jesse rubbed his hand across the back
of his neck. Damn, there it was again. The sensation hit
every time he walked into the barn, scraping over his
nerves with an icy caress. Why did this place set him on
edge? He took his time studying the inside of the barn, his
gaze stopping and probing all the dark shadows. He still
couldn't pinpoint the cause. He tried to shove the feeling
aside, but it always persisted and pushed back, nagging at
him, making his gut twist.

Grandma Boo would tell him it was just some restless
*waŋagi*, haunting the place. God knew DuBois had more
than its fair share of haunts. They still told stories on the rez
about some of the kids who had died at Indian schools. Stories about their ghosts that still walked the grounds, calling
out their Indian names so their mamas would recognize
them and take them home.

The old woman would also tell him that he felt these
things because of who he was, what he was, because he
was Lakota, because it was in his spirit, in his blood. Whatever the reasons or the truths, he had enough damn things
to worry about without putting ghosts on the list, too. He
looked up at the hayloft one last time and whispered,
"Leave me alone."

"Hey, what about horses and wagons?"

Tooter's voice wrenched Jesse's thoughts away from old
ghosts.

"We gotta have 'em," Tooter added, peering into an
empty stall. "Realism, man, realism."

"Quit harassing me. We're getting horses." Jesse joined
his friend, grateful to have his mind occupied with things
other than ghosts. "I talked with Richmond Brock. We get
as many horses from the academy's stables as we need. No
charge." He handed the light meter back to Tooter.

"They've also got some big old Belgian draft horses that they use to haul a Civil War cannon in parades. We get one of them, too." Crossing the barn aisle, Jesse opened the lid on one of the grain bins, not surprised to find it empty. "There are a couple of restored wagons and a surrey that would be perfect for a few shots. We get our pick."

"Fantastic. Horse, you amaze me. You're more organized than an old maid's panties drawer." Tooter enthusiastically punched Jesse's shoulder. "This flick is gonna rock!"

"Don't get too carried away; we've still got a few nasty wrinkles to iron out."

"Such as?"

"We're short on extras for the live shots." Jesse stopped at the double doors at the back of the barn, mirror images of those at the front of the building. He flipped the wrought-iron latch and pushed the doors open. A team of horses and a fully loaded high-sided hay wagon could easily be driven right through the building. "I called the American Indian Center in Indianapolis yesterday morning, and there are about thirty families who can help us out." His gaze scanned the parade ground as he spoke. "We're getting quite a group: Apaches, Navajos, some Comanches and Kiowas, a few Cherokees and a Tlingit." He glanced over his shoulder at Tooter. "A real mixed bunch, just like the original DuBois kids would have been." He leaned against the doorframe. "Still not enough, though, to fill out the scenes."

"Wow, I didn't think there'd be that many skins in Indiana." Tooter walked toward the back of the barn and stood next to Jesse. "We'll be okay. I put the deal through with Bobby Big Bow that we talked about." Tooter pulled a stick of gum out of his pocket, unwrapped the foil, and popped the gum into his mouth. "Bobby's bringin' two busloads of kids from the rez. They're makin' it a school field trip. We pay for the lease of the buses and gas." He paused, chewed for a moment, then added, "And thirty bucks each for the kids."

Jesse glanced at Tooter. "That's a pretty generous deal, *kola*!" He shook his head and laughed. "Have you figured out where these kids are going to stay? There's no way we can find or pay for all those motel rooms."

"Don't worry, Horse, I got that covered, too." Tooter's self-satisfied grin made him look like a cat that had found a flock of low-flying canaries. "They're bringin' tents. They're gonna camp out." He pointed to a flat span of ground south of the barn. "That spot'll be perfect."

"And what else?" There was always something else when it came to Tooter's deals, something that was always the last thing to get mentioned.

Tooter shrugged. "Bobby says we gotta feed them. If you don't want to pay for the catering people to do it, then we'll give Bobby some food money. They'll do their own cooking." He lifted his ballcap and gave his head a quick scratch. "There's just one hitch." He glanced at Jesse. "We're only gonna have the kids for a few days, so we gotta get all our student shots done in that time, rain or shine."

"No problem, the storyboards are done." Jesse scanned the grounds and watched a couple of the academy's gardeners pruning bushes along the driveway. "The school uniforms arrived two days ago from the costume company. Actually they're altered Civil War confederate uniforms but they'll work fine. We've got seventy-five in different sizes. That should be enough."

Jesse liked Tooter's deal. Giving the kids from Cold Creek Reservation the chance to see some of the history of their ancestors was a great idea. Giving them a little pocket change to spend on their trip was another one.

"Speaking of the storyboards, I was looking at some of 'em this morning." Tooter cast a sidelong glance at Jesse. "I still think you'd be perfect for the part of Night Shield."

"I told you before, no."

"Yeah? Well, who?" Tooter shoved his hands in his back pockets. "I know you'd still like to get Rodney what's-his-name from *Dances With Wolves,* you've called his agent twice and nothing, so now you've run out of time if you're planning to shoot in a couple of days. I'll say it again, Horse, you'd be better'n anybody." He clapped his friend on the shoulder. "Come on, if you do it we don't have to

cancel the shoot and the other actors we've hired. Just think
of the money you'll save our budget—no big Hollywood
actor to pay."

"Get it out of your head. I'm not an actor."

"Yeah, and your point? What acting? There isn't any di-
alog, Horse." The gum in Tooter's mouth made a loud pop.
"All you gotta do is walk around and look pissed off. You
know, just be yourself." Tooter dodged Jesse's friendly cuff
on the back of his head, and then a sheepish expression settled on his face. "I stopped by Grandma Boo's and picked
up your Indian clothes and feathers. I brought everything
with me."

"You did what?" Jesse quickly looked at Tooter. "I told
you that I didn't—"

"Yeah, yeah, yeah, I know what you said." Tooter put
his hands up as if to ward off another blow. "Horse, you'd
be better than anyone else we could hire—just look at yourself. You've got the looks, the hair, we got your clothes.
Besides, who's gonna know you ain't a dead ringer for
*Haŋha'pi Waha'caŋka*? Nobody knows what the guy
looked like." He shrugged. "We don't need a big-name
actor for the part, and we don't need to pay the big-name
actor's fee." He folded his arms across his chest. "And you
know what? I think it would take away from the film and
its message to have some famous actor sashayin' around in
it."

Jesse grudgingly agreed with Tooter, but if he played the
role, there was another problem. "My clothes are powwow
clothes. They're not accurate for the period."

"So? We make some changes." Tooter shrugged again.
"I brought my dad's old chief's blanket—it's navy-blue
stroud cloth with a super strip of beadwork, and Grandma
Boo packed your great-grandpa's war shirt. There are some
supplies in the suitcase, too; sinew, beads, some hairpipes,
that sorta stuff. No problem, we'll put something good together."

Jesse still wasn't convinced. Tooter's plan might work,
but one other problem remained, one that he'd just learned
about before breakfast, and one that had certainly thrown
him for a loop. "Okay, solve this one. I've got old Provi-

dence's part already cast, you want me for Night Shield, but have you got any bright ideas for the role of Rachel Divine?"

"What happened to the broad you had already lined up?"

"The agency in Indianapolis phoned this morning. The actress I'd hired bailed out."

"Why?"

"The costume won't fit. She's pregnant."

Tooter hesitated for only a moment before pointing up the hill toward the administration building that housed Kathleen Prescott's office. "What about—"

"Oh, no," Jesse interrupted, shaking his head and backing away. "Are you insane? No. Definitely not." He glared at Tooter. "You are kidding, right?"

"Nope." Tooter shook his head, straight white teeth flashing behind his crooked grin. "I'm not kidding. Why not ask her? She's perfect." He gave Jesse a quick jab on his biceps. "Whoever you get is gonna have to fit the costume. Small, right? Well, from the looks of your Miss Prescott, she's your Cinderella." Using his hands, he outlined the imaginary shape of a woman, then added a low wolf whistle. "Hell, man, she's Providence Divine's great-great-granddaughter. That's a great advertising coup for the film." He rested his hand on Jesse's shoulder. "Besides, she probably won't cost us anything, and hell, with her wire-framed granny glasses and that old-lady hairdo, she already looks the part. You'll save a bundle on makeup." He jabbed at Jesse again. "So, what d'ya say?"

Jesse rubbed his arm. "I'll think about it."

Tooter wouldn't let it go. "I bet it'd be the biggest event in her life."

"I said I'd think about it."

"I watched her last night at the restaurant. She was like a little bird, nervous 'bout being away from her nest." Tooter added another notch to his argument. "I bet she hasn't been asked out to dinner too many times in her life, if ever." He kicked at a clod of dirt with the toe of his boot. "Come on, give her something to remember in her old age. Ask her."

Jesse knew Tooter was right. He'd seen the excitement

in Kathleen's eyes when they'd toured the restaurant with its northern Canadian hunting-lodge theme. He'd seen her delight with the delicious meal, and her wistful expression as she'd looked at some of the other patrons—the couple at the next table holding hands, the young family across the room.

"I'll tell you something else," Tooter continued, cracking his wad of gum again, "while everybody was gawkin' at us wild, long-haired prairie princes, once she'd looked at everything in the place, she couldn't take her eyes off you for the rest of the evening. You've made another conquest, Horse." A grin spread his face wide open. "You know what?" He elbowed Jesse in the ribs. "I bet she'd do anything you asked . . . well, perhaps not *everything* . . . but . . . hell, man, you know what I mean."

Jesse shot a glare at Tooter. "I'm not asking."

"You know, you're the damnedest, most stubborn Injun I've ever met." Tooter tried to bulldoze through Jesse's resolve. "I'd bet with a little makeup, and loosening that damned tight knot of hair at the back of her head, your prim little Miss Prescott would be a real looker."

"In your dreams." Jesse forced a laugh. "There are miracles and then there are *miracles*." He didn't want to tell Tooter he'd already had a glimpse of the miracle himself.

Tooter chuckled. "I bet it'd be just like that straitlaced librarian in those shampoo commercials when she throws her glasses away, lets her hair down, and becomes a hot babe." He tossed his own hair, imitating the commercial. "So, what do ya say, huh?"

"Damn it, Toot, I told you, I'll think about it." Jesse scowled at his friend. "Can we drop the subject now?" He hit his friend with a hard glare. "And she's not *my* little Miss Prescott."

Tooter put up his hands, his eyes widening in counterfeit innocence. "Okay, okay, whatever, but I think—"

"Enough! Don't think." Jesse turned away and looked at the brace of windows on the second floor of the museum building. Kathleen Prescott's office. He'd seen her standing in the window, watching them, and he'd seen her duck behind the drapes when Tooter pointed in her direction. If a pointed finger could make her hide, then what would happen when he asked her to stand in front of a camera? *If* he asked her. She'd already said no, but that had been the first time they'd met and he'd been teasing. What would she say now?

Too many questions harassed him. How would she look in the hunter-green costume with the tightly cinched waist and the long, full-bustled skirt? Would the camera be able to see her large expressive eyes, her flawless complexion, the graceful way she moved, and those unbelievable lips? The idea started to intrigue him. Hell, more than that, the idea flat out bedeviled him.

"Okay, if you're not gonna talk about that"—Tooter jerked his thumb in the direction of Kathleen's office—"did ya find out anything yet about Grandma Boo's uncle, *Tokalu Sapa*?" He glanced at Jesse.

Thankful for the change of subject, Jesse pulled his attention away from Kathleen's windows, away from small waists and gray eyes. "Nothing more than I already knew," he replied. "He's on the enrollment records for March 22, 1884, the day he arrived. There's one other mention of him in February of 1885. By then they were calling him Adam Black Fox."

"What, no name-giving ceremony?"

Tooter's cynical remark made Jesse laugh. He slipped his sunglasses out of his breast pocket and put them on. He walked out of the shade of the barn and into the bright afternoon sun and looked at the rows of white headstones in the cemetery behind the school dormitories. "I went through the old class photos hoping I might find some listing the names of the students, hell, I even studied each face trying to find a family resemblance in one of those kids." He shook his head and began to walk away. "Nothing."

"How about the cemetery?" Tooter asked, following Jesse's gaze to the tree-lined knoll. "Did you check there?"

"Of course I did. I read every tombstone in that place . . . twice."

"Nothing?"

"Nothing about him, nothing with his name on it."

Silence fell between them, broken only by the chattering

song of a red bird in the nearby spruce. Jesse glanced back at the barn and then at Tooter, wondering if his friend would think he was losing his marbles if he asked the question that was on his mind. What the hell, he'd ask it anyway. "Toot, do you feel anything kind of different . . . odd, when you're inside the barn?"

"Yeah." Tooter sniffled. "My allergies give me hell with all that dust and hay. I'm eatin' antihistamines like they're M&Ms."

"No, that's not what I mean. I'm talking about something sort of . . . spooky, something that makes you jittery?"

Tooter's jaw stopped working on the gum. "What in the hell are you talkin' about?"

Yeah, it had been foolish to ask. Jesse gave a slight shake of his head. "Never mind." He looked back at the barn again. "It's nothing." He'd said it; he just didn't know if he believed it.


HAD IT BEEN her imagination? No, definitely not. Tooter Poolaw had pointed at her, and Jesse had looked, too. Surely they couldn't see her standing in the window. It was a little late to duck behind the drapes, but she did it anyway. Why were they talking about her? "Good grief, this whole film thing has driven me to paranoia."

Pulling the edge of the drapes back a few inches, she watched the two men as they stood together in the barn doorway. It was easy to see they were friends, good friends, as close as brothers. The way they walked together or stood talking with each other showed an ease that was only possible between men who were family, or the next best thing to it.

A stab of regret sliced deep into her heart. Being home-schooled at DuBois didn't offer many opportunities to meet other children or make friends. The closest she'd come to a best friend had been Mary Hanson, but the Hansons moved away from Pritchart during the summer when Kathleen was twelve.

She'd never had a close family, either. Her parents loved

her, but there had always been a cold reserve that didn't
leave much room for hugs or loving touches.

Kathleen's gaze rested on Jesse. She would be able to
recognize him at any distance. The way he stood, his
height, the shape of his body, the way he moved with lan-
guid ease. It was all distinctly Jesse Spotted Horse. And she
confessed that she was very attracted to the man . . . in a
purely platonic way, of course.

She had met handsome men before, men who had toured
the school and museum or collected information from the
archives, but none stayed in her mind and filled her
thoughts and dreams as Jesse did. In just the short while
that he'd been at DuBois and she'd been working with him,
her world had changed, expanded, become more special,
more exciting.

*Quit being a silly old prune. The only reason he spends
time with you is because he wants information. The moment
his film is finished and he and his film crew leave, you'll be
back to . . . what?* She didn't want to think about it. *You
know what—nights watching television, or reading, or . . .
wishing you were anywhere but here.*

Kathleen reached up, her fingers tucking a few wayward
strands of hair back into the tight knot at the back of her
head, and reset a hairpin with a determined jab. *It's an old
woman's hairdo.* No, old women didn't even wear their hair
like this anymore.

She smoothed her hand over the waistband of her skirt
as if she could straighten out her life with that simple gesture. A white high-collared, long-sleeved blouse, a long
dark-colored skirt, and a pair of sensible shoes; her dress
never varied. Not true, she mentally argued. Today the skirt
was navy, not brown like yesterday's, or black like the day
before. *Brava, Kathleen, you're a regular fashion sensation.*

She released a deep sigh and let the curtain fall back.
*Mother always said I was plain. Even Richmond Brock, with
all of his leering, doesn't find me attractive. He just thinks I
might be available.* She reached up and touched her cheek.
*But Jesse said I looked like Mama, and she wasn't pla . . .*

"Kathleen."

Yanked from her thoughts, she wheeled around. "Oh, Jesse." She felt the immediate trip and skitter of her heart, and as if in defense, her hand moved to her high collar. "I didn't hear you come up the stairs."

"Sorry if I startled you. When I didn't find you in the museum, I figured you might be up here." He stepped farther into the office. "Got a minute? I'd like to talk with you about something."

She stepped away from the window and, clasping her hands, nervously twisted the plain gold ring she wore on her right hand. "All right." She pointed to the few file folders on her desk. "I don't have much time to—"

"Yeah, I know," Jesse interrupted, his full mouth moving into that easy teasing smile he used so often, the one that made her feel warm all over. "You're busy."

"Coffee?" Kathleen lifted the pot from the hot plate. If she could keep busy, keep moving, maybe he wouldn't see how nervous he made her.

"Thanks," Jesse replied. "Black. I've sworn off sugar in my old age."

She passed the full mug to him, her fingers grazing his, her breath lightly catching in her throat.

Jesse slowly raised the mug to his mouth.

She watched his lips touch the rim of the cup, watched them purse slightly as he took a sip, then felt embarrassed as he raised the mug in a mock salute.

"It's good."

She ducked her head. "It's instant." She silently chastised herself for her inane response.

The teasing grin returned.

Kathleen sought safe refuge behind her desk. "Did you need something?" She had purposefully put a prickly tone to her voice, a shield she could always count on when she was nervous. She sat. "Is there a problem?"

Jesse settled into the chair across from her, casually crossed his legs, his left ankle resting on his right knee, and balanced his coffee mug on his knee. "Just one, but Tooter seems to think you might be willing to help us out."

"I don't know what more I can do. I am already taking too much time away from my work to help you."

"You might enjoy this. It's more fun than work."

All right, he'd made her curious, and if truth were told, there wasn't that much work for her to do. And if further truths were told, she had been looking for an excuse to spend more time with him. "What is it that you need?"

Jesse leaned forward in his chair. "We've planned a scene showing Providence and Rachel greeting Night Shield when he visited his children in 1885." He took a sip of coffee. "I've already hired an actor for the part of Reverend Divine, but the actress I'd hired to play your great-great-grandmother got herself . . . uh . . . she's pregnant. We had to have the costume custom-made." He shrugged. "It doesn't fit her anymore."

Kathleen tightly clasped her hands together in her lap. What was this all leading to?

He glanced down at his coffee cup. "Tooter thinks the dress would fit you and that you'd be perfect for the part."

Kathleen's stomach felt as though it had flipped upside down. He'd made the statement as smoothly as if it were nothing more than a comment on the weather. *Hi, hello, it's a lovely day, isn't it, and by the way, will you be in my movie?* "No. Absolutely not." She raised her hand as if that simple gesture would stop him from asking again, or stop the excited trill that cascaded through her body. "I thought you were being facetious the first day you were here and asked me."

"I was, then, but I'm very serious now." He didn't move except to lift his mug and take another sip. His dark eyes watched her over the rim of his cup.

"It is a preposterous idea."

He didn't say anything for second, just watched her, and then, "Kathleen, please," he said. "At least give it some thought. We're just shooting film; you won't have any lines to learn. It could be fun." He gave her an encouraging nod.

She left the security of her desk and going to the window, she gazed out at the school grounds. "Surely there's someone else, an actress—"

"We don't want an actress."

"But—"

"We want you."

She hadn't heard him leave his chair or walk across the room, but suddenly he was standing behind her. She could smell the fresh scent of the pine soap he used, and there was another underlying scent as well, a scent that was all Jesse.

She turned to face him, immediately struck by his height, the beautiful contours of his face, the warm color of his skin and the broad span of his shoulders. She denied the urge to reach out and touch him. "Do you want me, or just someone who can wear the dress?"

He grinned, putting an intriguing set of creases beside his mouth, and she braced herself for the teasing that always accompanied that appealing smile.

"Of course we need someone who can fit into the costume. . . ."

"And that's your sole reason?" she asked, swallowing a pang of disappointment. She didn't know what reason would have satisfied her. Maybe it was the one that her heart was beginning to yearn for.

"My reasons for asking are simple," Jesse replied. "I'm asking, Kathleen, because there is so much of you already in the project. Because I think you'd be perfect for the part." He hesitated for a moment, his eyes holding hers hostage. "And because you're the great-great-granddaughter of Providence Divine."

He might as well have physically backed her into a corner, the result was the same. In a voice she barely recognized as her own and knowing she would probably live to regret her decision, she answered him, "All right, I'll do it."

# Chapter 5

The children will be hostages for the good behavior of their
people.

—COMMISSIONER HYDE,
WAR DEPARTMENT, AUGUST 6, 1879

"TAKE A DEEP breath and suck in your tummy."

"Excuse me?"

A little over an hour before, an out-of-breath, tattooed
and pierced, magenta-haired creature who had introduced
herself as Egypt Goldenbird had breezed into Kathleen's
apartment toting a large makeup case and a garment bag.
She wore a red sequined halter top, a pair of red satin
shorts, and high-heeled silver sandals with glittery ties that
wrapped around her calves and all the way up to her knees.
Each toe had been decorated with little gold rings. Egypt
Goldenbird had immediately begun Kathleen's transformation.

"Come on, sweetie, suck it in." Egypt adjusted the stiff
corset over the delicate chemise that Kathleen already
wore. "I can't lace up this torture chamber unless you do."

Kathleen had never, in all of her life, seen anyone who
looked like Egypt. The woman left her speechless. How did
someone find the freedom to be so unique? Where did the
courage come from to stand out so boldly in a crowd?

A trio of earrings pierced the upper shell of each ear and
two more dangled from each lobe. A tiny dumbbell perfo-
rated her left eyebrow, and another decorated her navel.
When Egypt spoke, Kathleen was positive she'd even seen
a glint of metal on the woman's tongue, and the very pro-

nounced peaks under the halter top on the tips of Egypt's breasts made Kathleen wonder what else had been pierced.

Kathleen stared, fascinated by the tattooed array of vibrant colors that wound around the woman's arms. A lush tapestry of leafy vines and flowers, red poppies and purple orchids, began at her wrists and ended over her shoulders on her back. What possessed someone to endure the pain to decorate her body like that? Freedom and self-confidence, that's what.

Kathleen couldn't imagine what it felt like to be that free, to totally be your own person. The school, the museum, and her duty to her family's legacy had been the catalyst that had molded and demanded so much of her. *Outside of DuBois I have no idea who I am.* The thought cut like a razor.

She didn't want the pierced nose, or eyebrow, or tongue, or whatever. She didn't want to be brightly tattooed, but she did want more, so much more, than she had. She wanted to step out of the tight boundaries she'd been raised to accept. She wanted the courage to taste all the flavors life offered, not just vanilla. And yes, she wanted bright colors, maybe not reds and purples tattooed on her skin, but her own bright colors, wherever she wanted to put them.

Terrified that these new wild ideas challenged the Divine family's standards, Kathleen pushed them away. But the ideas returned, bringing with them new arguments, new excitement.

Was it possible? Could being in Jesse's film be the first step she'd take toward the freedoms she craved, toward the colors? And maybe a red or purple or bright green once in a while would be okay.

Other changes were worrying her, too. In just a few short days she had gone from being vehemently opposed to the film, to freely giving Jesse information and photographs from the archives that would only make his film better. There had been no coercion; if anything, he'd seemed surprised that she would help him. She had surprised herself. But now she worried that maybe she had foolishly sacrificed her family's reputation for a few moments of selfish pleasure.

Madness, it was all madness. But agreeing to be in Jesse's movie, agreeing to play the role of her great-great-grandmother, was the maddest thing of all.

"Hang on to something. It might be easier." Egypt moved behind Kathleen. "Are you ready?"

"Oh, okay." Kathleen grabbed the edge of her bureau and held on as Egypt drew the laces tighter and tighter. "Oh, please . . . ugh . . . I can't . . . breathe."

"I don't think you're supposed to." Egypt giggled. She placed one hand between Kathleen's shoulder blades and pulled on the laces again with the other. "I bet that some little wimpy man with ambiguous testosterone who couldn't keep his wife happy invented this damned contraption. It rates right up there with the chastity belt, for God's sake." A laugh erupted. "Whoa, where did those little gems of militant feminism come from?" Still laughing, she tugged again at the laces.

Kathleen gasped. "Jesse didn't tell me I'd be cut in half!"

"Suck it in again, sweetie, I'm almost finished."

"Oh, please, does it have to be so tight?" Kathleen adjusted her grip on the bureau. "Can't we forget about the corset and leave it off? Nobody would know."

"Honey, the way this dress is made," Egypt said, glancing at the emerald green gown hanging from the door frame, "you'd never get into it without the corset." She yanked on the left lace, then the right. "This costume is almost authentic, from the hem to the neck to the tip of the sleeves. There's no elastic, no zippers or snaps, just hooks and eyes. It needs all of the underthings, even that ridiculous flounced underskirt and bustle pad, to make it fit and look right." She gave one final tug, then tied the laces in a bow. "There you go, snug as a bug."

"I don't think there's room in here for a bug," Kathleen croaked. She pulled at the whale-boned garment and prayed for even a hairbreadth of relief.

"Honey, don't fight it." Egypt patted Kathleen's hand. "Try to relax, you'll get used to it."

Kathleen tried to relax. She tried to breathe. And she knew she wasn't ever going to get used to it. A series of short, shallow breaths that quickly turned into gasps and pants were all she could manage.

"No, no, don't breathe like that. You'll hyperventilate and then you'll really be in trouble. Just breathe normally."

"Normally? Ha!" Kathleen tried to laugh, but there wasn't enough room.

"Relax, you'll be fine." Egypt gave Kathleen a quick hug, then reached for the garment bag. "Are you ready for the next layers?"

"Did you say *layers*?"

"Yup, sure did. How do you like these?" Egypt giggled and held up a knee-length, lace-trimmed pair of drawers.

"Bloomers?" Kathleen quickly glanced at them, then gave a second look. She gasped. "My goodness, there's no . . . um . . . uh . . ."

"The word is *crotch,* darling." Egypt laughed, waving the drawers like a flag. "And I think if you're wearing these, your goodness kinda depends on who you're with." She gave the drawers another wave. "I bet *these* weren't designed by that chastity-belt guy. Talk about your women's lib!" She gave Kathleen an exaggerated wink and tossed the drawers at her.

Next came the lace-trimmed corset cover and the full underskirts from the garment bag. "We'll hold off on the bustle pad until you're ready for the dress." Egypt pointed at an odd-looking item that resembled an overstuffed pillow with tie strings and flounces.

"If women wore all this padding, no wonder they looked so angry in those old photographs," Kathleen groused.

"But you are gonna be absolutely gorgeous. Wait and see." Egypt steered Kathleen to the chair she'd drawn in front of a mirror. "Sit."

"Impossible."

"Sit."

"I can't."

"Sit!"

Protesting with a long sigh, Kathleen reluctantly eased herself down until she perched precariously on the edge of the seat. There was no way to be comfortable while whalebones squashed her ribs and squeezed her waist until her liver and her stomach traded places. She tried to block out the agony while Egypt opened the makeup case. Maybe counting the times this wild, magenta-haired creature had called her honey or sweetie or sugar would help.

"Okay, just relax, I promise, you're going to like this part." Egypt held up a large cotton ball.

Kathleen closed her eyes as Egypt's fingers fluttered and stroked, applying cleanser, then a creamy foundation over her cheeks and forehead.

"Have you ever had your eyebrows plucked?"

Kathleen opened her eyes. "No. Are you adding that to my list of tortures?"

"I think you'd look better on camera with a neater arch. It'll just take a minute," Egypt said, clicking the pair of tweezers she held in her hand.

"Jesse didn't say anything about this. Does it hurt?"

"No, not at all, just little tugs and pinches."

"But I really don't think I—"

Egypt laughed. "Sweetie, if I thought I'd have a chance with that gorgeous, sexy studmuffin, I'd pluck everything I have . . . well, everything that isn't plucked already." Holding the tip of her tongue between her teeth, she concentrated on working her tweezers for the next ten minutes, ignoring Kathleen's wincing and fidgeting. "There, all done." Egypt smoothed her fingers over Kathleen's brows. "Now, that wasn't too bad, was it?" Dropping the tweezers into her makeup bag, she then pulled out a few more items. "The rest won't hurt at all, I promise."

"What is a . . . studmuffin?"

"Hmm?" Egypt swept a light touch of gray eye shadow on Kathleen's lids then drew an eyeliner pencil across the edge of each eye. "What did you say?"

"You called Jesse a . . . studmuffin. What does that mean?"

Egypt's mouth fell open. "You're kidding, right? Oh, honey, where the hell have you been . . . Siberia . . . the middle of the Gobi?" She propped her hand on her hip. "Let's see . . . a studmuffin is a gorgeous guy, a man who trips your trigger, heats up your hormones, loosens your libido, caresses your cli—"

"Okay, okay," Kathleen interrupted, quickly lowering her eyes. She felt the hot blush rush up her cheeks. "I think I get the picture." She wished now she'd never asked.

"You don't think he's a studmuffin?" Egypt swished a big fluffy brush in a pot of face powder, then dusted Kathleen's face.

The woman wasn't going to let the topic drop. Kathleen folded her hands in her lap and straightened her shoulders as best she could. "I've never thought about it."

"Liar." Egypt laughed as she deftly wielded a lipstick brush on Kathleen's mouth, then handed her a tissue. "Blot." Using another soft brush, she added a light blush to Kathleen's cheeks. "You might not have known he was a studmuffin, but I bet you gave it a lot of thought." Egypt leaned closer and whispered in Kathleen's ear. "A lot."

Kathleen flinched. Egypt was right. *I am a liar.* Jesse Spotted Horse had definitely filled her waking thoughts, and for the past four nights he had tiptoed through her dreams as well. She knew better than to hope he might be dreaming about her. She doubted if he thought about her at all . . . at least not in *that* way. A devilish notion trotted into her mind before she could rein it in. *I wonder what trips his trigger.*

She had no illusions. Their time together had been and would continue to be strictly business. Even their dinner at Loon Lake Lodge had been business, right down to the bill that Jesse would use for a tax deduction. But knowing that did absolutely nothing to stop her dreams or her wishes.

Egypt added a few more strokes of mascara to Kathleen's lashes, then stepped back to examine her handiwork. "Good. No, better than good, beautiful. Now, let's do your hair."

Kathleen felt a twinge of guilt. "I've never been pampered like this."

"Well, you just sit there and enjoy it." Egypt laughed. "Maybe not the corset, though." She patted Kathleen's shoulder.

Surely it was wrong to enjoy all of this so much. And all this makeup; she'd never worn anything more than a very pale and neutral shade of lipstick. But Kathleen refused to listen to the ghost whispers of disapproval that filled her head. If anything, the voices made her all the more determined to delight in every self-indulgent moment. *I'm going to enjoy it all, because tomorrow everything in my life goes back to normal.* Well, not exactly everything, Jesse and his film crew would still be here for another two or three weeks.

She closed her eyes again, luxuriating in the touch of Egypt's brush and hands in her hair. Moments slid by.

"I'm done. Take a peek. What do you think?"

She must have dozed off, impossible to believe considering the corset's bite, but she quickly roused at the sound of Egypt's voice. Kathleen peered at herself in the mirror and couldn't believe what her eyes were telling her. Sometime during the past hour, a magical transformation had taken place. Not only did she barely recognize herself, but the person who gazed back at her from the mirror was from a different life, a different century. The person who gazed back at her from the mirror was . . . pretty.

"Well?"

"Oh, my." Kathleen's voice barely reached above a shocked murmur. She turned her head to the left and then the right, leaned closer to the mirror, and stared. "Is that me?" She cautiously touched her cheek with the tips of her fingers, then glanced over her shoulder at Egypt. "I never imagined I could look like this." Tears welled up in her eyes as she touched the curls at her temple, then the intricate soft twist of hair on the back of her head.

"Good grief, honey, don't cry! If you do I'll have to start all over again." Egypt carefully dabbed at Kathleen's eyes with a tissue.

"I can't believe how you've made me look. Egypt, you're a magician."

"No, I'm not. I'm just an underpaid dresser and makeup artist," Egypt replied, gently touching the tissue to Kathleen's eyes one more time. "Lemme tell you something, sweetie. I can only enhance beauty, I definitely can't create it if it isn't already there." She gave Kathleen another quick hug, then glanced at the rhinestoned Mickey Mouse watch on her tattooed wrist. "Crap, we're running late. You're supposed to be in the barn and ready for your shoot in twenty minutes." She reached for the bustle pad and then the emerald gown. "Let's get you dressed."

Kathleen stood, glad to feel the pinch of the corset let up a little.

"Okay," Egypt said, "first the skirt. Thank God they made at least one concession and made this gown in two pieces. So much easier to get in and out of."

Full and bustled at the back, the skirt fell to just above the floor with three rows of knife-pleated ruffles at the hem. An overskirt, draped just below Kathleen's hips, gathered about the gown, ending in a large, flat bow at the small of her back. Even the fabric, a polished cotton, amazed her. It whispered with her every move.

The form-fitting bodice came next and followed every line the corset helped create, allowing for the soft curve of her breasts, then tightly dipping in at the waist. The sleeves, long with a slight puff at the upper arm, ended at the wrists with ruched ivory-colored cuffs. A steep row of brass fili-gree buttons marched upward from her waist and ended at the upright military-styled collar.

Ten minutes later Kathleen stood before the tall antique cheval glass and slowly assessed herself from head to toe. The dress was severe in cut and the emerald color was un-like anything in her closet. She had never worn a gown so beautiful in her life.

Lifting the edge of the skirt, she stared at the black, high-topped, buttoned boots on her feet. The supple kid leather hugged her ankles. She twisted her foot to the left, and then the right, surprised to find the boots fit her perfectly.

"Just a few more things," Egypt said. She set a perky green bonnet with a sprig of ivory flowers on the back of Kathleen's head, then drew the grosgrain ribbon ties up under her chin and tied them off to the side in a soft bow. A pair of ivory lace gloves was next. "Ladies always wore their gloves." She handed one last item to Kathleen. "Hang this from your wrist."

Kathleen took the small beaded drawstring purse from Egypt.

"I've put some tissues in the bag along with the button

hook for your boots, in case you want to slip them off. There's a small comb and brush and some extra hairpins, too." Egypt began to repack her makeup kit. "I'll be on the set for any touch-ups that you may need." Dropping in one last tube of mascara, she closed the case with a loud snap. "Okay, I think that's it. Let's go."

Kathleen hesitated. When she'd first seen the dress, the idea had quickly formed. If she didn't ask now she knew she'd always have regrets. "Please, can you wait just a moment?" She opened the top drawer of her bureau and withdrew a small black jewelry box. "Do you think I could wear this?" She lifted the beautiful cameo brooch from its velvet nest and held it to her throat. "My great-grandfather, Elijah, gave this to his bride, Charlotte, on their wedding day. It was my grandfather Jacob's wedding gift to Louisa, my grandmother. And my mother wore it on her wedding gown." Embarrassed, she lowered her head. "I don't expect to ever have my own wedding day, so I won't carry on the tradition." She looked up. "But I was hoping . . . could I . . . do you think it would be all right if I wore the brooch in the film?"

"Oh, sweetie, you bet. It's a fabulous piece, just the right touch," Egypt replied. Taking the cameo and diamond brooch, she pinned it at Kathleen's throat, then stepped back and inspected her one more time. She frowned. "Do you have contact lenses?"

"No."

"Can you see at all without your glasses?"

Kathleen wasn't sure where this line of questioning was going. "Enough that I don't step out in front of buses or large trucks. Why?"

"They're really great for the period with those cute little wire frames, but I think you'd look better in the shot without them. We don't want the lights to reflect on the lenses, either." Egypt slid Kathleen's glasses into the small drawstring purse. "You've got them with you in case you really need them."

A twist of jitters began to uncoil in Kathleen's stomach. Never had she ever imagined she would be in a movie. This was truly going to be the high adventure of her life.

"Oops," Egypt said, taking hold of Kathleen's wrist. "Here's something we almost forgot, your watch." Undoing the leather strap, she placed the watch on the dresser.

"Can't I put it in the purse with my glasses?" Kathleen asked. She gave an apologetic shrug. "I know it sounds silly, but I've always liked to know what time it is."

Egypt didn't hesitate. "Sure, no problem." After dropping the watch in Kathleen's purse, Egypt gave her a quick thumbs-up. "Now you're perfect, absolutely perfect."

Kathleen lifted her fingers to the cameo at her throat and gave a small, nervous laugh. "No. Now I'm terrified, absolutely terrified."

JESSE STEPPED INTO the barn and watched Tooter make some last-minute height adjustments to the light bars. Two banks of lights had been set on high tripods, one on either side of the barn aisle, with reflectors positioned right behind them. Two other bars were positioned in the middle of the aisle beside the camera. Tooter's crew had unpacked and set up all the equipment to his specifications.

About twenty-five feet inside the front of the barn, the main camera stood on a track in the middle of the aisle. The fourteen-foot track extended halfway through the barn. A second camera was on an eight-foot high scaffold to the left. The scene would be shot from both angles and then edited and spliced together later.

Thick cables from the lights and cameras, black and tangled like snakes, ran back across the barn floor to the electrical outlets on the walls on either side of the barn behind the cameras. The storyboard for the shoot was propped on a table off to the left. A tub filled with ice, soft drinks, and bottled water, a coffee urn, and five bakery boxes of doughnuts and bagels took up every remaining inch of the tabletop. Tooter's crew ate like starving hyenas.

Six horses, delivered earlier by the academy's stable master and his helper, now occupied the stalls that would show in the scene. Another, a huge Belgian draft horse in full harness, patiently stood cant-hipped in the aisle behind the cameras. His scene would come later.

Items that would have been found in a barn in the late 1800s had been added as well. A straw-bristled push broom leaned against the wall, coiled ropes and leather halters hung on the wooden pegs outside of the stalls, and two sets of harness hung from hooks beside the grain boxes. Wooden buckets and old oak barrels were stacked at the far end of the barn and antique kerosene lanterns hung on hooks along the wall. A layer of straw hid the concrete floor, and overhead, the hay had been heaped close to the edge of the loft. No detail had been forgotten.

Pleased, Jesse nodded. Everything looked perfect for the shoot. And then it returned. The insidious phantom touch sent a chill to his bones. Maybe he should have purified the place, smudged it with cedar smoke and prayers the way his grandfather and his grandfather's grandfather would have done. Maybe that would have appeased whatever restless spirits still roamed DuBois and vied for his attention.

Jesse tried to dismiss the odd feelings, tried to explain them as being nothing more than worry about making the best film he could. But the teachings of Grandma Boo and the beliefs of his people were too ingrained, too much a part of Jesse Spotted Horse. The haunts didn't budge.

Everything was going okay, wasn't it? Nothing bad had happened. It was only a ridiculous feeling . . . right? For the last couple of days, he'd helped Tooter film the photographs from the archives that Kathleen had allowed him to use. Some of the editing had already been done, too, putting the shoot a couple of days ahead of schedule. Yeah, there were no problems. Everything was fine.

Jesse watched Tooter give some last-minute instructions to the cameraman on the scaffold. He worked easy, nothing made him rush. He was lucky to have Tooter. He'd never have considered filming *Stolen Childhood, Stolen Culture* without him. Not only was Tooter Poolaw his best friend, he was the best damned cameraman Jesse had ever worked with. The Oklahoma Kiowa might have a personality that was over the wall, but Tooter also had a sixth sense about lighting and angles.

At first Jesse had wondered if the barn was the right place to shoot this scene. According to all accounts, Providence Divine had tried to keep Night Shield from visiting DuBois. The Reverend had written in his journal that his staff believed the tribal leader's visit would cause an uprising among some of the older students who wanted to go home. None of the students had been told of Night Shield's arrival, not even the man's own two sons. Not even his sickly daughter. The driver who met the Lakota leader at the train depot had been instructed to take him to the stables. He would wait there for the Reverend to meet him.

After careful thought, Jesse knew the barn scene had to be in the film. It was the perfect way to show the disrespect and the contempt that the school faculty actually held for the Indians.

"How's it going?" Jesse stepped further into the barn.

"We're just about ready." Tooter didn't take his eyes off the adjustments he was making to the light bar. "Has Kathleen shown up yet?" He tightened a bolt with a twist of his wrench.

"Not yet. Egypt's with her now."

"Yeah?" Tooter tested the light bar, then set his wrench to the bolt again. "So, tell me about that gorgeous hot and kinky wild woman you hired to do makeup." Tooter wiggled his butt. "I wouldn't mind doin' a little *makeup* on her myself when we're done here." He gave a wicked chuckle. "Do ya think she'd be interested in some good 'n' hot Kiowa lovin'?"

"Careful, don't trip over your hormones." Jesse chuckled. He'd figured Egypt would whet Tooter's appetite. They'd certainly make quite a pair. He'd also have paid a bundle to be a fly on the wall in Kathleen's apartment when Egypt Goldenbird walked through the door.

Five years ago, when he'd first met Egypt, she'd been plain Sara Louise Gildenkrofft with mouse-brown hair, braces on her teeth, and a Ph.D. in anthropology. There hadn't been a tattoo or a piercing in sight. A two-year study of the culture of the punk and Goth music scenes had changed all of that. "We may be surprised with Katie-girl's transformation, you never know."

"Yeah, right. Anyway, when they show up, everything's

ready to go . . . if the guy you hired to play Providence Divine is here, too."

"He's in the trailer getting dressed. Well, actually he's getting redressed," Jesse answered, stepping over the knot of cables. He rested his hand on the rump of the big draft horse as he passed behind it. "He tried to do his own costuming and showed up looking like Ichabod Crane." Jesse stood behind Tooter. "I see Bobby and the kids are all settled in."

"Yeah," Tooter replied, giving the wrench another twist. "They got in this morning. Thank God he brought his wife and sister with him. He'd never get those youngsters dressed in their costumes without them. The group we'll need for this shoot are just about ready; the others will be in about an hour."

"Good. That'll give us time to get the scene done here, and then we can move outside for the shot of the kids on the parade ground."

Tooter shifted the tripod and tested the clamp on the reflector. Satisfied, he slid the tool into his back pocket. He glanced over his shoulder at Jesse and did a double take. "Holy Saint Tonto, Horse!" He slowly walked around Jesse. "You are unbelievable." Tooter hummed a few bars of the *Twilight Zone* theme and, with his arms folded over his chest, slowly inspected Jesse from head to toe. "Good gawd, man, you look like you just stepped through a time warp from the 1880s."

"Don't get too carried away." Jesse laughed. It had felt strange to put his Indian clothes on. The last time he'd worn them was four years ago at the dance the tribal council had held for Grandma Boo's seventy-fifth birthday. Since then, they'd been packed away. The clothes still fit, but he'd had to spend time the night before working on them until they looked less powwow and more historically accurate.

The moccasins had been his father's. Beaded in traditional Lakota colors and pattern, they'd been worn only once before, at the farewell dance for Carl Spotted Horse before he went to Nam. The buckskin leggings hadn't lost any of their suppleness, and the fringes on the edges swayed softly with each step. His great-grandfather's war shirt, with its beaded strips over the shoulders, scalplock drops, and brass trade-bead trim, fit as though it had been tailored just for him. He'd felt uncomfortable putting it on, though. In the old days a war shirt was an honor that was earned. Now the old ways were gone. No one had the right anymore.

His porcupine-hair roach was in with the things that Tooter had packed, but he'd decided to forego the headgear. Night Shield would have tied eagle feathers in his hair, a display of his prowess on the battlefield and his power among his people.

After tightly plaiting a narrow scalplock braid at the crown of his head, Jesse had used an eight-inch length of leather thong to tie the three black-and-white feathers snugly against his head at the base of the braid. He had wrapped a buckskin thong around the tail of the braid and decorated it with a trio of brass hawk bells. The rest of his hair hung almost to his waist in two braids and he'd wrapped narrow strips of red trade cloth around each braid, securing at the ends with a single looped knot. A pair of old silver ball and cone earrings hung from his ears.

The old chief's blanket that belonged to Tooter's father was a perfect addition. Folded lengthwise, he'd draped it over one shoulder and across his chest to display the beautiful strip of beadwork that spanned the fabric edge to edge.

Before he had dressed himself, Jesse had cleansed the clothes, purifying them as his ancestors would have done with cedar smoke and prayer. He had prayed that his film would bring honor to his Lakota people and to the children whose lives had been changed forever at DuBois, he had prayed that his people would find pride in his work, and he had prayed that he could take news of *Tokalu Sapa* home to Grandma Boo.

Tooter touched the fringe on the old war shirt, then adjusted the chief's blanket. "Holy crap, man. Lookin' at you is like looking into the past." Tooter rubbed the back of his neck, then slowly shook his head in wonder. "*Suŋgléska*," he breathed. "You'd have made a hell of a warrior, Horse."

"Hey, guys."

At the sound of Egypt's voice, Jesse and Tooter turned.

Outlined by the frame of the barn door and highlighted by a touch of sunlight, Kathleen Prescott stood next to Egypt and looked as though she had stepped out of a fine painting. Beautiful. Breathtaking. Beyond belief. Stunned, neither man spoke. Jesse didn't think he could, even if he tried.

# Chapter 6

The purpose of the school is to lead the Indian from a life of poverty, dirt and ignorance.

—ONTARIO INDIAN,
VOL. 3, NO. 10, 1880

KATHLEEN SLIPPED HER glasses from the drawstring purse and put them on. After one look she could barely draw a breath and knew it had absolutely nothing to do with the tightly laced corset. The wild, erratic rush of her heart had nothing to do with the corset, either.

She knew Jesse would portray Night Shield, but she'd given little thought to how he would look dressed in his Indian clothes. With or without her glasses, Kathleen wished that she had given it more thought and had better prepared herself.

She nervously twisted her fingers in the draw cord of the little purse and stared at him. No, there was absolutely no way she could have prepared herself. *Oh, Kathleen, be careful. This is something you don't know how to handle.* She searched her mind for words to describe the Jesse Spotted Horse who looked as though a century had disappeared into thin air. Only one word came to mind. *Magnificent.*

He seemed taller, his shoulders broader, his manner more imposing, his bearing regal. There had been no doubt about his heritage before when he'd worn his boots and jeans and his favorite Henley shirts. But now that the layers of the present-day world had been peeled away and modern clothing discarded for traditional, there wasn't an inch of him that wasn't pure Lakota. The warriors who had been

his ancestors seemed to have come forward and shaped him
into what his blood demanded.

"Oh, my." Kathleen sighed, unable to speak above a
whisper.

"Easy, girl." Egypt poked Kathleen. "He's just a man."

"Oh, yes, he certainly is." Afraid to look at Jesse for too
long, afraid someone might see the blush that burned her
cheeks, she slid her glasses back into her purse. "I had no
idea."

Egypt gave a snort. "Yeah, right." She tugged on Kathleen's arm. "Come on, sweetie. Time for *you* to dazzle
'em."

They both gave wide berth to the huge Belgian horse
tied to the wall-mounted hitching ring and stopped in front
of Jesse and Tooter. Moving aside, Egypt swept her arm in
a wide arc that ended with a flourish in Kathleen's direction. She spoke in the worst English accent that Kathleen
had ever heard.

"Gentlemen, may I present the star of the day—the
lovely, the beautiful, the incomparable Miss Kathleen
Prescott." She nudged Kathleen to step forward. "Ta-
daaaa!"

Stunned, Kathleen didn't move. No one had ever used
her name and *beautiful, lovely,* and *incomparable* in the
same sentence before. Her gaze flew to Jesse and she anx-
iously waited for his reaction. His eyes seemed to widen a
little, but that was the only change in his expression. Did he
agree with Egypt? Was he pleased or disappointed? She
couldn't tell.

She glanced at Tooter and found a similar look on his
face. Where were his usual jokes, his usual teasing?

*Do I look that bad?* The question hit hard and pushed a
resigned and ragged sigh through her lips. *Of course I do.
Why should some paint and powder make any difference,
no matter who had applied it?* Maybe if Egypt redid her
hair and makeup? No. Why bother? Jesse's silence spoke
volumes.

With the bitter ache of disappointment, she surrendered.
Why waste any more of Jesse's time and money? There
was only one thing to do.

Swallowing what felt like an elephant-sized lump of defeat, she finally found her voice. "I don't look the way you hoped I would, do I?" Out of nervous habit, her trembling hand moved to her throat, where her fingers fidgeted, tracing the edge of the cameo brooch. "Please don't blame Egypt. It's not her fault. She did everything she could." She glanced at Egypt for validation, but found only a puzzled frown.

Kathleen set a resolute upward tilt to her chin and squared her shoulders. She'd dealt with disappointment like this before. It hurt, but she'd always survived. *You'd think I'd learn.* She grazed her fingers down over the buttons on the bodice, then clutched the little drawstring purse with both hands to her waist. She looked at Jesse. "I'm sorry I wasted your time and money." She began backing away. "I'm sure you won't have any trouble finding someone more attract . . . suited for your needs." Her smile was half-hearted and counterfeit. "I'm sorry." The lump pushed back up her throat. *I'd die before I let him see my disappointment.* "Now, if you'll excuse me."

Without waiting for Jesse's response, Kathleen lifted her head and, with all the dignity she could muster, turned to leave. The lead weight in her heart made every step of her retreat difficult, but she pushed herself toward the door. How could she have been foolish enough to believe that an hour or so with Egypt and her paints and brushes could actually produce a swan where for thirty years there had been only an ugly duck?

The touch came, feather light, warm, nothing more than a whisper of skin against skin, grazing her hand, then taking hold of her fingers. The voice, like the touch, was soft and gentle.

"Please, Katie-girl, don't go."

Jesse had come after her. Jesse had asked her to stay. He still held her hand. *Dear God, please don't let this be pity.* She couldn't stand it if it was.

She turned and immediately began to melt under his dark gaze. She'd never felt the sensation before. Something sweet, delicious, and fragile flowed through her body like sun-warmed honey. Her knees weakened and for a moment she thought she would crumple to the floor. Even her heart had reacted, beating at an erratic pace. The tight grip she always held on her self-control was slipping. It all felt so glorious and it terrified her.

Gathering her wits, she flew to safety, stepping behind the prim and staid battlements she'd surrounded herself with all of her life. Once there she found her familiar cool, resolute composure. She found sanctuary. *Kathleen, you're acting like a silly love-struck ninny. And he called me that stupid, horrible name again . . . Katie-girl, indeed.* Her brow arced sharply. "I believe I've asked you before, don't call me that ridiculous name. My name is Kathleen."

The most marvelous grin she had ever seen met her biting words and released the delicious honeyed heat again, changing it into wild and fiery lava as it renewed its amazing journey.

"Yeah, I know it is, Katie-girl. I know it is."

He tugged lightly on her hand, forcing her to take short reluctant steps toward him. She stopped when she dared go no closer, when her wide skirt touched his legs and tipped, when she could smell the light pine fragrance that was his alone.

"I don't want anyone else, Kathleen, I want you."

Her eyes were level with his lips. She watched him say the words and felt the light, warm caress of his breath that came with each one. She forgot to stifle the wistful sigh that rose in her throat. Moonlight and thoughts of a lover's embrace tiptoed into her mind. *Stop this instant! Fantasies and dreams are a waste of your time and have absolutely no place in your life.* Ah, yes, another snippet from the Divine-Prescott creed, how typical for it to raise its prudent head at a time like this.

She suddenly felt the sharp bite of guilt sinking its teeth. She'd never questioned her life's service before. Why now? Why the sarcasm? But the truth was that besides her life's work, all she had were fantasies and dreams.

*I want you.* His words thrilled her, but Kathleen wasn't so naive to believe they were about anything but the film. Looking up, she became hopelessly caught in the depths of his dark eyes again. All sense of time disappeared.

"Ahem . . . yoo-hoo . . . anybody?" Tooter shuffled his feet in the straw-strewn floor and waved his hand. "Over here. Hello. Are we gonna make a movie here today, or what?"

The silence continued for a breath or two, and then, as if he'd suddenly awakened from a trance, Jesse glanced over his shoulder. "Uh . . . yeah . . . sure, as soon as Ichabod gets here."

Tooter laughed. "Now that you've insulted the man, I probably should tell ya. He's been standing beside Egypt for, oh, about five minutes."

Embarrassed, Jesse greeted the actor he'd hired. "I'm so sorry." He smiled and lifted his shoulder in an apologetic shrug. "How do I look with a size twelve moccasin in my mouth?"

"Looks good," Tooter replied, "just don't choke on the beads."

"Thanks," Jesse murmured. He placed his hand on Kathleen's arm and gently turned her around. "Kathleen, meet your great-great-grandfather."

"Actually, it's Arthur Summers, or Ichabod, whichever you prefer," the man said, a friendly smile filling his face. He extended his hand. "I'm very pleased to be working with you, Miss Prescott."

Stunned by the actor's appearance, Kathleen stared much too long. Embarrassed by her lack of manners, she took his hand. "Hello, it is so very nice to meet you, too."

Though perhaps not as tall as she knew her great-great-grandfather to have been, the man's resemblance to the photos of Providence was uncanny, even unsettling. Suddenly dizzy, she felt as though time had flipped in a wild twist and leaped backward, taking her with it. She grasped Jesse's arm to steady herself.

"Are you all right?" He gave her hand a slight squeeze.

After gulping a breath or two, she stepped away from him. "It must be the tight cor . . . costume."

"Okay, everyone," Tooter interrupted, clapping his hands. "Let's do this in one or two takes. We're gonna do a walk-through first so everybody knows what they're supposed to do."

As Tooter explained the scene about Providence and his wife, Rachel, greeting Night Shield, Jesse kept his eyes on Kathleen. What had happened in this woman's life to make her question her own self-worth? She was so direct, so determined, and even damned feisty when it came to anything about the school, the museum, or her family. But when it was just about her, just about Kathleen, she seemed to fold into herself. Did she really think that she had no value unless she was coupled with Providence Divine's legacy? He remembered the thought he'd had a few days before. DuBois *was* Kathleen Prescott's prison.

"Kathleen," Tooter said, leading her to Arthur Summers's side, "you're gonna take Arthur's right arm, and I want you both to come into the barn through the back door and walk toward camera one." He stepped about twenty paces from the camera and scuffed some straw aside. "When you get here, you're gonna stop." He bent down and stuck an eight-inch strip of red tape to the concrete floor. "This is called a mark. So if I say 'hit your mark,' you make sure you're standing where the tape is."

He turned to Jesse. "Okay, Horse, you're gonna walk from behind camera one, on the left side, and meet up with Kathleen and Arthur at their mark. Have y'all got that?" He glanced from Jesse to Arthur and then to Kathleen. "Good."

Tooter pointed out the back door. "Some of the kids that Bobby brought from the rez will be in the shot, too, outside in the background walking across the lawn—just like any normal day at good old DuBois High." Tooter chuckled at his own joke, then moved back to his camera. "Night Shield and Providence had quite a showdown when they met that day. So I want you guys to stand and face each other so the shot will show you both in full profile. That way it'll look more confrontational. Camera two up on the scaffold will get another angle. Okay?" He paused for a moment, looking from Arthur to Jesse. "Any questions? No? Good. Let's run through it and then we'll shoot."

Jesse shivered. The uneasy feeling slid under his skin again. Tangible, as though someone, or something, were breathing on the back of his neck. Every nerve in his body tightened and burned in response.

*What in the hell is going on?* He looked around the old barn, trying to find the answer. In the bright sunlight common sense told him there was nothing to worry about, that it was nothing more than camera jitters, but it was being raised on a reservation by an old traditional Lakota woman that had him thinking about ghosts again, thinking about the *waŋagi.*

"Horse, are you ready? Horse?" Tooter stepped forward, a worried frown creasing his brow.

"Huh? Yeah, sure. Let's do it." The ominous feeling stayed and seemed to press down on him as he walked slowly toward Arthur and Kathleen. Stopping on his mark, he still felt its touch.

"We're not shooting audio, but I don't want you to just stand there like sticks and not talk. Arthur, introduce Jesse to Kathleen." Tooter nodded. "Kathleen, just greet him with a nod. Now, Jesse and Arthur, I don't care if y'all take turns saying 'Mary had a little lamb,' just make it look like you're talking and things are getting hot and angry between the two of you." He turned back to the camera, then scanned the setup once more. "Good. I think you've all got it. Okay, let's shoot." He raised his fingers to his lips and loudly whistled. "Places everybody . . . let's see if we can get this done in one."

One of Tooter's crew stepped in front of the camera with the clapboard. "Scene one, take one." The hinged top of the board closed with a loud pop.

Before the word *action* had cleared Tooter's lips, a thunderous boom, and then another, resounded from the front of the barn. Egypt shrieked. Jesse moved first and, in less than twenty strides, was beside the large Belgian horse as it kicked out at the wall a third time. "Whoa, boy, easy now." He grasped the halter with one hand and slowly stroked the horse's massive neck with his other. The gelding squealed, tossed its head, and then struck out with its hind leg once again. "Hey, easy, whoa now, easy," he cajoled, running his hand down over the horse's shoulder and across its ribs, quickly inspecting the Belgian's belly and hind legs. "The clapboard might have spooked him, but I think it could've been a wasp or a bee. I don't see anything now."

Tooter called over his shoulder to one of the grips, "Hey, Mike, baby-sit the horse, will ya?" The man hesitated. "Just stand there and keep him quiet, dammit." Tooter turned back to Jesse. "Now, let's get back to work."

After another walk-through, they were ready to shoot. Jesse watched Kathleen. She was clearly nervous, but there was a radiance about her that was fresh and brand-new. A lovely rosy blush tinted her cheeks and her eyes sparkled with excitement. *I'm glad I asked her to do this.* The declaration had marched strong and solid into his mind. It was like watching the opening of a blossom, the bud going from something tightly wrapped, protecting its inner being, to the graceful unfurling of its petals, opening up, taking more and more chances on life. Another thought struck, just as strong and just as solid. *She has absolutely no idea how lovely she is.*

"Ready?" Tooter asked, looking around at his crew, then back over his shoulder at the large horse. "We won't use the clapboard." He pointed at one of the crew standing at the back door. "Okay, Eddy, stand outside and give the kids their cue to begin walking by the barn. Tell 'em not to look in when they go by." Tooter double-checked his camera setting, then looked up and nodded at the crew on the scaffold. "Okay, places, everybody, we're ready to go." He raised his hand and held up three fingers. "Three, two, one . . . cameras rolling, now . . . action."

Following Tooter's direction, Jesse walked toward Kathleen and Arthur. Standing on their marks, they faced each other.

"Good. That looks great," Tooter said. "Now, talk."

Jesse felt ridiculous, but he began saying what he imagined Night Shield might have said to Providence. Arthur quickly picked up on the idea. The confrontation seemed so real that Kathleen looked startled.

"Great, fantastic everyone, film's still rolling," Tooter declared. "Kathleen, that look on your face is a perfect touch."

Jesse felt the intensity grow between his character and Arthur Summers's, and just when he figured they'd get the scene in one take, all hell broke loose.

The barrage of hooves hitting the wall and angry, pain-filled squeals from the big gelding at the front of the barn started all over again. The sound of the horse's shod hooves striking the wall and stomping on the concrete floor sounded like cannon fire.

"Mike, what in the hell is going on back there?" Tooter yelled.

Before the man answered, the big horse reared back. Fighting against the tie rope, pulling it taut, the gelding plunged and bucked. With a loud bang, the hitching ring, its long bolt still attached, pulled out of the wall and hit the horse on the nose. Terrified, it wildly tossed its head, sending the halter rope with the hitching ring on the end whipping through the air like a medieval weapon.

"Mike, grab the damned rope! Get a hold of the bastard!" Tooter yelled. "Egypt, look out!"

Loose, the Belgian spun away from the wall. It scrambled for footing on the concrete floor, then swerved, missing Egypt by inches. Mike jumped in front of the horse and tried to grab the rope, but the Belgian dodged to the right, hitting the tub of drinks. Ice and bottles flew, spooking the horse even more, sending it skidding into the tangle of cables. Trying to rid itself of the wires that had become snarled around its legs, the huge horse kicked out again and again. With a final squeal, it bolted for the open front door, the cables still wrapped around its legs.

Yanked off the scaffold by its taut cable, camera two fell and smashed on the floor before the plug pulled loose. Tooter's camera toppled from the track and bumped into two of the lighting tripods. Jesse lunged for the tripods but couldn't reach either of them before they pitched over, knocking over the other lights. The exploding bulbs sounded like gunfire.

Jesse prayed that he could snatch the light stands off the floor before the hot bulbs touched the straw. If he didn't reach them in time, the barn would become an inferno.

As his fingers were about to close around the first set of lights, a *whoosh*, a sound like nothing he'd ever heard before, filled the air. Flames shot up, feeding on the straw on the floor, and he jumped back, feeling the searing heat on his face and hands. He grabbed at the lights again, but it was impossible to get near them. The fire was already out of control.

Flames spiked up either side of the barn and raced along the upper deck of the hayloft, devouring the hay in its path and licking hungrily at the dry barn wood. Smoke billowed, thick and black. It poured over the edge of the hayloft and down the aisle and engulfed everyone and everything in its path.

"Water! Get some water on this damn fire!" Jesse shouted over the roar of the flames. "Someone help me get the horses outta here!"

"Jesse!" Kathleen cried, her scream becoming a strangled cough.

"Kathleen! Get out here!"

"Jesse!" she shrieked. "I can't see. Help me!"

"Where are you?" Why hadn't she run out the back of the barn when the fire had first started? Holding the end of the chief's blanket up against his face, he tried to breathe through the fabric without choking on the smoke.

"Jesse!"

"Kathleen, where are you? I can't see you."

"Please . . . oh, God . . . help me!"

Turning toward the sound of Kathleen's voice, he blindly reached out for her through the smoke. "Where are you?" The acrid cloud burned his eyes, and he quickly rubbed each eye to get rid of the tears before he swept his arm through the smoke again. "Kathleen? Talk to me . . . where are you?" He heard her choking. Straight ahead, maybe a little to his right. He took another step and another and reached out for a third time. On the fourth try his fingers grazed her body. Thank God! Tightening his fingers around her arm, he hauled her against him and put the blanket over her nose. "Breathe, sweetheart, keep your head down." Damn it, damn it! Which way was out?

The smoke had become so thick he could feel it moving against his skin as though it were a living thing. He shuddered and pulled another draught of air through the blanket. The material was a poor filter, but it did help a little.

He'd never seen burning hay and straw give off so much

dense, dark smoke. He could understand if the hay had
been fresh cut, green and damp, but it was tinderbox dry.
The speed with which the smoke had filled the barn was
odd, too. He held Kathleen tightly at his side. The smoke
was so thick that if she stepped away from him, he'd never
find her again.

"Tooter! Where the hell are you?" He pulled another
breath through the blanket. "Damn it, Tooter, answer me."
Jesse listened for a reply. Nothing.

There were no sounds at all, just an eerie silence within
the caul of smoke. Even the crackling sound of the fire had
disappeared. Had everyone else made it out safely? Why
couldn't he hear them trying to fight the fire or trying to
find him and Kathleen? The terrified horses imprisoned in
their stalls should be screaming and kicking the walls down
trying to escape, and yet the only sound he'd heard was
Kathleen's voice.

"Jesse, I can't . . . breathe."

He felt her body tremble as she gasped and coughed.
She clutched his arm and fell against him. He knew time
was running out. If he didn't get her out of the smoke, she
might not make it.

"Hang on, Katie-girl, I'm going to get us out of here."

For half a second the noxious cloud parted. In that brief
moment he saw the rear door of the barn, the green grass
and blue sky beyond. In the next half-second the smoke
closed around them once again, but now Jesse knew where
he was going. "Come on. Hang on to me." He wrapped his
arm around Kathleen's waist and then, half pulling and half
lifting her, dashed toward the back door. The sound of her
gasping made him all the more determined to get her safely
outside.

The gravel of the driveway crunched under the soles of
his moccasins and felt like a blessing. They'd made it outside. They were safe.

He drew Kathleen into his arms. "It's okay, it's okay,"
he gasped. "Come on, breathe. It's okay to breathe, we're
out of it." He took gulp after gulp of fresh air until his head
swam. He never imagined that air could taste and smell so

good. He tipped Kathleen's head up so he could see her face. "Are you okay? Katie-girl, answer me. Please."

Kathleen opened her eyes and gave a slight nod. "Yes, yes, thank you, I'm all right." She shuddered. "Jesse, we need to get help. We need to call nine-one-one." Pushing out of his arms, she took a few running steps up the hill toward her office, her wide skirt wildly swaying. And then she stopped. "Oh, my God." She covered her mouth with her hand and took one backward step after another. "Jesse, I don't understand. What's happening? What's going on?"

He stepped beside her. "What? What's the matter?"

Kathleen's hand shook as she pointed up the hill. "Look."

Jesse's gaze followed her pointed finger, and he watched some Indian kids walking across the lawn by the administration building. "Those are just some of the kids that Bobby Big Bow brought with him."

"I don't think so," Kathleen replied, her voice little more than a shaky whisper. "Look. There."

Jesse followed her pointing finger once again, and in an instant, his heart battered frantically against his ribs. His knees almost buckled, and he took a step to keep his balance. Surely what he was looking at was a hallucination. What else could it be? He shot a glance at Kathleen, then looked back up the hill again. "That's impossible."

Two dormitory buildings, redbrick with white wood shutters, with white-railed wraparound porches and upper balconies, now stood where only an hour ago the DuBois Military Academy's new gymnasium had been. A third building, identical to the first two, had also sprouted over the academy's outside basketball court.

"I don't get it . . . buildings don't just grow like weeds," Jesse said, shaking his head. "This doesn't make any sense."

He quickly looked behind him, and although the barn had been engulfed in smoke and fire only moments before, it now stood empty, no fire, no smoke. There wasn't a camera, a light bar, Tooter, Egypt, Arthur, or a film crew in sight. A chill uncoiled within his gut and wrapped around his sense of reality, touching every nerve in his body and making him reel. Was this what that uneasy feeling had been all about? Had he been given a warning . . . a warning delivered by a *waŋagi*?

He shook his head as if that simple motion could dislodge the ridiculous thought from his mind. "This is all a bunch of crap. I'm going to find out what the hell is going on." Hesitating only a moment, he stepped back into the barn. Different horses dozed in the stalls, and the hanging light fixtures in the rafters had disappeared. He ran his hand over the wide-planked walls, finding clean white wash where he'd expected to find scorched boards. Sweet clover and timothy hay filled the loft, and not a wisp of smoke hung in the air.

He slowly raised the edge of the blanket he wore up to his nose, afraid what he might find . . . or what he might not find. He sniffed the fabric twice and then a confirming third time. No smoky odor, just the light scent of cedar and sage. "This is totally insane." He slowly walked the length of the barn, studying every inch along the way. "Or *I'm* going insane."

He ran his hand over the rusty iron pump. Only a little while ago a new lever-action faucet had been in the same place. The kerosene lanterns still hung on their pegs, the wooden buckets were still stacked on the floor, but the large barrels and the two sets of harness had disappeared. Lifting the lids, Jesse looked into the grain bins. Two days ago they had been empty. Now each was filled almost to the brim—not with the kind of mixed feed of crushed oats, corn, and molasses that was popular with the horse owners he knew—but with old-fashioned whole oats.

Glancing back toward the open door, he watched Kathleen take a few wobbly steps. Her body swayed as she reached for the doorframe to steady herself. "God, don't faint on me, Katie-girl." He rushed to her side and she whimpered when he touched her. "It's okay, it's okay. I promise, we'll figure this out."

Shaking, she turned and pressed her face against Jesse's shoulder. "I think I already have."

# Chapter 7

I felt as if I were dead and traveling to the Spirit Land; for now, all my old ideas were to give place to new ones, and my life was to be entirely different from that of the past.

—CHARLES EASTMAN,
SANTEE SIOUX

"WHAT? SAY THAT again."

Kathleen took her wire-framed glasses out of the small purse and settled them on her nose. Now that she could see, she felt more like herself—if she would ever truly feel like herself again. The very idea of what might have happened terrified her. A slip through the barriers of time. It went against all reason, against every sensible thought she'd ever had.

She tried to remain calm, but her heart continued to beat at a frantic pace. The disappearance of Tooter, Egypt, the film crew, the cameras—the sudden reappearance of the school's buildings and the changes inside the barn; what other explanation could there be? She looked at Jesse. "It's the only thing that makes sense."

"Makes sense?" He shook his head. "You can't be serious." He walked a few paces away, then suddenly stopped, pivoted on his heel, and faced her again. "Let's see if I've got this straight. You're saying that the smoke was some sort of portal . . . a door we passed through and traveled back in time." He firmly shook his head. "No. Impossible. I've read H. G. Wells's book, Kathleen. I've even seen the movies. It's fiction."

"Jesse, for just one moment put common sense and reality aside." She moved back to the barn door and looked up the hill. "Those buildings are solid. They're not a mirage, you can't see through them. One burned down in 1923, the other two were demolished in 1999; and yet, there they are." She stepped back into the barn. "And in here; where are the electric lights, the chrome water faucet, and the concrete floor? Half an hour ago they were here and now they're gone."

"There's got to be some reasonable explanation."

Kathleen sighed, determined to prove her point. "I've studied photographs of this place from the 1880s. You've seen them. This is exactly how it was then." She carefully chose her next words. "I really do think we've experienced some sort of time shift." She watched him struggling to accept her theory. "I can't explain it any other way."

"Tooter and Egypt . . . my whole film crew has disappeared into thin air. It's as though they don't exist."

"And they don't. Not yet."

"Are you listening to yourself?" Jesse passed his hand over his brow. His laugh rang hollow. "Doesn't what you're saying scare you? I know you've got me spooked."

Scared? She'd never been more scared in her life. But in the last few minutes she'd found a new strength in herself that amazed her. Where had it come from? Where had it been all of her life? Maybe it had just been waiting for the right time to show itself. "Of course I'm scared, but unless we're both having the same hallucination, we are going to have to deal with this."

"So, you want me to believe that somehow, through some kind of mystical *abracadabra,* we're in the 1880s?"

To answer his question she had to face the unnerving fact herself. Finally she gave her answer. "Yes, I do."

Jesse looked around the barn again and gave a quick shrug. "Okay, suppose you're right. Let's say we've been zapped back in time." His choice of words and the way he said them made his doubt clear. "Let's suppose that this is over a hundred or so years from where we were fifteen minutes ago. So, now what? We don't know what year it is, or the month or the day. We don't know how to get back and we don't know why the hell we're here."

"I've never read H. G. Wells," Kathleen said. "You have?"

"You mean *The Time Machine*?"

"If that's the book you were referring to, yes."

"A long time ago, why?"

"Because I *have* read Jules Verne, the book about Captain Nemo and the Nautilus."

"That's great, Kathleen, we've both got library cards?"

She ignored his cut. "As improbable as that story was when Mr. Verne wrote it, today almost every navy in the world has submarines." She paused, hoping he'd get the point. "Maybe there *are* answers in Mr. Wells's book."

He shook his head. "It's fiction, not a textbook. It's not *Time Travel for Dummies.*"

She raised her hand as if her gesture could stop his resistance to her theory. "Did the time machine always take the person backward or forward to the same date but different year?" He looked at her as though she'd lost her mind. Maybe she had.

"I think so, unless the time rider changed the date on a dial on the machine." He gave an exasperated groan. "This is nuts. Why are we even talking about the damn book?"

"Hear me out. What if we've changed years but not the month or the day? We didn't have a time machine, so we didn't have any dials to change, right? So it's possible that today is still the fourteenth of June, just the year has changed."

She moved to the open back door of the barn and looked up the hill. A woman walking along the path caught her attention. At first startled to see a live human being, Kathleen could barely contain her excitement and whirled about to face Jesse. "I not only know what the date is, I know the year."

He joined her at the door. "What magical law of physics and fiction are you conjuring up now?"

Kathleen pulled him into the shadows and pointed up the hill. "Do you see the woman going into the administration building? Can you see the white bandage on her left arm?"

"Yeah, so?"

"That is Margaret Lester. I recognize her from the photos in the archives." She glanced up the hill again, excited that she could finally prove her theory to Jesse. "Remember, you asked me about her the other day?"

"You said she'd been here from . . . what, 1883 to sometime in '86. Right?"

Kathleen saw the spark of excitement in his dark eyes. Maybe he was beginning to believe her.

"So, what is the year? You've got three to choose from."

"No, just one." Kathleen felt giddy. Her life spent studying every item in the archives and reading all the journals was about to pay off for more than tourist dollars. "According to an entry in the school's infirmary records, on the eleventh of June 1886 Margaret Lester burned her left arm on a gas lamp."

A frown creased Jesse's brow. "How can you remember . . ."

"I've lived with these records all of my life. There's a lot of information that I remember, and probably a lot I don't." She shrugged. "But I remember the date she burned her arm because it's my birthday. So, if this is the same date from where we began, then today is the fourteenth of June 1886."

Jesse folded his arms over his chest, leaned back against the wall, and closed his eyes for a moment. When he opened them, she saw uncertainty in their depths.

"This is all so damn unbelievable," he said. "I don't know if you're right, but if you are, how do we get back where we belong?" He pushed away from the wall. "Where's the magic door, the damned stargate?" He walked to the place where Tooter had put the red tape on the floor and moved the toe of his moccasin in the hard-packed dirt as if hoping to find a scrap of tape. After a moment he looked up at Kathleen and gave a compliant shrug. "Okay, maybe you're right."

Kathleen felt an odd vibration shimmer through her body. Excitement? Apprehension? Maybe a cocktail of both. She looked at the buildings on the hill again, and then turned to Jesse. "This isn't just whimsy. Fate doesn't make something like this happen just for a joke." She thought quietly for a moment. "I think there is a very special reason for the time slide, and I think Fate arranged it just for you and me."

Jesse shot a skeptical look. "Kathleen, what possible reason could Fate or anyone else invent that would put us together on this wild time ride?"

"I firmly believe the answer to that question is quite obvious. We are here so you will see the truth about DuBois and finally have to admit to the wonderful works my family did."

Jesse snorted. "Not very damned likely, Miss Holier-Than-Thou." He pivoted on his heel to walk away but quickly turned back. He leaned close, pointing his finger at her. "*You're* the one who's going to get the harsh lesson in reality. I can't wait to say I told you so."

Kathleen recoiled. Whatever reality remained had slipped away, and she found herself confronted by an angry Lakota warrior. All that was missing was the war paint.

Jesse's shoulders sagged. "I'm sorry. That was uncalled for." He stepped back. "Considering the circumstances, we need to put our differences aside and work together on this."

Kathleen searched his face, trying to find the sincerity of his words and found it in the softened expression in his eyes. She drew a steadying breath. "Even though we don't agree about DuBois, we both have strong connections, emotional and physical, to the past of the school." She touched his arm. "Maybe we're both right, but we'll just have to wait to find out."

"For how long?" Jesse still didn't look convinced. "So, you think that once we figure out why we're here and do whatever we've been sent to do, then we go back to the future?"

"I don't know." Her teeth worried with her bottom lip. "I don't know when or even how we'll go back, but something in my heart tells me to believe that we will."

"I like your optimism, Katie-girl. So, we'd better get busy and figure out how to survive till then."

His gaze traveled over her. "The way you're dressed, you'll have no trouble fitting in. Besides, you know the history of the place and its people." He spread his arms out and the fringes on the sleeves of his buckskin shirt swayed. He laughed, the sound hollow and totally humorless. "I guess I'm dressed for the period, too, aren't I?" He lowered his arms. "But there's only one damn place I'll fit in." He jerked his thumb toward the school. "I'm a little old for the classroom and I don't have a uniform, so I'll have to take my chances."

"Jesse, you know that sometimes older sons of the tribal leaders went to the schools to learn to read, to learn a trade."

"Kathleen, believe what you want. Truth is they came to watch over the younger children from their tribe."

"I'm just saying that your arrival wouldn't be that unusual."

"For them, maybe, but it would be all new territory for me." He draped the stroud blanket over one shoulder, crossed his arms over his chest, and let out a deep breath. "All right, let's hear the rest of your theory."

Excited, Kathleen felt a grin about to break open on her face. "Okay, consider this." She paced a few steps, then stopped and faced Jesse. "The proof, and the answers, are all in the date—June fourteenth." She stuck her thumb in the air. "Number one—in the very early morning hours on the fourteenth of June in 1886 a large group of Indian boys who had been collected from a number of tribes out West arrived in Chicago. There the boys were divided into three smaller groups. One was sent to Hampton, another to Carlisle, and twenty were sent here."

"And?"

"Just hear me out." She drew a breath and raised her index finger. "Number two—in the afternoon on the fourteenth of June 1886, twenty Indian boys arrived at the train depot in Pritchart. They were met by Josiah Wilks and two wagons that would take them to DuBois. Wilks, a geography and history teacher, was also the supervisor of the older boys' dormitory." She paused for a moment and her smile widened. "When they arrived at DuBois, Wilks discovered he actually had twenty-one new students."

Her middle finger joined the first two. "Number three—

on the fourteenth of June 1886, Delia Shore was supposed to arrive on a later train from Ohio, instead she had run off with the Topeka shoe salesman." Her ring finger joined the first three. "Number four—on the fourteenth of June 1886, another teacher arrived at DuBois and was hired to take Delia's place." She paused before she raised her little and final finger. "And number five—on the fourteenth of June 2003, you and I took a fantastic journey to 1886."

"Nothing but coincidences," he rebutted.

Kathleen cautiously peered out the door. "Jesse, we need to decide what we're going to do because I'm sure that Josiah Wilks and the wagons will be coming soon."

"Do you really believe that?"

"Yes," Kathleen replied, her voice soft. "I do."

Jesse shrugged. "You're the one with all the knowledge of this place. Do you have an idea?"

"Yes, I think I do." Her plan was so perfectly simple. "I think that hiding in plain view is the answer."

"What? What are you talking about?"

"Jesse, if you slip into the group of boys when they get off the wagons, everyone will think you came with them." She carefully watched the expression on his face and found doubt.

"What about the Indian agent's papers that were sent with each child? There won't be any to match up with me. What about the head count?"

"Weren't you the one who told me that the records weren't always accurate?" She saw him nod. "Sometimes the paperwork was wrong and sometimes it got lost. Maybe this time it can work to our advantage." She touched his arm. "Jesse, what if you really are the twenty-first student?"

"What?" He stepped away and then quickly turned to face her again. "That's ridiculous!"

"No, it's not. It's very possible. Listen to me, if slipping through time is possible, anything is possible." She moved toward him. "I truly believe you'll be safe."

"Safe? Kathleen, I'm thirty-two years old and I'm six foot two. I'll stand out like an elephant in a herd of gophers." He shook his head. "My age and size will give me some advantage if there's trouble, but an Indian, no matter how old or how tall, was never safe in places like this."

She watched the muscle along the edge of his jaw tighten. "I know how much you hate the school—the whole system, but with the way you're dressed and the fact that you *are* Indian, I can't think of any other way for you to safely stay here until we can figure out how to get back where—or is it when, we came from."

Jesse knew he had to make some sense out of this damned time jumble. God, what an unbelievable mess. He looked at Kathleen. Did she have any idea what faced him if he tried to pass himself off as a student? He'd bet that even after seeing the photos and reading the archives, she didn't know what those two wagonloads of Indian kids were going to go through. And if they went through it, so would he. But, yeah, her plan made sense.

"Okay, Katie-girl, we'll do it your way." He moved back to where she stood and toyed with the grosgrain tie ribbons on her bonnet, letting them slide through his fingers. "But what about you? I can't leave you hiding here in the barn. I'd have to bring table scraps out each night to feed you and the cats."

"I won't be hiding." Kathleen grinned, then pointed her gloved index finger at herself. "I'm Delia Shore's replacement."

Jesse watched her face light up with excitement, her smile too smug for his liking. "Oh, no. I won't let you do it." He firmly shook his head. "It's too dangerous. What happens when the other teacher shows up?"

"Just like it's possible that you're the twenty-first student, what if there is no other teacher? What if *I* am really Mrs. Shore's replacement?"

"You're kidding, right?" he quickly countered.

"No, I'm not. It's *very* possible."

"Oh, come on, Kathleen, it's ludicrous, and you know it." Where were all these damn wild ideas coming from? He wasn't sure if he felt comfortable with the new-and-improved Kathleen.

"Think about it. There are only a few entries about her in Providence's journals. She's never referred to by any name other than Katherine, and she disappeared without a trace."

"When? When did she disappear? If you believe this crazy idea that you're her, if you can remember when she disappeared, we might know when we can—"

"I don't remember an exact date." Kathleen slightly shook, then lowered her head. "Sometime in 1886."

"Well, the idea is absurd. Besides, you're not a teacher. How are you going to pull that off?"

The fire was back in her eyes. "I was homeschooled. I remember my curriculum very well. I can pass as a teacher."

"I don't like it. Besides, you're Kathleen, not Katherine."

"It's not that big a slip-up. I've been called Katherine dozens of times by people I didn't know, even by some I thought I did." She shot a challenging look at him. "If you don't like my suggestion, then what is *your* idea?"

*God, I wish I had one.* He'd never felt so damned helpless in his life. How could he keep Kathleen safe, especially when she kept coming up with all sorts of outrageous theories? How could he get them both out of this nineteenth-century nightmare? What if he couldn't? *You're a damned pitiful superhero, Horse.*

He looked at Kathleen and suddenly felt as though he'd been sucker-punched. When had the metamorphosis happened? *Breathtaking.* The word immediately filled his mind, quickly followed by another. *Beautiful.* High color tinted her cheeks and excitement shone bright in her smoke-gray eyes. *Well, I'll be damned! She is enjoying this! Keep your mind on the problem, Horse. Don't go creating any more.*

"I don't have a plan, but I also don't think you've grasped the danger we're in." He peered out the open door. "Reading or studying about things that happened in the past is one thing, but living it is another." He watched a slight frown crease her brow. "Do you realize how many things could go wrong, things we could goof up on?

"Such as?" She lifted her chin a notch.

"Do you know how to light a gas lamp, light a wood-stove, prime a pump?"

"Not really, but—"

"And you really think that your homeschooled classes have prepared you to teach?"

"Of course it's not like I took a teaching class, but I'm sure I could do it well enough to get by."

He pointed at her clothes. "You can't even get dressed in that getup without help, can you?"

"No." She sighed and turned away.

"Who's the president?"

"Ah-ha!" Kathleen exclaimed. Whirling back to face him, she poked him in the chest. "That one I do know. Grover Cleveland!"

Jesse laughed. "Okay, you're right, I'll give you ten points for Grover, but you're a D on the rest." His smile left his face. "Katie, you're right, I'll fit in easier because I'm Indian. But because I'm Indian the price I'll pay will be greater than you can imagine." He straightened the blanket over his shoulder and stood tall. "Look at me. I want you to remember how I look in my Indian clothes." He touched his braids. "I want you to remember how long my hair is, the eagle feathers, the color of my skin. I want you to remember the scent of cedar and sage on my clothes." He stepped closer and, holding her chin between his thumb and forefinger, tipped her head up until her eyes met his. "I want you to remember because the way I am now is not how I'll look when they get finished with me."

The frown reappeared. "What do you mean?"

He drew his hand away, allowing his fingers to softly brush across her cheek with gentle compassion. "Remember the photographs? Remember the haircuts, the shoes, the starched collars and dark gray military-styled uniforms?"

"Yes, but that all was for the students' benefit."

He saw the challenge in her eyes. Providence Divine's prudish great-great-granddaughter hadn't gone too far away.

"The students were taught good hygiene and how to dress appropriately."

Jesse fought the urge to tell her that it was pretty damned presumptuous of a white man to tell an Indian that his clothing was inappropriate or tell him that dousing himself with cologne to mask body odor was better than bathing; but now wasn't the time to argue. For the first time since she'd unraveled the time puzzle, Kathleen looked uncertain. "Come on, Katie-girl, it'll be okay. We'll figure this out." He drew her into his arms. She felt like a timid bird, small and trembling as she collapsed against him, her hands clutching his shirt.

"I'm scared," she whispered against his chest.

"I know. Me, too."

"You can't be scared, Jesse Spotted Horse," she sniffled. "You are the great and powerful Oz." She struck his chest with the palm of her hand. "You're the one who got me into this mess. 'Be in my movie, Kathleen. It will be fun, Kathleen.'" She lightly pummeled him again. "You said absolutely nothing about visiting the *Twilight Zone*."

Jesse gently lifted her chin, forcing her to look up at him again. "Okay, we'll do it your way. We'll hide among them until we can go home."

He rested his cheek against her brow, the stiff, narrow brim of her bonnet pressing against his temple. How had the day gone so wrong? It was supposed to have been a simple shoot, one four-minute segment of film, not a trip to Never-Never Land.

His thumb caressed the edge of her jaw. "I guess I should wish you happy birthday."

"You already did."

"When?"

"You took me out to dinner."

"But I didn't know it was your bir—"

"Jesse, shh, listen." Kathleen lightly touched her fingers to his lips. "The wagons." She rushed to the front door and cautiously peered out. "They're coming." She turned to face him, wide-eyed with panic. "What are we going to do?"

She was right, he could hear the sound of the wheels on the dirt road and the clanking chains of the tug straps on the horses' harness. "Come on. We'll go out the back, and double around to the front through the trees. When the kids get out of the wagons, I'll slip in among them." He placed his hands on either side of her face and made her look up at him again.

"Kathleen, you've got to understand. Once I'm a student I won't be able to help if you get in trouble or if they get suspicious of you." Her skin felt hot beneath his touch. "I won't have any freedom to help you." He paused, not wanting say his next words. "I'll be one of the DuBois Indians."

He watched her cheeks blanch. "If anyone suspects we know each other or we're caught talking, I'll be punished and you'll be sent away. We've got to be careful and you're going to have to take care of yourself. Can you do that?"

She nodded. "Yes, I can." Squaring her shoulders and with a purposeful step, she moved toward the door. "Let's go."

"Wait!" Jesse grabbed her wrist and pulled her back. "You've still got makeup on your face." He began wiping her skin with his fingers. "You know damned well that the good Reverend Providence Divine isn't going to hire a painted hussy as his new English teacher."

Her smile returned, although less assured. She reached into the drawstring purse and pulled out a couple of tissues. "Egypt put these in here. She said I might need them."

"She was right." He wiped her face, but when his fingers grazed the softness of her lips, a tightness spread through his chest and he heard her draw a ragged breath. In an instant his gaze found hers—smoky gray eyes, wide with wonder. "Oh, Katie-girl," he whispered just before he straightened the perky bonnet on her head, just before he leaned forward, just before he placed a kiss on her forehead.

Gathering his senses, Jesse stepped away. *What the hell am I doing?* Kissing Kathleen Prescott was only going to confuse things, and everything was too confusing already. He tucked the tissues into her purse and led her out the door.

He peered around the corner of the barn, then motioned for Kathleen to follow. "Okay, come on." Holding her hand, he led her through the trees and bushes on the north side of the barn. He could see the first wagon coming up the road. "Get down."

Crouched low in the bushes, they watched the two drivers pull their teams to a halt in front of the barn.

"Who's the guy in the derby?"

"That must be Josiah Wilks," Kathleen whispered. "I think the drivers were two men who did general chores around the school, a Mr. Blunt and a Mr. Slocum." She shook her head. "I don't know which is which, though."

Jesse glanced from Wilks to the passengers of the wagons. Indian boys of all ages huddled together on the floorboards, the young ones sticking close to the bigger boys. Kathleen's hand began to shake in his and when he curled his fingers around her wrist, he felt her racing pulse under his fingertips. "It's okay, you'll do fine," he said quietly, turning to look at her. He lifted her hand to his lips and kissed her knuckles, gave her fingers a light squeeze, and then let go. "Time to go to school."

Kathleen watched him steal through the underbrush, then stop and wait at the edge of the trees until all the boys had climbed out of the wagons. They huddled together, watching every move that the two drivers and Josiah Wilks made. She looked at Jesse again. If his charade was going to work, he had to move now.

Jesse took a furtive glance to the left, the right, then after one last look back at her, he stepped out of the woods. As he walked toward the boys, he tugged at his breechclout as if he'd just slipped into the woods to relieve himself. Without looking at any of the boys, he joined the group near the second wagon.

Kathleen realized she was now truly alone. *Can I do this?* Panic flared, sending the burn of adrenaline throughout her body. *You have to.* Another traitorous thought struck. *What if my plan is wrong?* She nervously bit down on her lip. *No, don't even do the* what-ifs, *just do the plan. You can do anything,* she reached up and touched her forehead, *because Jesse kissed you.*

Not waiting another moment, Kathleen picked up her long skirt and petticoats and quickly headed north through the trees. She didn't stop until she reached the elbow in the lane. If her plan to become the new English teacher was going to work, she would have to make everyone believe that she'd had a ride from town and had been dropped off at the end of the lane.

A painful stitch bit into her side. She stopped to catch her breath and peered through the trees, gauging the distance from where she stood to the wagons in front of the barn. It would probably take her more than five minutes to walk the distance. Positive that no one would notice her, she drew a deep breath and stepped out onto the road.

CAREFULLY PICKING HIS time and the spot, Jesse moved out of the trees and into the middle of the group of boys. The three closest to him were Lakota, others that he could identify were Apache, maybe a couple of Kiowa and the three at the other end of the wagon looked like Comanche. Five, maybe six tribes, but the boys all had one thing in common. Fear. He could smell it.

"Line them up, Mr. Blunt," Josiah Wilks said, waving his walking stick at the man who stepped down from the first wagon. "Give him a hand, Mr. Slocum." Wilks tapped the second driver on the arm. "Time for these heathen brats to learn their place."

Anger surged through Jesse's body. *Stay cool. Don't lose it.* Keeping his head down, he obediently moved into line, avoiding the wrath of Blunt's hand. The boys who didn't move fast enough felt its hard whack. Slocum followed close behind, making sure he got his fair share of hits, too.

"What's your count, Mr. Blunt?" Josiah Wilks held a small booklet in one hand and a stubby pencil in the other.

"Twenty-one, sir."

Wilks checked his tally book one more time. "We're one over, Blunt," Wilks stated. "I thought you'd counted these bastards at the depot."

"Well, dammit, I did." Blunt's belligerent tone brought a sharp look from Wilks as he drew a sheaf of papers from his breast pocket.

Jesse recognized the documents: records sent by Indian agents with each child they'd put on the train to hell. Keeping his head down, he watched as Wilks matched each piece of paper with each child and suddenly remembered

Kathleen's words. *On the fourteenth of June there had been twenty Indian boys that had arrived at the depot, but twenty-one arrived at DuBois.* Was she right? Was he really student number twenty-one?

"That one, Blunt." Wilks pointed his walking stick at Jesse's chest. "That tall bastard."

# Chapter 8

> Once there our belongings were taken from us, even the little
> medicine bags our mothers had given us to protect us from
> harm. Everything was placed in a heap and set afire. Next was
> the long hair, the pride of all Indians. The boys, one by one,
> would break down and cry when they saw their braids thrown
> on the floor.
>
> —LONE WOLF,
> BLACKFEET

FOR EACH STEP she took toward the wagons, Kathleen
thought of at least five reasons to turn around and take
twenty in the opposite direction. Without money where
could she go? The cameo brooch was the only thing of
value that she had, but need would win over sentiment.
She'd sell it if she had to.

She glanced ahead looking for Jesse. Taller than all the
others, she found him immediately. No, she wouldn't run,
she'd see this fantastic adventure through to the end—
whenever and whatever that might be. Her step took on a
renewed purpose. She watched Josiah Wilks walk back and
forth in front of the line of Indian boys as though he were a
general inspecting his troops. Kathleen slowed. Her hand
trembling, she straightened her bonnet, smoothed her skirts,
and with each remaining step, practiced the words she
would say.

Excitement blended with apprehension. Before the end
of the day, she would meet the beginning of DuBois. She
would meet Providence Divine.

"First things first, Kathleen," she whispered, trying to

keep her mind on the task at hand. Only ten yards now separated her from the two wagons, and once more she focused on what waited for her ahead.

The high-topped boots didn't feel too comfortable anymore. Stepping on a small rock, her ankle twisted once again, the third time in her short walk. The tie ribbon on her bonnet chaffed her neck, but the worst misery, the corset, still painfully cramped her ribs, making her wince with every breath. Adding to her discomfort, the afternoon sun beat down; its hot and unrelenting rays sent a trickle of perspiration down her spine. Another slid between her breasts. *So far there's nothing good about the good old days.*

Josiah Wilks continued to walk back and forth in front of the boys, but when he stopped in front of Jesse, Kathleen's steps faltered. Wilks lifted his walking stick and poked Jesse in the chest, and she saw Jesse widen his stance, much like a boxer would before throwing a punch. *Jesse, please. Don't let him rile you.*

The other two men joined Wilks, and all three stood in front of Jesse. She could hear their conversation.

"Well, he ain't on any of these," one of the men said, shuffling through a stack of papers before handing them back to Wilks. "I don't remember him bein' on my wagon, either. Was he on yours, Slocum?"

The second man shook his head. "As tall as he is, hell, if he was, I'd have surely seen him."

"He's standing near the end of the line, so he must've been with your bunch."

"Gentlemen, gentlemen, don't quibble," Wilks said, interrupting the two men by tapping his walking stick on the ground. "The savage didn't magically appear, so obviously he rode on one of the wagons." Using the tip of his stick, Wilks flipped one of the scalplocks on Jesse's shirt.

"I sure don't remember seein' him at the depot, either, and believe me, Mr. Wilks, this ain't a bugger you'd miss."

"Well, Mr. Blunt, obviously this is one *bugger* you did miss." Wilks motioned for Jesse to step out of line, then slowly walked around him.

"He's a little old for us, ain't he, Mr. Wilks?" Blunt

looked up at Jesse and squinted. "I'd say he's at least twenty-five."

"Dressed kinda dandy, too, if you ask me," Slocum said. "Not many of 'em come gussied up like that, wearing feathers 'n' such. Maybe he's the son of one of them important chiefs."

"Ain't no such thing as an important chief anymore." Blunt laughed.

"The Reverend don't like 'em to be this old. Trouble-makers," Slocum grumbled.

"Possibly." Wilks pushed Jesse back into line with the tip of his cane. "He'll definitely be a handful, but he'll learn to be civilized—one way or the other. It might be quite enjoyable . . . well, maybe not for him, of course."

Kathleen watched Jesse's eyes narrow. The muscle along the edge of his jaw tightened. If she didn't distract Wilks and his men now, Jesse was apt to tear into all three of them.

Battling her raw nerves, Kathleen stepped closer. "Excuse me, gentlemen. Hello."

Wilks and the two drivers continued to sort through the paperwork. They hadn't heard her, but a hurried glance told her that Jesse had. She nearly missed the slight, impercepti-ble nod of his head, but she definitely saw the quick up-ward turn of his lips and the roguish wink that followed. In the next instant his expression sobered, becoming blank again as though he hadn't seen her at all. But with just that momentary connection, he had bolstered her courage.

"Mr. Wilks? Are you Josiah Wilks?" Kathleen took a de-liberate step closer to the sandy-haired man. His height matched hers, perhaps only an inch taller, and the pungent lemon scent of macassar hair oil wafted on the air around him. He was impeccably dressed; highly polished shoes, a stylish brown derby, and a finely tailored suit. An elabo-rately engraved silver head decorated his walking stick. His wardrobe looked expensive, more than she thought he'd be able to afford on a teacher's salary. He slowly turned to-ward Kathleen and she drew a slight gasp. The angelic beauty of the man's face came as a complete surprise.

"Yes, I am Josiah Wilks," he said, passing the stack of

papers in his hand to Blunt without looking at the man. "And you are?"

Kathleen found his smile to be disarming, a strange dichotomy to the imperious tone shading his voice. She moved closer. "Mr. Wilks, my name is Kathleen Pres—"

"For God's sake, madam, quickly, step away," Wilks commanded with an impatient tone usually saved for an unschooled child.

"What?" Startled, Kathleen jumped back.

"Aside from the fact that these heathens would love to cut your throat or take your scalp, it's best to keep your distance. Unless of course, you have a liking for lice." He brandished his stick in the air, causing a couple of the boys to cringe and turn away. He met her gaze with another disarming smile. "You were saying?"

"Mr. Wilks, my name is Kathleen Prescott." She extended her hand only to have it ignored. At first the man's rudeness shocked and angered her until she wondered if maybe she had made a faux pas. Maybe it was improper for a Victorian lady to shake hands with a man to whom she hadn't been properly introduced. Jesse was right, there were many things that could trip them up.

"I'm looking for Reverend Divine. Would you please tell me where I might find him?"

Wilks's eyes narrowed. "Prescott, you say?"

Kathleen nodded. "Yes, Kathleen Prescott."

"And what is your business with the good Reverend? He told me nothing about expecting a . . . Miss Prescott." He flicked a speck of dust off of his jacket, then glanced up at her, obviously not very interested in who she was or what she wanted.

Josiah Wilks's handsome face had suddenly lost all of its appeal. She drew a deep, settling breath and tried to coax her temper down below a boiling point. *Come on, Kathleen, play the game.* "I would like to see Reverend Divine about applying for a position. I'm an English teacher."

Wilks's gaze, slow and with a deliberate course, traveled from the ribboned and flowered bonnet on her head to the hem of her skirt and then back up again. "I see," he said, adding an aloof arch to his brow. "Well, Miss Prescott, I'm afraid you've made the trip for nothing. Reverend Divine is not here, and there are no openings."

Without a good-bye or a polite nod, Josiah Wilks turned away as though she weren't worth another moment of his time.

Kathleen refused to be dismissed so easily. Without her getting a job at DuBois, her entire plan would fall apart. Besides, where would she go? She stiffened her spine and set a sharp edge to her voice. "Mr. Wilks, another moment, if you please."

Wilks faced her once again. "Yes, Miss Prescott, what now?" he droned.

"I believe that Reverend Divine is expecting a Mrs. Delia Shore." She saw the flash of interest in his pale blue eyes.

"Yes, as a matter of fact, he is. What does that have to do with you, Miss Prescott?"

Choosing to ignore the man's arrogance, Kathleen glanced up the hill toward the school's administration building. "Mr. Wilks, in Reverend Divine's absence, is there someone else in charge? If so, I believe my business would be with them." She lifted her chin a notch, and peered down her nose through her wire-rimmed glasses at him. Wilks's manner reminded her too much of Richmond Brock for her liking.

Wilks stepped in front of her, slowly swinging his walking stick at his side like a pendulum, the tip coming closer and closer to her skirt with each swing. Unsure of his intent, Kathleen took a step backward and then another. The cane continued to swing. A glance at the expression on Josiah Wilks's face told Kathleen all she needed to know. *He's testing me. He's seeing how far he can push me. Stand your ground, Kathleen. Stand your ground.*

A sound, a quiet cough, coming from close behind her broke into her thoughts. As much as she was tempted, she didn't turn around. She didn't have to. She knew who it was. Jesse. He was encouraging her in the only way he could.

She pressed again for an answer to her question. "Who is in charge, Mr. Wilks?"

A Cheshire smile curved Wilks's mouth, lifting the mustache that covered his top lip. "That would be me, Miss Prescott. I am in charge when Reverend Divine is away." He offered a quick salute with his cane.

Kathleen's hopes sank. There was little chance left now for the plan to succeed, but little was better than none. "Mr. Wilks, Reverend Divine hired Mrs. Shore to be the school's new English teacher."

For a moment or two, Wilks idly watched his walking stick as it continued to swing. When he finally looked up he appeared to be bored by the conversation but the expression in his eyes proved the opposite to be true. Kathleen knew she had Josiah Wilks's undivided attention.

"I am well aware of Mrs. Shore's future position at DuBois, Miss Prescott." His eyes narrowed, giving his handsome features a cunning, fox-like appearance. "How is it that *you* are?"

Kathleen was beginning to enjoy the game, the thrust and parry of their conversation. Maybe everything would work out. Keeping her stiff pose and the confident tone to her voice, she began to tell more lies in one conversation than she'd told her entire life. "Mrs. Shore is a colleague of mine. We taught at the same school in Cleveland. Mrs. Shore won't be coming. A week ago she married Mr. Marcus Baker and moved to Kansas."

Kathleen watched the surprised expression take shape on Wilks' face. He believed every word. Kathleen was delighted that she had dropped a bomb in the middle of Josiah Wilks' sunny afternoon.

"And the woman didn't believe it necessary to inform me . . . Reverend Divine? No letter, no message?"

"I have brought her message, Mr. Wilks. I am here in her stead."

The walking stick stilled. Wilks looked beyond Kathleen and down the line of Indian boys. "How did you arrive, Miss Prescott? I know, without a doubt, that *you* did not ride from town on one of our wagons." He pointed down the dirt lane with his stick. "I didn't hear another wagon . . . a buggy."

Kathleen heard Jesse cough again, a tight, almost

cautious-sounding cough. Good grief, did he really think she would tell Wilks the truth? "I have just arrived on the train from Dayton," she replied, praying that Wilks didn't know the schedule any better than she did. "Unfortunately, it pulled into the depot just as your wagons were leaving."

She turned to quickly acknowledge the boys, realizing too late that she'd made a mistake. She found she couldn't turn away. She scanned the line, face by face, finding boys of every age. Toddlers and teenagers stared back at her; some with dark eyes filled with fear, some their eyes bright with unshed tears, some with chilling defiance. This time she did look at Jesse. As though he could read her dismay, he slightly shook his head, his caution clear. The blood in her veins suddenly chilled and she felt cold to the bone. *My God, what lunacy have we gotten ourselves into?*

"Miss Prescott, how did you get here?"

She quickly turned back to Josiah Wilks. "A delightful family, the Hillsons, or was it the Hillmans"—she pressed her index finger against her lips and shrugged—"were kind enough to give me a ride from town."

"I didn't see or hear a wagon."

Kathleen's pulse began a frantic race. Lying was not one of her better skills. *Think! Think!* "After so many long hours on the train, I told them I would prefer to walk from the end of the lane to stretch my . . ." *No, you can't say legs, I don't think it was proper for Victorian women to say legs in mixed company.* "I felt the need to walk."

Wilks nodded, never taking his gaze from her face. "Hmm, I don't believe I know the Hillsons or the Hillmans. Do they live far from here?"

Kathleen's stack of lies grew higher and higher. She prayed it wouldn't topple. "I don't know, Mr. Wilks. I didn't ask."

For a moment or two, Wilks didn't speak. He peered around her skirt and then looked up, his expression reminding Kathleen once again of a sly fox.

"Where are your bags, Miss Prescott? Surely you brought some luggage if you intended to stay?"

She felt another jolt of adrenaline. Why hadn't she thought about her lack of luggage? "Of course I have bags . . . well, *had* bags. They were lost." The lies were getting easier to tell. "My bags were probably lost when I changed trains in Dayton." She tightened her grip on the small drawstring purse, hoping Josiah Wilks wouldn't notice her trembling hands. "The stationmaster said they would be sent to me when they were found."

"English, you say?" He tugged idly at the sideburns on the right side of his face. "Do you have your credentials with you?"

Another lie. "Unfortunately, they are in my lost luggage."

"Of course they are. How inconvenient." Wilks straightened his shoulders, his posture becoming imperious once again. "We will discuss the teaching position further after I get our new arrivals processed."

"Would you like me to wait for you in the administration office?" She pointed to the building up the hill.

"No, Miss Prescott, if you intend to become a teacher at DuBois Indian School, I believe it would be most beneficial for you to be familiar with the transformation of our students from their arrival as ignorant savages to trained and educated, useful and civilized citizens." Josiah Wilks gestured toward the line of Indian boys with a wide sweep of his hand. "They come to us stinking, filthy, bug-ridden, and feral. It is only through the dedication, perseverance, strict discipline that often requires the rod, and the curriculum devised by Reverend Divine that their lives are changed forever."

Astounded by Josiah Wilks's words, Kathleen felt a roll of nausea hit her stomach. Surely these weren't the beliefs of everyone at DuBois. Did they think so little of the children that punishment and degradation came before education and kindness? Did her great-great-grandfather know that some of his teachers believed this way? She tried to calm her anger, but an unsettling thought pushed into her mind. Were these Providence Divine's own doctrines? Is this the legacy her family had honored for so many years? Shame pricked her conscience. As though Jesse had actually stepped forward and whispered in her ear, she could hear his voice, his *I told you so*, passionately deriding DuBois and every place like it.

Without thinking, she took another look at the boys.

Wilks stepped closer. "Take a long look, Miss Prescott, especially at this tall, older one." He lifted his walking stick and pointed it at Jesse. "Look at his arrogance, his defiance." Wilks laughed. "He's quite insolent for someone who is ignorant of proper etiquette, can't understand English, can't read or write. He probably stuffs his food into his mouth with his hands." Wilks lowered the stick. "So look hard, Miss Prescott, look hard at them all, for within the hour they will all be as babes, reborn."

Jesse fought to keep his expression blank, to play his role, to keep his loathing for Wilks under control. Looking at Kathleen, he watched her face blanch as she listened to Wilks's sermon. Her gaze met his and he saw the exact moment her painful understanding took hold. And in that moment he knew she had lost the innocence of a life-long believer.

He ached to step forward, to comfort her, and to gently wipe away the tears that suddenly glistened in her eyes. *My God, where did that idea come from, Horse? Two hours ago you would have enjoyed seeing her realize the truth.* He saw her shudder. Was she strong enough to last the hours, days, weeks, or months that they were at the whim of this insane twist of time?

Jesse watched her wipe her eyes, pull her emotions into check, and straighten her posture. *Good for you, Katie-girl, good for you.*

"It is fine and noble work that is being done here, Mr. Wilks," Kathleen remarked, her voice sounding tight and hollow. "I'd be most proud to be a member of this splendid institution."

Wilks performed another courtly bow. "Your admiration for my work is humbly accepted."

Jesse almost choked on the laugh that welled up in his throat. *Arrogant bastard.* As disgusted as Wilks made him feel, listening to the man speak made him realize something that would work to Kathleen's benefit. The way she normally spoke, professorial and straitlaced, had seemed so archaic and out of place in 2003. But here and now—if it really was 1886—her ten-dollar words and her prim, old-fashioned manner fit perfectly. Maybe she'd do all right, after all.

*"Wagni kta wacin."*

Jesse looked down at the small boy standing beside him. Fear brightened the child's dark eyes. In an instant he realized he had another problem, a big problem, one that he hadn't thought of, one that could jeopardize *his* safety.

He'd heard Lakota all of his life, had spoken it fluently as a child until he'd learned it wasn't cool to be Indian. After he'd moved to the city, the only times he'd heard Lakota were on his trips home to the rez. He might not have any trouble passing himself off to the school authorities, but his rusty Lakota wouldn't fool his own people for a minute.

*"Wagni kta wacin!"* the boy cried again.

*"Shh . . . nihiŋciyapi śni ye,"* an older boy responded.

Jesse began sifting through the Lakota words he remembered. Taking longer than he'd expected, he finally pieced together what the boys had whispered. *I want to go home* and then the reply, *Don't be afraid.*

He cursed himself. Why hadn't he listened to Grandma Boo when she spoke their language or when she told him that if he didn't keep speaking it—if any of the young people didn't speak it and use it often—the language would die? Now, here he was at one of the very places that would take the language away, and he didn't have it to lose. The irony was laughable.

*"Nihiŋciyapi śni ye."* He whispered the words to himself, letting their sounds roll off his tongue. How soon would he be able to remember enough of the language?

Jesse felt a tug on his leggings. Looking down, he found a small Lakota boy looking up at him with wide eyes. *"Táku eŋiciyapi he?"*

Once more he searched his memory. This time the translation came quicker. *How do they call you?* Fortunately this was one question he remembered how to answer. Touching his fist to his chest in the old way, he answered, *"Suŋgléska emaciyapi."*

The boy nodded, then striking his own chest, replied, "*Kéya Iŋyaŋke.*"

*Running Turtle.* Jesse smiled. A child's name. It described a boy who was so slow that he always had to run to catch up.

"Silence."

Wilks's command startled every boy in line, and they all shrank back as he strode down the line looking for those who were talking. Jesse's anger rose again. *So, the education begins.*

"Blunt," Wilks called. "Is Mr. Watson ready?"

"Yes, sir. Ready and waiting."

Wilks studied each boy and then pointed to one after another with the tip of his stick. Slocum pulled each child out of line.

"These five will do," said Wilks, shooting an uneasy glare over his shoulder at Jesse.

"Ya don't want the big one?"

"No, Mr. Slocum, I do not."

The five boys that Wilks had chosen huddled together, furtively glancing over their shoulders, as Slocum herded them into the barn. The boys left outside moved restlessly, crowding closer to each other, whimpers coming from the smallest. Without thinking of his own safety, and knowing what was likely going to happen to the boys, Jesse moved out of line and took a few steps toward the barn. From the corner of his eye he saw Wilks swing his stick, and heard the whoosh it made as it cut through the air. The blow hit him across the stomach and caught the ridge of his hip bone. Gasping, he staggered. Bent over and pressing his hand against the pain in his belly, he tried to catch his breath. Gritting his teeth, he waged war with his rage and battled the impulse to strike back.

"Keep the bastard in line." Wilks turned away, obviously convinced that Jesse posed no threat. "I won't tolerate disobedience. He'll learn that here or in the cold house."

Jesse saw Kathleen's eye grow wide with alarm. She began to rush toward him. Still bent and gasping for breath, he slightly shook his head and prayed that she understood what he was telling her. *Don't give them any reason to be suspicious. Stay away, you can't stop them.* Pain racked his gut and, grasping the edge of the wagon, he pulled himself up and turned away.

"Ah, Miss Prescott, how sweet, you're a tender heart," Wilks cajoled. "But you will soon learn that discipline is of utmost importance to the education of these savages. Sometimes harsh punishment is all that they understand; sometimes it is all that reaches their inferior minds."

Glancing over his shoulder, Jesse swore he'd seen a smile on Wilks's lips, but he'd definitely seen Kathleen quickly look back at him, her brow furrowed. Worried. *I understand, Katie-girl. I won't do anything stupid. Ha*, he thought, *I already have.*

The small boy at his side pressed closer. *"Nikhuja he?"*

*"Hau."* Jesse nodded. "I'm all right."

Wails, loud and keening, filled with the sound of indescribable terror, suddenly came from within the barn and ripped through the quiet afternoon. Running Turtle gripped Jesse's leg. He lightly placed his hand on the boy's head. *"Nihiŋciyapi śni yo."* He quickly glanced down the line of boys, some no older than five or six. If he could barely say the words in Lakota, how the hell could he tell them all— the Kiowa, Comanche, all the others—not to be afraid?

Another cry came from the barn, and even though he had a good idea what was going on, Jesse felt his gut twist and the blood in his veins run cold. Amazed, he watched as one-by-one the boys in line, even the youngest, swallowed their fear, gathered their courage, and stood tall and stoic against the unknown. These were boys who had been raised by their families and their tribes to be warriors. Today their people would be proud.

# Chapter 9

Allowing for an exceptional case, the Indian child is of lower physical organization than the white child. His forearms are smaller and his fingers and hands less flexible; the very structure of his bones and muscles will not permit so wide a variety of manual movements . . . and his very instincts and modes of thought are adjusted to his imperfect manual development.

—ESTELLE REEL,
SUPERINTENDENT OF INDIAN SCHOOLS, 1900

SHAKEN, KATHLEEN TOOK a step toward the barn, then stopped, afraid to go any closer. She had never heard such horrific screams. *My God, what's happening to those children?* Why wasn't the man named Blunt or Josiah Wilks rushing to the barn to stop it? Another wail rose and fell, then rose again, the sound lifting the hairs on the back of her neck.

An unmerciful twist gripped her stomach, the knot giving a hard jerk with each new cry. She clutched the drawstring purse against her breasts and drew on every reserve of courage that she could muster. "Please, someone, tell me . . ."

"I should have warned you. Pay no notice to that hullabaloo, Miss Prescott." Wilks stepped close and touched her elbow. "There is absolutely no need for alarm."

The sounds coming from the barn made his casual words sound ludicrous. If the children were being abused, he should be doing something about it. The man's indifference was unforgivable. "Mr. Wilks, aren't you concerned—"

"Truthfully, Miss Prescott, there is nothing to worry about." A condescending smile twisted his mouth. "Randall Watson always takes photographs of some of our new arrivals for the school's records." The smile became a laugh. "They don't seem to like it."

"This must be terrifying for them," Kathleen countered, disgusted that she had to point out the obvious.

"Oh, pishposh. It's only a camera, not a gun."

"And you assume they know the difference?"

The look Wilks shot at her held what she could only interpret as righteous indignation. She tried again to reason with him. "Why is it necessary to take the photographs when the children first arrive, when they're scared and disoriented? Can't you wait until after they have been here a few days?"

Wilks harrumphed, showing his opinion of Kathleen's suggestion. "The idea, Miss Prescott, is to record how these uncivilized boys looked when they arrived. In a year Mr. Watson will photograph them again to show the public and bleeding-heart skeptics the wonderful transformation that DuBois Indian School has wrought."

"But the cries." Kathleen felt the weight of guilt fall heavily on her heart. All of Randall Watson's photographs of the Indian children in their tribal clothes were part of the archives that she, and those before her, had treasured and proudly taken care of for generation after generation. She had never imagined these sounds were part of those pictures.

"Ah, yes, the cries." Wilks dared to chuckle. "Well, I warn you, shortly there will be more. A lot more." He casually polished the silver knob of his cane on the sleeve of his jacket. "That's why this step of their indoctrination is held here in the stables, away from the school." He lowered his voice as if sharing a secret. "We wouldn't want those unpleasant sounds heard by any visitors the school might have. After all, a lot of our funds come from generous donors."

"Why would there be more cries?" She glanced toward the barn. Quiet. Perhaps Watson was finished. "You only took five boys to Mr. Watson."

"For their photographs, yes. But it's Mr. Watson's scissors that cause the most crying."

"Scissors?"

"Mr. Watson is also our barber. And believe me, Miss Prescott, the boys definitely don't like having their hair cut." Wilks's shoulders lifted in an uncaring shrug. "That is when they do the most caterwauling. But fortunately, for our ears, the kerosene doesn't bother them as much."

"Kerosene?" She remembered seeing the monthly allotments of kerosene itemized in the ledgers, but she'd always assumed it was just for the lanterns. "I don't understand. Kerosene?"

"Lice, Miss Prescott, lice. Nasty, filthy little critters, but kerosene kills them."

Hadn't the photos in the archives shown girls with long hair? She frowned. "Do you cut the girls' hair as well?"

Wilks looked at her as though she had lost her mind. "Of course not."

"Surely you aren't inferring that only the boys have lice, if any child has them at all?" Kathleen regretted saying the words the moment they had left her lips. If she had any chance of securing a teaching position at DuBois, it wouldn't be wise to antagonize Josiah Wilks. He held the key to her safety.

"A woman's hair is her crowning glory," Wilks declared, apparently choosing to ignore her impertinence. "But society declares that a gentleman's hair be cut short." He snorted. "Only ruffians and heathens allow their hair to grow long." He paused, tucked his fingers into his coat pocket, and began pontificating once again. "One of the main tenets of DuBois and schools like it is assimilation. We take the Constitution at its word that *all* men are created equal. So, in our plan of assimilation, our students are all made as equal as possible to those in our society. They all dress alike—the boys in military-styled uniforms and the girls in white blouses and long dark skirts."

Kathleen immediately thought of the style of clothing she'd worn all of her life—white blouses and long dark skirts. Her next thought struck as hard as a physical blow. *I, too, am a product of DuBois.*

"The rules are simple," Wilks continued. "Their hair is worn the same as every other boy's or girl's, and it is forbidden for them to speak anything but English.

"Assimilation is civilization, and it is our God-given duty to ensure that each of these heathens reach that goal." He tipped his derby and gave a curt nod. "Now, if you'll excuse me for a few minutes." Wilks left her side, joining Blunt a few yards away. "Let's begin, Mr. Blunt."

Kathleen watched him walk away. She had never heard the principles of DuBois presented in such a cold and unfeeling manner. *God-given duty . . . indeed.* Where was the nobility she had come to believe was the basis of Providence Divine's school? *These are lies, all lies. Why should I believe Josiah Wilks?*

"You're doing fine, Katie-girl."

Jesse? He'd spoken softly, barely above a breath. Why would he ignore the danger and talk to her? She fought the temptation to turn and look at him. Adrenaline skittered throughout her body, leaving a burning trail in its wake. She shot a look at Wilks and Blunt. Had they heard him, too?

"It's okay, don't worry. They can't hear us."

Kathleen began to turn to face him.

"No, don't turn around. Just stay calm and look toward the barn or the school buildings." He paused for a moment. "That's good, you're doing fine." He drew a breath. "Katie-girl, I'm proud of you."

His words fell gently on her ears, on her heart, and were as comforting as an embrace. She slightly nodded, letting him know she had heard him.

"We're going to get through this, I promise, but there are going to be some rough spots and we've got one coming up in a few minutes."

"What do you mean? What could be rougher than what's already happened?" Kathleen heard him step a little closer and wanted to reach out to him, needing to draw comfort and strength from his touch.

"Soon they're going to come back and take the rest of us into the barn. They'll cut our hair and take our clothes." He quietly laughed, the sound little more than an empty and humorless breath. "It'll be like a factory assembly line. We'll go in one end of the barn as Indians and come out the other as sad imitations of white men."

She bit her bottom lip, fighting the tears. "That isn't what it was like at all. Providence would never have allowed that. How dare you suggest such a thing?"

"How do you think the kids in those photos in your archives went from being Indian to red-skinned whites?"

"I never thought it was like this." Her breath caught in her throat. "The crying . . . I didn't know."

"Listen to me. Many tribes cut their hair when a loved one dies. It's a sign of mourning. When they take the rest of us in there and Wilks's men starting cutting hair, it will be the kids from those tribes that you'll hear. They'll think their families have died since they left home."

"Why doesn't someone tell them that's not true? Jesse, why don't *you* tell them?"

"There are five, maybe six Lakota in this bunch, Kathleen. The rest are Kiowa, Comanche, Cheyenne, and a few other tribes. Just because I'm Indian doesn't mean I can speak every tribe's language or they can understand me. Besides, my own Lakota is pretty damned rusty." Jesse paused as Blunt and Slocum drew another four boys from the line. When they moved away, he continued. "You can't show any emotion when they take me. Remember, if we're not good at this game, we won't get to pass Go, we don't get two hundred dollars . . . and it could mean we'll never get home."

Kathleen couldn't stand it any longer, she needed to see Jesse's face, she needed to touch his hand, she needed him to hold her and promise her that everything would be all right.

"Shh, careful, Wilks is coming," Jesse whispered.

She felt an odd sense of loss as Jesse eased back into line.

"Miss Prescott," Wilks said, walking toward her, "in just a few minutes the first step toward civilization will be taken by all of these boys." He motioned to Blunt and Slocum to begin herding the rest of the new students into the barn. "Just so you know, the arrival process is a wonderful thing." He spread his hands in an exaggerated gesture. "A rebirthing, if you will." He paused, as if he expected Kathleen to offer a "hallelujah," then swept his arm in a wide arc. "It will be the same for each one of these heathens.

"After we cut their hair, their heads are treated with kerosene." He gave a little shrug. "The smell is unpleasant, it burns their skin a little, but it kills the lice and the nits." Wilks laughed. "Although I believe it was General Sherman who said that it was the Indians who were the nits." His laughter subsided as he continued his lecture. "After their hair has been doused, they are scrubbed from head to toe with lye soap to rid their entire bodies of filth and disease."

Wilks delivered his words with a religious fervor that sickened Kathleen. She wanted to break his own walking stick over his head.

"For decency's sake, you must wait out here," Wilks continued. "The boys will be stripped of their filthy clothing, scrubbed, wrapped in blankets, and taken to their dormitories. Their discarded clothing and their cut hair will be burned. Not only for the sake of cleanliness, but it makes them dependent on the clothing we give them." He turned to join Slocum and Blunt, then paused and looked back at her. "Miss Prescott, I'll be going with the boys, but I'll either return for you within a half hour or I will send one of the other teachers to escort you to the office. You will need to provide some information for our records." He gave a salute with his walking stick. "I hope you feel up to the wonderful challenge DuBois has to offer."

"Are you saying that I have the job?"

"Miss Prescott, isn't that why you're here?"

"Come on, come on," Blunt growled, pushing two of the boys toward the barn. "Get movin', get movin'."

Kathleen stood rooted to the spot as one by one the boys passed behind her. None of them made a sound; even the youngest ones were strangely silent. She wanted to stop them, take them back to town, put them back on a train, and send them home. She began to shake, her knees threatening to buckle, and then she felt the slightest touch on her hand, the warmth of another's skin on hers. A touch that risked everything. Jesse.

After giving her fingers a light squeeze, he allowed his hand to rest over hers for a precious moment. Kathleen closed her eyes, drawing strength and comfort from him. As he moved toward the barn, his caress trailed over her fingers, across the back of her hand, her wrist, and then was gone.

KATHLEEN SAT ON the bench in the shade of a huge oak and tried to close her ears to the horrible sounds coming from the barn. How much time had passed? A minute? Fifteen? An hour? She looked up, catching glimpses of the bright blue sky between the canopy of leaves and branches. A gentle breeze toyed with the leaves and songbirds warbled a June-day chorus. The day seemed so normal, but it was a lie. There was nothing normal about it. It had taken little less than one hundred and seventeen years and an hour or so for everything she knew and relied upon to be turned upside down and inside out.

Shame wedged itself in her throat until she could barely swallow. Was everything that Jesse said about DuBois and all those other Indian schools true? Had her blind denial wasted her entire life? Had her father, her grandfather, her great-grandfather encouraged these practices, too? Tears spilled down her cheeks and she brushed them away with an angry swipe of her hand. The Indian boys weren't the only victims of the day.

The faint melody of a song, a hymn, being sung by children in one of the buildings on the hill, rode the current of a breeze. Without thought, Kathleen joined in, humming the familiar strains of "Rock of Ages." She suddenly stopped, but the sweet singing continued. And all she heard was the hymn, the rustling leaves, and the songbirds. She jumped to her feet and ran to the barn. Stopping just shy of the door, she listened. Silence. She stepped inside. Empty.

"They're not here," she whispered. "Gone."

She lifted her long cumbersome skirt, ran to the north edge of the barn, and peered around the corner.

Grouped in tight military formation, twenty-one new Indian students marched barefoot in mismatched cadence across the parade ground and up the hill. Josiah Wilks, holding his walking stick as though it was Moses' staff, led the group looking every bit like a messiah leading his followers to the Promised Land.

Blunt, Slocum, and a man she assumed to be Randall Watson followed, teasing the boys by lifting the edges of their blankets, and pushing stragglers back into line.

Kathleen immediately found Jesse, and her hand flew to cover her mouth, stifling a whimper. A drab blanket barely covered his shoulders and body, leaving him bare from mid-thigh down. His beautiful black hair now only reached the bottom of his ears. Mr. Watson's scissors had been cruel.

A persistent sob escaped from behind her hand.

As if he had heard, Jesse turned and looked back toward the barn, back to where she stood. Had he seen her? Without thought, she raised her hand and believed in her heart that she saw him give a slight nod.

She stepped away from the corner of the building, and as she passed the open barn door, curiosity made her step inside.

The odor of freshly spilled kerosene stung her nostrils, and as she ventured farther into the barn she had to sidestep a large soapy puddle beside the horse trough. Stopping, she listened for a moment. Not hearing anything but the occasional swish of a horse's tail and the faint scratching of a mouse or two, she relaxed.

Suddenly she drew a quick breath and stumbled to a halt. A cloaked figure stood near the back door.

"Hello." She hesitantly took another step. The figure didn't move, didn't reply. "Hello."

Taking a few more uncertain steps, her alarm turned to laughter. The cloaked figure suddenly became Mr. Watson's camera and tripod, still draped with the dark cloth. Kathleen carefully lifted the cloth. "Unbelievable." Her finger lightly traced the lettering on the brass plate on the front of the wood-box camera. "Rochester Optical Commodore. It's the same camera!"

When she had last seen the camera in the school's museum, the varnish had been scratched in a few places and the bellows had dried and cracked along some of the creases. It hadn't been new like it was now because it had been over a hundred and fifteen years old.

On the floor beside the camera were the spoils of Randall Watson's scissors. Struck by an impulse too strong to ignore, Kathleen bent down and retrieved two long braids, the ends wrapped in red trade cloth. Beneath them, she found the narrow braid with the brass bells still tied to the end. Jesse's hair. Holding the braids, she saw the pile of discarded clothing. Again impulse drove her and she knew what she had to do.

The beaded blanket and the buckskin shirt were easy to find; it took her a few more minutes to find his fringed leggings, breech clout, moccasins, the decorative pieces he'd worn around his neck, and the silver ball and cone earrings. After lifting and moving aside almost every piece of clothing in the pile, she couldn't find his eagle feathers. She wanted everything that belonged to him. Something drove her to it. She looked around. "Where could they be?"

A flash of white caught her eye and there, stuck under the brow band on one of the bridles hanging on a wall peg, were Jesse's feathers. She snatched them away and carefully laid them on the beaded blanket with the rest of Jesse's Indian clothes and his hair.

She hesitated for a moment. Why was the impulse to save Jesse's hair and clothes so strong? It was as though someone had whispered in her ear. Was it impulse or intuition? She glanced at everything she'd gathered and an idea took shape in her mind. Could it be that in order to make the trip back home to 2003, they needed to have everything they'd brought with them into 1886?

The theory made perfect sense. Believing it to be true, she rolled the blanket into a tight bundle. Now she had to find a safe place to hide it. But where?

The hayloft?

Kathleen eyed the ladder that led up into the loft. No. With the long full skirt, she knew she would have trouble climbing the ladder and Wilks could return at any moment.

The grain bin?

She lifted the lids, and tried digging into the oats. As quickly as she scooped out a hole, the grain slid back in and filled it up. That wouldn't work, and besides, in a day or two the bundle would be exposed. She dropped the lid and scanned the barn again. A closed door drew her attention.

Yes.

Without a moment's delay, Kathleen rushed to the small tackroom. The door creaked as she pushed it open, and the smell of saddle soap, mildew, and mouse droppings met her when she stepped inside. She reached for the light switch, then laughed. There'd be no light switch for almost a hundred years. She waited a few seconds for her eyes to get used to the dark before she began looking for a hiding place.

Harness and saddles lined one wall, and on the other was a workbench littered with scraps of leather, a few dust-covered bottles of homemade liniment, a couple of lanterns, and a jumble of currycombs and brushes. She circled the small room, hoping to find a safe place for Jesse's clothes.

She crouched down and peered beneath the saddles, but the mouse that scurried into the hole in the corner changed her mind. Jesse's clothes wouldn't be safe where mice could get to them.

A wide shelf jutted from the wall over the workbench. It was wide enough to hold the bundle, but at eye level it was too low.

Her gaze swept the room again. What about under the stack of burlap sacks in the corner? She quickly lifted a few of the bags only to find more mouse droppings. She looked at the striped tabby cat that had ambled into the room and now sat perched on the workbench. "Somebody's not doing their job."

How much time did she have before Wilks returned? She searched the room again, and saw it. A narrow ledge. The dark corner where the eaves of the roof met the side-walls was a perfect hiding place. Getting up to it was another problem.

The corner of a large wooden toolbox poked out from under the saddle racks. Grabbing its rope handle, she dragged the box over to the workbench. She tested the lid and then stepped up, steadied herself by holding onto the shelf, and stuffed the bundle into the crook between the eaves and the rafters. Done, she stepped off the box, shoved it back under the saddles, looked up and smiled. "Perfect." Jesse's hair and his clothes were safe. If only she could say those same words about Jesse.

# Chapter 10

Discipline is universally admitted to be easier than in white schools. This may be explained partially by the fact that there (in the Indian schools) the children are under continuous discipline, from which there is no appeal.

—THE RED MAN,
CARLISLE INDIAN INDUSTRIAL SCHOOL

KATHLEEN SAT ON the edge of the bed and glanced around the austere room she had been assigned. Simple furniture: a straight-backed cane chair, a narrow quilt-covered iron bed, a chest of drawers, a bedside table, and an oil lamp completed the décor—if utilitarian could be called décor. The small mirror on the wall over the chest made it impossible to check her hair unless she crouched and leaned forward. A plain white china washbowl and a pitcher with a chipped handle sat on the dresser. One folded cotton towel, a washcloth, and a soap dish lay beside them.

She swept the toes of her high-button boots back and forth on the hand-braided rag rug beside the bed. A dingy mixture of reds and blue, frayed along one edge, and too small, the rug served little purpose. White sheeting sewn into drapes covered the window and could be held back on each side by a loop of cord hung over a hook.

Although not as severe as she imagined a cell in a nunnery would be, even by her own simple tastes, except for the window that looked out over the parade ground, Kathleen found the room to be lacking. She knew she shouldn't complain; the rest of the women teachers housed on the third floor of the senior girls' dormitory, with the exception of Margaret Lester, were housed two to a room. Kathleen decided she would gladly trade décor for privacy.

The generosity of the other women—the teachers, housekeepers, and cooks at the school—was certainly not lacking.

Although she'd been touched by their charity, Kathleen couldn't ease the weight of guilt that pressed against her conscience. Once the lie about her luggage being lost was heard and believed, each woman kindly brought her some item of clothing. Three gave her dresses, large enough, thank God, that she could forego the hellish corset. Miss Blessing, the art teacher, provided a black wool shawl. Mrs. Gilbert, the head cook, gave her a few handkerchiefs, hair combs and pins, and a few lengths of ribbon. The sewing teacher, Hannah Dobbs, a plump and friendly young woman whose brother Basil taught in the carpentry shop, gave her two sets of undergarments, everything from extra bloomers to chemises and corset covers, made by the senior girls in sewing class.

Margaret Lester, who had made it clear on the first day they'd met that she supervised all of the women teachers at DuBois, provided a white blouse and a long black skirt from the school's uniform inventory. Once again Kathleen found herself confronted with the similarity between the school uniform and the style of clothing she had always chosen for herself. Was DuBois so ingrained in her every breath that she unconsciously dressed like the students? The hollow feeling in the pit of her stomach provided the answer. Yes.

With a lot of preening about his own charitable nature, and the statement that Reverend Divine probably wouldn't have been nearly as generous, Josiah Wilks had given her a small advance on her salary. Although the money looked nothing like what she was used to, it did help to add some of the more intimate necessities to her wardrobe.

She smiled. The eight-dollar advance had gone surprisingly far at the general goods store in town, but then, she had been shopping with a 2003 perspective in an 1886 world.

She lightly caressed the hand-stitched bed quilt with the

palm of her hand. The room was plain but serviceable. How long would it be her home?

For the last four nights she had fallen into fitful sleep. And for the last four mornings had abruptly wakened, her skin damp with perspiration, her heart hammering wildly, before she was able to get her bearings and remember that she was still an unwilling visitor to the past.

She had quickly learned that to survive, she had to keep her wits about her every waking moment. And she had to resign herself to the possibility that she might never return to her own time. There was actually very little that she missed, perhaps a TV show or two, a few of her favorite books that wouldn't be written for many, many years, and her two selfish luxuries—Shalimar skin cream and Godiva Triple Chocolate Truffle ice cream.

Learning the daily schedule at DuBois had come easily, but one worry remained. Since they had made the time slide on Monday afternoon, she had not seen Jesse, not since she'd watched him walk away from the barn wrapped in a blanket. Was he safe? Was his room comfortable? Warm? Was he well? She placed her hand over her pounding heart. Was he as frightened as she was?

Kathleen spent much of her spare time looking out her window or sitting on the bench in front of the dormitory. She looked for Jesse among the students as they marched single file from class to class, to the dining hall, from building to building. She wandered down to the barn and peered into each stall, carefully looked at each face in the groups of older students as they did their chores. She searched the dining hall at each meal, peeked into classrooms as she passed along the halls, and visited the print shop, the harness shop, the carpentry shop, and the kitchen. Occasionally she saw some of the other boys who had arrived on June fourteenth, but Jesse wasn't among them.

It seemed as though he had completely disappeared.

One fear prodded at her more and more. Had he made the trip back? Had time reversed for him but not for her? *Have I been left behind?*

With a soft sigh she rose from the bed, gathered up her books and tablet with her class notes. She enjoyed spending time with her pupils, teaching them how to read and write and speak their new language. She had been nervous at first, not knowing what to do, how to do it, or even if she had the ability to teach. Each day her classes became easier, her tension eased, and she looked forward to the time she spent with the children. She discovered she was a good teacher, and she was beginning to care deeply for each one of her pupils. It had become her only consolation on this excursion.

Kathleen slid her watch from the pocket of her skirt, grateful she had tucked it in the drawstring purse the day of the film shoot. Wearing it in the film would have caused them to reshoot the scene, but keeping it hidden from view was now imperative. Her safety depended upon it.

Seven-fifteen. There was time for breakfast before her first class at eight o'clock.

Their greetings subdued, the Indian girls in the dormitory acknowledged Kathleen's friendly *good mornings* as she made her way down the stairs and along the promenade to the dining hall. Maybe Jesse would be there this morning. She entered the building and paused at the door. Looking for him among all the other students had become a daily routine.

The girls ate on the far side of the hall separated by a wide aisle from the boys, who ate on the side nearest to the door. She scanned the rows of boys. He wasn't there.

The clank and clatter of cutlery on tin plates, a cough or two, the sound of shuffling feet, or a muted sniffle was all that could be heard. Conversation among the children was forbidden unless it was in English. Margaret Lester had warned Kathleen that if children from the same tribe were allowed to talk among themselves in their own language, they could devise all kinds of horrific plots.

Student monitors, selected from the older students and rewarded with extra helpings of food or extra relaxation time, stood watch and made sure that all the rules were followed.

At one time Kathleen had agreed with the rule, thought she'd understood the principle, but her belief now veered in the opposite direction. Seeing children torn from brothers or sisters, or friends, or from their own people, from their own language, was cruel.

She made her way across the dining hall to the far corner where the teachers took their meals, noticing the food on the children's tables as she passed.

Since she had arrived, the teachers' menus had always been generous and delicious. Breakfast offered a full fare: eggs, fried potatoes, bacon or ham, hot bread, the choice of hot coffee or chilled milk, and fresh fruit. But the students' morning meal hadn't changed at all in the past three days. She suspected after seeing the disappointment and hunger on their faces that their menu hadn't changed in quite a while.

Thin oatmeal porridge, a slice of bread, a withered wintered apple, and a cup of watered milk were barely enough to fill the belly of an eight-year-old. Dickens couldn't have provided a more meager meal for Oliver.

"Good morning, Miss Prescott. You slept well, I hope?"

She greeted Margaret Lester with a small smile, noting that she still wore the bandage on her burned arm. She nodded to the men at the table, who slightly rose from their chairs in polite greeting. "Yes, very well, thank you."

"Sit here, beside me," Hannah Dobbs invited.

Kathleen sat and looked at the plate the cook set before her. Eggs and potatoes, a slice of ham, and warm, fresh bread. Quite different from what was on the students' plates.

"Delicious," Margaret Lester commented between a mouthful of eggs and a sip of coffee. "I'm sure you must find the food served at DuBois to be most palatable."

Kathleen glanced down the table at the plates in front of the other teachers. *For some, yes.* Raising her eyes, she scanned the room, taking in row after row of Indian children, some with their heads bent to the task of finding and eating every crumb on their plates, others staring with hunger at the food on the teachers' table. *For others, no.*

"The garden looks excellent this year, Mr. Wilks," Sara Blessing commented. "It would appear that the crop will be most beneficial for the school."

Josiah Wilks turned to Kathleen. "DuBois doesn't send

their senior students on outings to work for the local farmers during the summer like Carlisle and a few of the other schools do. We like to keep our boys and girls in class the year 'round." He poured a generous dollop of cream into his coffee, then vigorously stirred the brew, his spoon clanking loudly against the side of his cup. "During the summer our Indians plant and tend a very large vegetable garden that supplies not only food for the school but the surplus is sold in town to supplement school funds." Wilks took a noisy sip. "We also sell our excess hay and occasionally a hog or beef cow."

"I think that's a very excellent program," Kathleen replied, trying to enjoy her meal under Josiah Wilks's gaze.

The conversation turned to weather, then the women talked about new bolts of fabric at Gant's Dry Goods in town. The men discussed the new press in the print shop, the best-producing milk cow in the school's herd, and then the schedule for the first cutting of hay for the season. Not paying close attention to any conversation, Kathleen allowed their voices to drone in her ears as she picked at the food on her plate.

"He's a quick learner, this new one," Basil Dobbs said, nodding his head. "He's good with his hands; caught on to using a ruler quicker than most." Dobbs looked up at Wilks. "It's his size that bothers me, though. He's strong and muscular and could harm someone should he become so inclined."

"It's the size of his brain that's our concern. How the brain goes, so goes the body," Wilks replied, picking at his teeth.

"Well, I imagine he and his body will certainly be an asset on our football team," Marcus Bishop, the agricultural teacher, added. "His height will be intimidation enough, but if he can run fast and remember the rules, then our senior boys' team will be hard to beat next season."

Kathleen quickly looked up from her breakfast with the fork in her hand hovering midway to her mouth. Before the piece of ham could fall, she placed the fork on the edge of her plate. Were they talking about Jesse? Picking up her knife, she pretended to spread some jam on her bread, now listening carefully to every word.

"Just keep him under your thumb, Dobbs. That's a warning I'll give each and every one of his teachers. I don't trust this heathen and you shouldn't, either. I've already had to have Blunt remind him of his place." Wilks reached for another piece of ham. "As I've said before, none of them is too big or too small for the cold house if they get out of line. It's amazing how quickly that place gives their attitude a turn for the better."

"He's surprisingly compassionate, though," Dobbs continued, pouring cream into his coffee. "He's good with the younger boys. They look up to him as a leader."

"That could be dangerous," Marcus Bishop said, gesturing with a flick of his fork. "We don't need any of these redskins thinking he's Sitting Bull and is going to lead them on the warpath."

"Right you are, Bishop, right you are." Wilks stuffed a chunk of ham into his mouth.

Dobbs looked down at his coffee, wrapped his hand around the cup, and gave his head a slight shake. "Mr. Wilks, I doubt that anything like that will happen." He looked up. "There are times I'd swear he knows more than we think he does, or at least understands what I'm saying."

"Bah," Wilks snorted, continuing to talk as he chewed. "He's as ignorant as the rest of them." He pointed at Kathleen with his fork and chuckled. "In the meantime, our delightful new English teacher will have him understanding and speaking properly in no time. There'll be no more Indian gibberish coming out of his mouth." He swallowed his ham, his throat making an unpleasant gulping sound. "We're speaking of the Lakota who was in the group of students who arrived the same day you did, the tall, older one."

"Yes, of course, I remember him." Kathleen struggled between excitement to learn that Jesse was still here and the rage provoked by Wilks's attitude. She kept her gaze steady on his. "I assure you, I'll certainly do my best to teach him all I can. Will he be joining my class soon?"

Wilks gave a nonchalant shrug. "Possibly." His mouth

moved around another gob of half-chewed ham and settled
into something that resembled a smirk. "He's being taught a
few manners at the moment; otherwise he may prove to be
a bit of a problem for a wee woman, such as yourself."

Kathleen bristled, the "wee woman" comment grating
against her independent side, the side that had been honed
with the help of Richmond Brock. They were so much
alike; she couldn't help but wonder if Josiah Wilks and
Richmond Brock shared the same DNA. "Mr. Wilks, I'm
sure I will have no problem with him."

Dobbs saluted her with his coffee cup. "Very good, Miss
Prescott. Such confidence is to be admired."

"Or ridiculed," Wilks added, his tone suddenly sharp-
edged. "Time will tell, won't it, Miss Prescott?"

Kathleen lifted her chin and gave Josiah Wilks as severe
and direct a look as she dared. "Mr. Wilks, I assure you,
I've dealt with a fair share of unsavory individuals in my
lifetime and have always been able to remain unscathed.
I'm sure this won't be any more difficult."

Josiah Wilks had become one of those unsavory individuals in Kathleen's eyes, but he knew where she could find
Jesse. If she didn't ask now, she'd miss her chance, and she
didn't think she could pass another day, another hour, without knowing. "I haven't seen him since the day I arrived.
Has he taken ill?"

Wilks studied her over the folds of his napkin as he
wiped grease from his chin. The seconds ticked away before he answered, making her increasingly nervous. The
smirk returned to flaw his beautiful face. "He's quite well,
unless he's sick of the tasks he's been given."

"Is that the one you're talking about, Mr. Wilks?" Margaret Lester asked, pointing across the room. "That one by
the door?"

Kathleen's gaze followed Margaret Lester's pointed finger.
*Jesse.*

Had she said his name out loud? She quickly glanced
around the table. No. Satisfied she hadn't, she turned her attention back to Jesse. She felt as though an anvil had
dropped on her stomach. Had he been standing near the
door all along? Had she walked by without seeing him?

She watched him elbow his way between two other boys at one of the tables and sit down. As if he had heard her thoughts, he raised his head, and without searching the room, his gaze immediately locked with hers. A blank expression covered his face like a mask. Did he recognize her? God knows, she barely recognized him.

Randall Watson had cut Jesse's hair, the braids she'd hidden with the bundle of his Indian clothing proved that, but she wasn't ready for the crudeness of the cut. Watson had done little more than hack the braids off just below his ears. The uniform he wore didn't come close to fitting him, either. The sleeves ended somewhere near the middle of his forearms and the fabric pulled tightly across his chest and shoulders. Kathleen knew if he stood up, she'd probably see that his pants weren't long enough to cover his calves. She hated to think about the ill-fitting shoes he'd probably been given to wear. *Oh, my God, Jesse, my magnificent Jesse, what have they done to you?*

She quickly glanced at the other students in the room. A question that challenged everything she had ever thought was exemplary and noble about DuBois cruelly pushed into her mind. What had DuBois done to them all?

"He's not as grand-looking anymore, is he, Miss Prescott?" Wilks casually turned away from Jesse and began gobbling the remainder of his breakfast, decorating his mustache with bits of egg.

Had Wilks read her mind? She managed to contain her anger and put on the impassive expression she had worn like a mask for most of her life. "His clothes don't fit him very well," she stated, knowing and not caring that her words would probably rile Wilks. "I do hope that you plan on providing him with a uniform that fits properly."

"Whatever for, my dear?" Wilks glanced up, obviously surprised by her remark. "These people run around half naked before they come here; now you expect me to care that what he's wearing doesn't fit him like a Chicago-tailored suit? Ridiculous." Wilks began to laugh. "Besides, it is so much easier to keep these savages under control, to have them bend to our will, when their primitive sense of dignity is stripped away."

"Is this Reverend Divine's doctrine?" she challenged, giving a fervent silent prayer that it wasn't. "Should anyone from town or a visitor, a government official for example, see this student in these ill-fitting clothes, well, it certainly wouldn't be good for the school's reputation—or funding—would it?"

Wilks arched his left brow in disdain. "For someone who has been here such a short while, Miss Prescott, you seem to have quickly developed your own views on how DuBois should be run. I certainly hope you won't make me regret hiring you."

Veiled, though perfectly clear, the threat hung between them. She bit back other words she wished she could say to Wilks, offering an apology instead. "I have overstepped my bounds, Mr. Wilks, and am truly sorry." She gave a slight deferential bow of her head. "I'm a new student, myself, to the theories that you and Reverend Divine have established. Of course I'll follow your directives."

Wilks turned back to his meal and dismissed her with a quick flip of his hand. "You'll learn, Miss Prescott, you'll learn. You'd do well to follow Miss Lester's guidance." He pointed at Margaret Lester with the piece of bread in his hand then continued to shovel food into his mouth. He shot a sidelong look at her and added, "Perhaps the first lesson you should learn is that I am Reverend Divine's confidante, his second in command, and his mentor, if you will." He gave a grandiose gesture with his hand. "I taught at three Indian schools before coming here and have shared my extensive knowledge and experience with Reverend Divine. When I speak, it is as though the Reverend himself has spoken."

She quickly glanced at the other teachers sitting around the table. All sat silently, their heads bowed. Not one turned their attention from their meal or challenged Wilks's declaration. Kathleen had never heard anything so pompous, so preposterous. Obviously Josiah Wilks had no idea that Providence Divine kept detailed journals. And, according to her great-great-grandfather's writings, Wilks was nothing more than a history and geography teacher who was only mediocre at best. It was true, though, that Providence frequently left Wilks in charge when he was absent from the school.

Kathleen's appetite disappeared, both for the company and for the food.

She gathered her books and, forcing an affable smile, she stood. "Again, Mr. Wilks, I apologize." She glanced around the table. "Now, if you all will excuse me, I need to prepare for my morning classes."

Kathleen made her way across the dining hall, between the lengths of tables, and to the doorway as quickly as she could. As she neared the table where she had last seen Jesse sitting, her gaze fell to an empty spot on the bench. Had he moved to another table? She searched up one row of tables and down another, but couldn't find him. He had disappeared.

Kathleen took one last look over her shoulder at her fellow teachers. They were all deep in conversation, none looking her way. Grateful that she'd passed another 1886 moment without being found a fraud, she stepped out onto the porch.

Bright morning sunlight blinded her for a moment, and raising her textbook, she shielded her eyes and looked out over the parade ground with its large bandstand at the south end. How could anything so familiar to her be so unfamiliar in the same breath? *Don't even go there. Don't think about where you began four days ago and where you are now. There's nothing you can do about it but wait . . . wait and see what happens.*

Lowering the book from her eyes, Kathleen moved to the stairs and reached for the banister. Still unused to the full bustled skirt and high-button boots, she slowly began down the ten steps.

Before her booted foot touched the third riser, someone grabbed her arm. Then a hand covered her mouth, stifling the shriek that rushed up her throat.

"Katie-girl, hush, it's just me. Don't scream." The hand slowly lifted away from her mouth.

"Jesse?"

"Shh. Come on, follow me." He took her hand and quickly pulled her down the remaining stairs. At the bottom step he doubled back and led her between the honeysuckle bushes that flanked the high verandah. Lifting a loosened lattice panel, he took her through the opening.

Under the verandah, in the mottled light that filtered in through the bushes and the latticework, for the first time in four days, they stood face-to-face. The moment stretched between them and neither moved, neither said a word.

Unmindful of her surroundings, the cobwebs that hung from the joists overhead, or the musty smell of damp soil and rotting leaves under foot, Kathleen's gaze moved over Jesse from head to toe. An odd sensation washed over her. As if she had been hungry for a long time, seeing him and being with him somehow took the edge off that hunger. Tears filled her eyes and rolled down her cheeks.

"Jesse." His name slipped from her lips on a trembling breath. She slowly raised her hand. Her fingers lightly touched his hair, smoothing the uneven cropped strands back from his face. He didn't move. His gaze lingered on her mouth and her breath caught in her throat as a growing warmth rushed to envelope and ignite every cell in her body. Brand-new. Wonderful. Arousing. Unnerving. The moment seemed to expand, time taking another flip and twist.

Suddenly feeling self-conscious and embarrassed that she'd touched him, Kathleen breathed a soft exclamation and lowered her hand. But the texture of his hair remained a phantom feeling on the tips of her fingers.

Shadows created illusions of dark and light in the dim space under the porch, but what she saw on Jesse's face was neither shadow nor illusion. A bruise, still a little swollen, the edges beginning to change from blue to a faint yellow-green, discolored his left cheek. Lower, on the left side of his face, his skin was scraped and scabbed over.

"Oh, my God, what have they done to you?"

# Chapter 11

All the boys in our school were given English names because their Indian names were difficult to pronounce. Besides, the Indian names were considered by the missionaries to be heathenish.

—FRANCIS LA FLESCHE,
OMAHA, 1900

"SHH," JESSE WHISPERED, "I'm okay." He pulled her further under the porch. "We've got to be careful. If we're caught . . ."

He paused, not finishing his thought. He didn't have to. She knew the consequences for her would be immediate dismissal, but for Jesse they would be much worse.

His full mouth moved into a slow, engaging smile. "Hey, Katie-girl, it's good to see you."

That silly name, she hated it, and yet the sound of him saying it caused a glorious warm rush. God, how she'd missed it.

She grasped his hand and twined her fingers with his, afraid he'd disappear if she let go. "I was terrified that you might have left without me. Where have you been?" Without waiting for his answer, she rushed on to her next question. "Are you really all right?" She took a quick gulp of air, then let it out in a long sigh. "I've been sick with worry."

"I'm supposed to be in the carpentry shop with Basil Dobbs, but Wilks and his boys have kept me working at the woodpile. I must have chopped at least eight cords already." He grinned. "I think they're trying to wear me down." Kathleen saw a rascal's twinkle in his eyes. "So, were you *really* worried about me?"

She ignored his teasing. She withdrew her hand from his and, throwing propriety aside, reached up and gently touched his bruised cheek. "Your face, what happened?" Being careful not to hurt him, she smoothed her fingers over his skin.

"It's nothing. I bumped into a 'blunt' object. Mr. Cecil Blunt, to be exact." He grinned. "I think that makes it blunt-force trauma, doesn't it?" He chuckled at his own silly pun.

Kathleen took her hand away from his cheek and lightly slapped his arm. "How can you joke about this?"

"I've got to, it's the only way to deal with it without pounding the crap out of him." He traced the curve of her cheek with the tip of his finger. "Mr. Blunt and I had a little scuffle, that's all. I told him in the best Lakota words I could remember that I don't like chopping wood. In his own special way, Mr. Blunt told me that I did." His smile reappeared and another millennium seemed to slip by as he looked into her eyes. "Touch my face again. It feels good."

An intriguing warmth spread through Kathleen's body, leaving feathery tingles in the most amazing places. Jesse wanted her to touch him. She began to raise her hand, then stopped. What was she thinking? No matter how wonderful it felt, she shouldn't be touching him so often in such an intimate manner. The first time was an error, the second was concern, but this time would be deliberate. Her mother's voice pushed with cold censure into her conscience. *Kathleen, women of loose morals will attract a man but never his devotion and love.* She dropped her hand and stepped away.

A rebuttal rose from her heart but quickly died. Love? She definitely had no illusions about love, although she couldn't deny she cared about Jesse as a friend. But, if that was all it was, then what were these new, delightful feelings all about? The feelings that made her breath quicken when she saw him, the feelings that made her heart race when he was near, the feelings that brought him into her dreams each night.

Romance.

The word pirouetted through her mind in a frivolous dance. She almost laughed out loud. Impossible. No, definitely not. Romance and love, they went hand in hand, so it certainly wasn't for her, and certainly not with someone like Jesse Spotted Horse. They disagreed on everything that mattered and most things that didn't. The one and only thing they did agree upon was their need to find a way to turn the time slide upside down and put them back where they belonged.

Saddened by her dry analysis and the desolate, empty feeling it left, she resolved to banish her silly musings. "Jesse, I'd better go. This isn't safe."

"Katie, no. Not yet, please." His hand encircled her arm, gently stopping her retreat.

She eased away from his touch and a tide of tears spilled down her cheeks. Frustrated, she fisted her hand, scrubbed them away, once, twice, and then pressed her closed hand against her breast. "I'm sorry I'm being so emotional. I'm not very good at this." Turning to face him, she shook her head and drew a ragged breath. "I've spent my entire life loving DuBois, believing in it and in the good that was done here. I've fought battles against those who said it had been evil." Her voice dropped to a quiet place near a whisper. "I've even fought you." With another brisk swipe of her hand, she attacked a few fresh tears, then looked at him once again. "And now, now I don't know what to think." Her voice wavered as she fought for precious composure. "I see what it's done to the children who sit in my class, the children who pass me in the halls, those poor hungry babies in the dining hall." She sniffled and pointed at Jesse. "Look what DuBois has done to you." Continuing in spite of her trembling bottom lip, she added, "In just four days everything I've believed all my life is tarnished and crumbling. There have been so many lies." She paused and waited for him to speak; when he didn't, she continued. "Aren't you going to say it? Aren't you going to say 'I told you so'?"

Jesse reached out to touch her, but she stepped away. Reflex. Ingrained and unconsciously practiced, it drove her away from him. No matter what pain and emptiness it brought, distance had always been safe. Distance always protected her. A silent cry tore from her soul. Distance was so lonely.

"Don't be so damned hard on yourself, Kathleen, and don't take everything at face value. Wait until Providence gets back. Talk to him, see what he has to say."

"Is this why Fate brought me here? Am I supposed to learn that this place was built on nothing but lies and suffering?" She searched Jesse's face for an answer. "What about you? What has there been here for you other than bruises and hard labor?" Kathleen touched his sleeve; a spark of hope filled her heart. "Have you found him yet? Have you found *Tokalu Sapa*?"

Jesse looked away before he answered, but she already knew what he would say.

"No. None of the Indian kids I've asked will say if they know him. I think they're afraid to say anything."

"I guess I should add your loss to the list of DuBois's disgraces." She sniffled. "Oh, drat." Fumbling with the drawstring on her purse, she retrieved a tissue and began wiping her face.

"Kathleen, look what you just did."

Puzzled by the sharp edge in his voice, she quickly looked up. "What?"

"What's in your hand? You've got to be more careful. You've got to get rid of anything that might give you away." He took the tissue from her, then removed the rest from her purse. Gouging the dirt with the heel of his boot, he dropped them into the hole, then pushed the earth back over them.

Her hand flew to her throat, covering the cameo brooch. "Please, not this."

"No, no, not that," Jesse replied, gently removing her hand from the brooch. "The cameo is an antique. It fits into the time. But if you've got anything else, a safety pin, a bobby pin, a tube of lipstick, anything, it has to go."

Her hand slid into her skirt pocket and touched the watch. She wouldn't tell Jesse about it because she couldn't give it up. Slowly withdrawing her hand, she promised herself that she'd be more vigilant. "I just didn't think about the tissues."

"You've got to. You've got to think about every . . ."

Voices and footsteps on the porch overhead silenced his words. Jesse touched his fingers to her lips for a moment. Neither dared to move.

"Damn it, Providence and his loving little family will be returning tomorrow," Josiah Wilks grumbled. "Just when things are running smoothly. It's much too soon for my liking."

"Aren't you the least bit worried?"

"About what? He trusts me." Wilks chuckled, his footfalls slowing on the stairs. "Ah, but you, Margaret, you've been a naughty girl, a very naughty girl."

"Yes, I have, haven't I?" Margaret Lester's laughter joined Wilks's. "And I'll probably be naughty again, Josiah. Yes, I think I will."

Jesse saw a frown crease Kathleen's brow as Wilks and Margaret Lester walked away from the dining hall. The honeysuckle bushes allowed glimpses of them through the branches, and Jesse didn't move until the sound of their footfalls on the ash-strewn promenade had completely faded away. He'd seen and heard enough of Wilks over the past few days to know that the man was up to something, but how did Margaret Lester fit into Wilks's schemes?

Jesse took hold of Kathleen's wrists. "Listen to me." He slid his hands up to her shoulders. "Wilks isn't to be trusted. He's working some sort of scheme, and I plan to find out what it is." He grazed her left cheek with his thumb.

"Don't worry. I *don't* trust him." Kathleen smiled for the first time since they'd slipped under the porch. "If he's a crook, I'm not surprised. Josiah Wilks is a self-righteous, pompous, egomaniacal ass."

He watched her eyes widened with surprise, and she immediately lost her smile. He'd bet every penny left in the film grant that the prim side of Kathleen Prescott hadn't realized she'd said *ass* until the word tumbled from her lips. Looking at her in the stippled light that pushed through the latticework, he saw the red blush on her cheeks.

"I'm sorry. Excuse me," she murmured, stepping back from him. Her slight smile proved she wasn't sorry at all. "Josiah Wilks has a face like an angel, but he is one of the most devious individuals I've ever met. The man is a consummate liar." She arched her brow and glanced in the direction that Wilks had gone. "Don't worry, Jesse, I intend to watch Josiah Wilks like an eagle."

"*Han, wasicu winyan,* you will be like the great *wanbli.*" Jesse stood tall, folded his arms over his chest, and looking arrogantly down his nose, imitated every bad Hollywood actor who had ever played an Indian in the movies. "White woman speaks with great wisdom." He made a horizontal gesture with his hand, moving it, palm down, away from his heart. "It is *wasté.*"

A smile captured her lips, and Jesse liked what it did to her soft, pretty mouth. Liked it a lot.

"*Wanbli. Wasté. Wasicu.*" She stumbled over the words. "What do those words mean?"

"Oh, no." He tried to quiet what would have been a deep, full-bodied laugh. "You're the English teacher. I'll be damned if I'll corrupt you with Lakota."

"Good grief! It's a good thing you reminded me!" she exclaimed. "I forgot. My class. I've got to go." She turned her back to him, then paused with her hand on the latticed panel. "When will I see you again?" She spoke without looking at him, her voice soft, her head bowed as though it embarrassed her to ask the question.

She looked so small, so fragile, and so vulnerable. Jesse battled the strong urge to pull her against him, to hold her close—not just for her, but for him as well.

Before he could answer her question, before he could reach for her, Kathleen whirled away from the panel and into his arms. Her books fell to the ground. Surprised, Jesse stiffened and then relaxed as the pleasure of feeling her body pressed against his swept through him.

She fit perfectly into his shoulder, and he pressed his cheek against her temple. Her hair was fragrant, reminding him of sunshine and lemons. She trembled as he closed his arms around her, and he held her as though she were made of delicate crystal.

"I'm sorry, Jesse," she said, her words muffled against his chest. "You're my only tie to who I am and where I come from. You're my touchstone." She looked up at him. "I can't do this without knowing I can see you or talk with you." She shuddered. "I can't . . . I can't do this alone."

"You won't have to, Katie-girl. I'll be as near as you need me to be." An unfamiliar feeling hit him with a punch, filling him with a warm, sweet ache. Her smoky gray eyes held him prisoner, and he knew that no matter what happened, no matter what the next hours, days, months, or years brought, he would do everything he could to keep this promise.

"Do you suppose Tooter and Egypt . . . do you suppose they think we died in the fire?"

Her question surprised him. He hadn't even thought about what Tooter and the others would think when they couldn't find either of them after the fire was put out. Another question laid a cold weight on his heart. How would the old lady take the news? He was Beulah Spotted Horse's only family. He touched a silken strand of Kathleen's hair that had come loose from the twist at the back of her head. "I don't know. I can't imagine what they think."

He watched her teeth worry at her bottom lip, and he gently placed his fingers against her mouth. "Stop that." The urge to kiss her swept over him, its force taking him completely by surprise. *Damn it, Horse, this isn't the time or the place.* His conscience railed at him, but his wanting won out. He slowly lowered his head, eager to press his lips against hers, to taste her intriguing mouth.

A mere sigh, an excited breath away, the words came loud and clear in his head. *Don't do it, Horse. You're asking for trouble, big trouble, if you do.*

At the last moment he turned his head and his lips lightly grazed her cheek. "You'd better go."

*I ALMOST KISSED HER. What the hell was that all about?* Unable to take his eyes away, Jesse moved closer to the latticed panel and watched her walk away. Prim Miss Prescott had absolutely no idea how enticing the swish and sway of her skirt was. And under that skirt . . . he imagined the swing of her hips and the lithe stride of her legs. He drove his fingers through his cropped hair. When had he begun thinking about kisses, legs, hips, and Kathleen Prescott in the same thought?

"Easy, Tonto," he cautioned himself. *It must be something like the Stockholm syndrome—the captive becomes emotionally involved with the captor.* "Only one problem with that idea," he murmured, "you're both captives."

He stood with his hand on the panel, watching, listening. Finally sure it was safe, he tipped the panel upward and ducked under it. Stepping through the break in the honeysuckle bushes, he stood in the open sunlight. With one last look in Kathleen's direction, Jesse turned in the opposite direction. If he didn't show up at the carpentry shop soon, Dobbs would probably send Blunt out to look for him.

"Ah, there you are."

*Too late.* A nervous chill skittered through his body, chasing away the warmth that Kathleen had left behind. *Now we'll see what kind of punishment gets doled out for being late.* He looked down at Dobbs, surprised to see a compassionate expression on the man's face.

"Are you lost?" Obviously not expecting Jesse to answer, Dobbs continued, slowly enunciating each word and playing charades with his hands. "I looked for you after breakfast. When I couldn't find you, I thought you might have gone to the shop. Come along, follow me."

Jesse began to take a step, the unconscious reflex of someone who understood what Dobbs had said. Thank God he stopped himself before making a foolish mistake.

Dobbs glanced up at Jesse and offered a friendly smile. "Come along, fellow, come with me." He beckoned with his hand, then lightly touched Jesse's arm. "There's no reason to be afraid, it's just time for you to go to school, that's all. Wilks thinks you won't behave, that you'll cause trouble, and that you're not smart and won't learn." He took hold of Jesse's sleeve and pulled him along. "You're a bright fellow. I think you'll catch on to things just fine."

Jesse filed Wilks's words away in his memory; maybe not today, but someday he'd show that pretty son of a bitch just how smart he could be. He held back from Dobbs, pretending to be afraid. He yanked his arm out of Dobbs's grasp and stopped, solidly standing in the middle of the promenade. *Okay, Tooter, you win. Are you happy? Now I'm an actor.*

"Come along, now. Don't be afraid. No one's going to hurt you, certainly not me."

Dobbs led him past the senior girls' dormitory and the administration building.

The morning bell clanged and butted into his thoughts. Each morning one of the senior students rang the bell on the north edge of the parade ground to signal the start of classes, each afternoon it rang to end classes, and at nine each night it rang again for lights out. The day at DuBois was organized to run like the Army ran its boot camps.

Dobbs stopped in front of the building that housed a number of classrooms. It was one of the buildings that had reappeared, one that hadn't been there in 2003, the building where the basketball court had been built.

"We'd better hurry," Dobbs said, puffing from their walk. "You don't want to be late for your first day in class."

Jesse silently followed Basil Dobbs inside. In the hallway Dobbs stopped and took a few moments to catch his breath, then led Jesse up the flight of stairs to the second floor.

"Ah, here we are," Dobbs said, pausing outside a closed door. He turned and inspected Jesse. A frown furrowed his brow and he shook his head as he tried to adjust Jesse's ill-fitting jacket. No matter how far he tugged, one way or the other, the front still gaped, the buttons holding by a thread or two. Dobbs's attention then moved to Jesse's trousers. He shook his head again. "No, this will never, never do. I'll ask my sister to have the young ladies in her sewing class fix some clothes for you, a shirt and pants that fit."

Jesse deliberately frowned as though he were trying to understand Dobbs's words. The damned charade was beginning to really get on his nerves.

Dobbs knocked on the closed door and quickly took off his hat. A few moments later the doorknob turned and the classroom door swung open.

Dobbs had brought him to Kathleen.

# Chapter 12

If the Great Spirit had desired me to be a white man, he would have made me so in the first place.

—SITTING BULL,
TETON SIOUX

"GOOD MORNING . . . AGAIN, Miss Prescott." Basil Dobbs fumbled with his hat, holding it by the edge of the brim and turning it inch by inch. "I . . . uh . . . I have a new student for you." He grabbed Jesse's sleeve and pulled him forward.

The moment Kathleen saw him, the expression on her face registered somewhere between disbelief and shock. Jesse watched her struggle for composure and knew exactly when she'd won the battle by the arched brow and commanding expression that settled on her face.

"Mr. Wilks didn't tell me that I should expect a new student today." She peered around Dobbs and adjusted her glasses as if she needed a better look at her new pupil. "Isn't he the new arrival that you gentlemen were discussing at breakfast?"

"Yes, as a matter of fact he is. I've had him in the carpentry shop for a few days. He's kind of stubborn but a hard worker nonetheless." Dobbs looked up at Jesse and then his gaze fell back on Kathleen. "He's a very handsome and imposing specimen, don't you think?"

While Dobbs stared at her, his infatuation clear to anyone who watched, Kathleen appeared to assess Jesse before answering. The opportunity seemed too perfect for him to pass up. With the most dazzling Hollywood smile he could muster, Jesse winked.

Kathleen's brow shot up and her eyes seemed to darken. Exasperation had a habit of looking very good on Miss Prescott.

"Well, he is . . . imposing, but I'm not sure I'd call him handsome." She shot him a how-did-you-like-that-answer look.

Ouch. Not handsome . . . just imposing? Jesse dropped his bottom lip in an exaggerated pout that almost did her in. He watched her fight the urge to laugh. Damn, he'd pushed her too far. Jesse watched her pull herself together and he breathed a sigh of relief. *Close call. Damn it, Horse, behave yourself.*

"I asked Mr. Wilks this morning when this . . . pupil was going to be starting in my class. Why didn't he tell me then that it would be today? Instead, he was very evasive."

"I don't know, Miss Prescott." Dobbs nervously fumbled with his hat again. "After you left the dining hall, Mr. Wilks asked me to bring him to you. That's all I know."

"Very well, Mr. Dobbs." She stepped aside and clasped her hands at her waist. "Come in."

Jesse followed Dobbs and, as he passed Kathleen, grazed his knuckles over the back of her arm. She drew a sharp breath, and from the corner of his eye, he watched her rub her arm as though she'd been singed.

"Where do you want him to sit?" Dobbs looked around the room, from one small desk to another. "I don't think he'll fit in any of these."

Jesse watched, mesmerized, as the expression on her face changed with her thoughts. Within the narrow confines of her world, she had obviously never become skilled at hiding her emotions. He could tell exactly when she'd settled on an answer that satisfied her. What was she up to?

She flashed a look at Jesse, the kind of look that Grandma Boo had always given him when he was a kid and had been bad. All kids at one time or another got "the look." He'd never had too much trouble dealing with Grandma Boo's look. The old lady's punishment had never been severe. She'd never spanked him; her methods were worse. Nothing could make a boy stay in line more than having to sit out on the front stoop and fringe powwow dance shawls for the ladies. Now, Kathleen's look, well, that was something completely different. There were unknown consequences, but he had a niggling feeling he was about to get the big payback for his wink and his touch.

He had to admit she had the right to yank his chain, especially after his mini tirade about the tissues in her purse. He didn't even bother to hide his grin. *Oh, yeah, I'm going to enjoy this class, a lot.*

Kathleen dropped her gaze to his long legs, a smile quirked the corners of her mouth, and then she pointed to one of three empty desks at the back of the room. "He'll have to try to fit, at least until other arrangements can be made."

Dobbs scratched his head and then shrugged. "It ain't going to work, Miss Prescott, but we'll give it a go." He led Jesse to the small desk, then patted the wooden seat with the palm of his hand. "You, Indian, sit."

The last time Jesse had seen one of these desks, the little all-in-one desk with the lift top and hinged seat, was in elementary school on the rez. He'd had trouble then fitting into them. But now that he was taller, bigger, fitting in one was going to be next to impossible.

Dobbs tried again. "You . . . sit." He struck the seat again.

Standing with his feet apart, arms crossed over his chest, and looking over the top of Dobbs's head, Jesse didn't move.

Dobbs sputtered, his frustration peaking, then pointed at the boy sitting at the next desk. "Look. See? Please . . . sit, like that."

Grabbing Jesse's arm, Dobbs tried to pull him down. Determined not to give in too easily, Jesse widened his stance and refused to budge. Next, Dobbs tried to scrunch his own rotund body into the desk seat, but his stomach kept hanging up on the desk lid. The whole scene reminded Jesse of a comedy show, and from the muffled giggles that cropped up all over the classroom, the kids in the class found it funny, too.

Wheezing, Dobbs pushed away from the desk and grabbed Jesse's arm. "Come on, Injun. Sit! Sit! Sit!"

"Mr. Dobbs," Kathleen said, stepping between Basil Dobbs and Jesse, "don't excite yourself so." She turned and faced Jesse, and touched him on the arm. "Please, sit down." She punctuated her request with a sharp lift of her left brow.

Okay, Jesse decided, he'd play along. After all, he'd antagonized Basil Dobbs long enough. He hunkered down and made a few honest attempts to sit and fold his long legs under the desk. Squeezing into the seat, he fit his left leg under the desk at a ninety-degree angle, but that left no room for the right. Stuffing an elephant into a breadbox would have been a lot easier.

The giggles grew louder, some even becoming full laughs. Turning around to face her class, Kathleen shook her head and placed her index finger against her lips. "Shh, children, that's not polite."

Jesse noted there hadn't been too much authority in her request. In fact, her voice held the strong hint of a giggle.

The last position he tried worked the best. Sitting almost sideways with one leg slightly bent and the other straight, his feet stuck out into the aisle. The only other problem was that the edge of the desk bit painfully into his bruised hip.

"How ever did you get him to do that?" Dobbs voice was filled with wonder.

"As you said, Mr. Dobbs, he's a quick learner."

Standing beside Dobbs, her arms folded across her breasts, Kathleen watched every minute of Jesse's misery. When he'd finally twisted himself into a pretzel, he looked up at her and silently begged for mercy. Damned if the little scamp didn't grin and wink at him!

With the serene look of an angel, she demurely clasped her hands as if in prayer and allowed the devil's twinkle to show in her eyes. "Oh, my." She pensively paused for a moment. "I suppose that's not very comfortable, don't you agree, Mr. Dobbs?"

Dobbs shot a sidelong glance at her, then looked back at Jesse, grimaced, and placed his hand on his rotund belly. "Best him and not me."

She studied Jesse's painful pose for another moment or two. To Jesse it felt like a lifetime. He moved his leg, praying for another inch of easement. *Come on, Katie-girl, please, have a little compassion.*

Kathleen drew a long sigh and shook her head. "I really don't think this will do." She lightly placed her hand on Basil Dobbs's arm. "Perhaps you would be kind enough to find me a small table and a chair that would be appropriate for him? Your sister might have such a table in her sewing class." She looked at Dobbs and seemed to wait until she had his undivided attention, then modestly lowered her lashes. "I'd be most grateful."

Jesse couldn't believe his eyes. Prim little Miss Prescott kept pulling out all these feminine wiles like a magician pulling scarves out of his top hat. The timid orchid was learning how to bloom.

"I would be delighted to help you, Miss Prescott," Dobbs gushed. "But did you mean right now?"

"Well, yes, of course. Now. Is that a problem?"

Dobbs glanced at Jesse, then back at Kathleen. "Yes, I suppose I could go now, but . . ." He looked at Jesse again. "I don't know whether it's safe to leave you alone with this fellow. He's not been in a classroom before."

Kathleen quirked her brow. "Thank you for your concern, Mr. Dobbs, but I'm sure I can manage." The devil's twinkle returned. "If he is determined to cause trouble, I believe it would take at least ten minutes for him to unfold himself from that desk. By then the students and I would be safely out the door and halfway to town."

"Oh, my, Miss Prescott." Dobbs chuckled. "That is quite humorous, yes, I see your point." Complete adoration filled Dobbs's face.

*Yup, things keep getting more and more interesting,* Jesse thought. *Tooter, you should be here, you're missing a great time.*

"What is his name, Mr. Dobbs?" Kathleen stepped closer to Jesse. "I need to know what to call him." She waited for Dobbs to answer. The moment lengthened and still no reply. "You do know his name, don't you?"

"Uh, well, no, not really . . . no, I don't," Dobbs stammered. "He arrived without agent papers. We don't know his name."

"Has anyone asked him?"

"He's Indian, Miss Prescott." Dobbs breathed an exasperated sigh. "No one on staff speaks Indian."

"I believe, Mr. Dobbs, that he's Lakota, not just Indian."

"Uh, well, yes, you're right about that . . . Lakota." Dobbs quickly nodded. "But no one at DuBois speaks Lakota." Dobbs continued to nod, apparently satisfied with his response.

"No one? Are you sure?" She impaled him with a pointed glance. "Aren't there other Lakota students at DuBois?"

"Well, yes, but—"

"I believe there are some in this very room."

"Well, yes, but—"

"I'm sure you could have asked one of them to find out what his name is."

"Well, yes, but . . . uh, what I mean is . . . no, that wouldn't do." Dobbs nodded, then shook his head, and then looked completely flummoxed. "I don't think . . . no, that definitely wouldn't do. The children are not allowed to speak Indian; it's against the rules. Mr. Wilks forbids—"

"Mr. Wilks forbids? Even in an instance such as this?" Kathleen's brow arched sharply. "Mr. Dobbs, what do you suppose Reverend Divine would suggest you do to learn this pupil's name?"

"I'm not . . . I don't know what . . ." Dobbs continued to stumble over his words, then threw his hands up in the air. "What difference does it make? In a day or so all of the new arrivals will be renamed, anyway." He shrugged. "I suppose you could just go ahead and name him yourself."

Jesse watched Kathleen's hands close into fists at her sides. Disgust, or something very close to it, turned the devil's twinkle in her eyes into the devil's fire.

"Name him? Like someone would name a dog or cat?"

"No, of course not, Miss Prescott. Forgive me for saying so, but that's a very poor analogy."

"I believe, Mr. Dobbs, that he already has a name."

Dobbs had the decency to look contrite. "But Christian names help them fit into white society much better than their Indian names. We can't pronounce their Indian names, and spelling them"—he shrugged—"well, that's almost impossible." A nervous chuckle gurgled from his throat.

"And do the children not have difficulty pronouncing the Christian names they're given?"

"Possibly," Dobbs pondered, then shrugged again, "but I don't know."

"No, I don't suppose you do."

Her response had been so quiet, Jesse doubted that Dobbs had even heard her.

Basil Dobbs waited as if expecting further argument from her. When none came, he continued. "Reverend Divine likes us to use names from the Bible." He pointed to some of the children sitting close to Jesse. "Such as Sarah, Abraham, Esther, Noah, and John. Just don't forget to tell Miss Lester what you choose . . . for the school records."

Kathleen stepped closer to Jesse, her gaze locked with his. "I wonder what name would suit him best."

"Oh, please be careful, Miss Prescott, don't go too close. It might not be safe until we know he's not going to cause trouble or hurt anyone."

Kathleen turned and looked sharply at Dobbs. "That is the second time that you've inferred I might be in danger. If you think he might cause trouble or harm anyone, why did you bring him to my class?"

Dobbs began twisting his hat again, this time looking embarrassed. He dropped his gaze to the floor. "Mr. Wilks suggested it would be a good test of your . . . abilities."

Jesse saw Kathleen stiffen, and her anger brought a bright flush to her cheeks. *Uh-oh, watch out, Dobbs, I think you're about to get yourself a genuine Kathleen Divine Prescott heart-to-heart lecture.*

"Mr. Dobbs." Turning, she gave a sweeping gesture with her arm. "These children are human beings, not tests of anyone's abilities. The charge we have been given is to open new doors, provide an education for them, and provide tools that will make a better life possible for them in a quickly changing world. That is where my *abilities* lie. They should not be wasted in ridiculous tests and challenges by my own peers." She paused, then coolly added, "Please, don't forget to bring the table and chair."

Jesse watched her pivot back toward the front of the class, dismissing Basil Dobbs without a backward glance, and possibly breaking his heart. Picking up a piece of chalk, she began to write some letters on the blackboard.

"One more thing, Mr. Dobbs," she said, without turning around.

"Yes, ma'am."

"Tell Mr. Wilks that I passed his test."

"Yes, ma'am."

Jesse heard the door close behind Dobbs and knew that Kathleen had heard it, too. She slowly turned back to her class and, walking down the aisle, stopped in front of Jesse. She tapped the top of the desk. "You may sit here for now."

He unfolded himself from the tight seat and perched on the edge of the desktop, and tried to ignore the painful tingling in his legs as his circulation returned.

"Are we ready to begin, again?"

Jesse saw a hand go up, second row, fourth seat.

"Miss, I help find name." The boy turned and pointed at Jesse with an upward tilt of his chin and pursed lips.

Kathleen moved to the boy's desk. "Are you Lakota?"

The boy nodded. "Yes. I help?"

"Of course," she replied. "Yes, please."

The boy rose and slowly walked toward Jesse with Kathleen following close behind. He stared, his dark eyes taking in Jesse's size. Finally, as if he had stoked his courage, he gave a slight nod. Jesse responded in kind.

"I ask now, miss?" He hesitated for one last look at Kathleen.

"Yes, you may."

The boy stepped closer and stared at the bruise on Jesse's face. *"Ani'pe kin he tu'we hwo?"*

The question certainly wasn't the one Jesse had expected. He shook his head and shrugged. What good would it do to tell the boy who had hit him? What good other than increase the child's fear of this place.

The second question came. *"Táku eniciyapi he?"*

This time his reply and the gesture came easily. *"Suŋgléska emaciyapi."*

The boy grinned. He glanced first to his left, then his

right, and leaned closer as if he were about to share a secret.

Touching his chest with his fist, the boy whispered, "*Maśtincala.*"

Kathleen tapped the boy's shoulder. "Matthew, what is his name?"

Jesse watched the light in the boy's eyes dim. His name was *Maśtincala,* Rabbit, not Matthew.

The boy hesitated for a moment, and then looked at Kathleen. "His name, *Suŋgléska,* means Spotted Horse."

Kathleen's gaze quickly left the boy and flew to Jesse. He shrugged his shoulders in an "I told you so" gesture and quietly mouthed his name, *Suŋgléska,* then touched his chest.

Kathleen quickly turned back to the class. "Shall we give him a new name now?"

The children nodded and a few answered aloud.

"All right, let's see." She raised her finger to her lips, giving herself a pensive look. "Now, it must be from the Bible, right?"

"Moses," the boy to Jesse's left suggested.

Kathleen looked at Jesse and then back at the class. "Moses?"

"No," most of the children replied and she shook her head, agreeing with them.

"Hezekiah," another child suggested. "Is good Bible name?"

"No," the children replied.

"Ezekiel," the girl to Jesse's right called out.

"Lazarus."

"Daniel."

"Goliath."

Jesse had a difficult time not laughing at the last suggestion and noticed that Kathleen suffered from the same problem.

"You name, miss," Matthew said, looking up at Kathleen. "You give *Suŋgléska* good white man Bible name."

"All right. What about Zacharius?" She looked around the classroom.

Too many scrunched up faces and shaking heads.

"No? How about . . . Meshach or Bartholomew?"

"No, miss, give *good* name," Matthew pleaded again.

Jesse could have sworn that a touch of guilt showed in the expression on Kathleen's face, and he couldn't help but wonder if she had had her heart set on naming him Hezekiah or Zacharius. Obviously winking at Kathleen Prescott could be very dangerous. He saw the moment she caved in and he sighed with relief.

Kathleen gently rested her hand on Matthew's shoulder and nodded. "Jesse." Her voice had softened when she'd spoken his name. "What about Jesse?" She glanced at the class again. "Is that a better name?"

Smiles and nods greeted her final suggestion.

"What it means—Jesse?" Matthew asked.

Kathleen smiled. "*Jesse* means 'the gift.'"

"*Wasté.* Jesse. Is . . . good Bible name . . . good gift that one." Matthew turned and looked at Jesse. "*NiLa'kota, eniciyapi* Jesse. *Wasté.*"

Jesse knew the moment Matthew realized he had spoken in Lakota without permission. The boy's eyes grew wide with fear, and he immediately stepped out of Kathleen's reach. Jesse groaned. *Oh, Katie-girl, please, please, don't disappoint me.*

As if she had heard his plea, Kathleen drew Matthew back to her side, her touch gentle. "*Wasté,* does that mean 'good'?"

The boy gave a timid nod.

"Thank you, Matthew. Thank you for teaching me one of your words." She looked at Jesse and grinned like a cream-filled Cheshire cat. "*Wasté* means 'good.'"

*Yes, it does, Katie-girl. Yes, it does.*

# Chapter 13

In the Indian civilization I am a Baptist, because I believe in immersing the Indians in our civilization and when we get them under, holding them there until they are thoroughly soaked.

—RICHARD H. PRATT,
CARLISLE INDIAN INDUSTRIAL SCHOOL, 1883

KATHLEEN STOOD AT her window and looked out over the promenade and parade ground. When no one was on the lawn or walking the promenade, it looked as though the time flip hadn't happened at all. But subtle clues told her the truth—the three buildings that had reappeared, the unpaved driveway, and the absence of the neat diagonal pattern on the parade ground that Richmond Brock's groundskeeper always left with his lawnmower.

On Saturdays classes were held only in the morning. The children were now in the dining hall at lunch but would soon spill out of the building and spend the next three or four hours doing their weekly chores. With floors to sweep and scrub, weeds to be pulled from the garden and flowerbeds, laundry to be done, windows to wash, and trash to be hauled, Saturday afternoons provided little respite for the students. Their only free time came after the work was done or after chapel on Sunday.

Providence and his family were expected home later in the day, but until then there was little for her to do. Free time, time to do as she wished, time to feel guilty because she could relax while the children worked, time to worry about Jesse, and time to worry that she might never go home.

*Home,* a common word, easy enough to say, but it brought such melancholy. *There's no place like home, there's no place like home.* A short-lived cynical laugh parted Kathleen's lips as she clicked her heels together, once, twice. Nothing happened. She tried again. Nothing. "I guess I need the ruby slippers." *Be strong, Katie-girl,* Jesse's words tiptoed through her mind. "I'm trying, Jesse," she whispered. "I really am trying."

Picking up the Jane Austin book she'd found in the desk drawer in her classroom, she pulled the straight-back chair close to the window and sat. Opening the book, she began to read, anticipating a quiet afternoon's diversion in Miss Austin's prose. Everything began well enough, but in a moment her concentration drifted elsewhere and she closed the book.

Would she have the chance to talk with Providence? Would she be able to ask him about the muffled sobs she heard each night in the dormitory, the children who gave Josiah Wilks a wide berth when he passed, and the meager meals they were fed? In the meantime, until she heard the words coming from his lips, she would believe that very little of what she'd seen in the past week was his philosophy for DuBois Indian Industrial School.

Once again the idea touched her. Was this the reason she had traveled back through time? What lesson or task needed to be completed? But what about Jesse? Why had he been sent on this trip? *I wish I knew.* There was nothing she could do but wait and see. She hoped the wait wouldn't be too long.

Kathleen opened the book and began to read again. Before she'd read a complete page, her concentration failed once more. Jesse.

The table and chair that Basil Dobbs had delivered to her classroom for Jesse had been empty all morning. With each sound in the hallway she had looked up, expecting to see him. But he'd never come.

Giving up on her book, she tipped her head against the high back of the chair. The day had turned into a scorcher and she'd left her bedroom door open, hoping for a cross breeze that would cool the room. Opening the top four buttons of her bodice, she spread the peach-colored fabric apart. She closed her eyes as a light refreshing current touched and cooled her skin. The breeze carried the fragrance of sweetgrass, and images of Jesse filled her mind. Without conscious thought, she allowed her fingers to follow the touch of the breeze, trailing down her bare throat and across her collarbone, causing a delightful frisson just under her skin. Is this how Jesse's touch would feel?

She bolted from her chair, dropping her book to the floor at her feet. She had once more stepped over the boundaries she'd lived within all of her life and done something totally out of character for Kathleen Divine Prescott.

Repentant, Kathleen refastened her buttons, all but the one at the top of her collar. That would be enough space to let the cooling breeze touch her skin. Her hand remained at her throat. *When did these changes begin and why?* Her final question trailed reluctantly behind the others. *Do I really want to stop them?*

The answer to the first question came easily. They had begun when Jesse Spotted Horse first walked into her office. Soon after, she was doing things, saying things, thinking things she'd never imagined herself capable of. She had never looked at a man and wondered what it would be like to kiss him, to feel his touch. It just wasn't proper to let your mind dwell on such things. But the most surprising change was stepping out of her safe cocoon and agreeing to be in Jesse's film.

Since the slip through time, the changes had escalated. With newfound nerve, she'd stood up to Josiah Wilks and taken advantage of Basil Dobbs's feelings to get something she wanted. She'd been able to fit into the new century, and she'd made friends, but at the center of all these changes was Jesse.

When she stood near him, she could barely breathe or think, and just the promise of a touch of his hand caused a yearning that was difficult to bear. And then there was that wink, that silly wink she'd given him. Who would have ever thought that Kathleen Divine Prescott would wink at a man. A smile teased at the corners of her mouth. No, she definitely wasn't acting like herself, but she was beginning to really like the new Kathleen. "Katie-girl," she whispered. "He calls me Katie-girl.

"Enough of these silly daydreams." Fighting the bustled skirt that constantly plagued her, Kathleen bent down and picked her book up off the floor, then sank back into the high-backed chair. Flipping through the pages, she found the last paragraph she'd read and began again, this time enjoying each word. Perhaps the afternoon wasn't going to be a total loss after all.

The knock on her open bedroom door interrupted and put a strong doubt in her mind.

Hannah Dobbs knocked a second time. "May I come in?"

Kathleen looked up, slid a piece of paper between the pages to mark her place, and closed her book. "Yes, of course. I'm just doing a little reading and hoping that a breeze will wander through my window."

"It is hot, isn't it," Hannah replied, dabbing at her upper lip with the handkerchief in her hand. "It's usually not this hot in Indiana until July and August." Hannah moved the handkerchief up to her brow and patted it across her forehead, then began to fan herself with it.

Hannah sighed. "I'm always at a loss how to spend my Saturday afternoons. If there are no ball games or band concerts by the senior boys, there's really nothing much to do." She sighed again, this one deeper and longer as she settled herself on the edge of Kathleen's bed. "I know it sounds ridiculous for the sewing teacher to say, but I don't crochet or tat, I've never enjoyed any kind of needlework, so I don't pass my time doing that." She pointed at Kathleen's book. "I'm not much of a reader, either." Hannah stood and wistfully looked out the window. "After Saturday morning classes and if the weather is nice, I like to go into town." She began to walk about the room, touching the items on Kathleen's table and chest of drawers with casual interest. "I love to stroll down one side of Jefferson Street and up the other and admire everything in the shop windows." She turned to Kathleen and giggled. "My last stop of the day is always at Cohen's General Store for a bag of peppermint candy."

Her plump cheeks were flushed with heat, and the handkerchief waved in the air again, stirring only enough current to ruffle a few loose wisps of her coppery red hair. She plopped back down on the bed, and the springs creaked in protest. "I was wondering if . . . well, I was hoping that you might like to go into Pritchart with me. We could ask Mr. Blunt or Mr. Slocum to take us—unless you know how to drive a horse and buggy." The handkerchief paused. "I hope you do, then just the two of us could go. I always feel so guilty keeping Mr. Blunt waiting for me." She gave a small derisive snort. "Of course, the Saturday before last he spent most of his time waiting in the tavern. The disgusting man belched clouds of whiskey all the way home."

Kathleen wondered how she could politely decline Hannah's invitation. She wanted to be here when Providence arrived home. She hoped to meet him and get to know him, to span the generations and learn all she could about his dreams and plans for the school. She wanted to meet Elijah, the child who would become her great-grandfather, and she wanted to meet Providence's second wife, Libby. His first wife, Elijah's mother, had died of consumption in 1882, when the boy was just four. It was Libby who helped raise the child to manhood.

*Unbelievable.* She slightly shook her head. This whole adventure was not only unbelievable, it was a precious gift. But the reason for the gift still eluded her.

"I was hoping to meet with Reverend Divine when he comes home this afternoon."

Hannah's handkerchief stopped for a moment. "Whatever for?"

Kathleen quickly found an answer that sounded plausible. "Although Wilks hired me, the Reverend is my employer. I'm sure he'd want to meet the latest addition to his staff."

"I doubt that he'll see you, Kathleen. He's been very ill, you know." Hannah lightly touched the handkerchief to the back of her neck. "Reverend Divine has been in Indianapolis for the past three weeks consulting with one doctor after another." She slightly shook her head. "He'll be exhausted when he arrives. There's no train and it's a long buggy ride from the city, at least three hours. No, I don't think you'll be able to meet with him today, not even for a few days." Hannah glanced toward the open door, then leaned closer to Kathleen and whispered, "It's so very, very sad. Jos . . . um . . . Mr. Wilks told my brother that Reverend Divine is dying and that he won't be with us much longer, probably not through the next month or so."

Dying? In a month? Impossible. Providence had lived almost twenty-five more years after 1886; Kathleen knew that for a fact. An exhibit in the school's museum displayed his death certificate dated August 12, 1911. He had also written a new journal each year. In the next moment she realized what Hannah was talking about. *My God, how could I have forgotten?*

In May and early June of 1886, Providence had written in his journal about his lingering illness that often left him incapacitated for days. Some of the entries had even been written in another hand, a feminine hand, and Kathleen wondered if on those days he had felt too sick, too weak to write, and had dictated his entry to his wife, Libby.

"That's ridiculous, Hannah. He isn't dying and certainly not within a month or two. He'll live for many more years to come." The words were out of her mouth before she could stop them. Apprehension quickly slid through her body.

Hannah's eyes gaped wide. "Whatever can you mean?" She quickly stood and pressed her hand against her breast. "Oh, Kathleen, death certainly isn't ridiculous and certainly nothing to joke about. Besides, how can you say that he won't die for a long time? Only the good Lord can grant Reverend Divine more time." Hannah's expression turned stern. "Just remember, the Lord giveth and the Lord taketh away."

"Yes, I'm aware of that passage."

Hannah twisted the handkerchief in her hands and scowled at Kathleen. "I'm sure you don't want people to think you're like that horrid woman, the fortune-teller, at the county fair last summer, pretending to predict the future," Hannah continued. "A few of the ladies from the Greater Zion Church were all ready to drive her out of town with sticks, but Sheriff Nelson sent her packing, just like that." She snapped her fingers. "You should be more careful about what you say, Kathleen."

Unsettled by Hannah's outburst, Kathleen was now more aware than ever how quickly anything she said or did could turn against her. "You're right, Hannah. I apologize. I don't know what I was thinking."

Hannah smiled sweetly. "I don't like talking about death. It's too sad." She dabbed at her brow again with the handkerchief and plopped down on the edge of Kathleen's bed once more. "Basil and I are all that's left of our family, so I'm sure you can understanding why I find the topic disturbing."

Kathleen leaned over and patted Hannah's soft hand. "I am so sorry. Of course I understand. My own family is gone and I'm the only one left."

A subtle smile lifted the corners of Hannah's mouth. "Then perhaps we should make a lovely afternoon of it and go to town . . . like sisters." She grinned. "Besides I'm completely out of peppermints."

Kathleen decided that total honesty provided the best reply to Hannah's invitation. "I'm sorry, but I really don't want to go to town this afternoon. I'd rather stay here."

"Oh." Hannah's smile drooped a little, then returned. "I suppose we could take a walk, that might be nice." She shrugged. "Besides, with Reverend Divine coming home, I'm sure that Josiah . . . Mr. Wilks plans to have an assembly on the parade ground to welcome him."

Kathleen had not missed Hannah's little slip. She had become almost breathless when she'd said the name. Josiah. Hannah Dobbs was clearly infatuated with the man. She hated to think of the consequences Hannah's heart faced if Wilks was truly the scoundrel she and Jesse believed him to be. She immediately thought about some of the comments Wilks had made about his importance at DuBois, and she remembered the odd conversation she'd heard between Wilks and Margaret Lester. "Hannah, whenever Reverend Divine leaves DuBois, is Mr. Wilks the one he always leaves in charge?"

"No, not always," Hannah replied. "One time he left Mr.

Price in charge. He used to work in the harness shop, but he no longer teaches here. And once he asked Basil to take charge, but my poor brother broke out in hives at the very thought. Of course, Josiah came to his rescue."

"Of course." Her cynical remark didn't draw any comment from Hannah; she obviously hadn't heard its barb. Kathleen studied Hannah, wondering how many questions she could ask about Josiah Wilks before Hannah began to get suspicious. "You seem to know Mr. Wilks quite well."

"Not as well as I'd like," Hannah tittered, holding the hankie over her mouth. "But isn't he wonderful?"

Kathleen ignored Hannah's rhetorical question and posed a new one of her own. "Where is he from?"

No doubt remained; they were now talking about Hannah Dobbs's favorite subject. She lightly wiggled on the edge of the bed until she found a comfortable spot and for the next fifteen minutes talked nonstop about Josiah Wilks.

"Have you met his parents? Surely they've come to visit him here. Pritchart isn't too far from Chicago."

"Oh, no," Hannah replied. "They were going to come for Easter, but his father suffered some pains in his chest and his doctor told him to cancel the trip."

*How convenient. I don't believe a single word of it.* "I'm surprised that such an attractive man is still single," Kathleen continued, fishing for as much information about Josiah Wilks as she could hook.

"Josiah told me that his mother and father's marriage is so perfect that he won't marry until he finds just the right woman who will make that kind of marriage and commitment possible for him."

*The man has certainly got all the right answers.* "That is very wise of him," Kathleen said. "Of course, being wise and educated are extremely important to a teacher and assistant school administrator. I don't believe I know where he went to school."

"Oh, that is so exciting," Hannah replied, her voice breathless with awe. "He won a scholarship to Indiana University when he was barely fifteen years old. Josiah told me that his teachers called him a child prodigy, a genius."

Kathleen gaped at Hannah. How could she, or anyone

else for that matter, believe a single word of Wilks's fairy tale? She wondered if there would be any way she could check on Mr. Wilks's record at the university, if one existed. Without the Internet or telephones, the mail would be her only choice and that could take weeks.

"He's taught at Hampton School in Virginia and then, so I understand, Richard Pratt at Carlisle Indian Industrial School in Pennsylvania insisted that he help with their program." She clasped her hands over her heart. "And now he's here with us. Aren't we lucky?"

Rather than answer Hannah's question, Kathleen posed another, softening it with a just-between-us-girls smile. "Do I detect a little attraction on your part for Mr. Wilks?"

The floodgates opened wide. "Oh, Kathleen, I think he is the most handsome, the most wonderful man I have ever met. I think about him day and night. I always try to sit next to him at the dining table, and he lets me take care of his clothes for him, his ironing and mending." She barely caught a breath before charging on. "At the Christmas ball last year he danced with me three times." She held up three fingers. "He only danced with Lily Webber—the daughter of Pritchart's mayor—twice." She giggled and covered her blushing cheeks with her hands. "I think I'm in love with him." A sigh punctuated her statement. "Surely you must know what it's like to be in love?"

Hannah's question stopped her cold. *Do I?*

For the very first time in her life, Kathleen found herself wondering about love. Of course she'd loved her parents. She loved DuBois and all it stood for, she loved sunshine and long walks in a gentle rain, but Hannah was talking about a very different kind of love; love that involved a man and a woman, love that filled one with desire and passion.

"I feel all warm and giddy inside whenever I'm near him." Hannah sighed. "And when he touches me, even accidentally, my skin tingles and my heart races wildly." She placed her hand over her breast. "Even talking about Josiah makes my heart pound." She sighed. "Oh, you must know what I mean."

Jesse. His name stirred in her mind as though a quiet

voice had whispered it to her heart, sending the sound on a wave of warmth throughout her body. *Ridiculous. I'm drawn to him only because we share this extraordinary experience. He's my travel companion, nothing more, absolutely nothing more.*

She brushed a few strands of hair back from her face, as if the simple motion could brush Jesse from her thoughts. But she knew he wouldn't budge. She'd spent too many nights lying awake, thinking about him while she waited for sleep. And then, when sleep came, there he was in her dreams. To pay attention to these kinds of thoughts gave them validity, and there were some things she wasn't ready to have validated.

She stood and placed her book on the bedside table.

"Let's go for that walk now."

Kathleen closed her bedroom door and followed Hannah down the stairs. Once out on the verandah she immediately saw why she hadn't heard any children inside. Wilks had ordered them all to the parade ground, lining them up in regimental form.

Marcus Bishop and Gustav Felder hurried by, buttoning their coats and straightening their ties as they ran.

"The Reverend has been seen coming up the county road," Bishop called out to Hannah and Kathleen. "Mr. Wilks wants us all down by the administration building."

"I told you Josiah planned a grand welcome," Hannah said, glancing over her shoulder at Kathleen and pointing toward Wilks. "Let's hurry, he'll want us with the other teachers."

As they stepped down from the porch stairs, Basil Dobbs led six senior boys in single file along the promenade from his carpentry class. Kathleen found Jesse at the end of the line. Basil raised his hand, signaling for the boys to stop, much as a cavalry officer would halt his troops.

"Good day, Miss Prescott. My, don't you look lovely this fine day."

"How kind of you to say, Mr. Dobbs," Kathleen replied, never taking her eyes off Jesse.

"Let's walk along with Basil," Hannah suggested as they stepped aside and waited for the boys to pass.

Jesse passed close enough that her skirt touched his legs. "I think you look lovely, too," he whispered, pressing something into her hand.

Dumbstruck, she watched him walk away. She closed her fingers around what he'd given to her. Paper. A note?

# Chapter 14

This language which is good enough for a white man and a black man, ought to be good enough for a red man.

—JOHN D.C. ATKINS,
COMMISSIONER OF INDIAN AFFAIRS, 1887

KATHLEEN SLID THE piece of paper into her pocket, pushing it deep to the bottom. She didn't want to risk losing Jesse's note before she read it. And she certainly didn't want to have it end up in the wrong hands.

"Hurry up, children, take your places!" Josiah Wilks shouted, waving his walking stick in the air. "Move smartly now. I'm sure you don't want to displease me. Remember, this is for our beloved Reverend Divine." He turned to Blunt and Slocum. "For God's sake, go get the damned lot of them in order." He clapped his hands. "Hurry, hurry." As Blunt and Slocum began pushing the children into line, Wilks added another edict to the DuBois employees standing nearby. "I want all my staff to line up in the front here with me." He clapped his hands again. "Quickly now, quickly. Mr. Gilbert is standing on the widow's walk of the junior school. He'll wave his handkerchief when Reverend Divine's carriage comes up the road."

"Come on, Kathleen, hurry. I want to stand near Josiah." Hannah impatiently tugged at Kathleen's arm. "Hurry, please."

Wilks spent the next five minutes organizing the staff, lining everyone up in front of the administration building that housed the Divines' apartment on the third floor. Delivering one last order for everyone to keep their places, Wilks stepped into the middle of the front line, adjusted his coat, and straightened his cravat. Kathleen and Hannah found themselves in the second row behind him, and behind Margaret Lester.

Kathleen bristled at Wilks's words—"his staff." Why didn't anyone remind him Reverend Divine owned DuBois, not him? Why didn't anyone challenge his arrogance? Perhaps things would change now that Providence was coming home.

"Attention, everyone. There's Mr. Gilbert's signal!" Wilks shouted. He raised his cane. "I'll give the signal."

A hush fell over the crowd. Every eye turned toward Wilks.

"Oh, look! There they are!" Excited, Hannah bounced up and down on the balls of her feet and clapped her hands.

"Now, everyone, now." Wilks brandished his cane in the air, and a cheer began to roll through the hundred or so children. Beginning at the north end of the parade ground, it traveled row by row to the south, picking up voices and volume as it went. A quick look at the children's faces told Kathleen that their welcome was little more than following the instructions relayed by Josiah Wilks's upraised walking stick.

For a moment Kathleen saw the black surrey until it disappeared behind the barn. In a few seconds the horse and buggy reappeared. Traveling up the lane it passed the chicken house, the harness shop, and then rounded the southeast corner by the cemetery. The big bay moved at a smart trot. Sweat darkened its hide and lather that had built up under the curcingle and breast strap gleamed pearly white. As the cheering grew louder, the horse fought the checkrein and nervously tossed its head, sending flecks of froth from its mouth into the air.

Kathleen felt her heart pound with excitement, pushing adrenaline throughout her body at great speed. She tightly clasped her hands against her stomach, hoping to contain some of the butterflies that whirled like dervishes in her belly. Her elation turned to wonder as she caught her first glimpse of the four passengers in the surrey.

Impossible as it seemed, Kathleen found herself looking

at her great-great-grandfather and her great-grandfather. Over one hundred and seventeen years lay between her life and theirs, but a quirk of time had brought those years together. In a little while they would meet face-to-face.

Turning, she searched in the crowd for Jesse, desperately wanting—no, needing—to share this incredible moment with him. She found him less than thirty feet away, already looking at her. His soft smile and barely visible nod, both as tangible as a touch and a caress, told her that he knew what she was feeling. Replying with a smile of her own, Kathleen quickly turned her attention back to Providence and Elijah, not willing to miss a moment of this special event.

"He looks so frail," Hannah said, speaking close to Kathleen's ear. "I wonder if the doctors were able to tell him anything about his illness or give him some new medicine."

The driver, a young Indian man of about twenty or so and smartly dressed in a nicely tailored suit and hat, now dusty from the long road trip, drew the horse to a halt in front of the administration building. The children's cheers waned, then dwindled voice by voice.

Slowly leaning forward in his seat, Providence raised his hand in a feeble wave, his lips offering a slight smile that appeared little more than a grimace. "Thank you, thank you, everyone," he rasped, his voice barely louder than a hoarse whisper. "A wonderful welcome. Thank you." He lowered his hand, gently laying it on the dark head of the boy sitting beside him. "It is good to be home, isn't it, Elijah?"

Providence looked up again and allowed his gaze to drift from one side of the crowd of children to the other. Kathleen closely watched the expression on his gaunt face. As he studied one child and then another, a slight frown touched his brow. Pushing himself upright from his seat and bolstered by the Indian driver's steady hand, Providence stood up on wobbly legs.

"God bless you, children." He raised his hand as though he were giving benediction.

"The benevolent father has returned," Josiah Wilks said to Margaret Lester, his disrespect and sarcasm clear.

"Josiah, hush," Margaret hissed, quickly looking over her shoulder at Kathleen and Hannah.

There was no mistaking the bitter tone of Wilks's voice. What was he up to? Whatever it was, Kathleen knew it would be nothing she'd agree with and perhaps nothing Providence Divine would agree with, either. God had given Josiah Wilks such physical beauty on the outside, yet left him sadly lacking on the inside.

But was Margaret Lester involved as well? *You've been a naughty girl, Margaret, a very naughty girl.* The words she'd overheard Wilks say played through her mind again. What did they mean? And what did Margaret's reply mean? *And I'll probably be naughty again, Josiah. Yes, I think I will.* Kathleen realized she needed to learn much, much more before she could answer any of her questions.

Wilks quickly stepped up to the surrey. "I'll help the Reverend, David," he said to the young Indian driver. "I would suggest you take care of the horse. It's a very expensive animal, you know. Go along now." With a great flourish, Wilks elbowed the Indian aside and helped Providence step down.

Kathleen drew a quick breath. This man was her great-great-grandfather . . . she carried his blood in her veins, his philosophy in her heart. But he was a very different man than what she'd expected.

Taller than she'd imagined and thin to the point of emaciation, his clothes hung on his body as though they'd been made for someone twice his size. He clung to Wilks's arm, his hands bony, his knuckles blanched. Appalled, Kathleen pressed her hand over her mouth. Where was the robust man from the photographs she'd studied in the archives?

His gait unsteady and still holding on to Wilks's arm, Providence turned around, looking for his wife, Libby.

Kathleen watched as slender, dark-haired Libby Divine stepped out of the surrey, the young Indian driver helping to steady her. Kathleen had always wondered why there had been no photographs of Providence's second wife in the archives, and now she believed she knew the reason why.

A slight breeze lifted the woman's veil from her face, re- vealing a livid port-wine stain that covered her left cheek and disappeared into her hairline. Libby Divine ducked her head and quickly drew her veil back down over her face.

With Wilks bracing Providence's left arm and Libby on the right, Kathleen watched Providence slowly climb the steps. Margaret Lester followed close behind.

Reaching the verandah, Providence paused, turned, and gave the students one last puzzled look, then, moving in a slow and shuffling gait, disappeared into the building.

Having taken the stairs to the family's apartment on the top floor every day of her life, Kathleen knew that the climb would be brutal for Providence. Hannah had been right. She wouldn't be meeting with her great-great- grandfather today.

Everyone began to leave the parade ground, students re- turning to their chores, the staff returning to their Saturday leisures, but Kathleen didn't move. She watched Jesse leave with the others under Basil Dobbs's care. His clothes fit much better since Hannah's senior sewing class had added some length to the pant legs. Even the jacket sleeves now fit.

"Kathleen, you should be ashamed of yourself," Hannah twittered. "But I don't blame you for staring at him, he is magnificent, isn't he?"

Alarmed that she'd been caught watching Jesse, Kath- leen fumbled for words. "Really, Hannah, I don't know what you are inferring." She hoped her counterfeit indigna- tion rang true. "Besides, Jesse Spotted Horse is one of my students and he hasn't been to class for two days."

Hannah leaned closer and lowered her voice. "Mr. Wilks doesn't approve of us fraternizing with any of the students in an unofficial manner."

"I'll try to remember yet another of Mr. Wilks's rules," Kathleen replied, her indignation no longer camouflaged.

Her gaze fell to Elijah, the little boy who would become her grandfather's father. Instead of joining his family in- side, he'd chosen to stay on the verandah in one of the wicker chairs. Ignoring everyone on the parade ground as though they didn't exist, he kept his head bowed, causing his dark hair to fall over his forehead. Busily spinning the wheel of the toy wagon he held, he alternately swung one dangled leg and then the other, forward and back, forward and back. Elijah Divine appeared not only to be a serious child, but a very lonely child as well.

"He's a sad little boy, so all alone," Hannah Dobbs offered. "I don't think he's over losing his mama yet."

Kathleen couldn't take her eyes off of him. Had he not been her great-grandfather, her concern would have been just the same. "What about friends? He plays with some of the Indian boys who are near his age, doesn't he?"

"Oh, gracious, no," Hannah quickly replied, looking surprised that Kathleen would consider such a thing. "At least not that I'm aware. He's the headmaster's son; don't you think that would be beneath his station?" Hannah placed her hand over her mouth, hiding her words. "He doesn't seem to like his stepmother too much, either. He won't let her touch him or get near him. Did you notice her face, the horrible birthmark? I think Elijah is afraid of her." Hannah leaned close and whispered, "They call it the devil's mark, you know."

"It must be quite a burden for her."

"Well, she caught herself a husband in spite of it." Hannah quickly glanced around, then whispered. "Miss Rachel used to be the sewing teacher." She gave a silent "that's the truth" nod, then continued. "Reverend Divine had begun to court Miss Lester but when Miss Rachel arrived, well, you see the result." Hannah pulled back. "At least, that's what Alma Briggs told me. I wasn't here then."

"Miss Rachel?" Kathleen frowned. She glanced at Hannah. "Who is Miss Rachel?"

"Elijah's stepmother. Mrs. Divine, of course," Hannah replied, looking puzzled.

Kathleen realized she was now the one with the bewildered look. "I thought her name was Libby."

"Libby? Where did you get such an idea? Her name is Rachel."

Kathleen rubbed her forehead. Something was wrong. This didn't make any sense. In his journals Providence had talked about his wife Libby. He'd never mentioned anyone named Rachel. Had Providence been married *three* times?

"Shall we take that walk?" Hannah wistfully looked toward the administration building where she'd last seen Josiah Wilks.

Kathleen reached into her pocket and felt Jesse's note still tucked in the bottom corner. She felt guilty as another lie slipped from her lips. "Hannah, I'm sorry." She pressed her fingers against her temple. "All that cheering and excitement has given me a headache." She lightly touched Hannah's arm. "I hope you understand, but I'm going to go lie down for a while. Please forgive me." Kathleen saw Hannah's disappointment, and her conscience gave a hard jab.

"I have some headache powders if you need any. I could bring them to your room and then just sit quietly with you. Cool compresses always help me get rid of my headaches."

Hannah's kindness turned the jab into a punch. Kathleen toyed with the piece of paper in her pocket again. "Thank you, but no. I just need to rest for a while. I'll be fine after a little nap." She took a few steps toward the dormitory, then stopped and turned back toward Hannah. "Will you have supper with me? I'll knock on your door and we can go together."

LOCKING HER DOOR, Kathleen moved to the window and retrieved Jesse's note from her pocket. Her fingers trembled as she unfolded the small piece of paper. The handwriting was nearly illegible, and she had to peer closely to make out each word.

*Meet me in the woods on the north side of the barn—we need to talk. Midnight tonight. Be careful. J.*

"Jesse," she whispered, enjoying the sound and the feel of his name on her lips. Melancholy tightened her throat. She never thought she would admit it, never thought it possible, but she missed him, terribly. She missed working close, side-by-side with him. She missed his humor, his ability to tease her without hurting her feelings. And those feelings, ah, those unfamiliar, exciting feelings that had stirred since she'd met him. New, totally new, alarming and delicious feelings, like nothing she'd ever known in her life. They were quickly becoming an addiction.

"Stop this silly nonsense, Kathleen," she scolded herself, folding the paper and returning it to her pocket. *Tingle and get breathless over him all you like, but all you'll ever share with this man is this time slide and the problem of returning to where you belong.* She slowly paced from the window to her door and back again. *But there could be more, couldn't there?* The question had slipped unbidden through her mind and touched her heart with hope. But the answer had the touch of a gremlin to it. *Oh, yes, there could be more, more disagreements about places like DuBois, more arguments about the treatment of the children, more heated discussions about the need for the Indian schools, more disputes about the atrocities.* The last thoughts stomped on whatever hope the first ones had raised.

Halfway between the window and the door Kathleen suddenly stopped. The atrocities. She now knew they existed and she could no longer ignore them. In just the few days she'd spent in the past, she'd seen enough to shatter the golden illusions she'd held all of her life. The discovery left an aching hole in her heart. She dropped to the edge of her bed.

*But it wasn't—isn't—all bad. I won't believe I've been lied to all my life.*

She pulled her watch from its hiding place in the bottom of her drawstring purse. Four-fifteen. Where would she find the patience to wait another seven and a half hours to see Jesse? She rose from her bed and stood at her window once again.

Her gaze moved across the parade ground, falling on the whitewashed barn in the wooded grove. How would Jesse be able to sneak away from his room? Surely Blunt and Slocum watched him closely, and if she and Jesse were caught together, the punishments doled out would be severe. Even with that threat, the delicious thrill of anticipation still filled her. She had never had a clandestine adventure before in her life. Kathleen sighed. Her first, and most likely her last, would be with Jesse Spotted Horse. *Suŋgléska.*

SUPPER IN THE dining hall resembled medieval torture for Kathleen. Time crawled slower than a snail, and Josiah Wilks's determination to hold court, reminding everyone of his close and personal relationship with Reverend Divine, made the meal almost unbearable. He had spent the first twenty minutes regaling everyone with news about the Reverend's poor health.

"He's deathly ill and not a doctor in Indianapolis was able to tell him cause or cure." Wilks shook his head, his beautiful face a mask of sadness and pity. "Poor Mrs. Divine, she's so afraid her husband will die and leave young Elijah a true orphan." He reached for a warm roll from the basket in the middle of the table and slathered it with butter. "He won't be able to return to his duties for another couple of weeks or so, and maybe not even then." His gaze swept the table. "Of course he insisted that I remain in charge."

"Of course," Kathleen breathed behind her coffee cup.

Wilks sadly shook his head again, letting everyone see his distress and grief. Kathleen wasn't impressed.

"On a good note, though," Wilks continued, pressing his hand over his heart and offering everyone at the table a wide and insincere smile, "I was able to convince him to allow us to go ahead with the school picnic that I planned."

Hannah leaned closed to Kathleen. "It's an annual event. We had a wonderful time last year, boating on the lake, a marvelous picnic lunch, and games with prizes for the children."

"That's simply wonderful, Mr. Wilks," Margaret Lester brightly chimed. "We are so very grateful to you for your wonderful leadership."

A few quiet murmurs of agreement came from some of the other teachers at the table.

"In the meantime," Wilks added, "any problems or concerns you have must be brought to me; we don't need to burden the dear Reverend." The tooth-filled insincere grin reappeared. "I promise you all that our beloved school and the children will continue to flourish under my care."

He's appointed himself as the archangel imparting the word from on high, Kathleen mused. What she'd told Jesse had been right. Josiah Wilks was a pompous ass, but more than that, Josiah Wilks was possibly a very dangerous pompous ass.

"And he would like to meet with you tomorrow, Miss Prescott."

Wilks's comment had come out of the blue, taking Kathleen completely by surprise. She quickly looked up from her plate. "Excuse me?"

"I said, Miss Prescott, that Reverend Divine would like to meet you tomorrow."

"Yes, of course, I want to meet him, too," Kathleen answered, trying to keep her excitement in check. "Did he say what time?"

As though he hated to give her information that would admit her to the inner circle, Wilks hesitated a moment or two before answering. "Yes. The Reverend and Mrs. Divine would like to have you visit them in the family's apartment at three, for tea."

"Thank you." Kathleen hoped she'd been able to sound calm, when inside excitement bubbled high.

"I expect you to present yourself with the appropriate comportment befitting a gentlewoman and a DuBois teacher."

Her gaze snapped to Josiah Wilks, and she fought to hold back the words that screamed in her head. *You are definitely an insufferable, chauvinistic, pompous ass.* Instead, she pasted a submissive expression on her face. "Of course, Mr. Wilks, I won't let DuBois down."

The rest of the meal faded into a blur. Even Wilks's rude comments couldn't halt her excitement. Tea with her great-great-grandfather—the idea was mind boggling.

The sound of a scuffle across the room drew everyone's attention. Kathleen turned and her heart bolted into her throat. Jesse! Alarmed and helpless, she watched Blunt twist Jesse's arm behind his back and push him into the corner of the room. Shoving back, Jesse almost got away until Slocum stepped in.

"You'll sit where you're told, you heathen bastard." Blunt's words echoed throughout the dining hall.

Kathleen's hand tightened around her fork. *Jesse, please, don't fight back. Don't jeopardize your safety. Don't jeopardize tonight.*

She glanced around the table. No one stirred. No one rushed to interfere. No one complained. She scanned the room. Every one of the students sat quietly, their heads bowed, looking down at their plates. Not an eye was lifted toward Jesse, not a fork was lifted to their mouths.

"I told you, he's a troublemaker, Mr. Wilks," Gustav Felder said, finally breaking the silence.

"He's assigned to my carpentry class," Dobbs replied with a frown. "I don't understand Mr. Blunt's continuing problems with Jesse; he works quietly for me." His face immediately blanched, and he nervously glanced at Wilks, obviously believing he'd overstepped his boundaries. He quickly turned away and dropped his attention to another helping of mashed potatoes.

"Jesse?" Wilks asked.

"Uh, yes," Dobbs answered, his hand trembling as he transferred a large blob of potatoes from the bowl to his plate. "Miss Prescott and her class named him Jesse."

"He's quite large, isn't he?" Alma Briggs, the penmanship teacher, added. "You're very brave, Mr. Dobbs. I'd be nervous to have that savage around. Better he be taught his manners before he sits in a lady's classroom." She breathed a righteous-sounding snort and resumed eating her supper.

"He has been attending one of my English classes," Kathleen countered. "Jesse Spotted Horse is a very agreeable student, and like Mr. Dobbs, I don't see the necessity for the harsh treatment that Mr. Blunt and Mr. Slocum are allowed to inflict upon him."

Dobbs dropped the serving spoon and it clattered loudly as it careened off the edge of the large serving bowl. He did little to hide the strickened look on his face as he glanced from Kathleen to Wilks.

Wilks snorted, dismissing Kathleen's words as ridiculous. "He's nothing but trouble, that one." Wilks bit into a fried chicken leg and then pointed it at Jesse. "He'll end up in the cold house, there's no doubt about it."

Disgusted, Kathleen refused to remain silent. She primly folded her hands in her lap. "If someone is treated with human kindness, that is what he will give in return. If he experiences abuse, that will be his response."

Wilks's cynical laugh grated on Kathleen's ears.

"Ah, Miss Prescott, I was correct the other day when I called you a bleeding heart."

"I believe, Mr. Wilks, that you called me a tender heart." She glanced in Jesse's direction again and watched Blunt shove him down onto a bench at one of the tables and drop a plate of boiled turnips and beans in front of him.

Josiah Wilks's manner immediately cooled, and his words came with a sharp edge. "I've learned too well that if you treat these buggers with any kindness, they're likely to scalp you in the middle of the night."

"Mr. Wilks, are you saying that you have experienced such a situation where . . ."

Wilks turned on Kathleen. His wild expression alarmed her, his words even held a threat. "I think this conversation is over, Miss Prescott." He slapped the table with the flat of his hand. "You seem to forget your place. I'm sure Reverend Divine would approve of my decision to terminate your employ. Don't force me to take that step." He glanced around the table as if reminding everyone that he held their jobs in his hands, as well. "You are hardly in the position to tell me how to run my school."

Her every movement deliberate, Kathleen lifted her napkin from her lap, lightly dabbed the corners of her mouth, and then placed the linen beside her plate. She pushed back from the table and, rising from her chair, looked down at Josiah Wilks. She made no effort to hide her contempt, and spoke quietly, forcing Wilks to lean forward to hear her. "How odd of you to say *your* school, Mr. Wilks. I was under the distinct impression, as I'm sure everyone at DuBois and anyone familiar with the school was, that DuBois is Reverend Divine's school."

There were one or two gasps from the others at the

table, but for the most part they sat, silently staring down at their plates. Disgusted by their blind acceptance of Wilks's lies and dictates and cruelties, Kathleen added one parting salvo. "Shame on you. Shame on all of you."

Without waiting for a response, she pivoted on her heel and headed for the door.

Jesse looked up from his plate, and in the few moments that their eyes met, Kathleen saw the anger and pain. His resolve was beginning to slip. And, for the first time since their time slide, she was truly frightened.

# Chapter 15

But they kept teaching ... the books told how bad the Indians had been to the white man. We all wore white man's clothes and ate white man's food and went to white man's churches and spoke white man's talk. And so, after a while, we also began to say Indians were bad. We laughed at our own people and their blankets and cooking pots.

—SUN ELK,
TAOS PUEBLO

AFTER THE LIGHTS-out bell rang at nine, Jesse lay awake on his cot. He knew that no matter where he went, either in this time or his own, he would never forget the smell of the boys' dorm. The pungent sweaty bodies of the boys, the sour smell of spoiling food hidden in pockets or under the beds to appease hunger during the night, the musky smell of vermin attracted by the food, and the strong, biting odor of thin mattresses stained with urine would always be just an unpleasant memory away.

A trickle of sweat slid across his neck. Even three hours after the sun had gone down, he guessed that the temperature in the room still hovered close to eighty degrees. Being fully dressed under his blanket made it worse.

*Maste.* Hot. He rolled the Lakota word around on his tongue. If nothing else good was happening for him at DuBois, while all the other kids were losing their language, he was reclaiming his.

After Reverend Divine's homecoming, Jesse had spent three exhausting hours splitting and stacking firewood for the school's four cookstoves. Later Blunt had strong-armed him to the kitchen, where he'd washed dishes and hauled trash for another three hours. He ran his hand down his belly. He'd lost weight, but there was a new hardness to his muscles. DuBois was a hell of a health club.

The work hours had also given him something else—time to think about something that had bothered him since the day he and Kathleen had slipped backward in time. Somebody was embezzling from DuBois.

He didn't have any hard proof . . . yet, and he wondered if any really existed, but he sure intended to find out. He didn't give a rat's ass for himself or for the school, but it was the kids who were paying the price, and he intended to do his damnedest to stop it. Any fool could see something was wrong; had Kathleen seen it, too? Would she, could she, accept the possibility that Providence Divine was pilfering his own school's funds? *I guess I'll find out soon enough.*

The large Regulator clock on the far wall ticked off each minute at a snail's pace, like the slow beat of a metronome, enticing sleep with its rhythm. The snores and sleep-laden breathing of the boys in the cots coaxed him to fall asleep. Drowsy, Jesse struggled to stay awake, fighting yawns and rubbing his eyes when they threatened to close. He dozed off once or twice, each time waking with a start, each time checking the clock to make sure he hadn't overslept.

At fifteen minutes past eleven he slowly peeled back the scratchy blanket and swung his legs off the cot. Sitting quietly for a moment or two, he scanned the other nineteen beds in the room. The boys were too busy snoring to worry about him leaving. Picking his boots up off the floor, he tied the laces together and slung them over his shoulder. He'd move a lot quicker and quieter on the hardwood floors in his socks.

He stepped between the rows of narrow cots, and after one last quick glance over his shoulder at the sleeping boys, he opened the door and peered out into the hall. Dark shadows along the walls provided perfect cover for his escape. He slipped into the corridor. Quietly closing the door behind him, he pressed against the wall and listened for a moment.

Earlier, Blunt and Slocum had come back from town with two quarts of whiskey. Sitting in Slocum's room on the top floor, they were earnestly seeking the bottom of both bottles. Their slurred voices rang throughout the dorm as they sang one bawdy song after another, drunkenly laughing after each lewd chorus. Their caterwauling would cover any noise Jesse might make.

He moved through the shadows to the staircase, stopping outside of Dobbs's room. If Blunt and Slocum's singing didn't cover any noise he'd make, Dobbs's snoring would do the job.

Jesse eased down the stairs, staying close to the wall where the tread would be more solid and not creak with each step. He'd promised himself that no matter the consequences if he were caught, the beating that Blunt and Slocum would dole out would be the last he'd take without fighting back. For some reason the two had chosen him as their special project, delighting in "teachin' him a goddamn lesson," as Blunt so eloquently put it each time the fist fell. The infractions were impossible to define; Jesse never knew when a "goddamn lesson" was coming.

Reaching the first floor, he hesitated. The front door would take him out on the promenade side of the building; the back door would lead to the less traveled utility lane that stretched from building to building. No contest.

Jesse slipped out the back, closing the heavy door behind him. Stopping for a moment, he tried the latch to make sure that the door hadn't locked. It easily swung open. Satisfied that he'd have no trouble getting back in, he closed it again.

Sitting on the stoop, he pulled on his boots. Dobbs had found him a larger pair. Basil Dobbs was a good man, a little inept at his job, but a good man nonetheless.

He sat quietly for a moment, allowing the night to embrace him. Inside, Slocum's and Blunt's voices still rose in drunken disharmony, but outside nature's night critters' choir performed a much better concert. The air felt fresh and clean on his skin. It smelled of sweetgrass, memories of home. A half-moon and the canopy of stars offered just enough light to help him make his way to the barn.

Moving silently, he left the back porch and traveled in the dark rim of the shadows, staying close to the buildings. It felt as though a lifetime had passed since he'd last had such freedom.

Jesse moved stealthily from building to building, shadow to shadow. A noise, something moving behind the junior girls' dormitory, sent him ducking deeper into the dark. Was it Kathleen? The thought of bumping into her behind a bush somewhere made him chuckle. No, she'd go the other way, around the south end of the grounds. From the senior girls' dormitory it would be the shortest way for her.

A fat raccoon on a late-night foray for food ambled along the lane. Pausing in front of the bush where Jesse hid, it stood up on its hind legs and chattered an evening greeting before meandering on its way.

Heading north, then turning west, Jesse passed behind the three buildings that held the classrooms. Next came the print shop and then the large garden where the tender leaves of newly planted vegetables were breaking through the soil. The younger students had hoed and weeded earlier in the day and the rich smell of fresh-turned earth perfumed the air.

Jesse slipped through the fence and into the cow pasture. The wide-eyed stares of the school's dairy herd followed him across the field. One or two curious cows moved with him until he reached the fence on the opposite side of the pasture.

He eased through the strands of barbed wire and stepped into the woods that stretched all the way south to the barn. Less than twenty steps past the edge of the tree line, a doe and her fawn broke from the brush. Startled, nearly colliding with them, Jesse jumped back. Pressing his body against a tree, he tried to catch his breath. "I thought this Indian stuff was supposed to come naturally," he muttered, pushing away from the tree and cautiously continuing south.

Reaching the barn, Jesse quickly scanned the area. Kathleen hadn't come yet. He hunkered down, leaned against the north wall of the barn and waited for her, trying to ignore the undeniable spark of anticipation that plagued him.

Since they'd arrived at DuBois 1886, he'd watched Kathleen, watched the changes taking place in her. He'd seen the pain in her eyes as she learned more of the truths about the school, and he'd seen the joy as she'd met and worked with the children. Somewhere between these two there had been even more changes.

Her formal manner had eased and she seemed to be more confident. He'd watched her make friends, oppose Wilks's dictates, and treat the kids with compassion and genuine affection. There were outward changes as well. The dresses she wore weren't the usual drab colors. The pretty blue, pale peach, and soft mint green all complimented her dark hair and brought a glow to her complexion.

He'd noticed that she'd also begun wearing her hair in a softer twist at the back of her head, more like Egypt had styled it for the film. A couple of times she had even tied it back with bright-colored ribbons, something that the Kathleen Prescott he'd first met never would have done. He liked the slightly curled tendrils that softly framed her face and wondered if they'd feel as silky as they looked. *Easy, Horse. How many times do you have to remind yourself? This is definitely not the time—whoever's time it is—nor the place to be thinking like this.*

Off to his right he heard a twig snap, and then another. A deer? No, he didn't think so. The bushes rustled and he heard the whoosh of a branch whipping through the air and then the solid swat as it hit something or someone.

"Ouch!"

Jesse chuckled. Obviously a someone.

In the next moment he heard what could only have been a trip and a stumble.

"Ugh . . . ouch . . . drats!" came another whisper.

Conveniently forgetting his embarrassing encounter with the doe and her fawn, Jesse decided that he'd have to show this pretty *wasicu winyan* how to walk through the woods like a Lakota woman. Pretty? Did he really think she was pretty? *Yeah, Horse, you do.*

He stayed hunkered down against the barn wall and watched Kathleen tiptoe around the corner, waiting until she was within inches of tripping over him before he spoke. "Good evening, Miss Prescott. Fancy meeting you out and about on this fine evening."

Kathleen's hand flew to her mouth and muffled what would have been a loud shriek. As Jesse stood, she slapped his shoulder. "Don't ever do that again, Jesse Spotted Horse. You scared me to death!"

He ducked as she readied for another blow. "Aw, Katie-girl, don't take all the fun out of my life." He laughed. Taking her hand, he began leading her through the trees. "Come on."

"Where are you taking me?"

"Where do you think, white woman? I'm hauling you off somewhere to ravish and scalp you. Isn't that what us wild Indians are supposed to do?" He paused for a moment and frowned. "Or is it scalp and then ravish, hmm, never did get that part right." He squeezed her hand. "Come on, let's find that bench."

"From the looks of things earlier, you would have gladly taken Blunt's scalp. Wilks even said so."

"I'd gladly take Wilks's, Blunt's, and Slocum's, but there isn't much call for skunk, weasel, or polecat hides these days."

Kathleen suddenly gave a hard tug on his hand. "Oh, ouch! Jesse, please, wait a minute."

"What's the matter?"

"My hair, it's caught on a branch or something."

"You're just not the outdoorsy type, are you?" Working slowly, he gently freed her hair from a bramble bush, strand by strand. A smile unwittingly curved his lips. Her hair did feel as soft and as silky as he'd imagined. Its length surprised him, though. He hadn't realized that there was so much wrapped into the twist at the back of her head.

When the last few curls fell free, he tucked them behind her ear and slowly moved his hand down the side of her face, cupping her cheek in his palm. Her skin felt warm, velvet soft and slightly damp from her trek through the woods.

Moonlight gave subtle highlights to her hair, and the
smoky gray of her eyes had almost disappeared and become velvet black. Yeah, he thought, she is pretty. Within
the next moment he'd changed his mind. No, not pretty.
He'd found the right word the day they'd slipped through
time. *Beautiful.* He trailed his fingers along the soft edge of
her jaw to her chin, pausing just below her mouth.

She shivered and breathed a sigh as she lowered her
lashes. Her tongue quickly flicked across her lips, drawing
Jesse's attention. *Why did I ever think that gorgeous mouth
was a waste on Kathleen Prescott?* The impulse to taste it
hit him hard.

He would have called anyone a liar if they'd told him a
month ago, when he'd first met her, that he'd be secretly
meeting her in the woods late at night and thinking she was
beautiful. Thinking about kissing her hadn't been anything
he'd have thought possible, either. But there it was, a craving. But it was the hard awakening of his body that really
surprised him.

*Kiss her? Touch her? Make love to her? You're asking
for big trouble, Horse.* Jesse stepped away, hoping that a
little distance would help clear his head and ease his
hunger.

"Come on, follow me." *Damn, Horse, you don't have to
snap her head off. It's not her fault you can't control your
hormones.* He led her to the bench and brushed a few
leaves and twigs off the seat. "I don't think anyone will see
us here."

Kathleen settled herself, carefully arranged her full skirt,
then demurely clasped her hands in her lap. She tried to appear calm, but inside her nerves were tied in knots. When
Jesse sat down beside her, she almost bolted and an old
habit immediately returned. She raised her hand to her collar and her fingers trembled as they skimmed over the buttons. "We shouldn't stay too long. If we are caught—"

"Don't worry, I'll get you home before bed check."

She heard the smile in his voice and felt her nerves ease
a notch or two. "Miss Lester retires each evening by ten.
I'm sure she wouldn't suddenly choose tonight to act like a
den mother."

"Don't misjudge Margaret Lester," Jesse countered. "The woman is too close to Josiah Wilks for my liking." He fell silent for a moment, leaning forward and resting his elbows on his knees. "I've seen them together and so have a lot of Dobbs's boys . . . places away from the school buildings where they figured they wouldn't be seen." He glanced at Kathleen. "There's a certain look, a kind of tension that's between two people when they're scheming together."

"You must be mistaken. If they were plotting something, wouldn't they make sure they weren't seen by anyone . . . not even the boys . . . not even you?"

Jesse shook his head. "They don't want to be seen by any of the staff, that's why they meet by the cemetery, behind the print shop, down by the creek . . ."

"But you said that you and some of the boys have seen them."

"Kathleen, the Indian kids are invisible," he replied, his voice a tight whisper. "No one cares what they . . . what we see."

Kathleen watched the muscles tense across his shoulders. She wanted to reach out and touch him, to help ease the pain she was beginning to understand. In the past week she'd seen too many things that her heart didn't want to believe.

She drew a deep faltering breath and looked through the trees to the school buildings beyond. "Jesse, have I been wrong all my life? Wasn't there *some* good at DuBois?"

Jesse sighed as he pushed himself to his feet. He moved a few yards away from the bench, then turned and faced her. *Way to go, Horse, now you're going to add to her misery with your suspicions.* After a long, quiet moment he finally answered. "I don't know, Katie, I really don't know." His fingers plowed through his hair, creating havoc with its crude cut. "I've seen kids getting excited because they've learned how to add, subtract, or multiply. I know they can use what they learn to help their people. By learning to read and write they can help their tribes understand treaties and laws before their leaders agree to them." He moved closer to her. "I've seen the pride the boys in the carpentry shop have for a chair they've made, or Felder's boys when

they've completed a new harness for one of the local farmers." He glanced back at the school. "I know you've seen
this in your kids, and I bet it's there in Hannah's girls, too."

He settled back on the bench beside Kathleen. "They'll
use everything they've learned, but I also see their fear.
There isn't one of them that isn't afraid of Wilks or his
boys, Slocum and Blunt." He laughed, the sound contemp-
tuous. "I eat the disgusting slop that's fed to the kids each
day, and I live in the dorm with boys who at the age of
twelve and older are still wetting their beds at night because
they're so damned scared." He glanced at Kathleen. "I'm
sorry if my answer doesn't make you feel better."

He took her hand and folded his fingers around hers.
"You have to face the truth that some of the brutalities I've
talked about were real. But abuse isn't always physical or
sexual. Sometimes the emotional is the worst of all." He
shook his head. "It's damned ironic, isn't it? It seems we've
both been wrong."

Kathleen silently nodded. "Thank you." She withdrew
her hand from his. "Thank you for your honesty." Tears
filled her eyes. One escaped, sliding down her cheek, only
to be followed by another and another.

"No, don't, Katie-girl." Jesse gently wiped her cheeks
with his fingers. "You can't cry; I threw all your tissues
away."

She replied with a meager smile.

He swept his fingers across her cheeks. "Maybe this is
the lesson we're here to learn. Maybe we're supposed to
change what we each think about places like DuBois." He
shrugged.

Kathleen nodded. "Maybe."

"So, is it true?"

"What?"

"Are you going to spend some time with Providence tomorrow afternoon?" Jesse shot her a sidelong glance.

"How did you—"

"I heard Wilks talking to Margaret Lester about you as
they left the dining hall this evening."

Kathleen tried to see his face, but night shadows kept

his feelings a secret. It was the tone of his voice that made her uneasy. "Yes, it's true. Why?"

Jesse left the bench. Hunkering down in front of her, he took both of her hands in his, resting his wrists on her knees. "Katie, I can't imagine what it must feel like to meet an ancestor face-to-face. I'd like to know . . ." He shrugged, choosing not to finish what he was saying.

She knew what he was thinking and immediately felt guilty. *Tokalu Sapa. Jesse deserves a chance, too . . . maybe more than I do.*

Jesse dropped his head, not meeting her gaze. "I just don't want you to expect too much."

She tried to pull her hands away, but his grip tightened. "I don't understand. What do you mean? He's my great-great-grandfather, he's my family."

"You can't count on that making any difference, Kathleen. He doesn't know the connection, and you certainly can't tell him. Just be careful, that's all, be careful. You know him from family stories, his journals, and the archives, but you don't know the living, breathing man."

"Was this why you wanted me to meet you tonight, to warn me about Providence, to imply that—"

"No," he interrupted. "No, it's not. I wanted to talk with you about something else. I didn't know you were meeting Providence until *after* I passed you the note." He gently squeezed her hands, placed them back in her lap, and stood, staring through the trees at the stars overhead. "All I'm saying is don't get your hopes up for a grand family reunion."

"Okay, I see your point." A sadness touched her heart, taking some of the shine off the chance to meet Providence. She drew a deep breath. "What *did* you want to talk with me about?"

He leaned back against the trunk of the maple that grew at the end of the bench. "Do you remember anything from the financial ledgers in the archives?"

She studied his face, looking for a clue that might tell her where his question was leading. "Some, perhaps. Why?"

Jesse reached up and tore off a leaf from an overhead branch. He wouldn't look at her but instead watched the leaf as he twirled it on its stem between his thumb and index finger. "Do you remember anything about the school's monthly income, where it came from, how much usually came in?" The leaf continued to twirl. "How about the expenses . . . the orders for food, clothes, or other things?"

Jesse's questions puzzled her. Where was this going? "DuBois had its own dairy herd. There was also a small herd of beef cattle, and some hogs and sheep. There were both laying hens and fryers in the poultry shed. There was a small smoke house behind the dining hall and the cook staff smoked hams and bacon for the school." Her shoulders lifted in a slight shrug. "I don't know how much meat came from the town butcher, maybe just fish." She studied his face. "Jesse, why are you asking about this?"

"Have you paid any attention to the menus since we've been here?" He folded his arms across his chest. "Have you seen what the staff eats and the slop the kids get?"

A twinge of guilt gripped her conscience. She nodded. She had noticed, at every meal.

"Before the time flip, I spent one morning skimming through some of the financial records. DuBois received government subsidizing of what, a thousand a month to feed and clothe these kids? And then there were charitable donations on top of that, right?"

She nodded. "That sounds about right."

"And some of the student programs brought in money for the school, too. Right?"

"Yes. Felder's class sold the harnesses they made, the carpentry class sold furniture. The senior girls' sewing class sold some of their needlework in town." She thought for a moment. What else? "They sold their excess hay, in the summer sold vegetables at the farmer's market in town on Saturday."

"And all this money went into the school's accounts?"

"Yes, of course. What are you getting at?"

He looked away before he answered. "Well, from the numbers I saw recorded in the books, what I know of the cost of things in 1886, and what I can see by being here, whoever has access to the money is skimming from the school's accounts."

An uneasy feeling had already been niggling at her, but with Jesse's last comment, she completely lost her temper and white-hot anger exploded to the surface. "How dare you!" She quickly stood, her hands clenched into fists at her sides, and took a step or two toward him. "How dare you imply that Providence was a . . . a thief!"

"I didn't say that." He held his hand out in petition. "But we need to consider all the possibilities until we have proof. Proof—one way or the other."

"And while you're looking for that proof, you're holding Providence to blame."

"You've seen these kids. They're too thin, they aren't getting enough to eat." He drew a haggard breath and shredded the maple leaf he held in his hand. "My God, Kathleen, I've watched some of them scrounging in the woods behind the carpentry shop for wild berries, acorns, any damned thing they can eat." He dropped the pieces of the leaf on the ground. "Did you know that yesterday two boys were caught cooking a squirrel in the fire in the blacksmith shop?"

"No." She could barely breathe.

"Where's the money going, Kathleen?"

"I don't know, but I refuse to believe that Providence is stealing—"

"I'm not naming names. I don't know who is doing it." Jesse's dark eyes searched her face. "All I'm saying is that *someone* is stealing from these kids."

"I won't believe that he's the one." She shook her head. "I watched him today looking at the children. I think he was upset by what he saw."

Jesse's reply began with a mere lift of his right brow. "Katie, he's only been gone two weeks. What has happened to these kids began months ago."

"But Hannah told me that he's been ill for a long time, at least two months. During that time he's hardly left his apartment. Wilks has been in charge." She paused, and then quietly added, "I would venture a guess that if there is a problem, Josiah Wilks is your suspect, not Providence. And because she works in the office and does the bookkeeping, I'd say it's a safe bet that Margaret Lester is involved, too."

Jesse nodded. "You might not be far off the mark." He pushed away from the tree and took her back to the bench, waiting until she sat down before he joined her. "Perhaps that's another reason that Fate gave us this little side trip. Maybe we're not only looking for answers for ourselves, but for the kids, too."

"What can we do?" Jesse's hand moved into her field of vision and she watched, spellbound, as he covered her hand with his own.

"I haven't figured out yet how we find out what's going on, but we need to take another look at the ledgers." His fingers twined with hers. "Yesterday Dobbs sold three rocking chairs from the carpentry shop for five dollars each, and I know that Felder's boys delivered a new tandem set of fancy harness to the undertaker in town this morning. I heard the price was fifty. Both were cash deals. That money should be on the books." He lightly squeezed her hand. "We need to get a look at the ledgers."

He lifted her hand to his mouth and lightly touched his lips to her fingers. She watched, mesmerized, wondering how such a simple gesture could have started the flow of sweet honeyed warmth throughout her body. He frowned, as if concentrating on a plan, and she wondered if he was even aware that he'd kissed her.

From the high branches the hoot of an owl cast an eerie pall over the small clearing. Trembling, Kathleen quickly pulled her fingers away from Jesse's grasp. "I'd better go." She smiled, hoping to ease the tension between them. "By the way, the note you gave me . . ."

"Yeah, what about it?"

"Your penmanship is atrocious. I'll ask Alma Briggs to spend some extra class time with you."

Jesse laughed. "Come on, Katie-girl. I'll walk you back." He stood, pulling her up with him. "I always see my dates home safely."

Kathleen suddenly felt the hot flare of a blush on her cheeks. She'd never been anyone's date before. Of course, she knew she wasn't really Jesse's date, but it felt nice to have him say so, even if he was just teasing.

Face-to-face they stood in a shaft of pale moonlight that filtered through the trees. Looking up, Kathleen searched his face. She studied the black wings of his brows, the high planes of his cheekbones, the strong line of his jaw and stubborn chin. She spent moments staring at his wonderful, full, and inviting mouth.

She didn't know what she was looking for. Maybe it was as little as wanting acceptance from this man who had managed to turn her life upside down. Maybe it was as much as wanting one moment of her dreams of him to come true. Whatever it was, Jesse Spotted Horse had changed her life forever. He had exploded into her world and taken her to emotional places she never knew existed. They had approached each other from opposite ends of that world, and now they were dependent on each other for their safety . . . for their lives. The thought was mind-boggling. But then, how could two people slip through the gates of time and find themselves in a place in history that was the core of both of their lives? That was even more mind-boggling.

She allowed a sigh to leave her heart, and when she spoke, her voice splintered with emotion. "I . . . wish . . . I wish this would all end and everything could go back to the way it was."

"No, you don't, Katie-girl. No, you don't." He drew her into his arms, held her close, and pressed her head to his shoulder. His hand gently stroked her back, riding up and down her spine.

His embrace had come as a surprise, but even more surprising, she didn't resist, she didn't pull away. This was that one moment of her dreams coming true.

"I know you don't want to go back to being Little Miss Mousey. You've already changed too much, and, sweetheart, there are more changes to come, you'll see. You owe yourself those changes and so much more." He lowered his head and kissed her forehead.

"Little Miss Mousey?" Her temper flared and she pulled back. "Do you think I don't know how people think of me, how you think of me?" She firmly planted her hands on her hips. "Well, I'll be sent to Hades in a hand basket before I'll be anyone's Little Miss Mousey anymore." She took a deep breath. "Maybe this will change your mind."

Without hesitating for the moment it would take to change her mind, Kathleen stood on tiptoe. She placed her hands on Jesse's face, one on each cheek, and pulled his head down to her. With her eyes tightly shut, she drew another bracing breath, and blindly pressed her mouth firmly against his.

The kiss, close-lipped, chaste, and almost an inch off center, lasted no more than four seconds before it ended.

"There," she proudly declared and stepped back. She ignored the old prudish Kathleen that struggled to surface and scold her and she tried to ignore the wild skips and jumps her heart was taking. She put a haughty upward tilt to her chin, reset her hands on her hips, and felt darned proud of herself. "Now, is *that* something a Little Miss Mousey would do?"

An easy grin quirked Jesse's lips. "Nope, you're right. Definitely not a Miss Mousey kind of thing." The grin widened. "And I bet that Little Miss Mousey doesn't know about the consequences she has to face for that kiss."

A quiver, a mixture of excitement, apprehension, and expectation, skittered through Kathleen. "What . . . what consequences?"

Jesse's answer came on a slow, soft breath. "Consequences like this."

Kathleen stood mesmerized as his gaze locked with hers and he slid his left hand around her waist. His right moved up her arm. Each inch traveled drove the beat of her heart faster and faster. He took his time drawing her closer and Kathleen's anticipation rose with each millisecond. In less time than a sigh she was pressed against his hard chest, her breath soundless as she stared at his mouth and thought she would die a thousand times over. Was he going to kiss her? Or not? Was he? Jesse bent his head down. Oh, my, yes . . . yes, he was. Drawing a ragged breath, she closed her eyes.

And he did.

# Chapter 16

A lot of our tribes don't know their traditions, teachings or ways. And it's a shame . . . because someday your children will ask what their purpose is on Grandmother Earth.

—ABE CONKLIN,
NUDA HONGA, PONCA HETHUSKA, PONCA/OSAGE

KATHLEEN IMMEDIATELY RECOGNIZED the difference between the closed-mouth peck she had called a kiss and the magnificent melding of lips and delight that Jesse gave her in return. Oh yes, consequences such as this she'd gladly endure.

Holding her chin between his thumb and index finger, he tipped her head up, making full and easy access to her mouth. His lips touched, feather light, the sensation sweet and warm, and tender. Oh, yes, definitely, yes.

His fingers moved slowly up the side of her face and then plunged into her hair, holding her against his mouth, and scattering her hair pins on the ground. He slanted his mouth against hers and coaxed and cajoled, teased, tempted, and then demanded. And suddenly the warmth in her body escalated and turned into something different, something hotter and hungrier. She leaned against him. Raising her arms, she clung to him, surrendering gladly what he silently claimed.

At first the glide of his tongue against her lips startled and then captivated her, urging her to open her mouth and accept his intimate caress. Denying Jesse would be denying herself. Kathleen granted his request.

His fingers slid from her hair, moved lightly across her

cheek to the juncture of their lips. His mouth moved on hers again, settling and resettling, teaching her how to give, to take, to share, teaching her every nuance, every delight of a lover's kiss.

She felt the vibration in his chest and then in his mouth as his low, hungry groan filled her with more excitement than she had ever known. A new awareness blossomed, spurring her senses, expanding her world. She hadn't expected the tingling in her breasts or the feathering sensation between her thighs. She uttered a small whimper of surprise as an unfamiliar needful burning pooled in her body's secret places and turned into a blaze she feared would melt her bones.

Jesse raised his lips from hers and looked down at her.

Kathleen held her breath and tried, without success, to read his mind. "Why . . . why did you kiss me like that?"

He placed a trail of nibbling kisses along the edge of her mouth, then, barely lifting his lips from hers, he answered, his voice a whisper, his breath a tantalizing warmth on her skin. "Because I've wanted to kiss you for a long time. Because you've got the most kissable lips I've *ever* seen."

Her breath left her. "Ever?"

"Yes, ever."

"Me? Ever?"

"Katie-girl, quit fishing for more compliments and just kiss me again."

And she did.

Light-headed, all reasonable thoughts fled. Then suddenly all she could think of was Jesse . . . Jesse . . . Jesse.

She felt his hands move to her shoulders, and a sense of great loss filled her as he pulled away.

"So, that was a consequence?" Kathleen gasped, placing her hand flat against his chest, trying to regain her balance, trying to breathe.

"Just one of them." Jesse prayed that his voice sounded light, that she wouldn't hear the wanting that boiled inside him. *Get a hold of yourself, Horse, before you really do something you'll regret.* He hated it when the voice of reason in his head was right, especially when it sounded just like Tooter.

"Jesse, I—"

"Shh, Katie-girl." He pressed his fingers against her freshly kissed lips, surprised to discover his new vulnerability where Kathleen Prescott was concerned. "I don't know what just happened." His fingers left her mouth and brushed across her cheek. "I liked it. No, I liked it a lot and I think you did, too." His finger traced the curl of her ear. "I don't know where this takes us or even if we should go there." He searched her eyes for some sense of what she was feeling.

Her breath still uneven, Kathleen solemnly nodded. "I know." She dropped her gaze and then softly added, "Thank you."

"For?"

A demure smile curved her lips. "A very memorable first kiss."

He grinned and something exploded inside him, filling him with ridiculous delight. *I'm her first kiss.* He wasn't surprised, but it still felt like he'd won the lottery. "Believe me, it was my pleasure." If he had a flashlight and shone it on her face, he knew he'd find a bright pink blush on her cheeks. "Come on, sweetheart, time to get you to bed . . . I mean . . . get you back to your room." *Gawd, I'm acting like a hormone-juiced teenager.*

He didn't want to take her back. There were many other places that he'd like to take her, but that wasn't one of them. Damn. Why couldn't this have happened when they were still in their own time, when all these complications didn't exist? *Because, Horse, you were fighting each other from opposite sides of the fence and because at that time you were out to take everything you could get from her for the film.* Jesse was getting damned tired of Tooter's voice butting into his conscience as though he were Jimminy-F'n-Cricket.

He led her along the south driveway, staying just inside the line of trees. They passed the blacksmith shop, darkened and still for the night. A few more paces to the north, sleepy murmurs came from the henhouse, and overhead a few night birds joined in, barely pausing their song as Jesse and Kathleen passed by. Through a break in the trees they saw the harness shop up ahead. A light glowed in the window.

"Damn. Gus is still up," Jesse cautioned. "We'll have to be careful. The man can hear a pin drop from a mile away."

They crouched low and, with Jesse leading, slipped around the back of the building. Passing an open window they heard Gustav Felder happily whistling a tune.

"Bach," Kathleen whispered.

"What?"

"Bach. He's whistling the Brandenburg."

Jesse almost choked silencing his laugh. Only his Katie-girl would play *Name That Tune* while sneaking around in the middle of the night and trying not to get caught. *My Katie-girl? Oh, Horse . . . you're getting in way over your head. Shut up, Tooter.*

He suddenly grabbed Kathleen's arm and pulled her deeper into the shadows of the trees. "Shh. Don't move."

"What's wrong?"

"Be quiet."

Footsteps, light and tentative, fell one after another along the lane, the faint crunch announcing each step. As the footfalls neared, Jesse heard Kathleen draw a deep breath and he gave her hand a reassuring squeeze. Whoever was stealing through the night was just as nervous about being caught as they were.

Jesse carefully pulled aside some branches, and with Kathleen looking over his shoulder, they watched Alma Briggs tiptoe down the lane. With a quick furtive glance back to the senior girls' dormitory, she picked up her skirt and began to run toward the harness shop. She rapped a quick tattoo on the door. The whistling strains of Bach stopped. The door opened, and Gustav Felder quickly drew her inside. In a few moments the harness shop was dark.

"Well, I'll be damned. Surprise, surprise." Jesse chuckled. "It looks like my penmanship class will have to wait. Gus has already signed up for some private lessons."

He heard Kathleen giggle and he almost shouted for joy. He'd bet that he'd just heard Kathleen Prescott's first out-and-out giggle. *Add that to your list of firsts, Horse.*

They made the rest of the trip back to the senior girls'

dorm without any other disruptions and all too soon stood in the shadows of the honeysuckle bushes beside the back stairs.

"Good night, Katie." Jesse didn't fight the urge. Reaching up, he cupped her cheek in his hand. "Please think about what I said about the school ledgers." He felt her stiffen. "The books will help us find out who is responsible. Okay?" Her nod against the palm of his hand was reluctant at best. Damned if he didn't want to kiss her again. *Stop it, Horse. You're gonna get yourself in too deep.* A deep sigh escaped his lips. *Go to hell, Tooter.* "Get some sleep. You've got a busy day tomorrow."

"When will I . . . we . . ."

"Shh," he whispered. "Soon."

She turned to leave. Without hesitating, he reached out and took hold of her hand, drawing her back to him. He leaned down and kissed her one more time. Not just for her, but for him as well. In an instant he knew he could easily become addicted to kissing Kathleen Prescott. Hell, he was hooked already.

Jesse reluctantly pulled away and watched her climb the stairs. Hesitating at the door, Kathleen looked back at him for an instant before slipping inside. Before he left, he stood at the bottom of the stairs and listened to her slide the bolt and lock the door. With each passing moment, this time slide was becoming more and more complicated.

He hated the thought of going back to his cot in the hot and stuffy room. If he could get away with it, he'd gladly sleep on the porch. Reaching the back stoop of the dorm, he sat and removed his boots. Tying the laces together again, he slung the boots over his shoulder, stood, and twisted the doorknob. It refused to turn. Jesse pushed against the door. It didn't budge. He tried the knob again. Nothing.

"Damn, the door's locked."

Had he accidentally locked it when he'd sneaked out? *No. I made sure it wasn't locked.* He'd have to go around and try the front door. If it too was locked, hell, he might just get his wish for a night on the porch.

A niggling, edgy feeling slid up his spine and tapped

him on the shoulder. In an instant he knew he wasn't alone. *Damn, this isn't good.*

"My, my, Mr. Slocum. Look what we have here."

Jesse eased around, his blood turning to ice water. Cecil Blunt stood at the bottom of the stairs, still drunk but blocking any chance for him to escape.

"I think this red bastard just earned himself a visit to the cold house, don't you?" Blunt swayed then grabbed the stair rail to steady himself. "Sounds like a party to me."

"Maybe the little buggers who're already there would like to have a new pal," Nate Slocum replied through a sneer. A sour belch slid from between his lips and he wiped the back of his hand across his mouth. "Ain't nothin' like getting some company, even if it is scuffed up a little."

Hoping they were still too drunk to catch him, Jesse tried to vault over the porch rail, but Slocum, who outweighed him by at least fifty pounds, grabbed him around the legs. They toppled over the railing, crashed into the bushes, and rolled out into the open. Blunt rushed in and gave Jesse's ribs a few hard kicks.

As Blunt drew his leg back to line up his boot again, Jesse grabbed his ankle and threw him off balance. Blunt crashed to his knees. Bulldozing over the top of Blunt, Jesse staggered to his feet only to find Slocum in front of him. Slocum threw a punch and Jesse reeled back as it glanced off his shoulder, sending a pain shooting down his arm. Determined to get at least one solid blow in before they overpowered him, Jesse pulled back, cocked his elbow, and drove his fist into Slocum's face. Dazed, Slocum staggered, blood spurting from his nose and mouth. Without waiting another moment, Jesse clipped Slocum a second time, hitting him on the jaw and sending him over backward.

Jesse's knuckles felt as though he'd hit a brick wall, and he shook his hand trying to rid himself of the agony. Swaying on his feet, he drew a breath only to have it immediately knocked out of his lungs as Blunt tackled him from behind, driving him to the ground. Blunt dug his knee into the small of Jesse's back and continued to pound his ribs.

Pulling together every ounce of strength he possessed, Jesse pushed himself to his knees, toppling Blunt to the ground. But before he could stand, Slocum's next punch, an undercut to the jaw, sent Jesse sprawling.

"Lemme get a few licks," Blunt gasped, reeling to his feet. He drove the toe of his boot into Jesse's side.

Jesse knew if he didn't give in, he'd end up with some broken bones. At the moment broken ribs worried him more than the infamous cold house.

Pushing to his knees, Jesse lowered his head. His boots lay on the ground in front of him, and he quickly grabbed them, hung them over his shoulder, and then raised his hands over his head.

"Lookit the big, brave warrior now," Slocum snorted, wiping the sleeve of his shirt across his bloody nose. He kneed Jesse in the shoulder. "You son of a bitch, that one's for Custer and the boys of the Seventh."

"Come on, help me get the bastard on his feet, Nate. I ain't gonna letcha pound him till he can't walk, 'cause I ain't gonna drag him all the way to the cold house."

Pain shot through Jesse as Slocum twisted his arm behind his back and yanked up, forcing him to his knees. Afraid that the next yank would dislocate his shoulder, Jesse gathered his feet beneath him and stood, then tried to twist free.

"Dammit, Nate, hold on to him. I'd hate for our new guest to get lost in the dark."

"I wonder what he was doin' out and about."

"Ain't no tellin', probably sniffing out one of them young squaws." Blunt belched, the stench gagging Jesse. "I hear these redskins breed like rabbits."

Oh, yeah, maybe not tonight or tomorrow, but someday soon, Jesse promised himself, he'd take care of Blunt and Slocum.

The two men grabbed Jesse's arms, one on either side, and hauled him down the lane. Sharp rocks bruised and bit into his feet but he was numb to the pain. Thank God he'd picked up his boots. Thank God they had just caught him and not Kathleen, too.

On the far side of the junior boys' dormitory they dragged him off the utility lane to a narrow path that wound through the dark woods. In a small clearing about seventy feet down the path, Jesse had his first glimpse of the cold house. The squat building had probably been built as cold storage for vegetables or a milk house. In the mottled night shadows it jutted out of the ground, reminding Jesse of a hunched monster. He guessed the building to be about twenty-feet square and couldn't help but wonder how many other guests waited inside for him.

"Got the key?" Slocum slurred as they stopped at the heavy wooden door.

"Yeah, right here." Blunt fumbled in his pocket and withdrew a cluster of keys tied together on a leather thong. He searched through them all before selecting one.

Jesse waited for Blunt to slide the key in the lock. If he made a run for it now, could he get away? Slocum wouldn't be too hard to overpower. *Hell, where would I go? It's not like I could blend into the population of 1886 Pritchart without being noticed.* The last reason was the real reason. *I can't leave Kathleen.*

The door swung open and the stench almost knocked him over. He heard a noise, a whimper, coming from the dark interior. There was also the sound of a furtive scamper as though a wild animal were trying to hide.

*"Ila'lapi."*

Jesse heard the words, a feral hiss, coming from the bowels of the building. Lakota. It translated into two simple fear-filled words: *Go away.*

"Shut up, you little bastards. We brung ya a new pal." Slocum laughed as they pitched Jesse forward into the black maw of the cold house.

Jesse stumbled and landed on his knees on the dirt floor. Throwing his hand out to brace himself, he felt cold, clammy flesh. One of the boys? Alive? Dead? He quickly drew back. Sitting on his haunches, he tried to breathe as rush after rush of adrenaline fed his body.

The hard slam of the door behind him and the metallic click of the closing padlock sounded like cannon fire in the black void. A lifetime seemed to pass and then another before a noise, little more than something living drawing away from another living thing, shattered the suffocating silence.

Jesse waited for his eyes to adjust to the dark. One small shuttered window on the south side of the building permitted only the smallest breath of fresh air and moonlight inside. The place smelled of human waste, sweat, and fear. The bare dirt floor dipped and rose unevenly as if dozens of hands with little else to do had scraped and dug away at its surface.

"*Le taku he*? Who are you?"

The question came from his left, the voice young and filled with apprehension. *So, one of my cellmates is Lakota.*

"*Sungléska,*" Jesse replied.

"*NiLak'ota?*"

"*Hau.* Yes, I'm Lakota."

The silence expanded and then was split by faint whispers. From the pitch-black corner the voice came again. "*Tonik'iyataŋpi he?*"

Jesse struggled with the translation, listening for Grandma Boo's voice in his head. For some reason if he could imagine her saying the words, their meaning came quicker. Yes, there it was—where are you from. "*Dakota ema'taŋhaŋ.*"

"*Dakota uŋki'taŋhaŋpi.*"

Jesse smiled to himself. Dakota homeboys. Just a hundred and seventeen years apart. "*Le taku he?*"

"*Hoksi'la Ca'pa,*" the boy replied. "They call me Isaac. You may call me by that name; I have become used to it." The boy's English was clear and well practiced, but the hint of a Lakota accent remained. A moment passed before Isaac spoke again. "You say you are one of us, Lakota, and yet your words are pitiful, not beautiful as Lakota should be."

*Hoksi'la Ca'pa,* Beaver Boy, Jesse mused, no wonder he preferred Isaac. The kid was brave, though, calling him out on his bad Lakota. "Isaac, you're right, I haven't spoken our language for a long time. Maybe you can help me speak better."

A grunt was Isaac's only reply.

"How many boys are in here?" Jesse asked, quickly changing the subject.

"*Unya'mnipi,* three of us," Isaac answered. "Do they still call you *Sungléska?*"

"No, I'm Jesse."

"*Hau.* I guess Jesse okay name. You sound . . . big."

A quick chuckle fled Jesse's lips, forcing him to hold on to his sore ribs. "Yeah, I guess I am. Who are the others?" Now that his eyes had grown accustomed to the dark, he could see the shapes of the three boys.

"*Hitu'ŋ kaasaŋ,* Weasel," answered the boy to his right. "I have been given the name Luke. I like Weasel better."

"I'll call you Weasel, then." Jesse looked at the boy in the middle, the one who had yet to say a word.

"*Kola, le taku he?*"

His question went unanswered for what seemed like forever. Jesse heard the boy shift his legs and draw a deep breath. The silence expanded, and just when Jesse figured he would never learn the boy's name, the answer came strong and clear.

"*Tokalu Sapa.*"

# 17

No longer Indian and certainly not white, they became what the Indians called aintsikn ustombe, the lost people.

—GERTRUDE S. BONNIN,
YANKTON SIOUX, 1910

KATHLEEN WOKE WITH a start. Had she overslept? Taking her small purse from the drawer in the table beside her bed, she fumbled in the bottom for her watch. Seven forty-five. She would have to hurry. Sunday chapel began at nine o'clock sharp, and Reverend Divine liked to have all of his staff attend.

She quickly dressed in a pretty blue gown. Stopping to check her appearance in the small mirror, she leaned closer for a better look at her reflection. "I've been kissed." She didn't try to contain the smile that sent her mouth up at the corners. She touched her lips with her fingers. "Oh, yes, I've been kissed very, very well." Every beat of her heart and every breath she took told her she wanted to be kissed again.

A door slamming down the hall chased her daydream away. She quickly left her room and rushed down the stairs. There might still be time enough for a quick breakfast.

A bright sunny day greeted her as she stepped out onto the porch. Walking along the promenade to the dining hall, she began to softly whistle a jaunty tune to herself, adding a few silly dance steps to her gait.

Realizing what she was doing, she laughed gaily. Whistling and dancing in public was not like her at all. Her parents would have been dismayed by her behavior. She glanced around. Had anyone heard her? Seen her?

She grinned. Jesse would think it was funny. Jesse. His name filled her mind and touched her heart. He was the reason for this happiness and the wonderful way she felt. Her steps faltered. *Am I falling in love?*

The staid Kathleen, protector of the Divine legacy, suddenly returned to reject the possibility. One kiss is not love. *Are you sure? It was a wonderful kiss.* The practical side of her told her that she had absolutely no hallmark to measure Jesse's kiss against and that it had been little more than a lust-filled opportunity for Jesse Spotted Horse. But the newly awakened side of her played traitor, and her hopes and dreams took flight.

What was Jesse thinking about this morning? She touched her lips again. Was he thinking about her? Was he remembering, too? And when he remembered, was he singing silly love songs and doing silly dance steps?

Still humming the happy melody, she turned off the promenade at the dining hall and bumped into a group of Dobbs's boys. They looked grand, their cropped hair slicked down, and their freshly scrubbed faces ready for church. Jesse wasn't with them.

"Good morning it is today, Miss Prescott." After offering his greeting, the boy shyly looked down.

"Thank you, Ezra, the same to you and your friends."

The boys all gave their own mumbled replies, then quickly made their way down the promenade toward the chapel.

Taking her seat at the teacher's dining table, Kathleen nodded her greeting to all. She'd looked for Jesse when she'd passed the long tables, but he wasn't in the dining hall, either.

"You're late this morning, Miss Prescott," Josiah Wilks remarked coolly, passing her the large platter of pancakes. "I hope you didn't have a restless night."

She glanced up and sensed an immediate threat as both Wilks and Margaret Lester watched closely for her response.

She refused to be intimidated. "No, Mr. Wilks, I spent a very peaceful night, thank you." She dropped two pancakes on her plate and added a drizzle of syrup from the pitcher that Hannah had placed in front of her. "It must be the wonderful Indiana air that aids my sleep." She smiled, hoping neither could hear the anxious trip and thud of her heart. "It is a lovely morning, isn't it?" she cheerfully added. She enjoyed a mouthful of her breakfast before Wilks interrupted her again.

"Please try to be more punctual for meals. Eating cold food is not healthy. Besides, it is thoughtless of you to expect Mrs. Gilbert to keep your food warm."

"Yes, of course, you're right, Mr. Wilks. In the future I'll strive to be more timely."

"Chapel in fifteen minutes, everyone," Margaret Lester snapped, rising from her chair, holding her bandaged arm.

"Now that he is home, will Reverend Divine be giving service this morning?" Hannah asked, politely folding her napkin and placing it next to her empty plate.

"Of course not," Wilks replied, as though he were speaking to an irritating child. "The man is still very ill. Reverend Shelbourne from Pritchart will be joining us again today."

"He delivers wonderful sermons about purity of heart and mind, and about the importance of a sin-free life," Alma Briggs added, her eyes meeting Gustav Felder's across the table.

"I can't wait," Hannah Dobbs whispered under her breath, apparently assured that only Kathleen could hear her.

"Did anyone else hear some strange noises last night?" Wilks's question may have been directed to the whole gathering, but his eyes remained on Kathleen.

"I was in bed sound asleep by ten," Basil Dobbs replied. "Didn't hear a squeak until this morning."

"No," Gustav answered, dropping his attention to the near empty plate in front of him. "Of course, from my room in the harness shop, I don't hear nothing from up here on the hill." His eyes darted to Alma Briggs again. "Didn't hear nothing."

"Miss Dobbs?" Josiah glanced at Hannah, gifting her with the most charming smile the handsome man had in his arsenal.

Kathleen watched Hannah melt under his blue-eyed gaze.

"Oh, no, Mr. Wilks. All I heard were the sweet sounds of the night birds singing outside my window."

Kathleen almost groaned listening to Hannah's overly poetic reply. The poor girl's infatuation was impossible to miss.

Kathleen felt Wilks's attention settle on her again.

"Miss Prescott, surely *you* heard something unusual in the night, even though you say you slept so soundly."

What was Wilks's game? He obviously didn't believe she'd slept well or had even slept at all. Jesse's words played in her mind. *Be careful.* "No, Mr. Wilks," she firmly replied, setting her cutlery on her plate. "Let me repeat, I slept very soundly all night long. So why don't you tell us what we all missed. It's clear that you want us to know."

She heard Hannah draw a sharp breath, then felt her friend's booted foot lightly tap her own ankle. The warning was clear. Another "Be careful."

Wilks leaned forward, placed his elbows on the table, and rested his chin on his steepled fingers. His mouth was drawn in a smug smile. "Well, Miss Prescott, it seems that you and Mr. Dobbs will be missing your favorite student for a while."

"Favorite student?" An icy fist gripped her stomach and cruelly twisted it into a knot. "I don't prefer one student over the other, Mr. Wilks, and I doubt that Mr. Dobbs does, either."

Wilks ignored her response. "For your enlightenment, your model student, the one you named Jesse, was caught sneaking around the grounds last night well past the lights-out bell." Wilks paused, but kept staring at Kathleen. He arched a brow as if waiting for a confession. When none came, he continued. "He was first seen slinking away from the senior girls' dormitory."

The fist in her stomach gave another hard jerk, and Kathleen suddenly felt nauseated. Had someone seen her and Jesse together, or was Wilks just on a fishing expedition for more information? *Well, I'm not taking his bait.* "Really? That's very interesting." Struggling to stay calm, she lifted her shoulders in an ambiguous shrug and took a sip from her coffee cup.

"Really," Wilks countered. "*Your* Mr. Spotted Horse was discovered last evening by our ever-vigilant Mr. Slocum and Mr. Blunt." A twisted grin breached the beautiful planes of his face. "*Your* Mr. Spotted Horse is now a guest in the cold house."

Speechless, Kathleen stared at Josiah Wilks. She couldn't have been more shocked than if someone had poured a bucket of ice water on her head. *Composure, Kathleen, composure.* "Yes, well, I'm sure you felt the punishment to be just." She picked up her fork, speared a bite-sized portion of pancakes, and put it in her mouth. That part was easy, but appearing nonchalant and swallowing the pancakes with the lie wedged in her throat would be the true test.

FILLED WITH THREATS of fire and brimstone, demons and agonies, the Reverend Mr. Shelbourne's sermon droned on and on. Kathleen shuddered. The nine o'clock service was just the first of three that would be held throughout the day to accommodate everyone at DuBois; seniors and teachers first, juniors and other staff, second and third. Kathleen pitied those who were coming to the following two services; the Reverend Mister Shelbourne was just getting warmed up.

Despite the minister's ardor and volume, Kathleen's thoughts kept drifting, replaying Josiah Wilks's words over in her mind. Jesse was in the cold house. She'd heard of the place a few times from Hannah and Basil. She frowned. In all of Providence's old journals he'd written about it only once or twice and then only about its use as the old milk storage house or where they stored vegetables if the garden had yielded a generous crop. *If the place was used for punishment, why hadn't that been in his journals, too?*

She had to see Jesse for herself. She had to know that they hadn't hurt him. *But I don't know where the cold house is.* She glanced at Basil Dobbs and then at Hannah. *But I'll find out.*

Her attention moved to Josiah Wilks, who dozed at the end of the pew in front of her. His chin rested on his chest and his lips and cheeks were slack with sleep. Her disdain for the man exposed itself in a short, derisive snort. *It would appear Mr. Wilks believes he's exempt from Reverend Shelbourne's warnings.*

As the strains of the final hymn faded and Reverend Shelbourne's hand fell at the end of the Benediction, Kathleen stood, hoping to talk with Basil Dobbs before he left.

"Don't go so quickly," Hannah said, taking hold of Kathleen's wrist and pulling her back down. "I want you to meet Reverend Shelbourne." She cupped her hand over her mouth. "He's single, you know." She giggled, then glanced at Josiah Wilks. "Of course, he's not half as handsome as Josiah, but I think you two would be a perfect match."

Kathleen stifled a groan. The last thing she needed was cupid in the guise of Hannah Dobbs. She glanced over her shoulder and watched Basil Dobbs leave the chapel. *Well, it looks as though I won't be getting my answer from him.*

Unwilling to give up so easily, she looked back at Hannah. Could she be trusted? Would Hannah tell her what she wanted to know? Leaning close, Kathleen whispered, "Do you know where the cold house is?"

"Yes, but why . . ." Hannah's eyes popped wide. "Oh. Surely you're not thinking of going there, are you?" She glanced to the end of the pew in front of her, but Wilks had already gone. "Kathleen, you can't. Josiah . . . Mr. Wilks wouldn't allow it."

"I don't think he has much to say about it." Kathleen stood again and moved out of the pew. In the aisle she stepped aside and allowed Hannah to join her. "Are you going to tell me or do I have to ask someone else?"

Hannah glanced around, causing the puff of feathers in her bonnet to sway back and forth. "I don't approve, and I can't imagine why you'd be interested." Her eyes widened again, and her hand flew to her mouth to cover an escaping twitter. "Oh, please don't tell me that you have feelings for that tall Indian, that Jesse. That is just not proper. He's a heathen. I can't believe this, it is just too . . ."

Worried by the direction that Hannah's remarks were

taking, Kathleen took Hannah's arm and drew her three rows closer to the front of the chapel. All the pews were empty; no one would hear them. "Hannah, do you care at all about these Indian children?" The question came direct and firm, and Kathleen wanted her answer from Hannah Dobbs to be exactly the same.

"Of course I do. I love my wild little Indian girls. They're so sweet and . . ." Anger suddenly flushed her cheeks and colored the tone of her voice. "What are you suggesting, Kathleen? I don't like what your question is inferring."

Kathleen lifted her prayer book. "Hannah, I'm going to tell you something that you can't repeat to anyone and that includes your brother and especially Josiah Wilks. Lives will be in danger if you do. Do you understand?" She waited. "I need your word, your promise."

Hannah pressed her hand on Kathleen's prayer book. "Yes, of course, I promise." Avid excitement colored her voice. "What is it?"

"I think the children are being shamefully mistreated, but I need help in getting solid proof." There, she'd said it out loud, and God forbid that it should turn against her.

"Mistreated? Certainly not by me! I treat them kindly."

"Hannah, please, hear me out." Kathleen raised her hand to stop any further denials. "What about the rule that forbids them from speaking their own language?"

"You of all people, their English teacher, should see the sound reasoning to that."

"But when they are caught breaking the rule, does it warrant washing their mouths out with soap, or a paddling, or the cold house?"

"Well, I remember when Basil was a boy and said a bad word, my mother—"

"Hannah, they are not speaking bad words. They are speaking their own language." Exasperated, Kathleen continued. "I've heard that some have even been punished for talking to their own sisters or brothers—family members who are here." She had hoped for some sort of denial, or a reaction of disbelief from Hannah, but received neither. "Yesterday, Mr. Felder made one of his boys run around the promenade four times with one of the draft horse collars around his neck."

Hannah looked away. "I'm sure there was a good reason. Gustav Felder is a very good man. Maybe the boy had been lazy, or stolen something, or lied."

"Hannah, I guarantee that you couldn't carry a draft horse collar a hundred feet, and yet this child was forced to run almost a mile with it around his neck." Kathleen drew a ragged breath. "And their meals, Hannah. What about their food? The portions are barely generous enough to feed the youngest and certainly not enough to feed the older ones."

"It's good food," Hannah countered.

"Is it? Has anyone on staff eaten it? Have you eaten it?" Kathleen shook her head. "No, you haven't. We're served fried chicken or roast beef, green beans and mashed potatoes, apple pie, and yet you call boiled turnips and potatoes with a piece of fatty unidentifiable meat good food."

"Oh, Kathleen, glory be," Hannah volleyed. "Since Reverend Divine took ill, everyone has had to suffer with poorer food. With his inability to travel, the charitable contributions have lessened. Mr. Wilks also said the money that the government is supposed to send each month has lessened as well." She shrugged. "Something to do with budgets in Washington."

"Mr. Wilks said that, did he?" Kathleen's left brow arched. "Are you saying that the food the staff eats now is different compared to what used to be served?"

Hannah appeared to be stricken. "Josiah said that—"

"When we have pancakes and eggs and bacon for breakfast, they get a thin oatmeal gruel, maybe a slice of bread with lard. Their milk is watered until there is no food value left."

"But Josiah said they are used to that kind of fare. He said that—"

"And when did this all begin? When did Mr. Wilks first tell you this?" She felt her hand close into a fist. "Think about it, Hannah. These changes all happened after Reverend Divine got sick and after Josiah Wilks took charge, didn't they?"

"Kathleen, why are you poking your nose where it

doesn't belong? It's not our place to question. Surely you don't think you know more about these things than Mr. Wilks." Hannah squared her shoulders. "And as for the way these children are treated, they are treated very, very well." She paused, tilting her chin a little higher. "They were undisciplined, filthy, and ignorant until they came here. DuBois has been their salvation."

Ready to heatedly rebut Hannah's argument, suddenly Kathleen felt a catch in her breath. Nausea hit her stomach and she thought she would lose her breakfast. *Their salvation?* A sob tightened her throat. *Oh, dear God, those are the exact same tenets I believed in all my life.*

Indignant, Hannah tipped her chin upward. "Josiah says it takes discipline, sometimes even places like the cold house, to help some of them learn their lessons. The troublemakers are a lot easier to manage since the cold house was put into use. And I would say that *your* Jesse is a troublemaker." She moved away, then turned to face Kathleen again. "In case you don't know, the staff are also doing the best we can to help Reverend Divine and his family. Everyone has stepped forward to help."

Kathleen stepped closer. "What are you talking about?"

"When Josiah told us that because of his illness Reverend Divine was unable to pay some of the bills, including our whole salaries. For the last two months we all agreed to a pay cut of ten dollars a month to help."

Kathleen almost laughed. Ten dollars wasn't very much, and then she remembered. No, it wasn't much in 2003, but in 1886 it was almost a full third of Hannah Dobbs's monthly salary.

"Kathleen, you aren't going to say anything about this to Reverend Divine this afternoon, are you? Please, oh, please don't. Margaret Lester discovered the shortage of funds after Reverend Divine took ill. Josiah said that the Reverend wasn't to know because it would embarrass and worry him, and with his health being so poor . . ."

There it was, another connection between Margaret Lester, Josiah Wilks, and school money. Now it was more imperative than ever that she talk with Jesse. "No, I won't say anything today, I promise." *Not this afternoon, but I will talk with Reverend Divine about this as soon as I have more facts.*

Hannah sighed, her relief obvious. "Good, very good." She began to walk down the aisle toward the door.

"One last thing?" Kathleen took hold of her arm and stopped her again.

"Yes, what is it?"

"Where is the cold house?"

KATHLEEN TOOK THE path around to the back of the chapel. *Maybe I should wait until after dark.* She hesitated before stepping onto the utility lane that ran behind all of the buildings. *No, now is best. If I'm caught, I'll say that I'm out for a stroll, exploring the grounds.* She nodded, agreeing with herself. *If I got caught at night, I'd have no excuse.*

Following Hannah's directions, she left the utility lane and took the narrow but well-worn pathway that led away from the school. Underbrush grew close to the path and brambles grabbed at the hem of her skirt. She carefully picked her way along the path, determined not to ruin the pretty blue dress that Alma Briggs had loaned to her.

Her steps faltered and stopped as the footpath ended at the edge of a clearing. The cold house seemed to grow out of the middle of the small field: dark stone, a low tiled roof, and a heavily padlocked door. Dark and hulking, it reminded Kathleen of a crouching beast. She shivered and rubbed her hands over her arms, hoping to dispel the odd chill that had washed over her.

Cautiously approaching the rough-stone building, she noticed a wooden shutter on the south side. Hinged at the top, it covered the single small window. A sad attempt to beg fresh air and light into the building had been made. What looked like a rolled-up shirt had been stuffed between the window and the shutter. The shirt only lifted the shutter about six inches from the sill.

Placing her hand on the cold stone, Kathleen leaned close to the narrow open space between the shutter and the window. The stench from inside burned her nostrils. She tried to ignore it, to breathe as though it didn't exist. "Jesse?" Silence. "Jesse, are you in there?"

*"Wiηyaη kiη he tu'we he?"*

She heard the panic the whispered words carried. Bodies scurried, changing places, drawing back further into the dark, their furtive movements acknowledging the occupants' fear.

The Indian words were said again. *"Wiηyaη kiη he tu'we he?"*

"Don't worry, guys. She's a friend."

Hearing Jesse's voice, Kathleen felt an odd mixture of dismay and relief.

"Katie, I'm going to lift the shutter. Grab my shirt. It's not Armani, but I'd hate to lose it."

"Wait, let me find a couple of sticks to hold it up." She quickly searched the ground around the foundation of the house. At one time someone else had had the same idea. Next to the building she found two pieces of wood that looked as though they had been cut especially to hold up the cold house shutter.

"Jesse, help me, push it up." She struggled for a moment, working around his arms, finally setting the two pieces of wood in place. Sunlight rushed through the window, spilling light to the interior of the cold house, but it was the iron grillwork, bars set less than eight inches apart, that came as a surprise.

Kathleen stood in the shade of the shutter, her gaze traveling slowly over Jesse. A fresh bruise colored his chin, and a livid scrape marred his left cheek. His bottom lip was cut and swollen, and another half-inch cut split the flesh over his left eye. A smudge of dirt darkened his forehead and crossed the bridge of his nose.

Her inspection traveled lower, and she suddenly realized he was naked, at least to his waist. A small sighing breath slipped through her lips. She'd never seen a man's naked chest before, on television, yes, and in the movies, but never in real life, never in warm bronzed flesh. Too enthralled to politely look away, she stared, her gaze following every ridge, every muscle and contour. *Oh, my, so this is what a naked . . . well, almost naked, man looks like.*

*Well, perhaps not Richmond Brock or Josiah Wilks . . . but Jesse . . . oh, my.*

"Hey, Katie-girl, out for a Sunday stroll?"

Embarrassed to be caught staring, she immediately looked up. "Are you all right?" She reached through the bars and gently touched him. He winced. Afraid she had hurt him, she began to withdraw her hand, but Jesse grabbed it and closed his fingers around hers. A sigh left her lips. How odd; she had come to comfort him, and yet his touch gave her consolation.

"Yeah, I'm fine. Of course, the accommodations could be better." He quickly glanced over his shoulder. "This isn't the Sheraton Royale, and"—he looked at his grubby hands and the dirt imbedded under his nails—"I'm sorry, I'm filthy—I probably shouldn't even touch you. A three-hour bath would be nice, maybe even one of those air-freshener gadgets, too." Cynicism coated his short-lived laugh. He pressed his face between the bars. "God, it smells great outside." Another bitter laugh fled his lips. "You're taking quite a chance coming here, aren't you?" An easy smile lifted the corners of his mouth. "You didn't happen to bring a Big Mac with you, did you?"

"Oh, Jesse." Kathleen felt the sudden bite of guilt. "I didn't think. I should have brought some food."

"It's okay, sweetheart, you're forgiven." His smile didn't last. "Blunt doesn't bring any more food or water just because there's another mouth in the house." A sneer curled his lips. "They pass the slop to us through the window in jars. I think the bastards are afraid to come inside." He gave her hand a squeeze. "And it gets awfully cold in here at night."

She knew what he was asking and yes, she'd definitely risk getting caught if it meant bringing them blankets and food.

"I'll be back tonight with blankets and food. I promise." She craned her neck and tried to see farther inside the cold house. "How many boys are with you?"

"Three," Jesse replied. "They're all under twelve years old, as best I can guess. They've been here about nine days."

"Nine days!" Kathleen's blood ran cold. "My God, how could anyone do that to a child? Why?"

"Margaret Lester caught them taking some apples from the bowl on the teachers' table."

"Nine days. Jesse, that's medieval!" The horrors kept growing in number. She hadn't believed Jesse before, but now she had little choice.

He patted her hand. "I know, Katie-girl, I know."

"Jesse, about what you said last night about embezzlement?" She watched him nod. "Remember I told you that besides teaching mathematics, Margaret Lester works in the office for Providence. She is the bookkeeper." She drew a shuddering breath. "This morning Hannah told me that the school is almost out of money because of budget cuts in Washington and a drop in contributions. It seems that Margaret *accidentally* discovered this, and it was Wilks who told the staff and implemented all sorts of money-saving schemes."

The muscle along the edge of Jesse's jaw tightened. "Before or after Providence got sick?"

"It was after."

"What else?"

"Margaret and Wilks have also talked the staff into giving up a large portion of their salaries to help the school stay open. Hannah said this is also the reason that the students' meals . . . changed."

"Son of a bitch," Jesse hissed.

"What should we do?"

He toyed with her fingers, taking a long moment before he answered. "I don't want you doing anything." He lifted her hand to his lips and held it there. "I'll figure something out. In the meantime, just keep your pretty ears and eyes open."

Caught in his dark gaze, she felt her heart pound in a wild rhythm under her breast. Not wanting to leave, but afraid to stay, she slowly withdrew her hand, feeling an aching sense of loss when they no longer touched. "I'd better go."

"Why are you always running away from me?"

His question surprised her. She couldn't tell if he was

teasing or not. Either way, her answer was the same. *Because it's the safest thing to do. Because if I stayed I'd risk my heart.* "I don't know what would happen if I got caught talking with you. For some reason Wilks and Margaret are already acting suspicious of me. I'm afraid that someone might have seen us together last night."

"That's possible." Jesse nodded. "But please, stay just a little longer. There's someone I want you to meet." He turned away from the window and she heard him whisper. "*U ye, u ye.* Come here."

A young boy, no older than nine or ten, stepped beside Jesse, a puzzled frown on his face. Big dark eyes stared up at Kathleen as his teeth worried at his bottom lip.

"*Nihiŋciyapi śni yo,*" Jesse cajoled. "Don't be afraid."

He put his arm around the boy's thin shoulders and drew him closer. "Kathleen, this is *Tokalu Sapa.*"

A feather could have knocked her over, and for what seemed like an eternity she stared at the wide-eyed, dirty-faced boy. She could see little, if any, excess flesh on his gaunt body, but he stood tall and defiant. She looked back at Jesse and found a smile curving his mouth. "Oh, Jesse, this is so wonderful." Tears filled her eyes, happy tears that promised to spill onto her cheeks. "I'm going to cry."

"Don't do that, Katie-girl, I don't want it to become a habit and have you crying at every little thing." His smile became a wide grin. "But then, this isn't just a little thing, is it?" Jesse looked down at *Tokalu Sapa* and tousled the boy's hair.

"I'm so glad that you found him." Her gaze traveled back down to the boy, who would one day in the future become Jesse's great-uncle. "Does he know?"

Jesse shook his head. "How could I tell him without scaring him half to death. Us Lakotas may have a few different beliefs than you *wasicus*—we're more spiritual than religious—but I think telling him who I am would be difficult for even him to accept."

Kathleen saw the shadow of fear in the boy's eyes. "He's already that frightened, isn't he?" Her question had fled her lips before she could soften the words, and she watched their impact on Jesse. "I'm sorry, I shouldn't have—"

"No, you're right. You're right." Sobered, Jesse glanced down at *Tokalu Sapa*.

"And the others?" She stepped closer to the window. Placing her hand on the window ledge, she tried to peer inside.

"Two others. Lakotas. They're the same," Jesse answered with a flat, hollow sound to his voice. "Perhaps worse." He looked over her shoulder toward the woods, plainly battling his emotions. "An apple, Kathleen, a goddamn apple."

A covey of birds exploded from the trees behind the cold house. Kathleen gasped, then quickly glanced over her shoulder.

"You'd better go, Katie-girl." He took her hand from the window ledge and raised it to his lips again. "Please, be careful." He kissed her palm, then tightly closed her fingers, trapping the kiss in her grasp.

The turmoil caused by Jesse's simple gesture reminded her of the kiss they'd shared the night before. She watched his beautiful mouth lift in a smile. Was he thinking the same thing? *I hope so . . . oh, yes . . . I definitely hope so.*

In that instant she knew. She knew what all the songs were about, what all the romance novels were about, and what she had been dreaming about. *Is this what falling in love feels like?* "I'll be back, Jesse. I promise, I'll be back."

"I know you will."

# Chapter 18

If a prophet had come to our village and told us that things were to take place which have since come to pass, none of our people would have believed him.

—MA-KA-TAI-ME-SHE-KIA-KIAK
(BLACK HAWK), SAUK AND FOX

KATHLEEN SLIPPED BACK into the dormitory and quickly made her way to the upstairs linen closet hoping to find four blankets. If Blunt and Slocum never went inside the cold house, there was a good chance the blankets would never be found. Only three were in the closet, but the one on her bed would make four. She took a pillowcase. It would be perfect to carry the food.

Safe in her room, the door locked, Kathleen slid the blankets under her bed and then sat in the chair near the window. Making careful plans for her trip to the cold house was crucial. *I'll probably have to make a couple of trips to get everything to them. There is no one I can trust to help me, not even Hannah.*

She pulled her watch out of her purse. There was just enough time to put on the pretty hunter-green dress she'd worn for Jesse's film, fix her hair, and be at the Divines' apartment for tea by three o'clock. Although the green dress carried the threat of the dreaded corset, it was the one most appropriate for afternoon tea. If worse came to worst and it wouldn't fit without it, she would have to find one of the Indian girls, or Hannah, to help lace her into the blasted thing.

In less than fifteen minutes she'd freshened up, brushed

and fixed her hair, and it was now time to see if she could hold her breath long enough to get the bodice of the dress fastened. In moments she had her answer. One by one the buttons fastened without having to pull the fabric into place. Egypt had lied. She *could* wear the dress without the whale-boned torture chamber.

Each minute brought her closer and closer to meeting her great-great-grandfather. The flock of whirling butterflies that had lately taken up residence in her stomach seemed to grow in number and become more active. Her hands trembling and with her fingers almost useless, it took three tries before she was able to pin the cameo brooch at her throat. After peering in the small mirror on the wall to make sure that the brooch was straight, she stepped back, smoothed her hands down over her skirt, then nervously drew on her ivory lace gloves. "I guess I'm as ready as I'll ever be."

Leaving her room, she locked the door, then slipped the key into her small drawstring purse.

"Off to tea, are you?"

Startled, Kathleen whirled around and found Margaret Lester standing in a shadowed corner of the hallway. "Uh . . . yes, I am." What was the woman doing lurking in the hall? "I'm looking forward to meeting Reverend Divine and his family."

Margaret scanned Kathleen from head to toe, her gaze falling on the cameo brooch at Kathleen's throat. Stepping forward, she reached up and touched it with the tips of her fingers. "So lovely," she whispered. "Yes, very lovely." She looked up, her eyes meeting Kathleen's, then she quickly drew back. "I suppose you'll do." She eyed the brooch again as she turned toward the stairs. "Come along, I'll walk the way with you. Perhaps there are a few things you'd like to know about the Reverend and his wife before you meet them. I can answer all of your questions for you, and perhaps even give you some advice."

They descended the stairs in silence, their footfalls echoing in the stairwell. Stepping out onto the verandah, Kathleen glanced at Margaret Lester. Something about the woman set her on edge. Plain with dull brown hair, brown eyes that narrowed when she spoke, and a sallow complexion, Margaret Lester didn't seem to be the kind of woman who could attract a man like Josiah Wilks. What was it that drew them together? Something more, perhaps, than physical attraction? Something like a scheme to embezzle money from DuBois?

As they made their way along the promenade toward the Divines' apartment, Margaret Lester finally spoke. "Reverend Divine can be a very difficult man, Miss Prescott. He has been known to lead people on, making them think he is in agreement with their thoughts and plans and then showing his true colors later." Margaret Lester's voice tightened. "If you wish to stay on at DuBois, don't do or say anything that may give him cause to find fault with you." She paused for a moment. "Remember your place, Miss Prescott. You are, after all, just an employee."

*And just what are you, Margaret?* "Thank you, Miss Lester, I certainly appreciate your advice."

"As for the new Mrs. Divine, I'm sure you've noticed the horrid flaw on her face." Margaret Lester gave an indignant sniff. "She doesn't deserve him, you know . . . Reverend Divine, that is." She leaned closer to Kathleen. "She terrifies young Elijah; the child won't go near her. But that seems to matter little to her." She glanced about, then leaned even closer. "I've heard she has struck the child, punishing him severely when Prov . . . her husband is not around." She quickly lifted her hand to her mouth. "Oh, my, please excuse me, you must think I'm a terrible person, gossiping like this."

Kathleen heard little in Margaret Lester's voice that sounded like an apology. The disdainful lift of the woman's lip made her remorse all the more unbelievable.

Margaret stopped. "Well, here you are. I'm sure you'll do fine." Without another word she turned on her heel and left Kathleen standing alone in the middle of the promenade.

She hadn't missed the drops of venom in Margaret Lester's voice when she spoke of Rachel Divine. Kathleen frowned. *Perhaps Josiah Wilks was Margaret Lester's second choice and not her first.* She watched the woman disappear into the junior girls' dormitory. *Jealousy is a treacherous master.*

Kathleen climbed the stairs to the Divines' apartment on the top floor, the same apartment that she had lived in all of her life. It felt as though she was going home. How different would it look? Of course, the small television and radio she'd bought in the city at Sam's Club wouldn't be there, but most of the furniture had been passed down from generation to generation. Fresh coats of paint every few years, a new set of drapes, a more modern commode and bathtub, electricity, and kitchen appliances were the only changes that she knew of. Her pulse bounced and jumped with each step that took her up the stairs to Providence's apartment, her apartment.

In the hall landing she stood quietly for a moment before knocking. On the other side of the door were two generations of her family that had died many years before she'd been born. Her heart raced in another melee of rapid thuds. Would she be able to keep her wits about her? Would she be able to comport herself as a genteel Victorian lady? She smiled. *Of course I can, it's what I've been raised to be all my life.*

She raised her hand to knock, then dropped it back to her side. Scolding herself for her cowardice, she drew a stabilizing breath, lifted her hand, and rapped on the oak door. Her breath caught in her throat as the knob turned and the door slowly opened.

"Welcome, Miss Prescott, how good of you to come." Rachel Divine greeted her with a warm smile, then stepped back and allowed Kathleen to enter. "My husband and I have been looking forward to meeting our new English teacher."

"Thank you for the invitation and for the opportunity to meet you both."

Following Rachel Divine into the sitting parlor, Kathleen was immediately struck by its familiarity. Her chest tightened with an unusual emotion. *I'm homesick. I'm standing in my own living room, and I'm homesick.* Though newer and the colors brighter, the tables, the chairs, the two settees, even the carpet beneath her feet were the same.

"Ah, Miss Prescott, come in, come in." Sitting in the high-backed chair near the window, Providence Divine raised his hand and beckoned to Kathleen. "Come, sit here beside me." He gestured toward the chair beside his own. "It is very ungentlemanly of me, but please forgive me if I don't rise to greet you. I've . . . not been feeling well." Pulling a handkerchief from his pocket, he dabbed at the sheen of sweat on his forehead and cheeks.

"I fully understand, sir. No apology needed. I hope you are now on the mend." Afraid she would be completely tongue-tied, Kathleen was pleased that a coherent phrase or two had slipped through her lips.

"Sit, sit, my dear. Let's get to know each other." He glanced at his wife, his smile filled with warmth. "I think we're ready for our tea, my dear." He turned toward Kathleen, shifting stiffly as though it pained him to move, and smiled. "My wife makes the very best tea and biscuits." Looking to the opposite corner of the room, Reverend Divine nodded. "Elijah."

For the first time since she had arrived, Kathleen noticed the boy, Elijah, sitting quietly in the corner. With a visible sigh, he slowly slid off the chair and made his way across the room to stand in front of his father.

"Elijah, please say hello to our guest." Providence leaned forward and gently drew the boy closer. "Miss Prescott, this is my son, Elijah."

Kathleen glanced at her great-great-grandfather and saw the worried frown on the man's face. Turning back to the boy, she extended her hand. "Hello, Elijah. I am so very pleased to meet you." The boy hesitated for a moment before he slid his small hand into hers. "Miss Briggs tells me that you are an excellent penman and that you also like to draw."

"Yes, ma'am." He withdrew his hand and kept his head down, not meeting Kathleen's gaze.

"I like to draw, too, pictures of birds and flowers." Still no spark of interest. "What do you like to draw?"

He continued to keep his eyes down. "Animals, ma'am. I draw animals."

"Such as horses and deer?"

"Yes, ma'am."

"Elijah, did you know that there is a doe and her fawn that sometimes, very early in the morning, nibble their breakfast on the parade ground?" For the first time his eyes lifted and Kathleen saw interest. Smoky-gray eyes, her eyes. "You could probably see them if you were up early enough and watched from your window. But you mustn't make any noise to frighten them."

His gaze fell again. "Yes, ma'am." He shifted, taking one small sideways step after another until he stood in front of his father once again. He lifted his head and looked at his father.

Kathleen saw Elijah's silent plea.

"Yes, son, you may go. Mind now, stay out of the woods."

Elijah bolted through the door like a terrified rabbit, and Kathleen could hear his boots landing on each stair as he ran down to the first floor and out onto the porch.

Providence turned to Kathleen, and she saw the sadness in his eyes. "Please forgive my son. He is very shy."

Kathleen wasn't sure what to say. She couldn't tell him that Elijah would grow up to graduate at the top of his class from Indiana University, that he would marry a young woman from Peru, Indiana, and that they would have a son, Jacob. She could only offer a simple reply. "He seems to be a sensitive child."

"He doesn't make friends easily. I'm afraid he's still not over his mother's passing." Providence looked up. "Ah, here's our tea." Perspiration coated his forehead and upper lip again, and with trembling hands, he lifted his handkerchief to his face.

Sitting primly with her hands folded in her lap, Kathleen noticed the looks and subtle touches that took place between Providence and his wife as Rachel set the tea tray down on the table. There was warm and genuine affection between the two.

The complexion on the right side of Rachel Divine's face was flawless which made the large birthmark on the left all the more startling. It was obvious, though, that Providence no longer saw the blemish, he saw only the woman he loved.

"Cream, sugar, lemon, Miss Prescott?" Rachel Divine asked.

"Just cream, please," Kathleen said, then accepted the fragile cup and saucer. She took a sweet biscuit off of the offered plate. "Thank you."

The pleasantries continued for a half hour with comments on the weather, the beautiful blooms on the honeysuckle bushes, and the budding flowers in the beds around the buildings.

"I understand that you are from northern Ohio," Rachel Divine said. "I have relatives near Cleveland."

Kathleen's pulse raced at a furious pace. Lies, lies, and more lies. "Yes, my family is from just outside of Akron." *If you can call Pritchart, Indiana, just outside of Akron, Ohio.*

"Mr. Wilks tells me that you were acquainted with Mrs. Delia Shore and that she suggested you take her position at DuBois."

Again her heart tripped and plummeted. "Just barely acquainted, sir. And yes, I learned about the opening from her."

Providence Divine silently nodded. "Well, I'm most pleased that you took her advice. I am also pleased with the progress I hear you've made with the children in just a short while. You have very quickly become one of their favorites." He frowned as he studied her face. "You look familiar to me, Miss Prescott. Do we know each other? Have we, perhaps, met before?"

It took every ounce of strength that Kathleen possessed to keep her seat and not tip her cup. "I am certain that we have not, Reverend," she replied, quickly placing the teacup on the table so she wouldn't drop it on the floor.

"The moment I saw her at the door, my dear, she reminded me a great deal of your mother," Rachel Divine said, looking at Kathleen over the rim of her cup.

Providence nodded. "Ah, that must be it." He looked at Kathleen for another long moment. "Yes, of course, I see it now. You're absolutely right. You have my mother's coloring, her eyes and hair, and the shape of your face is quite like hers."

Kathleen thought her nerves would snap under his close inspection.

"Miss Lester also told us that your luggage was lost and never found." His smile was slight, but the look in his eyes proved his concern. "I did approve Mr. Wilks advancing you a month's salary, but if there is anything, anything that you need, please don't hesitate to ask either my wife or me. Our staff is like family to us."

"Thank you, that is most kind of you . . . both." *Ha! So, eight dollars is a month's salary, is it? There is another clue to Josiah Wilks's guilt.* Quick on the coattails of that thought came another. *And I bet Margaret Lester willingly posted Wilks's deceit in the ledgers.*

After adding some more sugar to his tea, Providence lifted the cup to his mouth. Before he was able to take a sip, his hand began to shake. Rachel quickly left her chair and took the cup from him. "Here, let me refill that for you, dearest."

*She loves him.* Kathleen watched Rachel ignore her husband's tremors and pretend that all he needed was more tea. She loves him enough that it pains her to let anyone see his weakness.

"Do you have any questions that you would like to ask about DuBois?" Providence ignored the fresh cup of tea that Rachel had placed on the table beside him. "Perhaps you have questions about the school's purpose, regulations that I've found necessary, or the like?"

Providence had opened the door, but Kathleen hesitated. To pose the questions she really wanted to ask—about the cold house, and Wilks, and the food—during their first meeting might jeopardize any chance she had of helping Jesse and the boys. But there were a few questions she could ask.

"Will Elijah be joining my class?"

"He's a tender child, Miss Prescott, full of daydreams. It would take a gentle hand to draw him out."

"Sometimes a teacher who considers a child's special needs can produce wonders. She can supervise new friendships until they are solid and provide the right team projects to allow a shy child to learn, to open up and enjoy children his own age." She paused and tried to determine how well Providence was accepting her idea. Finding nothing to discourage her, she continued. "I also think it would be beneficial for the Indian children to see that you entrust your son to the same education they are receiving. It would give them confidence and trust." *There. I've planted the seed. No, I've planted a whole garden.*

Complete silence filled the room, growing until Kathleen thought it would suffocate her. She glanced from Providence to his wife and then back again.

"He did have a couple of friends among the Lakota boys, but I didn't see any of them yesterday when I arrived home." He paused and looked at his wife.

Kathleen saw the slight nod he gave Rachel and her reply.

"I believe you're right, Miss Prescott. My wife and I like your idea very much." Providence smiled. "He has been working with Miss Briggs and Miss Lester, here in the parlor, but I believe that beginning tomorrow morning you will have a new student in your classroom."

His smile opened his face, and a younger, handsome man emerged, and Kathleen knew she had just seen the true Providence Divine.

A deep sigh fled Providence's lips, and he shrank back into his chair. "Miss Prescott, again I must beg your forgiveness. I've become very tired. You're welcome to stay and chat for a while with Mrs. Divine, but I must retire."

"I fully understand," Kathleen replied. A glance at Rachel told Kathleen that the woman would rather care for her husband than make parlor talk. She rose from her chair. "Thank you for the lovely afternoon and your hospitality, but I must be going."

"I'll see you out, Miss Prescott." Rachel stood and followed Kathleen to the door. With the door half open, Rachel laid her hand on Kathleen's arm. "Miss Prescott, if I may be so forward, I believe you are a very perceptive person."

Kathleen couldn't dispell the touch of apprehension and

steeled herself for whatever Rachel Divine's next words
might bring.

"My husband has been very ill for a couple of months,
but this school is his life's calling. Perhaps you've noticed
that he tends to make some very strange choices in his staff,
choices based on sympathies and kind-heartedness."

Rachel Divine smiled and Kathleen knew that whatever
those choices were, the woman thoroughly approved of
them.

"You might say that he collects lost souls. Our sewing
teacher doesn't like needlework, the carpentry teacher is
rather inept with tools." Rachel's smile broke into a
chuckle. "The penmanship teacher is lacking in spelling
skills, the gentleman in charge of the print shop is half
blind. Mrs. Gilbert is a convi . . ." Rachel Divine's face immediately lost its smile, a look of alarm taking its place.
Her complexion blanched, causing the birthmark on her
face to appear bloodred. "I . . . uh . . . I believe you understand what I'm saying. Lost souls." Her hand trembled and
she quickly removed it from Kathleen's arm.

Two weeks ago Kathleen had been positive that she
knew everything there was to know about DuBois. Today,
nothing was familiar, nothing made sense. She had so many
questions to ask, but who could she ask? Who could she
trust? Certainly not Wilks, but what about Hannah, or Basil,
or even Gustav Felder? What about Rachel? What about
her own great-great-grandfather?

Solidly, almost defiantly, meeting Kathleen's gaze,
Rachel Divine spoke again. "You, I believe, are one of the
few exceptions. You appear to be a fine, solid young lady,
and I thank you for suggesting that Elijah join the other
children. I think it is something the boy really wants and
something that will be very good for him."

Plucking a kernel of courage from her reserves, Kathleen decided not to leave without asking one last question.
"Do you know the names of the Lakota boys that were his
friends? I'll try to find them and let them know Elijah is
back home."

"I don't remember all of them, but there was one boy,

Elijah's favorite, they called him Adam . . . Adam Black Fox."

Kathleen had been expecting that answer, but it still took her breath away when she heard Rachel say the name.

"Please tell Elijah that I will find his friends for him."

Rachel opened the door and stepped out into the hall with Kathleen. Their quiet talk was over.

"Thank you again for your hospitality, Mrs. Divine. I enjoyed our conversation very much."

"It was our pleasure, Miss Prescott." She began to return to the apartment, then paused. When she turned, a chilling, hard expression had settled on her face. "Another word, Miss Prescott." Rachel Divine lowered her voice to a whisper. "Be careful, be very careful."

# Chapter 19

... not a word of Indian is heard from our boys after six
months.

—REVEREND MR. WILSON,
NINETEENTH-CENTURY COMMENTATOR

DINNER TOOK FOREVER, and being seated next to
Josiah Wilks ranked as the second worst torture that Kathleen had ever endured. The hellish corset was a solid third.
But trying to make conversation while her mind raced with
plans for her midnight trek back to the cold house won first
place, hands down.

Wilks insisted on grilling her about her visit with Providence and Rachel.

"And what did you and Reverend Divine talk about?"
Wilks asked around a mouthful of roast beef.

Determined not to satisfy his curiosity, Kathleen side-
stepped his question. "We had a lovely conversation. He is
such an endearing man."

"Did you talk about anything specific?" Wilks persisted.

"Such as, Mr. Wilks?" She took a sip of coffee.

"Did you talk about his health? Did he happen to say if
he is recovering?"

Kathleen stabbed a few green beans with her fork. "No."
She popped the beans into her mouth. "We didn't speak
about it, but he looked quite rested." She could see by
Wilks's reaction that she hadn't given him the answer he'd
been looking for.

"Well, then, did he happen to say when he might retire?"

"No." She casually shook her head. "He definitely didn't say anything about that."

"Uh . . . well, did he happen to mention how much he relies on my help to run DuBois and what an excellent job I'm doing?"

She waited a moment before answering, hoping she looked as though she were trying to remember. Wilks sat forward, eager for her answer. Kathleen shrugged. "We spoke of so many things, Mr. Wilks, I can't remember each word." She paused for no longer than an infuriating moment. "No, I don't believe he mentioned you at all." She watched Wilks's puffed-up chest deflate. "I especially enjoyed discussing my ideas with him for some changes to the curriculum, though."

"You did *what?*" Wilks sputtered.

Battling to keep an innocent expression on her face, Kathleen slowly and deliberately placed her knife and fork on the side of her plate. "I plan to meet with him again soon." It wasn't a complete lie; she did plan to talk with Providence again, and yes, soon.

"I'd certainly be interested in hearing your ideas," Wilks wheedled. "Perhaps you'd care to share them with me, and I could help you with your presentation to Reverend Divine."

"How gracious of you," Kathleen replied, offering Josiah Wilks a smile that went flat. "But no, thank you." She rose from the table. "Now, if you'll excuse me, I've had such a busy day. I believe I'll retire early. Good evening, everyone."

Leaving the table, Kathleen wondered when she'd begun to change. She'd never toyed with people before. She glanced back at Wilks and found his face brightly flushed, a hard line to his mouth. She'd made an enemy, or riled one that she already had.

But there was no time to worry about that. Tonight there were other more important matters. She had to put her plan to help Jesse and the boys in motion.

She needed to find out where Mrs. Gilbert kept all the food so she wouldn't have to search later in the dark. Instead of leaving the dining hall, she slipped into the kitchen. Thanking the cook for the delicious meal provided the excuse.

Making friendly chatter, Kathleen watched as Mrs. Gilbert's two helpers put away the leftovers and tidied the kitchen. In minutes she knew where the wintered apples were kept. She knew which bin held potatoes, and discovered plenty of canned vegetables in the pantry. A wooden box on the table in the center of the kitchen held the loaves of bread. Kathleen watched Mrs. Gilbert put the leftover roast beef and vegetables from the teachers' table into the large, double-sided icebox in the corner near the back door. There were more than enough leftovers to make an excellent meal for Jesse and the boys.

After saying good night, Kathleen waited in the shadows at the back door until no one was watching. She quickly withdrew a small folded piece of paper from her pocket and slid it into the lock. With luck, it would keep the lock from catching, and she'd be able to get back into the kitchen after midnight.

Back in her room Kathleen took her watch out of her purse. Seven-fifteen. Twelve o'clock seemed to be a lifetime away.

At nine the lights-out bell rang for the students. Three hours remained. As midnight neared, her uneasiness grew. With an anxious sigh she sat in the chair near her window and tried to read another chapter or two of Jane Austen's *Pride and Prejudice* but found herself checking her watch over and over again. Rachel Divine's words kept niggling at her, elbowing their way into her thoughts as well. *"Be careful, be very careful." What was she warning me about?* Kathleen tipped her head back against the chair and closed her eyes. *Maybe I should rephrase that to* whom *was she warning me about.*

At ten-thirty Kathleen shut off the gas lamp and sat in the dark by the window and waited.

Midnight. The dorm had been quiet for hours. Time to go.

Standing at her bedroom window, she peered out to make certain that no one was outside and would hear or see her. Satisfied, she dropped the pillowcase and then the blankets, one by one, to the ground below. It would be safer to retrieve them once she was downstairs than get caught in the hallway with the bedding in her arms.

Kathleen nervously smoothed her hand over the skirt of her gown. She had thought about changing into one of her other dresses, the blue one or maybe the peach, but only the dark green gown she'd worn in Jesse's film would blend into the night and underbrush and help keep her safe if she had to hide. One thing worried her, though, about wearing the dress and putting it in jeopardy. What if she needed it, with no alterations and no damage, to travel back to her own time? Wasn't that the reason she had saved Jesse's clothes and his braids from being burned?

She stood at her bedroom door and listened. Quiet. She slipped into the hall and closed her door. With one hand over the lock to muffle any sound the tumblers might make, she turned the key and then dropped it into her pocket.

At the top of the staircase she paused and listened one last time. Still quiet. *It seems I have a talent for sneaking about.*

In the lower hall Kathleen stayed in the shadows close to the wall and slipped out the back door. It would be safer to retrieve the blankets by going around the building under cover of the bushes than to walk out onto the front porch to get them.

After gathering the blankets under her arm, Kathleen retraced her steps through the shadows to the back of the building and hastily made her way to the school's kitchen in the dining hall. The building was in total darkness. She placed the blankets under a bush and, taking the pillowcase, silently climbed the stairs to the kitchen door. With a twist of the knob and a little push, the door swung open. Elated, Kathleen slipped inside.

The moonlight shining through the kitchen window offered enough light for her to see without worrying about a candle or a lantern. Stepping into the middle of the room, she came to a sudden stop. On the table in the middle of the room, a collection of food covered the surface. *That's odd. I watched Mrs. Gilbert put all these things away.* Two loaves of bread, half a dozen apples, two canning jars of beans, and potatoes sat on the worktable. Two packages wrapped in waxed butcher paper lay beside them. Kathleen unwrapped the corner of one package. Roast beef.

Why was everything set out on the table as though waiting for someone? Who? Why? Suddenly uneasy, the hairs on the back of her neck rising, Kathleen quickly glanced around the kitchen.

"Don't be alarmed, Miss Prescott, it's just me."

Kathleen gasped, then spun around at the sound of Mrs. Gilbert's voice.

"Oh, honey, don't you get all worried none." Mrs. Gilbert stepped out of the dark corner. "When I had trouble locking the door tonight and found that piece of paper you'd jammed up inside, well, I just kinda figured out what you was up to." She took a couple of jars of milk out of the icebox and wrapped them in a towel. "Don't want these to break or clank together," Mrs. Gilbert said, setting the wrapped jars on the table. "I've tried a couple of times to slip some extra victuals in the pail that Mr. Blunt takes to those poor darlings, but he or Mr. Wilks always took the extras out and fed 'em to the dogs."

"I don't know what to say," Kathleen whispered, emotion robbing her voice of its strength. "Thank you."

"No need for any thanks, miss." Mrs. Gilbert hugged Kathleen. "Starvin' them babies just ain't right. And now there's that big fella out there with them." Mrs. Gilbert pointed to the pillowcase Kathleen held in her hand. "Let me give you one of them flour sacks. It's stronger and it won't matter if somethin' leaks." Mrs. Gilbert retrieved a sack from the pile in the corner of the kitchen. "I suppose you're wonderin' why I didn't sneak food out to them boys myself." She paused, placing the sack on the table. "I tried once, a bit over a week ago, and got caught. Mr. Wilks said he'd forgive me just one time 'cause he liked my cookin', but if I did it again, I'd lose my job." She stared for a moment at Kathleen, a worried frown deeply creasing her brow. "I can't lose my job, I got a sickly husband and—"

"Don't worry, I understand. I won't tell anyone that you helped me." Kathleen gently patted Mrs. Gilbert's arm, but her determination to learn more about the cold house persisted. "Are students often put in that place?"

"Lately there ain't been a week go by that some ain't put out there. 'Bout a week ago one of them little ones died in that awful place." Mrs. Gilbert sniffled and wiped her nose with the corner of her apron. "Mr. Wilks said it weren't so, but I seen 'em—Mr. Wilks, Slocum, and Blunt. They was puttin' that youngun in the cemetery." She glanced at Kathleen. "I seen it myself." She released a ragged breath. "I bet it weren't the first time something like that happened, either. . . . I just bet."

Dismay rose up in Kathleen, bringing with it a bitter taste that filled her mouth. "What about the police? You did tell the police, didn't you?"

Mrs. Gilbert couldn't meet Kathleen's eyes. "I . . . um . . . it weren't somethin' I could do."

Mrs. Gilbert's answer didn't make any sense . . . unless, of course, the police would also mean trouble for Mrs. Gilbert. Rachel Divine's unfinished sentence now made sense. One of Providence Divine's lost souls was, indeed, running from the law.

"Telling the sheriff might cause a whole lot of trouble and heartache."

What could bring more trouble and heartache than the death of a child and the mother who would never see him again? An ache filled Kathleen's heart to the brim. For years she'd denied that anything like this had ever happened at DuBois—and for years she had been so very wrong. *I can't believe Providence is to blame. I won't believe it.*

"I've got to get home, miss. My mister gets worried if I'm too late."

"Thank you again, Mrs. Gilbert."

They quickly loaded the sack, testing its weight and strength with each item added.

"Can you manage that?" Mrs. Gilbert asked. "You're such a tiny thing."

Kathleen lifted the sack off the table, staggered under the weight, and then shifted it onto her shoulder. "I think . . . uh . . . I can manage, but I'll have to come back for the blankets."

"No, you won't, honey. I'll carry 'em for you as far as where the path heads off the lane. Mr. Gilbert and me live in one of the little houses off the north pasture. That lane's on my way home."

KATHLEEN WATCHED MRS. Gilbert disappear into the night and suddenly felt alone and abandoned. She hid the blankets under a dogwood and hoisted the sack of food onto her shoulder. Staggering up the lane, grunting a few times from the weight of the sack, she knew she must be making enough noise to be heard four counties away. Unless she took half of the things out of the sack and made more than one trip, this was the only way to get the food to Jesse and the boys.

Stopping at the edge of the clearing to catch her breath, she lowered the sack to the ground and stared at the cold house. In the dark it looked even more evil. How many ghosts haunted this place? How many children had suffered here? How many had died in the belly of the beast? Kathleen couldn't stop shaking.

Sweat dampened her forehead and beaded on her upper lip. A trickle ran down her back and another slipped between her breasts. After drawing a deep, shuddering breath, she hoisted the burlap bag to her shoulder and staggered to the window.

"Jesse." She lowered the sack to the ground and leaned closer to the window. "Jesse, are you asleep?"

"No, Katie-girl, I'm wide awake. I think everyone else in Indiana is, too. You could have shouted, that noise wasn't in your repertoire."

"I'm not a pack mule, so don't get all fussy with me, Jesse Spotted Horse," Kathleen snapped.

"Aw, Katie-girl, I'm sorry, I didn't mean to bruise your feelings."

He stepped out of the shadows and Kathleen's heart did a perfect flip, a definite ten-pointer. Although no longer naked, the wrinkled shirt covered his chest and arms. And

that marvelous grin was back. Night shadows played about
his face, and it looked as though he still had his beautiful
long hair. Dumbstruck, Kathleen couldn't move. What wiz-
ardry did this man possess that could make her forget every
sense of propriety she'd ever been taught?

She reluctantly dragged her attention away. Struggling,
she finally succeeded in lifting the food to the window.
Careful not to knock the two supports that held the shutter
up, she braced the sack on the edge of the sill. In moments
she began passing the food, item by item, through the bars.
As Jesse handed them off to the boys, Kathleen heard the
rustle of the butcher paper as they discovered the roast beef
and the clank of the glass jars of milk. "I brought some
blankets, too, but I had to leave them back on the path."
She looked up and found his eyes watching her. "I couldn't
carry everything in one trip."

"You're amazing, do you know that? Absolutely amazing."

She had heard the expression once or twice, but now she
knew what everyone meant when they talked about their
hearts melting. Hers had just melted into a puddle of hopes
and dreams.

Jesse reached through the bars and lightly touched her
cheek with his knuckles. She leaned into his caress, unable
to draw her gaze away from his. His fingers cupped her
cheek, then curved around the back of her neck. He gently
drew her closer.

Kathleen knew he was going to kiss her. Her breath
caught in her throat, and she tried to brace herself for the
touch of his lips. Too quickly she discovered that fortifying
herself against Jesse's touch was impossible.

She felt the press of the cold iron bar on her cheek as his
mouth captured hers, but with a sigh Kathleen closed her
eyes and forgot it was there. Remembering the delicious
lessons he'd taught her the night before, she angled her
mouth against his and lost herself to the fiery tendrils of
heat that uncoiled and licked their way through her body.

The stone wall that separated them seemed to melt away
as she slid her hands up his arms and moved deeper into his
kiss. Hungry for him, she welcomed and met the thrusts of

his tongue. A need, unfamiliar, demanding, flared and burned hot, and Kathleen fell deeper and deeper into the fire of temptation. One by one her mother's words—be a good girl, don't allow a man to take liberties, they'll only use you for their gain, keep yourself pure—fell into that fire and burned to ash.

It was the boys' giggles that finally drilled into her conscience and brought her crashing back to reality.

Breathless, embarrassed, Kathleen stepped away from the window and Jesse's touch. Her hand immediately rose to her throat, and she drew her trembling fingers over the buttons on her high collar. Some things didn't change. She took another step back. Perhaps even more distance would clear her head. "I'll . . . uh . . . be back in a minute." Without a backward glance, she pivoted, picked up her long skirt, and ran back down the path.

"*Katie-girl, why are you always running away from me?*" Jesse's words knifed through her mind. Her heart beat wildly under her breast, and her lips tingled from his kiss. Why, indeed?

She slowed her pace and cautiously approached the junction where the narrow path met the lane. Standing in the shadows of a huge sycamore, she drew her arms around herself and tried to understand what was happening to her. Little more than a breath, a silent, cynical laugh escaped her lips. What her heart was beginning to learn, her head was unwilling to accept. *Kathleen Prescott, you know very well that dreams and wishes made upon the first night star don't come true . . . and especially not for you.*

Determined to deny any fantasies she might have about Jesse Spotted Horse, Kathleen steeled her emotions, pulled the blankets out from under the bush, and made her way back to the cold house.

As she passed the blankets to Jesse, another face appeared at the window. *Tokalu Sapa.* And then another and another.

Jesse touched one of the boys on the shoulder. "Kathleen, this is *Ca'pa Hoksila*, Beaver Boy. His DuBois name is Isaac." He drew the second boy forward. "This is *Hitu'η kaasan*, Weasel. His school name is Luke, but he likes Weasel better." Jesse smiled warmly at the children, then stepped behind them and rested his hands affectionately on *Tokalu Sapa's* shoulders. "Okay, guys, go on. Do it just like we practiced."

Together, the boys shyly whispered their words. *"Lila pilyama.* Thank you, Miss Prescott, for food. Good blankets." In the next moment two were gone, quickly disappearing back into the dark interior of the cold house. *Tokalu Sapa* stayed for a moment, then joined the other boys.

"He likes you a great deal," she said.

"We've become quite close." Jesse grinned. "Almost like family." Folding his arms over his chest, Jesse pointed to the boys with a lift of his chin and grinned. "So, how do you like my tribe?"

"I've never seen a whole tribe before." She tried to keep her voice light, but she had trouble meeting his gaze.

"And I don't think they've ever seen an angel before."

His voice had been soft, husky. Impassioned? Kathleen's heart took a wild bounce, and she felt a hot blush climb her cheeks. Thank God he couldn't see its bright color in the dark. "Jesse, I'm far from being an angel."

A grin spread on Jesse's face. He leaned close to the window, reached out, and brushed her mouth with the tips of his fingers. "Can I count on that, Katie-girl?"

Kathleen gasped and stepped back. No one had ever teased her with innuendos before. With every moment she spent with him, her staid life disappeared more and more. It was like a blooming, a becoming. It was the discovery of a new Kathleen Divine Prescott. And she liked it.

Kathleen glanced up at the sky. The moon had traveled across the clearing and was now disappearing behind the trees on the west side. "It's getting late," she said, moving back to the window.

"Yeah, I know. You need to go."

"One more thing," she said, turning to *Tokalu Sapa,* who had returned to Jesse's side. "Are you the one they call Adam, Adam Black Fox?"

The boy shyly nodded.

"Your friend, Elijah, misses you, all of you." She watched Adam's eyes quickly fill with fear. She shook her head. "Don't worry. His father knows you are friends and approves."

"What are you talking about, Kathleen?"

"It seems that Elijah and Adam are best pals." She watched the boy nod. "Reverend Divine would like that friendship to continue."

"And how do you suppose that can happen?" Jesse smacked the window bars with the flat of his hand. "We might be losing a lot of weight on our new DuBois diet, but none of us can squeeze through these yet."

"I'm going to get you all out of here. First thing tomorrow morning I'm going to talk with Providence." She banded her arms across her chest. "Elijah and these boys are playmates, and I'm going to see that they remain that way."

"And what if you go to Providence and find out he is the one who ordered that these boys be locked up?" Jesse argued. "What if you're going to the sinner to complain about the sin?"

"I don't believe for an instant that Providence knows where these boys are, but he will by ten o'clock tomorrow morning."

"Kathleen, no. Don't." He drove his fingers through his hair, then rubbed the back of his neck. "Don't talk to him. Wait until we know for sure if he can be trusted."

"Wait?" She glanced at the boys. "How can you suggest such a thing?"

"Right now you're the only one in Pritchart that I trust, and all you have to go on is hearsay and things that were written in a journal." He leaned closer to Kathleen. "If you can bring us a little food each night, we'll be okay for a few days. I know it'll be risky for you, but going to Providence right now would be much worse." He reached his hand out to her through the bars, and she took it. "Promise me, slow and easy until you find out who we can trust."

"Jesse, I can't walk away each night and leave you all here."

"You can, and you've got to. You need to know the whole truth, too."

# Chapter 20

In its infancy, the shaping was meant to transform American Indian children into carbon copies of their so-called civilized American brothers and sisters. As the experiment progressed, that purpose shifted to one of "influence" rather than transformation.

—FRANCIS LEUPP,
U.S. INDIAN COMMISSIONER, 1904

THE SOUND, RUSTY metal scraping against rusty metal, bored like an auger into Jesse's head. Startled, his reflexes propelled him away from where he sat against the wall. He found himself on his hands and knees in the middle of the cold house, staring at the door. He shook the cobwebs from his head. *Damn, I must have dozed off.* The bitter bite of adrenaline filled his mouth and burned along every thread of muscle in his body.

If there had been a warning, the sound of voices or footsteps, he hadn't heard it. He'd heard just the scrape of the key going into the lock, the *click, click, click* of the tumblers dropping.

"*He ŋayha'un he*?" Adam whispered, squatting beside Jesse. "Do you hear?" His fingers dug into Jesse's arm.

"Yeah."

Weasel scurried close, dragging his blanket with him. "*He tu'we he?*"

Jesse lightly placed his hand on the boy's trembling shoulder. "I don't know who it is." Kathleen had promised she wouldn't talk to Providence for a few days. Damn, he wished she'd waited longer.

Isaac scooted between the other two boys, his teeth chattering, his breath ragged and shallow. "*Tu'wa u.*"

A dull thud, the sound of someone pushing their shoulder against the door, sent Weasel and Isaac hurrying back to their corner. Another thud, a creak of wood, and the door burst open. Sunlight exploded into the cold house.

Two men, silhouetted against the bright light, stood framed in the doorway.

Cecil Blunt stepped inside, then reeled back a step or two. "Goddam, it stinks in here!" He covered his mouth with one hand and moved back into the dark building. He drove his knee into Jesse's shoulder. "Stand up, you red bastard." Reaching down, he grasped Jesse by the hair. "I said *up.*"

"*Ayustan yo!*" Adam threw himself at Blunt. "Leave him!" He pounded his fists on Blunt's arm, trying to break the man's hold on Jesse.

"Feisty little bugger, ain'tcha." The back of Blunt's hand struck Adam across the chest and sent him reeling into the stone wall.

Jesse pushed himself up from the floor, but Blunt's knee knocked him down once again.

"I ain't gonna take no shit from no Injun, big or little," Blunt spat, yanking Jesse to his feet.

"What do you wanna do with the little rats?" Slocum asked, peering into the darkness, his thumb and index finger pinching his nose closed.

"I'm gonna lock 'em up again for now. We'll find out what to do with 'em later." Blunt pushed Jesse out of the cold house. "Hang on to him, I wanna see what all they got in here."

Blunt's shove sent Jesse sprawling. Squinting against the sunlight, he threw his hands out to break his fall but still landed on his bruised ribs, his face pressed into the long grass. Pain knifed through his body. He could only take shallow breaths. He knew that Slocum and Blunt would beat him senseless if he fought them, and then they'd hurt the boys.

Jesse listened to Blunt rooting around in the cold house and knew he'd find everything that Kathleen had brought.

Barely lifting his head from the ground, he watched as one blanket after the other was tossed out the cold-house door. Next came the leftover food the boys had rationed for breakfasts and lunches, and finally the empty flour sacks joined the pile.

"Just like I thought," Blunt crowed. "I told ya so. I saw that damned shutter propped up the other night and knew we hadn't left it like that. I figured somebody'd been out here bringin' 'em stuff. Wilks figured the same."

Jesse cursed himself. *Damn, I should have dropped the shutter. Even though the boys didn't like the dark, I should've dropped it.*

Blunt turned back to the cold house. "Get back in there, you filthy nits." Pushing the three boys farther back in the building, he closed and locked the door. He turned and glowered at Jesse. "Yup, I'm gonna have a good time makin' the big chief here tell me who was bringin' 'em food."

"You said you knew." Slocum kneeled down and tied Jesse's hands behind his back with a piece of rope he'd pulled from his pocket. "Wilks caught old lady Gilbert doing it before." He grunted, pushing himself to his feet. "Maybe it's her again?"

"Naw, that old biddy's got too much to lose. She don't want no one callin' the law." Blunt scratched his whiskered chin. "Nope, I'm thinkin' it's somebody who showed up recent, somebody who's getting' herself quite a reputation for bein' real agreeable when it comes to these redskins." With a coarse-sounding laugh, Blunt cupped and pumped his crotch with his hand. "I'd sure like to find out just how . . . agreeable she can be."

Slocum's laughter joined Blunt's and then he sobered. His eyes wide, he pointed down at Jesse. "Aw, gawd, Cecil, you don't think that he and she . . ."

The expression on Blunt's face turned stone cold. "I wouldn't even want my spit to touch a woman who'd diddled an Injun." He looked down at Jesse. "Naw, she'll do her saintly work, but she ain't no whore." He laughed and touched himself again. "Not yet."

Anger boiled up from Jesse's gut. He pulled against the

bindings on his wrists, but they didn't ease up at all. If either of these bastards touched Kathleen, he'd gladly kill them. Hell, he'd kill them twice if it was possible.

"Get up, you son of a bitch." Blunt grabbed Jesse's arm and pulled him to his feet. "I've got some questions fer ya."

Fighting a sharp new wave of pain, he watched Blunt from beneath lowered lids. *Looks like I'm in for another one of their "goddamn lessons."*

"What makes you think he's gonna understand a word you say?"

Blunt glanced over his shoulder at Nate Slocum. "Oh, I think this bastard knows more'n he lets on."

Slocum shrugged. "Do ya think maybe he knew how to speak English before he come here, or maybe that pretty Miss Prescott taught him?"

"In a week and some?" Blunt's laugh grew and he poked Jesse in the stomach with the cold-house key. "Yeah, this Injun's a real genius."

Slocum's laugh sounded like a braying donkey. "Yeah, maybe he's been gettin' private lessons." He grabbed at his pants as Blunt had done moments before.

"Aw, shut up, Nate. I told you, that's disgusting." Blunt's eyes narrowed as he gave Jesse another poke in his ribs. "You gonna talk? Who brung ya the food and stuff?" He bent over, picked up one of the blankets, and shoved it in Jesse's face. "Where'd ya get it?"

Jesse looked down at Blunt as though he were looking at a gnat, and then turned away.

"Now, Chief, that ain't no way to be. I asked ya nice, but if'n you don't answer, I'm gonna get pissed, and you don't wanna get me pissed." Blunt pushed the blanket at Jesse again. "Answer me."

"He ain't gonna talk, Cecil. I told ya, he don't understand ya."

"Maybe he'll understand this."

Jesse saw Blunt pull back, and he knew the punch was coming. He tried to turn away, but Slocum held him from behind. As Blunt's fist drove into Jesse's stomach, he doubled over, battling a wave of nausea and gasping for breath. Every instinct goaded him to fight back, to beat Cecil Blunt

within an inch of death. His teeth bit into his bottom lip as
he drove his rage back down into his gut. *Not today. Today
you've got to play the game, Horse. Not today . . . but
someday.*

Red in the face, veins popping on his forehead, Blunt
grabbed Jesse's shirt, pulled him upright, and hit him again.
"You ready to talk yet?"

"He ain't gonna talk, Cecil."

"Maybe he needs a little more urging. Get me one of
them boys."

Ice water rushed and tumbled through Jesse's veins.
He'd take twenty beatings before he'd let them hurt the
boys. He pulled at the ropes on his wrist, trying to free his
hands, trying to get to Slocum before he got to the boys.
The rough hemp bit into his flesh and soon became slick
with his blood.

"Enough, Mr. Blunt. That won't be necessary. Leave the
little darlings alone." Josiah Wilks sauntered across the
clearing toward the cold house, his walking stick whipping
the tall grass out of his way.

"We was just tryin' to figure out fer sure who's been
bringin' 'em food," Slocum countered.

"That puzzle, gentlemen, has already been solved."
Wilks slowly circled Jesse. "He stinks like a pig. Clean him
up." He began to turn away, then stopped. "And don't . . .
interrogate him any further. When you're done with him,
send him back to Dobbs." Wilks waved his cane at Slocum.
"Release the others. I'm sure they'll need to be scrubbed
down as well." Lifting one of the blankets with the tip of
his walking stick, he grimaced. "Burn all of this stuff." His
gaze fell from Jesse to the boys as Slocum herded them out
of the cold house. "And clean out the cold house, just in
case anyone comes looking." He gave a slight nod, then
turned and left the clearing, whistling a jaunty tune and
twirling his cane.

"What the hell was that all about?" Slocum asked,
scratching his head.

Cecil Blunt watched Wilks disappear around a crook in
the path, and sneered, "I'd say that Mr. Wilks is showing
his tender side."

"Bullshit," Slocum spat. "He don't fool me none. Mr. Wilks is tryin' to save his own ass."

*My thoughts exactly,* Jesse mused.

MARGARET LESTER STOPPED Kathleen as she opened her classroom door. "Miss Rachel would like to see you in Reverend Divine's office." A smirk twisted her lips. "It would seem that you may have quite a bit to answer for."

Kathleen knew there was only one thing that could be sending her to the headmaster's office. She wasn't surprised. It had only been a matter of time until she was caught taking food to the cold house; what surprised her was that she'd gotten away with it for three days. She tried to read the expression on Margaret Lester's face. Was she the one who had turned her in? If not Margaret, who? "What about my class?"

"Miss Briggs will come and sit with them."

Margaret accompanied Kathleen down the stairs to the verandah and down to the promenade, keeping up a steady stream of conversation.

"I warned you not to trust her; now you'll see for yourself. She's evil. The devil's mark on her face proves it. She tricked Providence into marriage, and then the poor fool appointed her headmistress." Margaret's voice held razor edges and ice. "Until she came, it was all to have been mine. All. Mine."

Kathleen cast a sidelong glance and found the woman's face suffused with anger and something more. Hate? How could anyone be in the same room with Rachel and Providence and not see the love between them? Was it just the headmistress job, or had Margaret Lester had her sights set on Providence as well?

Margaret matched Kathleen's steps stride for stride and continued railing until they reached the administration building. "And the boy, he's terrified of her." Her voice dropped to a near whisper. "Last summer at the school outing at Marsh Lake, had I not been there to save him, he would have drowned. *She* had pushed him in the water."

Kathleen couldn't believe her ears. "Surely you're

wrong, Miss Lester. When I met her the other day, she certainly didn't impress me as the type to—"

"Don't let her fool you, Miss Prescott. I can assure you, Rachel Divine would sell her own family to the devil to get what she wants . . . and has."

Unease slipped through Kathleen. The contempt in the woman's voice had been perfectly clear. "Have you known her long?"

Margaret shrugged. "We were close once, but I believe that what you give out comes back tenfold. Her day will come, and the good Lord knows I want to be there to see her fall." She paused at the bottom of the stairs leading up to the school's office, and gently placed her hand on Kathleen's arm. "Don't worry. I'll stay with you. You may need a friend."

They climbed to the second floor in silence, and after crossing the hall landing Kathleen paused at the open office door. With the exception of the computer that sat on her desk, the electric lamps, and the telephone, the room was almost identical to how her office looked when she'd last seen it. The drapes had been drawn over the window on the left side of the room, and Rachel Divine sat at the desk. The shadow created by the closed drapes helped hide the birthmark on her cheek.

"Miss Prescott, please come in."

Moving toward the desk, Kathleen realized that the visitors' chairs were missing. She was obviously expected to stand, as any convicted felon would, to receive her sentence and her punishment.

"Margaret," Rachel Divine said, barely taking her eyes off Kathleen, "you may leave."

"Miss Prescott has requested that I stay." A smug smile lifted Margaret Lester's mouth.

"Miss Prescott, is this so?" With Kathleen's nod, Rachel continued. "Very well." She folded her hands together on the desktop and paused, as though gathering her thoughts. "First, please let me say that I am very disappointed to learn that not only are you a thief, Miss Prescott, but you have blatantly disregarded school rules. You have stolen food from the kitchen three nights in a row. Is this so?"

Kathleen knew there was no need to lie. "Yes, ma'am, that is true."

"And you took this food to students who were in detention."

"Yes, that's correct."

"You also stole blankets. Were you cold, Miss Prescott?"

"Not me, ma'am . . . the boys in the cold . . ." The unexpected touch of Margaret Lester's hand on her arm interrupted Kathleen. She saw the slight shake of Margaret's head, as if warning her not to say anything more.

"I see," Rachel Divine replied. "It is a pity, Miss Prescott. When we first met I was very taken with you, as was Reverend Divine. He has also been very pleased with your work with the children and Elijah. You've developed an excellent rapport with the students, and they've been learning well from you." She unfolded her hands and straightened her shoulders. "But you cannot expect that stealing and deceit would be acceptable. We also cannot permit our staff to defy the rules set by Reverend Divine."

"May I ask how you found out?"

"I was returning from tending to a sick child in the junior girls' dormitory last night. I saw you myself as you sneaked out of the kitchen. Then it was only a matter of asking the right people the right questions." Rachel Divine placed her hands flat on the desk and rose from her chair.

Her nerves tense and rigid, Kathleen could barely breathe. *The trial is over and now the sentencing.*

"You will be leaving DuBois, Miss Prescott. You are dismissed and no longer in our employ."

Kathleen's mind whirled. She had expected a reprimand, perhaps even some sort of punishment: no trips to town, maybe extra work, a temporary cut in pay, but certainly not dismissal. *How do I survive? What will I do? What about Jesse?*

With the few dollars she had left from the pay advance that Wilks had given her, she knew she could probably find a room in town. She doubted that any recommendation would come from DuBois, but perhaps she would still be able to find a job and stay close to Jesse. Her future might be doubtful, but she knew one thing, she wasn't going to leave DuBois without speaking her mind. Squaring her shoulders and standing as tall she should could, she angled her head in the imperious tilt that people usually found intimidating. "Mrs. Divine, do you really call being locked in the cold house for nine days 'detention'?"

"Kathleen, hush," Margaret Lester whispered. "Don't make it any worse than it is." Taking hold of Kathleen's arm, she tried to pull her away from the desk.

"The cold house?" A brief frown creased Rachel's brow. She quickly glanced to her left and then back at Kathleen. "What did you say about the cold house?"

"Come along, Kathleen." Margaret Lester drew her toward the door. "I tried to warn you. She could send for the sheriff. You did steal, after all. Leave now, don't say anything else."

"Wait a moment, Miss Prescott."

The voice, hoarse and feeble, yet still commanding, had come from the darkened left corner of the office.

Had she imagined the voice? Kathleen pulled her arm out of Margaret Lester's grasp and turned. Providence sat in shadows in one of the two visitors' chairs that had been moved to the corner.

He beckoned to her. "Come closer." He pointed at the chair beside his. "Sit, please."

Kathleen glanced at Margaret and saw the woman's eyes widen with what? Amazement? No. Alarm. With nothing to lose, she slowly crossed the room and took the offered seat.

Silence followed, making Kathleen more uncomfortable with each passing second. She found that Providence looked no better than he had a few days before. If anything, he seemed a little weaker. Why was he here? Did she have a chance to save her job? She tried to read the expression on her great-great-grandfather's face. What difference did his opinion about her make at this point? Whatever he thought of her was fine, but she wasn't going to leave without speaking her mind. "Reverend, I am sorry that I broke your trust. Yes, I did steal, but the boys were hungry and at night they were so cold." She paused and glanced up at Rachel, who had come to stand beside her husband. "I was afraid they'd become ill, or worse." She fisted her hands in her lap. "The building is an abomination."

Providence glanced up at his wife and then back at Kathleen. "An abomination? The detention room is clean and warm. The child is sequestered for a while to reflect on his transgression. There was no need for you to steal blankets . . . or food."

"Detention room?" Kathleen questioned. "Do you call the cold house a clean and warm detention room? Do you call taking a few apples because they were hungry an appropriate reason to be put in the cold house for nine days?"

"No, of course not," Providence replied, quickly sitting forward. "Why do you keeping talking about the cold house?"

"Because that is where these boys were."

"No, no, my dear, you must be mistaken. The detention room is in the junior boys' dormitory. That is where the boys are."

"No, Reverend. I'll admit to being a thief, but I am not lying; I know where I have been taking the food."

Providence's hands trembled as he clutched the arms of the chair. "My God, Miss Prescott, why didn't you speak with Mr. Wilks about this or come to me? I agree, this is unforgivable."

"It is little excuse, but being new, I didn't know if it was usual—"

"Josiah just found out himself where the boys were being kept," Margaret Lester interrupted, quickly moving forward, her hands piously clasped at her waist. "Needless to say he was appalled. He is overseeing their release as we speak."

Kathleen quickly glanced at Margaret. The woman was lying. Josiah Wilks knew very well where the boys were being kept. It had been Wilks who told her that Jesse was in the cold house. Margaret Lester and every other teacher at the table had heard him.

"How did that happen, Margaret?" Reverend Divine asked, his gray eyes closely watching his bookkeeper.

"It would seem that Mr. Slocum and Mr. Blunt," she said, spreading her hands in petition, "misunderstood the order to take them to the detention room and locked them in the cold house instead."

Providence pulled himself forward in the chair and, placing his elbows on the overstuffed armrests, rested his chin on his steepled fingers. He looked up at Kathleen, a pensive expression on his face. "It would seem that perhaps a couple of very grave mistakes have been made."

Grave. The word made Kathleen think about what Mrs. Gilbert had told her, about the boy who died in the cold house and had been secretly buried in the cemetery. Did Providence know about that? Did Rachel or Margaret know? And if they listened to her, could she prove it was true?

A new thought wedged its way into Kathleen's mind. *Is this another part of the puzzle that Jesse and I are supposed to work out before we can go home? Bide your time, Kathleen, bide your time.*

"Miss Prescott, I would hate to lose one of the best English teachers I've ever had. I find your methods to be commendable and quite progressive." With a trembling hand, he scratched his chin. "What is it that you call that one program that you use to help with their reading?"

Kathleen smiled. "Phonics, sir. It's a program called 'Friendly Phonics.'" *If he only knew it came from an infomercial on television.*

"Ah, yes, phonics. Perhaps, in your case, some concessions could be made?" He glanced up at Rachel. "What do you say, my dear?"

Rachel looked from Kathleen to Margaret Lester, then back to Kathleen again. "Now that these new facts have come to light, perhaps an allowance should be made." She moved to her husband's side and gently placed her hand on his shoulder. "Miss Prescott, my husband has always told me that everyone is worthy of a second chance." She leaned over and whispered quietly in his ear, rising only when he gave a few short nods. Rachel Divine's steady gaze met Kathleen's. "Miss Prescott, if you would be so kind, I would like to graciously withdraw my order for your dismissal. Your teaching abilities are invaluable to DuBois, and we would be sad to lose your talents. Your actions can certainly be excused, under the circumstances."

"Miss Prescott," Providence added, "it is improper for a young woman to be out walking the grounds alone well past dark. I hope, in the future, you will confine your excursions to pleasant daytime hours." He lightly touched his wife's hand, causing her to lean closer to him again. A few more whispered words were shared, some that apparently surprised Rachel Divine. When she straightened up, her expression was cold, and it didn't soften with Providence's next words. "I would also like you to spend some time with me every day," Providence continued. "I believe you can spare an hour in the afternoon."

Kathleen didn't know what to say. Everything had turned around, three-hundred and sixty degrees, and then some. She would not only keep her job, but would be spending precious time with her great-great-grandfather as well. Where was all this leading and what, if anything, did this all have to do with her and Jesse and getting back to their own time?

A quick knock at the office door interrupted, and Kathleen saw Rachel's posture stiffen as Josiah Wilks stepped into the room, his derby and walking stick in hand.

"The boys have been released back to Basil Dobbs. And both Slocum and Blunt have been severely reprimanded. It was an ignorant mistake on their part, but I'm positive it was innocently made." His petition for mercy was clear by the expression on his face and the gesture he made with his hands.

Although Josiah Wilks was lying through his pretty mouth, and his acting surpassing any Academy Award winner she'd ever seen, Kathleen only had one thought in her mind. Jesse was free . . . well, as free as any Indian student could be at DuBois.

# Chapter 21

I wanted to learn the white man's secrets. I thought he had better magic than the Indian.

—SUN ELK,
TAOS PUEBLO

"ALL RIGHT, CLASS." Kathleen clapped her hands, drawing the children's attention from their work. "That is all for today. Remember to study your spelling list. There will be a small test tomorrow." She watched the children gather up their books, amazed at how quickly she had come to deeply care for each one.

"Miss Prescott."

Elijah and Adam Black Fox stood side by side at her desk. Her great-grandfather and Jesse's great-uncle were best of friends. A few days and a hundred and seventeen years ago, she would have vehemently denied it was possible. Fate had certainly concocted all sorts of surprising twists and turns for her trip through time. "Yes, Elijah."

"My papa said don't forget to visit him today. He said today is important."

"Thank you, Elijah." She gently pushed a tumbled lock of dark brown hair from the boy's forehead. "And what are you and your friends going to do this afternoon?"

Elijah glanced at Adam Black Fox and grinned. "We're going to look for deer in the woods by the garden. Adam taught me how to look for their hoofprints." He puffed with pride and excitement. "I'm learning to talk Indian, too. I can say his name, *Tokalu Sapa*." He pointed to the other two Indian boys waiting by the door. "Isaac and Weasel are going to teach me how to hunt like real Indians." He leaned closer to Kathleen and lowered his voice to a loud whisper. "And soon they're going to show me how real Indians live."

She saw Adam give Elijah a quick jab with his elbow, but she found Elijah's enthusiasm such a delightful change from the solemn child she'd first met, she didn't wonder about its meaning. "Have you asked your mama if you could go?"

The glitter of anticipation left his eyes. "My mama is dead."

"Elijah, I'm sorry." Her hand grazed his cheek. "I meant did you ask Miss Rachel?"

His body shook for a moment as he traded grief for anger. "I don't ask her anything." His hands tightened into fists at his sides. "She's . . . not a . . . good lady." His mouth settled into a hard line.

"Then you need to ask your papa," Kathleen said, wondering what Rachel Divine had done, other than marry his father, that had made Elijah dislike, even fear her so much.

"I've already asked Papa." The boy's angry posture eased.

"Yes, ma'am," Adam added. "Elijah's papa said good play in woods."

"No, Adam, Elijah's papa said it was all right for him to play in the woods."

A frown creased Adam's forehead. "Yes, ma'am, that what I said so."

Kathleen smiled, charmed by the way so many of the Indian children strung their words together. "Yes, I suppose you did. Off you go. Just be careful."

"Yes, ma'am," the boys answered in unison.

"And don't miss supper."

She watched the boys—Elijah, Adam, Weasel, and Isaac—run from the classroom. Their feet beat a crazy tattoo on the stairs, and they jabbered and laughed the whole way.

In the two weeks since they had all been released from the cold house, the only time she'd seen Jesse was in the dining hall at mealtime and for the hour he sat in her English class each morning. But the three Indian boys and Elijah were everywhere. Like happy little peas in a pod, if you saw one, you saw all four.

Gathering her purse and her books, Kathleen locked her classroom door and then slowly descended the stairs. In a few minutes she'd have another meeting with her great-great-grandfather. Sitting with him, she occasionally forgot that a hundred and seventeen years and three generations of family separated them.

They discussed poetry, the works of Shakespeare, Homer's *Iliad,* and medieval history. He had been surprised and impressed with her grasp of politics and her detailed knowledge of the Civil War. But it was their conversations on current events that Kathleen found nerve-racking. She had to constantly keep her wits about her and was always worried she might slip and mention something that hadn't happened yet.

Near the end of their visit each day, Margaret Lester, who worked afternoons in the office for Providence, served tea that she brewed in the small kitchen across the hallway. Afternoon tea was a favorite daily event for Providence.

Each day Kathleen learned something new about Providence. She knew he'd been well educated, but his progressive thinking surprised her. If Jesse could join their discussions and see the true Providence Divine for himself, maybe he'd change his mind about Indian schools, about DuBois.

Kathleen climbed the stairs to Providence's office on the second floor. Sara Blessing's art class, Mr. Watson's barbershop, and the doctor's office filled the first floor. In 2003 the area housed the school's museum.

July heat pocketed in the upper hallway, but a lovely cross breeze always cooled the administrator's office. Sadly, she had seen no change for the better since Providence had come home, since she'd first met him. If anything, he seemed worse. His stomach cramps remained, sometimes so strong that he flinched and cried out. The tremors in his hands and severe nausea had stayed with him as well. The day before, while sitting close and reading aloud to him from Psalms, she had detected the odor of garlic. Kathleen couldn't help wondering if maybe his stomach would settle if he ate a more bland diet.

She rapped lightly on the open door.

"Ah, there you are. Come in, come in, Miss Prescott." Providence beckoned to her from behind his desk. His face was a gaunt, sharp landscape of high bones, and sunken cheeks with dark shadows under his eyes. Even his brown hair lacked luster.

Usually their afternoons were informal, sitting side by side by the window. But today the chairs had been moved back to their usual place in front of the desk.

As she stepped closer, Providence pointed to his right. "I believe you are acquainted with my other guest."

Turning, Kathleen stifled a surprised gasp. She would have expected anyone but him. Anyone but Jesse.

"Hello, Jesse." It took every bit of Kathleen's strength to sound calm.

"*Hau,* miss. Good I see you."

He played his part so well that sometimes she forgot it was all a charade. For the moment he was *Suŋgléska.*

Sunlight streamed through the window and glanced off his hair. Nothing had been done about the ragged cut, but no longer dirty and matted, his hair shone like polished obsidian. The bruise on his cheek and the one on his chin had faded, and the small cut by his lip had almost healed. The grime was gone from his hands, but the telltale signs of rope burns still encircled each wrist like obscene bracelets. Her silent inspection continued, and she drank in every inch of him as though she had been thirsty for a long, long time.

Inside, within the confines of the walls and ceiling of the room, he seemed taller, more imposing. Everything and everybody that shared space with him lessened. Her gaze traveled to his eyes, and in that instant she found herself lost in their black depths. It didn't take long for the mischievous twinkle to return, and she wouldn't have been the least bit surprised if he had given her another of his infamous winks.

The enticing warmth returned to her body, flaring up and flowing through her in a rush like wildfire through prairie grass. Clasping her hands at her waist as if trying to

hold herself together, she fought every impulse to rush to
him, to touch him, to hold him close.

"Miss Prescott."

The sound of Providence's voice startled her. She'd forgotten he was in the room. How long had she been staring
at Jesse? Embarrassed, she quickly turned, meeting Providence's interested gaze. "Excuse my amazement, but this is
quite an unexpected surprise," she finally stuttered.

"Not an unpleasant one, I hope."

"No, certainly not. He's one of my better students."

"I imagine that you're puzzled why I have asked him to
join us." Providence beckoned again. "Come, sit, both of
you." He pointed at the two chairs in front of the desk and
waited until both were settled.

Resting his elbows on the arms of his chair, Providence
templed his fingers and looked at Jesse. After a moment he
gave a thoughtful nod, then set his attention on Kathleen.
"David Yellow Tree, the fine young Cheyenne fellow who
has been my driver and helper for the past three years, has
also been a private student of mine. David is an accom-
plished pupil and has been studying treaties, and Indian Affairs documents and the law.

"Tomorrow, David leaves us and goes home, where he
can put his knowledge to good use, helping his people as
best he can. I'll be very sad to see him go, but his future
work is more important than my sentimentalities." His face
brightened with a smile. "Miss Prescott, I believe that your
Mr. Spotted Horse is an excellent candidate for David's replacement, if, of course, you would be willing to tutor
him."

Stunned by his suggestion, she quickly glanced at Jesse
and then back at Providence. "Reverend, I know nothing
about government policies, laws, or Indian treaties." She
glanced at Jesse again, unable to turn away. "Jesse has only
taken a few of my classes and has just begun to learn English." She watched the corner of his mouth twitch. *Oh,
please, Jesse, don't laugh.* "He has a long way to go before
he can read and write the language." That absurd lie almost
made Kathleen laugh.

"Ah, but you are an excellent teacher. I'm sure he will

make great strides under your tutelage. Your advanced teaching techniques are highly unusual—but marvelous. Phonics, isn't that what you told me they are called?"

"Yes, but—"

"Good, it's settled, then, Miss Prescott. Every afternoon after your regular class, you will meet Jesse here. There is a small room across the hall beside the kitchen that will be your private classroom." He leaned back in his chair, his shoulders drooping as though suddenly tired, but he continued. "You're wondering why, aren't you? You're wondering why I provide special education for a few?"

"Yes, of course I'm interested."

"I wish I could give every one of our boys and girls special treatment, but that's just not possible. I have to make a choice." He leaned forward again, his mood suddenly eager. "What the Indian people need now are educated leaders. Their leaders can no longer be selected from those who steal the most horses on raids or count the most coup in battle." He glanced at Jesse. "But every student who comes to a school such as DuBois isn't leader material. In fact, just as in their tribes, very few have that special gift."

"But why Jesse?"

"Look at him, Miss Prescott. Praise God that he doesn't understand what I'm saying because I fear it would give the fellow a swelled head. He is handsome, a magnificent and imposing young man. You can see his intelligence in how he carefully assesses his surroundings and the people in them. And most important, he's very charismatic. People are instantly drawn to him. I've watched how the other students look up to him, respect him, willingly follow his lead."

Kathleen found herself overwhelmed by Providence's words. "Reverend, because the majority of students are younger, smaller, isn't it possible that most of his . . . charisma might be nothing more than his age and his size?" Determined that Jesse wasn't going to enjoy Providence's accolades too much, she added, "Of course, size and age don't necessarily indicate intelligence."

"My dear, it is his size and his age that make people notice him, but it is the qualities I've mentioned that keep people interested." Providence's gaze swept over Jesse, his admiration obvious. "Yes, I believe he will be perfect." He then turned to Kathleen. "Without knowledgeable leaders in their midst, the Indians will not be able to save their race, their lands, or their dignity." He spread his hands in petition. "It's not that I don't believe the theory of assimilation has merit, I just don't believe it should be one hundred percent. If God had wanted us all to be the same, he would never have created so many wonderful variations."

Kathleen couldn't help but wonder how Jesse was feeling about what he was hearing. Providence's simple words dispelled so many of the beliefs he had brought to DuBois with him. From the corner of her eye she saw him sit forward as though he were going to speak. Without hesitating, she lightly touched her boot to his ankle—a warning. Careful. Keep quiet. He sat back. Kathleen released a little sigh, satisfied that he heeded her warning.

Providence lightly struck his palm on the desktop, bringing their discussion to a close. "Now, I think I'd like some tea, how about you?" Looking at Jesse, he lifted his hand and pretended to be drinking. He waited for Jesse's nod. "Ah, good." He turned to Kathleen. "Miss Lester isn't here this afternoon. May I impose on you, Miss Prescott? The little gas stove is really simple to use." He waited for her nod. "Wonderful. Then I guess that will be tea for three."

Kathleen returned from the small, well-stocked kitchen with the tea tray to find Providence trying to teach Jesse how to tell time.

"The big hand always points to the hour, just like an arrow." Providence looked up. "Ah, here's our tea." He waited until Kathleen had set the tray on the desk, then poured some of the steaming brew into one of the cups. Catching Jesse's attention, he pointed to the tray. "Sugar? Cream?"

Hard-pressed to hide her smile, Kathleen watched Jesse pretend to consider his options before he shook his head.

"No like," he said and held his hand out for the cup.

"Well, now, isn't that unusual," Providence remarked.

"Most of these Indians gobble sugar every chance they get."

"Speaking of which," Kathleen added, pointing at the almost empty bowl, "that is the last of the sugar." She took her cup from Providence and added a little cream. "I'll ask Miss Lester where she keeps the supply, or I'll get some from Mrs. Gilbert."

"I believe the sugar is kept on the second or third shelf of the cabinet, in a tin. But it's my wife who takes care of making sure my tea cupboard is stocked, not Miss Lester. I'll speak with her this evening." Providence added two heaping spoonfuls to his cup. Seeing Kathleen watching him, he smiled. "This looks as though I have quite a sweet tooth, doesn't it?" He swiveled his spoon in his cup. "This last order of tea that came from the grocer's in Pritchart is a bit of a disappointment—bitter. I always ask for a prime Ceylon, but I don't believe that is what they sent." He took a sip and then shrugged. "I find that it leaves a bit of an aftertaste. The sugar helps to cover it."

Kathleen took a sip, allowing the brew to slid over her tongue. In the time that she had been enjoying this afternoon ritual with Providence, the tea had always tasted delicious. She glanced at her great-great-grandfather as he added a third spoon of sugar to his cup. Perhaps his taste buds were being affected by his illness.

She reached for a biscuit, but the clatter of a cup against the saucer quickly drew her attention to Providence's trembling hands as he lowered his cup to the desk.

"I'm sorry. Please forgive me, but I'm suddenly quite tired." He tried to stand but fell back into his chair. His body sagged. "Perhaps Mr. Spotted Horse could help me upstairs."

Kathleen felt Jesse begin to quickly get up and she placed her hand on his arm. If he moved too quickly, Providence might suspect that he had understood what had been said. She stood and, taking hold of Jesse's arm, led him to Providence's side. She spoke slowly and added simple hand gestures. "Please help Reverend Divine upstairs." She pointed up toward the ceiling, feeling ridiculous playing this tiresome game with a man who fully understood every word.

"I'm so sorry, my dear," Providence rasped. "I'll see you tomorrow, tomorrow when you and this fine warrior begin your classes."

Kathleen watched Jesse help Providence to his feet, his touch gentle and kind, allowing the frail man to lean on him. He took him slowly out of the room and up the stairs.

The teacups rattled on the tray as she crossed the hallway to the kitchen. To her left, the door to Margaret Lester's small office stood wide open. *We wanted to look at the ledgers; what better opportunity could I have?* After a quick glance up the stairs, she ducked into the room and closed the door.

Careful not to disturb anything, Kathleen set the tray on the desk and began searching for the accounts ledger. She found it on the left side of the bottom drawer. Opening the book, she scanned each date from June fourteenth forward.

On the fifteenth she looked for the entry that would show the salary advance Josiah Wilks had given to her. Her eyes followed her finger as it slid down the page, past a blot of ink, and down to the last entry. Her name wasn't on the page.

"Maybe I missed it," she murmured, starting a new search. Her eyes skimmed past the ink spot again and then jumped back for another look. The blotch covered all but the last two letters of the individual's last name—*tt*— but the first name, Katherine, was easy to read. The amount was the same as Wilks had given her. Eight dollars. "The teacher who took Delia Shore's place was Katherine," she whispered, but the shiver that began at the back of her neck was insistent and soon covered her entire body. *When Margaret put my name in the ledger, she got it wrong. She wrote Katherine, not Kathleen.* "I *am* Katherine. Just like I told Jesse, I am Delia Shore's replacement."

She sat staring at the entry, stunned to see the proof before her. *Wait a minute, don't jump to conclusions so quickly. Her name could have been Scott; that ends in two t's.* "No, I know it's me."

A second number, twenty-two dollars, had been written

in the debit column under the eight dollar advance she'd received. "I think I've just found the first false entry." With the two amounts added together, it looked as though she had been paid thirty dollars, her whole month's pay.

Beneath it another entry itemized uniforms for the new arrivals, eight dollars each. She'd seen the uniforms the new boys had been issued, each well worn and definitely not new. Kathleen couldn't help but chuckle; even Margaret Lester's loan of a skirt and white blouse to her from the school's uniform inventory had been posted.

Suspicious entries had been posted on each page. The money received for the rocking chairs had magically shrunk to three dollars each and the harnesses to a mere twenty-five. The amounts seemed small, but in 1886 values it would quickly add up to a very comfortable sum.

She quietly closed the cover and began to slide the ledger back into the drawer, and then stopped. Opening the book up to January, she ran her finger down the page looking for Hannah's name. *There.* Her finger traced horizontally across the page to the debit column. Hannah's salary for January had been thirty dollars. Flipping through the pages to May, she searched again for Hannah's name. If what Hannah had told her about taking a cut in pay was true, then her salary should be listed as only twenty. Kathleen's finger stopped on the amount. Thirty dollars. She flipped back and forth from January to May, checking each teacher's pay. The deductions from the school's funds never changed, but apparently the money the staff actually was paid did.

After closing the book, she put it back in the drawer. "I knew it wasn't Providence, I knew it," she murmured. "But I promise, you won't get away with this, Margaret." Kathleen picked up the tea tray and left the room.

She dried the delicate china cups and put them back in the cupboard. A brightly painted tin on the second shelf caught her eye. *The sugar.* Using the small wooden stepstool from the corner of the room, she gingerly climbed onto the top tread. As her fingers touched the tin on the second shelf, she saw an identical one on the shelf above. It had been pushed into the back corner.

"Which is which," she murmured, taking the second tin as well. Lifting the lid of the first, she found it almost filled to the top with granulated sugar. She opened the second.

A brown paper sack, its top tightly folded over, had been pressed down into the tin. Kathleen pulled the bag out and began to unfold the top. On the side of the bag, in large black letters, someone had written one word. Stunned, Kathleen almost dropped the bag. It took her a moment or two to realize the import of that one word. *Arsenic.*

She peered inside the bag. Not as coarse and a slight grayish color, the crystalline particles sparkled like grains of sugar. Would anyone be able to tell if the two were mixed together?

*What am I thinking? Nobody is putting arsenic in the sugar. It's for the garden, for bugs or aphids, or whatever.* In the midst of her denials, another question squeezed its way into her head. *If it is for the garden, what is it doing in the kitchen cupboard on the second floor?*

Kathleen continued to hold the paper bag in her hand, trying to convince herself that what she was thinking was absurd. But the chilling thought wouldn't leave. *Arsenic poisoning. Was it possible? Is that why Providence is so ill?* She suddenly felt nauseous. *That means that someone is trying to kill him.* The idea left her numb. Surely she was wrong. Another thought quickly struck. *If it's true, they're killing him, slowly and painfully. But who is it? And why, why are they doing it?*

Once again Wilks's words to Margaret came rushing back. *"You've been a naughty girl, a very naughty girl."* Was murder part of a scheme cooked up between the two of them to embezzle money or take over the school? Was he talking about the arsenic, the lies in the ledger, or something completely different?

And then, with cold clarity, she remembered what Providence had said just a short while before. *" . . . it's my wife who takes care of making sure my tea cupboard is stocked, not Miss Lester."*

Rachel. Was that why there was no mention of her in Providence's journals or photographs of her in the archives?

When her murdering scheme was discovered and she'd been sent to jail, had Providence erased every mention of her?

Kathleen's mind whirled around each question, each possible answer. After a quick breath she refolded the top of the paper sack and slipped it into her skirt pocket. She pushed the empty tin back on the top shelf.

Whoever had hidden the arsenic would find the tin empty and know their scheme had been discovered. When they did, Kathleen intended to find out who that someone was.

Almost ready to leave, she remembered the sugar bowl. Was it pure sugar or did the bowl contain a lethal mixture? *I'm not taking any chances.* With a flick of her wrist, Kathleen tossed the contents of the bowl out the open window and into the bushes below. She tipped the sugar tin and poured a little into the bowl before returning it to the cupboard.

Now she had to find Jesse and tell him what she'd discovered—in Margaret's office and in the kitchen. Had he come back downstairs yet? He always walked so softly that if he had, she probably wouldn't have heard him. Kathleen rushed across the hall and back into Providence's office. Empty. *Maybe he thought I'd already left.* Glancing out the window, she saw him jogging across the parade ground, going back to the carpenter shop.

"Tonight. I'll get a note to him somehow and tell him to meet me tonight." She gnawed at her thumbnail and suddenly remembered the fine residue of arsenic that had fallen out of the bag and onto her hand. "If I don't kill myself before then."

# Chapter 22

We did not ask you white men to come here. We do not want your civilization. We would live as our fathers did and their fathers before them.

—CRAZY HORSE,
OGLALA SIOUX

KATHLEEN SLIPPED INSIDE her bedroom and bolted the door. She'd have to hurry; Hannah would be coming soon to walk with her to supper. With her back pressed against the door, a nervous sheen of sweat coating her palms, and her heart beating at triple cadence, Kathleen pulled the paper bag from her pocket. She'd given a great deal of thought to its contents on the way back to her room and now little doubt remained in her mind; arsenic hidden away in a cupboard in the small kitchen on the second floor was not there for gardening purposes. But until she knew who it belonged to, she'd keep it hidden. But where? She scanned the room, looking for a safe place.

The night table. No. Too accessible. She turned. Maybe under the bureau. No, that wouldn't work, either. The frame sat directly on the floor. She'd have to tip it up to slide anything underneath, and it was much too heavy to do it alone. Frustrated, she continued to search, but the sparsely furnished room offered few choices.

Footsteps in the hallway broke her concentration. *Please, not Hannah. Not yet.* She held her breath and listened as they moved on down the hall. Silence returned, and relieved, her breath slid from between her lips in a long sigh. "I'm not cut out for all this espionage."

She studied the room again, from corner to corner, floor to ceiling. And then, there it was. So easy, so ideal, it had stared her in the face the whole time.

*My bed.*

Pulling her skirts above her knees, Kathleen kneeled down on the braided rug. She lifted the coverlet and peered under the bed. *Perfect.* Unfolding the handkerchief from her pocket, she set the bag in the middle and knotted the corners over it like a hobo's sack. The ends of the knots were just long enough to tie the small package to a bedspring.

The bustled skirt bunched up around her waist, making wriggling around on the floor and trying to scoot under the bed next to impossible. Finally, with her head and shoulders under the bed, she looked up and tied the little bundle to a corner spring near the foot. She tied it high enough that even when the quilt was off the bed, no one could see the bundle.

Getting out from under the bed proved even more difficult, but Kathleen was finally able to slide out on the small braided rug. Gripping the white iron bedstead, she pulled herself to her feet, straightened her underskirt, and smoothed the wrinkles from her gown. Stepping back to the middle of the room, she studied her bed. Yes, she'd found a safe place.

The sound of more footsteps in the hall and on the staircase reminded her again that Hannah would soon be knocking on her door. Quickly opening the top drawer of the bureau, she reached inside for a fresh handkerchief. Her hand stopped in midair. Bewildered, she stared at her belongings. Confusion turned to anger that rose hot and thick, but cold dread quickly pushed it aside. Someone had thoroughly searched through the drawer.

*Who?*

The prowler had tried to be very careful. Her belongings hadn't been moved enough that someone who wasn't used to strict order and neatness would have noticed, but Kathleen immediately saw the little changes. Her stockings were no longer aligned with each other; her new chemise and delicate corset cover had been pushed a little to the right, and the index finger on one of her ivory gloves had been folded under.

It took little effort to guess who the snoop might be. Only two candidates were on the list. Margaret Lester and Rachel Divine. Head mistress or dormitory supervisor, they would both have a key to the room. Either one could have come in during the day while she was gone.

"Turnabout's fair play, I suppose," she murmured. But her invasion of Margaret Lester's desk had been a lot neater. She drew a quick breath. *Is anything missing?*

Her fingers dived into the drawer, searching for the cameo brooch. Since the slip in time, when she wasn't wearing it, she kept it tightly wrapped in a handkerchief and tucked into the left front corner. Her hand swept down the left side of the drawer and into the corner. Gone. The brooch wasn't there.

Her heart leaped to her throat. *It's got to be here.* One by one, Kathleen began to lift and move everything. A moment later she heard a light, muffled clank as something dropped against the bottom of the drawer. Lifting her pantalets, she found the cameo to the far right, its wrapping loose. "Thank God," she murmured, clutching the brooch to her breast.

An unsettling chill crawled over her skin. Nothing had been taken, but the invasion of her privacy was as palpable as if someone, secretly and unbidden, had touched her body. Kathleen's gaze darted to the bed. If they had been going through her things *before* she'd found the arsenic, then nothing was safe.

Now she had three things to talk with Jesse about.

PASSING THE NOTE to Jesse hadn't been a problem; in fact, it had been almost too easy. Basil Dobbs and his charges arrived at the dining hall only a few moments before Kathleen and Hannah. As they passed the line of boys on their way to the staff's dining table, she had pressed the slip of paper into Jesse's hand. Stealing out of the dormitory just before midnight hadn't posed any problems, either. She knew the routine very well after making her nightly visits to the cold house. She'd changed into the dark school uniform skirt and topped it with the white blouse and black shawl.

Storm clouds covered the sky hiding the moon, and the night air, humid and thick, carried the smell of approaching rain. Staying deep in the shadows of the trees, her journey to the barn tested every ounce of her courage. Every sound made her jump. She'd never been afraid of the dark before, but then, she'd never had a sack of arsenic hidden under her mattress before, either.

She moved as quickly as she could, hampered only by the damnable long skirt that kept getting caught on low branches and brambles. Her petticoat snagged and, giving it a quick tug, she heard it rip. In that instant Kathleen made herself a promise. If she ever made it back to her own time, she'd never wear a skirt longer than knee length again.

Just east of the harness shop she slowed and cautiously peered through the trees, praying she wouldn't bump into Alma Briggs on her way to another tryst with Gustav Felder. The harness shop was dark; maybe Alma was already there.

Out of breath, Kathleen rounded the corner of the barn. She'd wondered if Jesse would be sitting on the ground waiting to surprise her as he had done when they'd met before. Instead, she found him standing, leaning nonchalantly against the wall, his arms crossed over his chest.

"You sure do know how to make my life exciting, Katie-girl."

His voice reminded her of the caress of expensive velvet, deep and smooth and rich. He had a certain way of looking at her from under lowered lids that left her breathless. A lazy kind of smile moved on his lips, and did unprecedented things to her pulse rate. *Mama always called that an Elvis smile.* It was the kind of smile that either sent a girl rushing home to safety or tempted her to stay and play. And Kathleen knew that rushing home was impossible.

Half of the buttons on his shirt were undone, teasing her with a limited view of his chest and making it so very difficult to keep her wits about her. She tried to gather her senses, but mumbled anyway. "I'm sorry I'm late."

He laid his index finger across her lips. "The longer the wait, the better the reward."

Her breath caught in her throat and a silly little thrill zipped through her body. No one had ever said things like that to her before, and she had absolutely no idea how to respond.

He pushed away from the wall. "Shall we adjourn to our favorite bench, my dear?" He took her hand and, looking irresistibly ridiculous, waggled his eyebrows up and down.

A sudden attack of nerves nipped at Kathleen's heels and stifled the laugh she knew he'd expected. Any other time, holding Jesse's hand, would have been exciting and wonderful, but tonight there were other things—prowlers and murderers—that spoiled the thrill. Still, she couldn't help loving the touch of his hand in hers even if it did make her feel guilty. "Can we walk instead?" she asked, turning away from the bench. "I'm too jumpy to sit. We could go down the lane toward the main road and back."

They had traveled little more than thirty feet before Jesse's patience came to an end. He knew he'd go crazy if they took another step in silence. "Katie, I don't think you wanted me to sneak out and risk getting caught again, just to take a midnight stroll. What's this about?" He squeezed her hand, hoping to bolster her. "I already know it's not because I'm a charismatic kind of guy."

She offered a meager smile. "I knew that would come back to haunt me."

A chuckle welled up in his throat. Watching Kathleen Prescott come out of her cocoon was becoming one of his favorite pastimes. He loved seeing her opening up, learning to unbend; learning to use her newly discovered self-confidence, and learning to laugh. Her ability to make him laugh was an even more glorious discovery. But tonight she wasn't laughing.

"Jesse, I think I've discovered something far worse than your theory of embezzlement."

They passed the stand of sycamores, the outcroppings of boulders, and walked on around the sharp elbow in the lane beside the creek. Kathleen told him about someone searching her room, about the false entries in Margaret Lester's ledgers, and then she told him about what she'd found in the small kitchen. Throughout the entire time, her voice wavered and her hand trembled.

She suddenly stopped in the middle of the lane and looked up at him. "The handwriting in the accounts book proves Margaret's guilt, but I don't know what to do about the other, the arsenic. How can I say anything to Providence when it might be his wife?"

"How can you not when it might kill him?" Jesse certainly hadn't expected Kathleen's news. Embezzlement was enough to worry about, but attempted murder—or murder if they didn't find out who it was soon enough—was a completely different matter. And when the killer discovered that the arsenic was gone, what then? "You're sure Providence is being poisoned?"

"Yes, I am." They continued to walk toward the main road. "I've been thinking a lot since this afternoon about the signs of arsenic poisoning. From what I remember, Providence's symptoms all fit—the pain in his stomach and the sweating, the trembling, lack of appetite, weight loss, and the odor of garlic." She saw his puzzled look, and nodded. "Yes, garlic. At first I thought he'd been eating it, and then I remembered, a garlic smell is a sign of arsenic poisoning."

"But if someone is poisoning him, why are they dragging it out? He's been ill for months. Strong doses of arsenic can kill in a few days."

"I wondered about that, too."

Jesse glanced her. "And? You look as though there's definitely an *and*."

"There is." She slid her hand out of his, moved away a step or two, and then pivoted to face him. "I think whoever is doing this is being deliberately slow. It's unthinkably cruel, but I think he or she want him to suffer." A breeze lifted the tendrils of hair about her face, and she brushed them aside. "I think it is someone who is looking for some kind of revenge."

He prompted her again. "And that would be?"

She threw her hands up. "You know the possibilities. Rachel. Margaret Wilks." She folded her arms across her breasts. "He's worse now than when he came home from Indianapolis, and I think it's because when he was there, he wasn't being fed the poison. I think it started back up when he came home."

"But if it's Rachel . . ."

"If it is, then I don't think she'd risk giving it to him while the doctors were doing all sorts of tests."

"And Margaret?"

"She didn't see him at all while he was in Indianapolis. Again, Providence was poison free for about two weeks."

Jesse shrugged. "Where's the bag now?"

"Under my mattress."

"What?" He couldn't believe his ears. "Good God, Kathleen, don't you watch any crime shows on TV? That's the first damn place everyone looks."

She railed back at him. "Where else was I going to put it? I couldn't very well leave it where it was, now, could I? Maybe I should have just walked around with it in my pocket."

"You said someone had gone through your things . . ."

"Yes, but that was before I'd found the arsenic. Besides, I don't think they looked under my bed."

"But you can't be sure."

She hesitated for a moment. "No."

He saw her shiver. Kathleen had barely been out in the world in her own time, but 1886 was yanking her right into the middle of some damned frightening and dangerous circumstances. How much more of this could she take?

A strong gust of wind ruffled her hair, and her hands rose to tighten her hairpins. "I'm cold." She drew the wool shawl around her shoulders.

The temperature had dropped since they'd left the barn, and the wind coming out of the southwest had kicked up, whipping the leaves and limbs of the trees into a frenzied dance.

Jesse glanced up at the dark rolling clouds, angry and menacing against the night sky. "Looks like we're in for a hell of a storm." He took her hand again. "We'd better head back."

Kathleen hesitated. "Wait. We need to figure out how I can find out who is trying to kill Providence."

"Damn it, Kathleen, you're not doing anything on your own."

"Jesse, I'm the only one with the freedom to do it. It has to be me."

"No. It's too dangerous. We'll figure something—"

A blade of lightning sliced across the sky and illuminated the lane with a flat, dull light. The hard crack of thunder and strong smell of sulfur took only seconds to follow.

"And *this* is getting too dangerous. Come on, sweetheart, pick up your skirts and run. It's too damn close." A raindrop, large and heavy, plopped on the dirt road. One drop was soon followed by another and another. "Hurry! If we don't get out of this, we'll be drenched."

"We'll never make it back up the hill before it hits." Kathleen's breath came in rapid pants as she ran. The words had barely left her lips when the skies opened up and the wind rose, driving the rain hard against their bodies.

"The barn. Head for the barn."

JESSE LIFTED THE latch and opened the barn door just wide enough for them to slip inside. The smell of horses and hay, pungent, yet not unpleasant, hung on the damp night air. Overhead, the rain pounded on the cedar-shake roof, sounding like a thousand soldiers marching out of cadence. Jesse shook his head and rainwater flew in every direction.

"I've seen dogs do that," Kathleen said, pulling the hairpins from her own wet hair and wringing out the long strands.

"That's where I learned it. Who says you can't learn new tricks from an old dog." He glanced at her and his grin flattened. Mesmerized, he watched her comb through her hair with her fingers. Every impulse urged him to brush her hands aside and bury his own in that glorious thick mane.

Lightning cut through the dark again with the deafening roll of thunder at its heels, and Kathleen threw herself against him before the noise faded to a grumble.

"I've always been afraid of thunderstorms," she croaked, grasping his wet shirt, her fingers curling into tight fists. "We . . . we get tornadoes in Indiana." Another blaze shredded the sky, and without waiting for the answering thunder, she buried her head against his shoulder. "What if lightning hits the barn? Maybe we should go back outside."

"There are four lightning rods on the roof; we're more safe in here than anywhere else." He put his arms around her and felt her body shake as he drew her closer. "Are you cold?"

"F . . . f . . . freezing," Kathleen answered through chattering teeth.

"Here." He took the drenched shawl off her shoulders. Stepping back, he unbuttoned his shirt and slipped it off, wringing out some of the rainwater before wrapping it around her shoulders. "It's not as wet as your shawl, so it might help some."

Captivated, he watched the slow, sensuous glide of a drop of rain as it slid from her hair. He followed its journey down her nose and held his breath as it dropped off the tip onto her breast. *Easy, Horse, easy.*

"I . . . I'm soaked through to the skin." She ran her hand over his naked chest, the edge of her little finger grazing his nipple. "So are you."

Her innocent touch sparked a reaction he hadn't expected. It flared hot like the lightning and his pulse pounded like thunder through his veins. He couldn't stop the groan that slipped up his throat and prayed that the sound of the rain on the roof would mask its need-filled sound. He pulled away, hoping distance would ease the storm inside him, but she grabbed his arm and pulled him back.

"Please, don't leave me alone."

"Oh, Katie-girl, you don't know what you're asking." He drew her into his arms again, back into his hunger.

She pressed her cheek against his chest and he felt her breath touch his skin in hot rapid puffs. Her arms wrapped around him and she slid her hands up his rain-slicked back, the glide of her touch more sensuous than anything he'd ever known.

He stroked her hair, then crushed its wet silken strands in his hand. How long could he hold her like this before his resistance failed and he kissed her, stripped her clothes from her body, made love to her, and played out the dreams that had kept him hard and nearly insane each night in the cold house? *Keep your distance, Horse. This one's not about a casual fling; Kathleen Prescott is all about commitment. Don't do this if that's not what you want.*

Jesse firmly set Kathleen away from him before the impulse to press against her, to wedge himself between her thighs and let her feel his craving for her, became too strong to deny. *Okay, Tooter, are you happy now?* He touched her cheek, then quickly stepped away. "Wait right here. I'm going to go see if there are any blankets in the tack room."

Twin streaks of lightning lit up the inside of the barn as Kathleen watched Jesse walk away from her. Mesmerized by the sight of his bare shoulders, the play of muscles across his back, she didn't even flinch when the thunder cracked, shaking the barn. She didn't remember holding her breath, but when he disappeared into the tack room, it left her lungs in a slow sigh. Not wanting to let go of him, she closed her eyes and called up his image in her mind.

"I couldn't find any blankets, but this was in a wooden box under the saddle racks."

Kathleen jumped, her eyes flew open. How long had she been standing with her eyes closed? Even with the water-soaked school-issued shoes on his feet, she'd never heard him return. Looking at him standing so close, she immediately realized that the man in the flesh was far more magnificent than anything she could conjure up in her imagination.

"What do you think?"

His question yanked her back to reality, confusing her for a moment. "About what?" Flustered, she glanced down at the buffalo robe in his hands. "Oh, that. Okay, I guess."

"Maybe it's a woo-woo mystical sign of some kind," Jesse teased, shaking the dust out of the large hide. "My ancestors used buffalo hides for bedding in their tipis." He folded the robe over his arm and took her hand. "Come on, we're going to get warm, but we're going to be comfortable doing it." He led her to the wooden ladder on the wall. "Up you go."

"What?" She stepped back. "You expect me to climb up there in this?" She grabbed her skirt, heavy with rainwater, and gave it a toss.

"You're right. Take it off."

Her breath left her in a surprised whoosh. "I will not. And furthermore, I am not climbing into the hayloft."

"Yes, you are, Kathleen, on both counts. Don't worry, your underwear will save your dignity. It's warm and comfortable up there, and if anyone else shows up to get out of the rain, we'll be out of sight."

"Who else would be fool enough to be—"

"Quit arguing." He took her by the shoulders and turned her around, then placed her hands on the fourth rung of the ladder. Before she could argue again, he undid the buttons on the waistband of her skirt. With a couple of sharp tugs, the wet garment slid down over the bustled back of her underskirt and pooled around her feet. Resigned, she stepped aside.

Jesse retrieved and gave it a couple of solid shakes, splattering rainwater on the wall. "Come on. I won't let you fall, I'll be right behind you." He helped her hoist her underskirts and drape the bulk of them over her arm, then lay the wet navy blue skirt on top. "Slow and easy, one rung at a time."

Reluctantly Kathleen started to climb. Halfway up the ladder she stopped and cast a quick glance back down at Jesse. She caught him staring at her bustle and the bunched up underskirts. "What are you looking at?"

The delightfully wicked Elvis smile had returned. "You know, I've been wondering for days why your butt was all poofed out. Now I know."

Not hesitating a moment, Kathleen deliberately dropped the wet skirt and laughed when it fell over his head. "Oops, sorry."

He fought his way out from under the yards of fabric.

"Sorry, my ass." Tossing the skirt over his arm, he quickly followed her up the ladder.

Kathleen stepped off the top rung and into a soft cushion of sweet-smelling hay. Laughing, she turned and watched Jesse finish his climb, playfully backing away from him. "Shame on you. That's no way to talk to a lady. Someone definitely needs to teach you manners."

He came toward her with slow, measured steps as though he were stalking prey. "Well, you're my private tutor, aren't you?"

"Oh, no." She took another backward step. "I don't think Providence said anything about etiquette lessons."

He tossed the wet skirt at her. Stepping to one side, Kathleen reached up to grab it and her damp petticoats tangled about her legs. She wobbled precariously, and before she could catch her balance, she fell backward into the hay.

"Aw, Katie-girl, at least you could have waited till I'd spread out the blanket."

# Chapter 23

What is life? It is the flash of a firefly in the night. It is the breath of a buffalo in the wintertime. It is the little shadow which runs across the grass and loses itself in the sunset.

—CROWFOOT,
BLACKFOOT, 1890

THE LAUGH IN Jesse's throat immediately faded.

Lying on her back on the hay, one arm over her head and her glorious long hair fanned out around her, Kathleen reminded him of an exquisite wanton angel. There had been other women in his life, hell, one he'd almost married, but he'd never seen anyone so beautiful or wanted anyone as much as he wanted Kathleen. His eyes locked with hers and held for a long, tension-filled moment. He'd made a promise to himself, but keeping it was quickly proving to be a losing battle.

Driven by his conscience, Jesse turned away. It was one of the most difficult things he'd ever done. He spread the buffalo robe out on the hay, then leaned over and held out his hand to her. "Come on, I'll help you up." He tried to make his voice sound casual; instead, it sounded unreasonably harsh.

A brief frown creased Kathleen's brow, and then she slipped her hand into his. He pulled her to her feet, drawing her closer than he'd intended. The heat of her body singed his resolve, and he bit down on the inside of his cheek. Maybe one ache would stop the other. He began to pick the chaff out of her wet hair and brush it from her underclothes. She stood tall and straight and stiff the whole while, silently allowing his touch. His attention moved from her hair to her shoulders and then to her chemise. He immediately discovered his mistake. *You're a frigging idiot, Horse.* He'd trapped himself.

When dry, the chemise, made of delicate lace and fine cotton, probably provided some modesty, but wet it became nearly transparent. Beneath the thin veil of fabric, even in the dark loft, he could see the dusky circles of her tightly pebbled nipples. He watched her breasts slowly rise and fall with each breath, and his own body's response was immediate. He looked up and found her staring at him, her eyes wide and watchful, and her amazing lips slightly parted.

Guilt rose from his gut like bitter bile. He'd already chastised himself once this night. Obviously he hadn't heeded his own warning. He certainly hadn't had the seduction of Kathleen Prescott in mind when he'd suggested they climb into the warm loft. Or had he?

Jesse turned away and drove his hands into his pockets, trying to relieve himself of the phantom feel of her that lingered on his fingers. "I'm sorry, Kathleen. I should keep my damn hands to myself."

"Jesse, why am I Kathleen sometimes and other times I'm Katie-girl?"

Her words had been spoken no louder than a whisper, but he'd heard every one of them above the rhythm of the rain. "Just the whim of the moment, I suppose," he lied, hoping his casual shrug covered the truth. He knew damned well why. Calling her Kathleen put a comfortable distance between them, but what had begun as a joke, Katie-girl, was now the special password to feelings he never knew existed.

Determined to keep his promise to stay away from her, Jesse moved to the edge of the loft. Overhead the rain had settled into a steady pleasant thrum on the roof. The lightning had passed further to the east and the grumbles of thunder lagged far behind. He didn't turn around, but he knew she was still standing where he'd left her. He tried to eliminate the gruff tone from his voice, but a little too much remained. "Why don't you at least lie down on the robe and get some rest. There's no telling how long this rain will last."

"Aren't you going to join me?"

"In a little while. I'm still mulling over what you told me about the ledger . . . and the arsenic."

"No, you're not."

Her quick, blunt rebuttal hit him like a punch. *Dammit, Horse, you're as transparent as glass.* He heard the rustle of hay and assumed she'd taken his suggestion. Her light, open-palmed touch on his back proved him wrong. He tensed against the wonderful sensation. "Go, sit down, Kathleen."

"You sound just like my father used to," she said. Her hands moved in mirrored unison from his waist and up his spine.

"Kathleen, go sit down."

Her hand paused and then her fingers splayed over his bare skin, rising to his shoulder and then back down across his ribs. Settling her hands on either side of his waist, she pressed her cheek against his back. "Why?"

He'd felt her one word resonate through his body. And his body responded, quickly tightening with need. "Because I'm feeling anything but fatherly right now," he growled.

"Jesse, turn around. Look at me." She gently tugged his arm.

"Kathleen . . ."

"No, not Kathleen. Say it, Jesse. Please, say it. Call me Katie-girl."

He turned and watched a flash of lightning dance in the highlights of her hair. He groaned. "You don't know what—"

She touched her fingers to his lips, silencing his protest. "Jesse, I know who and what I am. I know I'm not . . . experienced. But that's just a technicality, not a flaw. I know my life has been dull and cloistered, and I'm not fool enough to think that under different circumstances you would ever look at me twice." She glanced away, as if gathering her strength. "But we're here, together, now."

Her hand slipped up his arm. Her fingers trailed over his

biceps, then moved up to his shoulder, his neck, and settled on the curve of his cheek. Her touch created a quickening that moved throughout his body, lighting fires wherever it went.

"Jesse, what I am feeling at this moment is something totally new to me." She shook her head. "I'm not stupid. I know what it is. I like how it feels and I want to explore and experience it all. I'm not asking for a commitment. All I'm asking for is . . . now."

Her laugh surprised him. It came easy, rolling off her tongue like sweet honey, and the sound of it struck him between the legs, making him rock hard.

"I've shocked you, haven't I?" Her fingers brushed across the edges of his lips. "I've got to confess, I've shocked myself a little, too."

He reached up and stilled her hand. "Shocked? You want to be really shocked? You have absolutely no idea how many times I've fantasized about you looking just the way you do now. Since the day I walked into your office and saw those damned wire-framed granny glasses perched on your nose, and you, all stiff and prim and proper, I wanted to find the one hairpin that if I pulled it out would release your hair. I wondered how dark your eyes would become if I could make you want . . ." He drove his fingers through his hair and rubbed the back of his neck, exasperated that he was losing control. "I think I've wanted to melt that cold exterior, heat you up, and ruffle your feathers from day one."

"Ruffle me." She grasped his hands and pressed them to her breasts, her advances unskilled, a little smile on her lips.

Firm and high, her flesh filled his hands. Her button-hard nipples pushed into his palms, and he moved his hands in slow, lazy circles, the surface of his skin lightly caressing just the tips. Her eyelids slowly fell and her lips parted in anticipation. He watched her face register every new emotion that hit her. He'd never seen a woman so unguarded. There was absolutely nothing coy or false about Kathleen Prescott.

Battling the urgency that shoved at him, his hands

moved leisurely, opening the tiny buttons down the front of her chemise. He pushed the diaphanous garment aside and slid his hands up from her waist. He cradled a breast in each hand and heard her draw a sharp breath as his thumbs stroked back and forth across their peaks.

Jesse touched his mouth to hers. He longed to crush her lips under his, but instead, trailed little kisses down her throat, across her collarbone and over the swell of her breasts. He slid his tongue over her flesh, lightly flicking at her nipples. She tilted her head back and arched her spine, lifting herself into his caress. Afraid she would tumble backward, he slid his arm around her waist and pulled her to him. Another mistake. The forward tilt of her hips drove her against his body, against his erection. Her soft moan pummeled Jesse's conscience and he eased away. If he didn't stop now, there would definitely be consequences.

He watched the tip of her tongue glide over her lips, and he knew what she would say next.

"Jesse, kiss me."

He hadn't been wrong. "Katie-girl, you don't know what you're asking.

"Yes, yes, I do."

She stepped into him, her bare skin against his bare skin, and slowly slid her hands up his chest, until she clasped them behind his head. She pressed her body tightly against him, settling herself between his legs. "Kiss me, now."

A groan, his audible surrender, fled his throat, and he slowly lowered his head. *Damned if I do and damned if I don't.* He touched her lips with the tip of his tongue, teasing her to open to him. And when she did, he slanted his mouth over hers and began to lose himself.

Kathleen couldn't even begin to understand the sensations that were rushing pell-mell through her body, bombarding her senses, and setting her on fire. When Jesse touched her breasts, a current, almost electrical, had raced through her, settling and igniting a delicious ache, an urgency between her thighs. And now, with his mouth on hers, his tongue exploring and caressing, the ache began demanding more and more.

He held her head, his hand at the nape of her neck, her

hair wrapped around his fingers, as his mouth ravaged hers. She fed off his hunger, drawing her fingers across the ridged plane of his ribs, his skin hot and smooth beneath her touch. She lost all sense of time and place. Jesse suddenly scooped her up and carried her to the buffalo robe. Gently setting her on her feet, he looked down at her, a silent question in his eyes. Kathleen touched his mouth with the tips of her fingers, and that, apparently, was answer enough.

He fumbled at the ties at her waist that held up the remaining underskirt. The garment loosened. Instead of tugging it down, Jesse slid his hands under the waistband and slowly began to push the skirt down over her hips. His hands rode with it all the way, smoothing it over the swell of her hips, her thighs, her knees. He knelt before her and helped her step out of the garment, lifting first one foot and then the other. Now only the silly bloomers remained.

Kathleen dropped to her knees on the robe and, taking Jesse's hands, pulled him down until they were kneeling, face-to-face.

He slid the open chemise off of her shoulders. "You're exquisite," he breathed. "Like a piece of delicate porcelain." He drew the back of his knuckles down the slope of her breasts and across their swollen peaks.

Feeling shy, yet driven by her own craving, Kathleen dropped her gaze. "I want to see . . . all of you." His hands led hers to his belt and her heart leaped to her throat.

"Are you sure this is what you want, Katie-girl? Are you sure?"

"Yes." The word had come on nothing more than a breath. Her fingers trembled, opening the buttons down the fly of his pants. She felt his penis, hard, jutting forward beneath the rough fabric and felt it pulse each time her fingers brushed against it.

With the last button opened, Jesse took her hand and closed her fingers around him. He was hard and hot and yet smooth like the finest silk. She explored the length, the breadth of him, her caress moving from the nest of hair at his groin to the smooth ridge of flesh and then to the hot satin tip beyond. She closed her fingers around him and slowly, with unpracticed ease, found the rhythm her own body craved and stroked up and down his velvet length.

Jesse stilled her hand. "Slow down, sweetheart. Give me the chance to breathe."

"Am I doing it wrong?" What if she was? Was she doing anything right or was she being a fumbling fool? She had no idea what someone did while making love. She knew the cold mechanics, but it was the other things, the hot things, the things that excited a man, that pleased him, that she wasn't sure about.

"No, Katie-love, you're doing it too well." Jesse grinned, placing a kiss on her mouth. "I want you naked." He began sliding the bloomers off her hips and, seeing the open crotch, stopped. "How convenient." He laughed and shook his head. "I'll never see you dressed in your pretty gowns again without being taunted by these naughty drawers. But I still want you naked." His hands began to slide them off her again.

"And do I get the same wish granted?"

"Oh, yeah. Definitely."

Totally bare and planning to get Jesse in the same condition, Kathleen didn't know why she wasn't feeling shy or embarrassed. Getting undressed at the doctor's had always been enough to scrape her nerves raw and make her nauseous. But tonight, with Jesse, she was eager, concerned only that he found her desirable.

He stood and kicked his shoes off. From where Kathleen knelt on the buffalo robe, she helped him take off the rest of his clothes. Her gaze slowly traveled from his eyes to his mouth, down his neck, across his chest, his hard stomach, and to his groin.

Touching him, closing her fingers around him, she reveled in the thought that she had made him this hard. Impulse—wanting—need pushed her and she leaned forward, kissing the tip of him, tasting him. She felt his hands move into her hair, as her tongue licked and teased.

"My God, Katie." His voice sounded husky, taut. "I want you . . . now."

The fur tickled her skin as Jesse gently laid her back on

the buffalo robe, and she waited, her body impatient for him to join her.

He stretched out beside her, and she felt his erection prodding against her hip. Propping himself up on his left elbow, he stroked her body, watching his right hand as it moved over her skin. His fingers slid over her breasts, teasing her by circling her nipples time and again before touching them, stoking the fire that burned inside her, and then rolling them between his fingers before taking them into his mouth. His hand moved lower, over her belly, dipping into her navel, and then teasing with the tight curls below. A gasp fled her lips as she felt his fingers move between her legs.

"Open up for me, Katie-love," he whispered against her lips, filling her mouth with the delicious shuddering breath of his moan when she complied. His kiss deepened and he slowly thrust his tongue into her mouth. The heel of his hand kneaded her and then his fingers parted her slick flesh and opened her to his intimate caress.

Instinct and want made her push up into his hand, and he answered by sliding his finger across the small, sensitive kernel of flesh he'd uncovered. A tremor more intense than anything she'd ever known sped throughout her body, awakening every cell, every molecule. It was like nothing she'd ever felt in her life and yet she knew there was more. This was only the beginning.

He settled himself between her legs. "Katie-love, tell me now if you want me to stop, because in the next breath, it will be too late."

"No, please, don't stop." She looked up at him, her eyes searching his. "Does it always feel like this, as though I'm hanging on a precipice about to fall?"

"No, sweetheart, it gets better and better." He placed a light kiss on her mouth. "Besides, you're not going to fall, you're going to fly."

Kathleen touched his face. "Jesse, I know this may hurt a little . . . the first time, but I . . ."

He silenced her with a kiss, covering her mouth with his own. Bending her knee, he lifted her leg to his hip and moved into her, slowly, steadily, pressing past the small tender barrier, filling her completely.

The pain lasted only a moment, and then she felt the wonderful pressure of him inside her. "Oh, Jesse, I never knew."

Jesse drew a quick breath. Holding back had taken every ounce of willpower that he possessed. She fit tight around him. "You don't know yet, Katie, but I'm going to show you."

He raised her hips up to him and began the exquisite thrust and parry, slowly pushing into her and withdrawing. She arched up against him, taking everything he offered, pacing to his rhythm. She slid her hand between their bodies, her fingers touching where they were joined. The simple gesture, innocent yet sensual beyond all reason, almost tipped him over the edge.

"Come with me, Katie. Let me show you how to fly." His strokes deepened and he heard her breath come in little gasps. She withdrew her hand and clung to him, her fingers digging into his back. He knew when she began to soar, to reach the clouds. Her body stilled and she pressed herself tightly against him, letting him send her over the edge. In that instant he joined her, shuddering as his climax came strong, surpassing anything he'd ever felt before. He spilled himself into her and prayed it would last forever.

Breathless, their bodies coated with a fine sheen of sweat, they spiraled back to reality in each other's arms. The storm had fled east and the rain had softened to a sweet and gentle rhythm on the roof. Still buried inside her, Jesse rolled to his side, taking her with him. He tenderly brushed a strand of hair from face, kissed her lips, her eyes, and knew that he had just made love for the first time in his life.

# Chapter 24

We were lawless people, but we were on pretty good terms with the Great Spirit, creator and ruler of all. You whites assumed we were savages. You didn't understand our prayers. You didn't try to understand. When we sang our praises to the sun or moon or wind, you said we were worshipping idols. Without understanding, you condemned us as lost souls just because our form of worship was different from yours.

—TATANGA MANI (WALKING BUFFALO),
STONEY TRIBE, 1871

JESSE OPENED HIS eyes, and a second or two passed before he caught his bearings. The coarse hair on the buffalo robe, the fresh smell of a morning cleansed by rain, the scent of sweet hay, and the beautiful woman lying snuggled next to him quickly reminded him. He looked down at Kathleen, her face soft and rosy with sleep, her hand resting on his chest. His sense of honor gave him a hard poke. *Aw, Katie-love, what have I done.* He touched her cheek, setting aside a silken strand of her hair, not wanting anything to hamper his view of her face. *You're a damned fool, Horse.* Tooter's voice rode his conscience like a tenacious cowboy on a bucking bronco. *What you've done, Horse, is fall in love. Plain and simple,* kola.

Love? Had he lost his heart to the prim Miss Prescott? Prim? Jesse almost laughed at the thought, remembering her eager night in his arms, the innocence she had freely given to him. She was now his Katie-girl, his alone. *Yeah, you're right, you crazy Kiowa, I love her.*

The pitch of night was fading, and Jesse knew they

couldn't wait another minute. Even under the shadows of
dawn the risk of being caught was too great, and he certainly didn't want anyone catching Kathleen slipping back
into her room. Too many early risers threatened their secret.
Mrs. Gilbert and her staff began work in the kitchen well
before daybreak and Gustav Felder and his boys would be
coming soon to care for the horses. They had to leave now.

"*Wa'na a'ηpa.*" He kissed Kathleen's cheek, and then
moved to her lips. "It's morning, Katie. Wake up," he cajoled. "We have to go."

She stirred, stretching, pressing her body against him. In
an instant he was hard again. He'd worried that she might
wake feeling remorse, regret, embarrassment, but she met
his light kisses and tipped her hips into him.

"I had the most wonderful dream," she murmured, tracing nonsensical patterns with her fingers on his chest and
following each with a light kiss. "I dreamed that I wished
on the evening star and my wish came true." She slid her
hand down between them and stroked him with long, gentle
sweeps of her fingers. "Love me again, Jesse."

And in his heart he answered her. "Forever, Katie-love,
forever."

JESSE HELPED HER pull the skirt over her head and settle it at her waist over the bustled slip. Still damp, the fabric
felt cool and clammy against her skin. "You'd better get
your pants on, Mr. Spotted Horse," she teased, surprised
that her words came easy and without discomfit. "Working
at the woodpile the way you're dressed could be very inju-
rious to your . . . health." She looked up and watched his
face as he winked at her and then buttoned his pants. Eyes
as dark as night, hair the color of a raven's wing, and a
smiling mouth that had thrilled and delighted her; her confession came easily. *Yes, oh, yes, I love this man.*

He touched her arm. "We have to hurry."

She smiled; he'd caught her staring at him. "Just a
minute, I have to find my blouse and shawl." She spied
them on a mound of hay near the wall. Bending to retrieve
them, something caught her eye. She pushed some of the

hay out of the way. "Jesse, look at this. What do you think this is all about?"

Hunkering down beside her, Jesse pulled back the rest of the hay and quickly rifled through the items she'd found. Someone had very carefully hidden two kerosene lanterns, some blankets, a flour sack with three loaves of bread, a half block of hard cheese, some apples, and a tin of matches. "Looks to me like someone's planning a trip." He covered everything up again, being careful to scatter the hay and make it look as though the items hadn't been disturbed.

"Shouldn't we tell someone? Providence?"

He glanced at her. "Why? Do you think punishment is going to stop whoever hid these things from trying to run away again?"

He steered her away from the hidden cache. "I think when you tell Providence about the arsenic, he's going to have enough things to worry about."

Climbing down the ladder posed a few new problems, but Jesse had gone first, to catch her in case she fell. He'd had little trouble unbuttoning her high-topped boots the night before, but without her buttonhook, she couldn't fasten them this morning. When she was five rungs from the bottom of the ladder, Jesse lifted her off and set her on the ground. She wobbled unsteadily in her loose boots. "Why don't I just take them off, it would be much easier to walk."

Barefoot, she followed him to the back of the barn. Lifting the latch, Jesse pushed the door open an inch or two and peered out. "Looks okay." He widened the opening just enough for them to squeeze through and they stepped out into the cool morning.

He led her to the stand of trees on the north side of the building. "I think it's best if we split up. If either of us is caught, at least the other will be safe."

"I'm not going to sneak through the bushes and fight brambles and bugs again. I'm going to stroll, just as bold as you please, across the parade ground," Kathleen declared, glancing at the wide lawn. "If anyone asks, I was unable to sleep, took a very early morning walk and got caught in the rain." She gave her hair a toss. "How else could I explain this?"

Jesse caught a handful of her curls. "You could always say that your lover messed it up."

A small poof of air fled her lips. "Is that what you are now? My lover?" She didn't know if she liked the sound of that at all, and in her heart she knew that she wanted more.

He took hold of her shoulders and smoothed his hands up to gently cradle her face. "*Ta'ku kin oyás'in isáŋbya cantéciciye.*"

"What did you say?"

"Someday I'll tell you. I promise," he whispered against her lips just before he wrapped his arms around her, just before he kissed her.

She lifted her arms around his neck and let the warmth and excitement wash over her. Her heart cried when he pulled away.

"You've got to go now, sweetheart. It's getting too light."

With one last glance at Jesse over her shoulder, she started up the short slope to the parade ground. Cresting the hill, she picked up her skirt and began to run, barefoot, across the wide lawn, leaving Jesse behind in the shadows.

The dormitory was quiet when Kathleen slipped inside. Hurrying up the stairs as quietly as she could, she fumbled with the key, unlocked her bedroom door, and stepped into her room. She dropped her boots on the floor beside her and closing her eyes, she leaned back against the door. Relieved she'd made it back to the dormitory without being caught, she drew three or four deep, calming breaths.

She placed her hand over her rapidly beating heart. A mixture of things caused its excited race, but one in particular gave her more joy than she'd ever known. "Jesse." She spoke his name on a sigh and sent a quick silent prayer Heavenward. *Please keep him safe, help him get back to his room without any trouble, just like I did.* "Jesse." Another sigh carried his name. *You have changed my life forever.* A light chuckle welled up in her throat. *This boring, plain old spinster has finally become a woman.*

The words had no sooner formed in her mind than she

felt the presence. Awareness slithered through her body.
Someone else was in the room.

A slight rustle of fabric and the squeak of a floorboard
shattered the silence. Turning toward the sounds, toward
the open window, Kathleen watched and held her breath as
the figure moved out of the straight-backed chair.

"Well, Miss Prescott. You've been a busy little harlot,
haven't you?"

Kathleen found it almost impossible to speak with her
heart lodged in her throat. She had to keep her wits about
her. Drawing a breath, she stepped farther into the room.
"Miss Lester. My, what a surprise." Her door key clanked
as she dropped it on the tall bureau. "You must be lost. Isn't
your room down the hall?"

"How dare you get self-righteous with me," Margaret
Lester spat, moving to the window. "I saw you. I saw you
and that filthy savage, his hands all over you, and . . . kissing." She pointed toward the barn, and her harsh gesture
suddenly changed to a casual flip of her hand. A smile,
smug and wily, curved her mouth. "Mind you, the view was
much better from *my* bedroom window." Her gaze traveled
over Kathleen from head to toe. "From the looks of you, I'd
say that you've had yourself quite a tumble. In the hay, I
presume?"

Kathleen refused to take Margaret's bait and forced herself to stay calm. She wouldn't provoke the woman, but she
wouldn't give her any more information than she already
had. There was little doubt about it, though. Margaret now
held the key to Kathleen's job and to her chances of staying
on at DuBois.

"I'm sure that Provi . . . that Reverend Divine would be
very interested in my discovery," Margaret wheedled. "Of
course he'd be most disappointed to lose his latest favorite." She stepped closer to Kathleen and sniffed the air.
"I can smell that dirty Indian on you." She gave a dismis-
sive gesture. "But that's what you get when you wallow
with pigs."

"I think, Miss Lester, that what you smell is your own
forsaken piety."

"And I think you should be very careful with your

clever words, Miss Prescott, very careful." She moved to the window, pulled back the drapes, and glanced toward the barn. "I do, after all, have the upper hand." She turned and the wily smile broadened. "But for the right reasons, shall we say, I might be persuaded to keep silent."

Her message couldn't have been clearer. "I believe what you're suggesting, Miss Lester, is called blackmail."

"Such an appalling word. Let's just say it is two people doing nice things for each other. And the fact that you have something I want makes the . . . arrangement more fitting."

*The arsenic. Was that what Margaret wanted?* Her eyes darted to the bed. *Had she found it?* The quilt didn't look as though it had been moved, and the little braided rug was still in the same spot. *No, it's still safe. This wasn't about the arsenic after all.*

Kathleen quickly aligned the facts. Margaret had been gone the day before, visiting in Pritchart with the ladies' guild at the Methodist Church and hadn't returned until just before supper. *She probably hasn't been back in the little kitchen across the hall from Providence's office.* If Margaret Lester hid the arsenic, she wouldn't know yet that her deadly scheme had been discovered.

The false entries in the ledger were another matter, and Kathleen wondered if she should tell Margaret that she had discovered her duplicity. Perhaps it would even the playing field, but the voice of reason slid into her mind. *No, not yet, bide your time until you have all the facts and can prove them.*

Kathleen knew there was nothing she could do right now except capitulate. "What do you want?"

"Hmm, what do I want?" Margaret placed her index finger alongside of her nose, pretending to give the question a great deal of thought. "Ah, yes. I believe I know." She crossed the room and rested her hand on the bureau. "I believe you have a pretty cameo bauble that might earn my silence . . . for a while."


JESSE PLACED HIS hand on Adam's shoulder and steered the boy toward the back of the carpentry shop. "You and I need to have ourselves a little talk."

"Not speak so fast, white words are crazy coming out of your Lakota mouth."

"Well, get used to them, you'll hear them a lot for the rest of your life." Jesse glanced over his shoulder, making sure that no one else was near. Satisfied, he turned back to Adam. "I think I found a few things this morning that belong to you and your pals." The sudden guilty look on the boy's face was all the confession he needed.

"How you know belongs to me?" The boy shrugged and tried to walk away, but Jesse's hand caught the back of his collar and pulled him back. "There be many boys at this place, that stuff could belong at them."

"That's right it could, but I saw three of those many boys slip up into the hayloft with a flour bag yesterday afternoon."

Adam shook his head. "What do I want with cheese?" He grimaced. "It not taste good."

"Funny that *you* should mention cheese, because I sure didn't." He watched the play of emotions on the boy's face—fear, hopelessness. "You've run away before, haven't you?"

"*Nu'ηpa ecámon.* I did it twice." Adam glanced away, and when he spoke, Jesse could barely hear his words. "That Slocum man, last time we run he catch us four. Other boy named *Tašuηke Lu'zahan,* Jonah Fast Horse. The one called Wilks, he *uηka'p'api,* he hits us many hard times with that stick he have." Adam trembled and his voice quavered.

Jesse's blood ran cold, his rage taking all the warmth from his body. He held his breath, afraid that he already knew what Adam's next words would be. He wasn't wrong.

"Jonah, die. We saw. They leave Jonah in the cold place with us." His voice finally broke and tears drenched his cheeks. "We try to remember songs to sing for him, to send him on to the Heaven place. Weasel take a stone from the ground and cut himself; Jonah his brother." Adam's body shuddered. "Them men come back in dark and take Jonah away." He looked up at Jesse, his dark eyes filled with anguish. "They hide him in hole in death place . . . whites call cem . . . cemetery." Adam looked down at the floor. *"Uŋgla'pi kta uŋciŋpi.* We want go home."

Jesse drew the boy into his arms. He didn't care if traditional Lakota boys needed or even allowed hugs, this kid, the boy who would become his great-uncle, was going to get hugged anyway. "I do, too, Adam. I do, too."

"You tell the fat one?" Adam pointed at Dobbs with a lift of his chin. "We get put back to that bad cold place?"

Jesse didn't know how he'd do it, but Wilks and his boys weren't going to get away with murder. If it meant his own life, his love for Kathleen, or any chance he had of going back to his own time, he'd make sure they paid. "No, I'm not going to tell anybody, and you will definitely not be going back to the cold house. I promise, I'm not going to let anyone hurt you."

AFTER CHANGING HER clothes and fixing her hair, Kathleen went directly to her classroom, avoiding the teachers' table in the dining hall. She wished that she'd at least stopped by the kitchen for a piece of bread and jam or an apple or peach. The morning passed at a snail's pace, and her stomach growled with hunger for most of that time. Leaning over one of the Winnebago boys to check his spelling paper, it grumbled again.

"You swallowed a bear, miss? I think he want out." The boy giggled, covering his mouth with his hand.

The class had quite a laugh at her expense, too, but the bear in her belly wasn't happy and growled again.

By noon she knew she couldn't avoid Margaret Lester and the others forever. She entered the dining hall and immediately sensed that Jesse was in the room. She saw him from the corner of her eye, but a glance at Margaret Lester warned her not to look at him.

"Ah, good afternoon, Miss Prescott," Basil Dobbs said, rising to help with her chair. "I . . . uh . . . we missed you at breakfast this morning. Mrs. Gilbert outdid herself with a wonderful dish of scrambled eggs with cheese, bell peppers, and just a pinch of onion. As usual," he patted his belly, "I had two helpings."

Hannah touched her arm. "I heard you were caught in the rain early this morning. I hope you haven't caught your death. Mrs. Lankford who used to work here, she went walking in the rain one day and died of consumption within the month."

Kathleen's gaze locked with Margaret's. The woman had the gall to smile and lightly touch the cameo brooch at her throat.

"I understand that Reverend Divine has asked you to tutor our troublemaker," Josiah Wilks remarked. "Why he insists on wasting extra time on these Indians is beyond me. Teach them enough till they think they're educated, then turn them loose."

"I'm sure that our Miss Prescott doesn't believe she is wasting her time at all, with this particular student." Margaret Lester's counterfeit smile showed too many teeth. "Do you, Miss Prescott?"

"No, of course not," Kathleen answered, thankful that she'd almost finished her meal.

"Miss Prescott," Alma Briggs called from the end of the table. "The Methodist Church ladies from town will be coming here for tea tomorrow, Wednesday. They usually bring their donation for the school every year on July seventh. It's the anniversary of the church's founding. Will you be joining us?"

"Thank you for reminding me, Miss Briggs," Kathleen said, rising from her chair. "I'll certainly try to be there." She glanced across the table at Margaret Lester and then at the others. "I have a busy afternoon, so if you will all excuse me."

All the way back to her classroom, something elusive kept niggling at her, staying just out of mental reach. It had been triggered by something that Alma Briggs had said. Kathleen replayed the lunchtime conversations through her mind, once, twice, and a third time before the piece of the puzzle began to slide into place.

Wednesday, the seventh of July. Why did that date strike her as being important? She ran down the list of possibilities, birthdays, anniversaries, national holidays, due car insurance payments. And then, as though it grew tired of teasing her, she remembered. On the seventh of July 1886, the barn at DuBois Indian School burned to the ground.

"Smoke," she breathed, her heart beginning to race with excitement. What was it that Jesse had called it? The portal? In that instant she knew. It hadn't been a split in the wall of time that had been the transporter, it had been the smoke.

*But the fire on July 7, 1886, had been a real fire,* she argued with herself. *But so was the one that sent you here.* Back and forth the argument raged. The three hours she had to wait until her counterfeit tutoring session with Jesse that afternoon would be cruel torture.

# Chapter 25

In a short time, the child comes to love and admire his captors ... a not uncommon adjustment made by those taken hostage; separated by all that is familiar, stripped, shorn, robbed of their very self, renamed.

—PAULA GUNN ALLEN,
(LAGUNA/SIOUX)

KATHLEEN LIFTED HER skirts above her ankles and ran up the stairs, praying with each step that Jesse would be there. Each day they met in the little room across from Providence's office for their sham tutoring sessions. She opened the door and stepped inside. Empty. A slight noise, nothing more than the creak of a floorboard, drew her attention. She turned to find Margaret Lester leaning against the door frame.

"Your eagerness to be with your pet Indian is really quite disgusting," Margaret sneered. She stepped away from the door and raised her hand to the cameo brooch pinned to her bodice. "I really liked our last conversation on the same topic, though." At the sound of footsteps on the stairs, Margaret quickly retreated to her office.

Jesse topped the staircase and Kathleen grabbed his hand. "Come on, hurry. Inside." She pulled him into the small classroom and shut the door.

Sweeping her in his arms, he laughed. "I could hardly wait all day to see you, too." She pulled away and his grin quickly faded from his lips. "What's wrong?"

Nervous, Kathleen moved to the middle of the room. She'd waited all afternoon to tell him, and now that he was here, she didn't know where to begin. She drew a bracing breath and began where it felt most comfortable. "Jesse, I think I know why we're here, why Fate or whoever, whatever, sent us on this wild time slide."

Jesse held up his hand. "Let me answer this one." The grin that spread across his face told Kathleen that was he pretty sure of himself. He swung one of the straight-backed chairs out from the table and, turning it around, straddled the seat and rested his elbows on the back. "I think we both needed to learn the truth about DuBois. I thought it was a hellhole and you believed it was the next best place to Heaven. Since the flip we've seen we were both wrong and we were both right. We started at totally opposite convictions, and were damned self-righteous about them, too." His laugh was soft. "I think we're both pretty much near the middle now." He winked. "So, how close am I to what you came up with?"

"That's just about what I was going to say." His wink helped ease her nerves. "Except, after all my tutoring, you said it better." She sobered. "There's more."

"What?"

"There are things that still need to be done before we leave."

"Let me guess. We need to tell Providence that someone is poisoning him and give him the list of suspects, and he needs to know that Margaret's been cooking the books."

Kathleen nodded. "That just about covers that, but there's something else." She nervously chewed for a moment on her bottom lip and then told him the rest. "I know when and how we go home . . . and we don't have much time left." She'd finally stopped him in his tracks. He didn't move, didn't say a word. "Remember I told you that the barn had burned down once before?" She didn't expect his response, and the look on his face told her she wasn't going to get one. "It happened on Wednesday, the seventh of July 1886. Tomorrow. It will happen tomorrow afternoon. I don't think it's a portal like a doorway that takes us across. It's the smoke. We need to be inside the smoke to go home."

"I won't be going."

"What?" Stunned, she reeled back a few steps as though he'd struck her, and she found she couldn't say another word.

He dropped his head, and in a voice quiet and cold as steel, he told her about Jonah Fast Horse. He looked up and his expression was so fierce, Kathleen drew a quick breath. "I'm going to stay and make sure that Wilks and the other two don't get away with murder."

"Jesse, I think that's also part of why we're here, to make sure that they don't. Providence's role is to get the authorities out here to take care of everything."

Jesse shook his head. "Without anyone showing them where to find the boy's body, they'd have to dig up the whole cemetery."

"So you say you're staying because you know where he's buried?"

"Yeah."

"Jesse, Mrs. Gilbert knows. She saw them bury Jonah. She can tell them where he is." Kathleen frowned. Intuition told her there was more to Jesse's reason for wanting to stay.

"She's afraid to talk, she's got her own troubles with the law."

Kathleen sat down across the table from him. "Jesse, look at me." She waited until his eyes met hers. "It's not just about telling the police and getting Wilks and the others arrested, is it?"

"I don't know what you mean." Jesse got up. He moved to the window and stood with his back to her.

"Oh, yes, you do. You know exactly what I'm talking about." She suddenly felt cold. Was he really willing to throw away what they'd found with each other for what . . . retribution? "You don't just want to see Wilks and his pals arrested, I think you want to have the chance to mete out your own punishment. You want to pay them back yourself, for the boys, for you, before the police get them, don't you?" She left her chair and stood behind him. Sliding her arms around his waist, she laid her head against his back. "No, Jesse, please. That's not right. Revenge always demands a price from the avenger. Let the police take care of them. Let justice be done by hands from their own time, not by hands that I love, not by the man that I love." She closed her eyes. "Jesse, please, come home with me."

He turned into her embrace and tipped her chin up. For a moment he lost himself in the love he saw in her eyes, and then he lowered his head, slanted his mouth over hers, and felt her love heal his soul. He knew then that no matter what time they were in, they belonged together, not apart. Never apart.

Lifting his mouth from hers, Jesse looked down into her eyes again. Oh, yeah, he'd been right. Love and passion did make them a dark, smoky gray. He gently cradled the side of her face in his palm, lightly rubbing her kiss-moistened lips with the pad of his thumb. "You're right, Katie-love, it isn't for me to do. We'll do it your way." His grin was slow in coming, but it filled his face. "But don't get used to me saying that, I don't want to spoil you." He stroked her cheek with the back of his hand and wondered if he should tell her what had worried him from the day they'd arrived in the past. Yeah, he should. "Katie, what if we need to take back everything that we brought with us? I know it probably sounds ridiculous, but I think it's a physics thing—keeping the universe in balance." He plowed his fingers through his hair and looked out the window at the barn. "And, if that's true, I can't go."

Kathleen grinned, but she didn't interrupt him.

"You've still got the green dress and everything else you brought. My clothes and my hair were burned, remember?" She began to speak, but he pressed his finger against her lips, silencing her. "Kathleen, I'm crazy in love with you and if I have to stay in this time I'd want you with me." He stepped away from her. "But I won't ask you to stay. Even loving you doesn't give me that right."

She touched his arm. "Jesse, we can go home together. Your clothes are safe."

"What are you talking about? They were burned along with my hair, the day we got here, don't you remember?"

"I remember it very well. I remember you and the other boys marching up the hill wrapped in blankets that barely covered your dignity. I remember going into the barn after you'd all left. I remember how it broke my heart to find your beautiful braids, even the narrow one with the little brass bells. I remember sorting through the discarded clothes and finding everything you wore, including your feathers. And I remember wrapping everything in the beaded blanket and hiding the bundle beneath the eaves in the tack room."

Without thinking he drew a long breath and was all set to let out a loud, wild, victory yell, and he would have, if Kathleen hadn't very prudently covered his mouth with hers and kissed the living daylights out of him.

The sound of the doorknob rattling sent them to opposite sides of the room. Jesse snatched a book from the table and pretended to be reading when Margaret Lester burst in.

"This door must be kept open at all times," she ordered. "Who knows what kind of sinful deeds could be going on in here?" She turned and left the room as quickly as she'd come, leaving the door open in her wake.

"What the hell was that all about?" Jesse whispered, craning his neck to make sure that the woman had returned to her office.

"She knows." A bright blush rose on Kathleen's cheeks. She took the book from Jesse's hands and turned it right side up.

"She knows about what?"

"Us." Kathleen dropped into one of the chairs at the table. "She knows about us. She saw me this morning coming back from being with you and was waiting in my room. She saw us together."

"What walking, standing, talking?"

Kathleen's voice dropped to a near whisper, and she looked up at him from under lowered lashes. "Kissing."

"And I bet the reason she's wearing your brooch has nothing to do with your kind nature." He paced to the window again then pivoted to face Kathleen. "And just how do you intend to get it back so you'll have it tomorrow afternoon?"

A sound coming from the small kitchen, a teacup rattling in its saucer, drew their attention before Kathleen could answer.

"She's fixing Providence's tea." Kathleen moved to the door to listen. "Thank God, his tea will be safe today. I've got the poison, and I also refilled the sugar bowl. The sugar that's in the bowl now is pure."

The sound of the small stepstool scraping along the floor, the creak of a stepped-on rung, was followed by Margaret Lester's loud gasp.

"I guess we know who the arsenic belongs to." Kathleen turned away from the door. "Now we need to find out why she's poisoning Providence, and what we can do about it."

"There's something else," Jesse added. "I also found out whose little stash you found in the barn this morning. I'd had my suspicions. Adam and his friends hid the stuff. Apparently they're planning to run away."

"And Elijah?"

"What do you mean?"

"Did Adam say anything about Elijah? Those boys are as thick as thieves. Elijah's even talked about Adam and Weasel showing him how to hunt and that they were going to show him how real Indians live." She touched Jesse's arm. "If Adam and the other Indian boys are planning to run away, then I would bet my . . . my pair of naughty bloomers that Elijah's planning to go with them."

Jesse shook his head. "I'd hate to see those bloomers go, but it looks like we're going to have a very busy twenty-four hours getting everything put right if we intend to catch the time ride home."

KATHLEEN CLOSED THE small classroom door behind her. Jesse had left minutes earlier to meet with the rest of Dobbs's boys and head to the dining hall. "Keep everything as usual," he had said. "Don't tip them off to anything."

She crossed the hallway to her great-great-grandfather's office. The late afternoon sun shone through the windows, casting an ethereal glow on Providence's desk and chair. The room was empty. Rachel had come earlier to help him upstairs.

Kathleen's throat tightened and her eyes filled with tears as she glanced about the room. She'd grown to love the gentle man who had founded and dedicated his life to DuBois Indian School. Providence Divine was a good man, with good ideas and honorable intentions; it was the people he had surrounded himself with who had blemished his reputation and his work. Not all were cruel or murderers or thieves, but it was the bad ones and their deeds that would be remembered. Children had been abused, beaten, starved, even murdered. That's what would be written in history and told in Indian homes for generation after generation. Very few would remember those who served well. Few would remember the kind man of God who privately tutored those who could lead their people, or the mild-mannered man who bumbled his way through classes in the carpentry shop, or the kindly cook who jeopardized her own safety to feed some hungry boys. It was the legacy that was tarnished, not the man, not his dreams.

Feeling a sadness that wrapped itself around her soul, Kathleen turned and slowly walked downstairs and out onto the promenade.

KATHLEEN ARRANGED ALL of the things on her bed that she'd brought with her into the nineteenth century. Everything, Jesse had said, everything. And everything meant the blasted corset as well. She'd ask Hannah to help her dress in the morning, using the afternoon tea with the church ladies as her excuse for wearing her best dress. Was anything missing? She mentally itemized everything she'd had when the time slide took place. Yes, there was something missing—the tissues that Jesse had buried under the dining hall porch. She'd get them when she went for dinner.

Dinner had been an abysmal experience with everyone commenting on Margaret Lester's beautiful new brooch, an inheritance from a relative, or so she'd said. Only Hannah had remarked how closely it resembled the one that Kathleen owned.

Leaving the table early, Kathleen stood outside at the bottom of the stairs and pretended to admire the flowers that grew next to the honeysuckle bushes. Waiting until no one would see her, she stepped behind the bushes, pushed the latticework panel aside, and slipped under the porch. The speckled patterns of light and shadows on the dirt made it difficult to find the place that Jesse had buried the tissues. Intent on finding the exact spot, she didn't see him until he spoke.

"Good God, Katie-girl, you're going to be the death of me yet." Jesse stepped out from the deep shadows, swept his arm around her, and silenced her scream with his mouth. His kiss deepened, his tongue lightly caressing the inside of her mouth. He pulled away, leaving her breathless. "That's what I wanted to do the first time we were under the porch."

"You . . . you did?" she stammered, her hand over her racing heart.

"I think you're looking for these." He held the dirty and crumpled tissues out to her and helped her tuck them into her purse. He steered her toward the loose panel and began to lift it, but the sound of footsteps on the porch above made him stop, and he drew her further back into the shadows.

"Just how did you get that gorgeous brooch, Margaret? Something tells me that little Miss Prescott didn't give it to you willingly."

Jesse leaned close to Kathleen and whispered in her ear. "Haven't we done this before?"

"Just like Yogi Berra said," Kathleen quipped, finding it impossible not to giggle, "déjà vu all over again."

Jesse fought to stifle his own laugh; the conversation on the porch overhead quickly made the battle easy.

"We have more important things to concern ourselves with than a piece of jewelry, Josiah. The tin is empty." Margaret's panic could easily be heard in her voice.

"What are you talking about?" Jesse and Kathleen could hear him impatiently tapping the tip of his walking stick on the floor of the porch.

"The tin is empty, the arsenic is gone. Someone has taken it. What are we going to do?" Margaret whined.

A moment or two passed before Josiah Wilks answered with a self-righteous tone to his voice. "What do you mean we, my dear? I'm sure the clerk in the store in Pritchart will remember that it was you, not *we,* who purchased it. For bugs in your rosebushes, wasn't that your story? I was here that day, never left the grounds."

"Josiah, you can't just leave me to take the blame for this," she hissed. "Our plans were dependent upon each other. You're as much a part of this as I am."

Kathleen and Jesse heard Wilks begin to walk across the porch to the stairs.

"If I were you, Margaret, I'd be very careful who I told my lies to." His footsteps retreated back to where Kathleen assumed Margaret Lester was standing. "As for me, well, I've done nothing but take care of Providence's school while he was ill. There's certainly no crime in that."

"And what about the cold house?"

"Providence knows that was Slocum's and Blunt's error. Not mine."

"He doesn't know about the boy you three conveniently buried. I'm sure he'd find that news very interesting . . . if someone were to tell him, of course."

Kathleen heard a sharp crack, followed by a gasp. She didn't have to see it to know that Wilks had hit Margaret.

"Don't threaten me, Margaret. You have no proof that it ever happened."

"The other boys are proof," Margaret whimpered. "They saw. They know what happened."

Wilks laughed. "They're damned Indians. Who's going to believe them?" His footsteps sounded on the stairs. "Have a lovely evening, Margaret. I hope you find your little lost package."

"You're a bastard, Josiah."

"Ah, yes, Margaret, an unarguable point."

Jesse and Kathleen watched through the latticed panel as Wilks and Margaret Lester went their separate ways on the promenade, neither giving the other a backward glance.

Jesse wrapped his arms around Kathleen. He pulled her back against him and rested his cheek against her temple. "The plot thickens," he whispered.

Kathleen snuggled in against him, and her breath fled her lips in a contented sigh. "Us, like this, is the best part of this whole wild excursion and drama."

"I know," Jesse replied, placing a light kiss on her forehead. "*Ta'ku kin oyás'in isáηbya cantéciciye.*"

"That's what you said to me this morning, isn't it?"

"Yes, I did, didn't I?"

"And you're not going to tell me what it means, are you?"

He ignored her question and steered her to the loose panel. "Good night, Miss Prescott. Sleep well; you're going to have yourself a very busy day tomorrow."

**JESSE WAITED UNTIL** she was out of sight before he slipped out from under the porch. If Kathleen was right, there were only a few more hours left in the wild time slide. Looking around the school campus, the wide parade ground where the boys played ball, the promenade, the redbrick buildings with their crisp white painted shutters and railings, the large gazebo, the barn—he knew he would take every bit of this with him when he left. In his own time it would look much the same, but the essence of the place would be very different. With all of the bad he'd seen a lot of good.

He'd met the man he'd hated all of his life and found his hate was unfounded. He liked and admired the Reverend Providence Divine, admired him for his vision and felt sympathy for his failure. It was the system Jesse hated. It was the system that had done the damage to his people. And like it or not, he'd found good things at DuBois, things that he knew must be told, things that would be added to his film.

# Chapter 26

If they (the Indians) possess one quality that is all but universal among them and in which they are our superiors, it is that of personal dignity.

—PROFESSOR "B",
CARLISLE SCHOOL PAPER, 1900

KATHLEEN HAD SPENT the night tossing and turning, her mind racing over the plan that she and Jesse had worked out. An hour before dawn she had stumbled out of bed and sat at the window, wondering if Jesse was awake, too. Mourning doves were just beginning their cooing for the day, and the sky was slowly changing from midnight pitch to morning blue. She watched the white-tailed doe and her fawn step from the woods and nibble their fill of dew-kissed grass. Was Elijah up and peering out his bedroom window watching them, too?

Her gaze traveled to the whitewashed barn. In hours it would be gone and, with luck, so would she and Jesse. The corners of her mouth lifted in a halfhearted smile.

In just a month her life had changed forever. She never would have imagined that any of the incredible twists and turns were possible. Perhaps she should thank Richmond Brock and the academy's board for approving Jesse's request to make his film at DuBois.

"I have to get home first," she whispered. "*We* have to get home." *Home.* The word was simple enough, but even if her theory about the time trip back home was right, even if they made it home, she could never go back to the way her life had been.

"Jesse." His name left her heart on a soft sigh. He'd said he loved her, had taught her how to love and be loved, gave her passion and gave her life, but no promises had been made. And she wouldn't ask for any.

"I DON'T KNOW why you bother wearing one of these," Hannah remarked as she tightened Kathleen's corset laces. "If I had your trim figure and could wear my clothes without one, I'd burn all of my corsets in the town square on a Saturday morning."

"Someday"—Kathleen laughed, hoping her voice sounded light and carefree—"that might become quite popular." Her nerves were still strung as tight as piano wires. *Six hours, that's all that remains. Six torturous hours.*

"There, all done." Hannah stepped back and admired her handiwork.

Grateful that Hannah hadn't tightened the laces half as much as Egypt had the first time she'd worn the wretched undergarment, Kathleen soon discovered that even a little constriction was uncomfortable.

She tried to look calm and collected, tried to act normal, sound normal, but inside tension, excitement, apprehension, hope, anticipation, and melancholy swirled and mixed, each vying for the upper hand. She paced a few steps, nervously twisting the fingers of one hand with the other. "What time are the Methodist ladies expected for tea?"

"Three o'clock," Hannah replied, plopping herself down on the edge of Kathleen's bed.

*Good, Jesse and I will be gone by then.*

"Reverend Shelbourne will be coming with them." Hannah giggled.

Kathleen held up her hand. "I think you should try to match him up with Alma Briggs or Miss Blessing."

"Oh, all right, I understand your hint." Hannah bounced off the bed and helped Kathleen pull the emerald green skirt over her head and button the waist. "Why are you putting your finest dress on now? You'll be in it for the whole day."

Kathleen had prepared an answer for just this question.

"I won't have time to change. Usually my tutoring sessions with Jesse Spotted Horse aren't over until about three." She quickly changed the subject, hoping Hannah's questions would go no further. "The school is very fortunate to have a group of generous donors such as the Methodist ladies." Hannah handed Kathleen the bodice, and she put it on, fastening the pretty filigreed buttons.

"I really think they're hoping for converts," Hannah remarked, stepping back to survey Kathleen from head to toe. "Hmm, something's missing." She chewed at her bottom lip as she inspected Kathleen again. "The brooch, that's what's missing. You wear it. You know that Margaret will be wearing her new one, and yours is so much prettier."

"No," Kathleen replied, hiding her amusement. "I wouldn't want Miss Lester to feel I was trying to best her."

"Oh, fiddles," Hannah declared with a wave of her hand. "Just breathing and walking, you already do that."

Melancholy pressed down on Kathleen. She would miss Hannah. In just three weeks Hannah Dobbs had become the best friend she'd ever had. She'd miss everyone. Well, maybe not everyone; Josiah Wilks and Margaret Lester were certainly not on the list.

Hannah opened the door. "I want to get to the dining hall early. Mrs. Gilbert is serving my favorite breakfast this morning, and I'm so hungry I could eat ten servings." She angled a look at Kathleen.

Kathleen hesitated for a moment before answering. She knew that Hannah had been expecting her company for breakfast. "I'm not really hungry this morning. Besides, I've got some class work I'd like to get done." Seeing Hannah's disappointment, Kathleen tried to cheer her up. "Tell Mrs. Gilbert that you can have my serving, too."

Leaving Hannah on the promenade, Kathleen hurried to her classroom and unlocked the door. She paced back and forth, from one side of the classroom to the other, her fingers trailing across the desktops as she passed. With each step her excitement grew, and with it her apprehension grew as well. *What if I'm wrong? What if the fire is just that, a barn fire with no magical properties, no escape from*

*1886, no going home?* She shook her head. *No, I won't accept that. It's going to work. It's got to work.*

"And when it does, I'm going to miss this," she murmured. "I'm going to miss these precious children. I'm
going to miss how good it feels to see them grasp and learn
something with enthusiasm." She stopped and looked out
the window, her gaze sweeping across the entire view.
"And I'm going to miss the real DuBois—not the damned
ridiculous shrine that my grandfather and father turned it
into."

"That's a very pretty speech."

She wheeled around to find Jesse sitting on her desk.
Her heart took a delightful little bounce. "I'm going to
make you wear bells so you can't keep sneaking up on me."

He grinned. "Just bells, eh? Now that could be real interesting. You in those naughty bloomers and me in bells."
He sobered. "Speaking of wearing stuff, I sneaked down to
the barn this morning and found my Indian clothes, right
where you said they'd be." His voice softened. "Thank you,
Katie-girl."

She smiled; that silly name always made her smile.
"You're very welcome."

"I hid them in the carpentry shop, where I can get to
them easier. I can't wait to get rid of these." He plucked
with disdain at the DuBois uniform. "I'm sick of this
damned uncomfortable outfit."

"Would you care for a corset and a bustle skirt in ex-
change?"

Jesse laughed. "What, no naughty bloomers?" He lifted
his foot and twisted his ankle first left then right, showing
every angle of the poorly made, thick-soled boots. "Okay,
I'll see your corset and bustles and raise you these wonderful dancing shoes."

"I think those are called clodhoppers."

He looked up from his shoes at Kathleen and his smile
slowly faded. "Now let's talk about the elephant in the
room. We need to talk about this afternoon." He pushed
away from the desk. "I guess the plan is simple—we walk
into the burning barn, step into the smoke, hope we don't
get incinerated, and get off the time slide in 2003. That's

about it, isn't it?" He waited for her hesitant nod. "Okay, Katie-girl, what time does the barbeque begin?"

*He's just as scared as I am.* The thought brought an ounce of relief. If Jesse weren't afraid, she'd have to question his sanity. "The archives said that the fire was first spotted about one-thirty."

"Have you given any thought to how dangerous this idea of yours might be? What might happen to us if you're wrong?"

She couldn't look at him when she answered, but glanced out the window at the barn instead. "I've thought of little else."

"And have you thought about what we're going to tell folks when we show up on the other side, alive, a month after everyone thought we'd died?"

She turned and her eyes locked with his. "I was hoping that maybe you'd have an idea."

"Yeah, right." He nodded with the quirky Elvis grin on his lips. "I'll meet you in Providence's office about noon. That should give us time to tell him about Jonah, about the arsenic, and show him the ledgers." He glanced over his shoulder at the growing number of students coming into the room. "We've got to be out of here before the police show up, and we've definitely got to be gone before the bucket brigade gets to work."

"Jesse?"

"Yeah."

"We are going to make it back okay, aren't we?"

"We'd better, because I'm pretty sure I'm going to marry you when we get home."

THE MORNING SEEMED to drag on and on forever, and Kathleen had trouble keeping her mind on her class. She had checked the time on her little watch at least ten times over, being careful not to be seen each time she'd taken it out of her purse.

Leaving her desk, she slowly walked up and down between the rows of desks, pretending to watch the children do their work. *Marry . . . did Jesse really say the word? Oh, yeah, he said it.* Hope rose to the surface and she reveled in its embrace.

She lifted her hand and unconsciously smoothed it over her hair, pushing a loose hairpin back in place. With her finger still pressed against the pin, a cruel thought sliced its way into her mind.

*I don't have everything that I brought with me. I've lost so many of my hairpins over the last weeks; I wouldn't know where to find them all.* She tried to deal with the fresh spate of panic. *No, I'm not going to tell Jesse.* Her decision was final. *If he gets through and I don't . . . at least one of us will make it home safe and sound.*

Just before noon she dismissed the class for lunch and followed them out of the building. There would be just enough time to go back to her room, collect her bonnet and gloves, and meet Jesse in Providence's office.

Movement on the porch of the senior girls' dormitory caught her eye. Margaret. Almost hidden behind one of the roof supports, Margaret Lester furtively glanced around a few times, then slipped inside the building.

Jesse's words suddenly filled Kathleen's mind. *"There's a certain look, a kind of tension that people get when they're scheming."* Margaret Lester had that look. *But why would she act as if she didn't want to be seen, especially if she was going into the building where she lived? It wouldn't matter . . . unless she didn't want anyone to know she was there.*

Walking faster and faster until she was almost running, Kathleen quickly reached the dorm and quietly made her way inside and up the stairs. Something, intuition perhaps, told her where she'd find Margaret, and she wasn't wrong.

Kathleen's bedroom door stood ajar, and she waited in the hallway for a moment, listening as Margaret stealthily opened and closed drawers, moved the chair, the washstand, checked behind the drapes, and then suddenly all was quiet. Pushing the door open another five or six inches, her heart leaped out of her chest and lodged in her throat as she watched Margaret lift the quilt and look under the bed.

With very little grace, her skirts billowing up around her, Margaret lay on the floor and peered under the bed at the springs. Her gleeful giggle told Kathleen what she feared most. The little bundle holding the sack of arsenic had been found.

Kathleen quietly slipped into the room and waited for Margaret to stand and turn around. And when she did, the shocked expression on Margaret Lester's face was one to be treasured.

Quickly recovering, Margaret took a menacing step toward Kathleen and held up the package. "Did you think I wouldn't figure out who had taken this . . . Little Miss Nosybody? Huh? Did you?" Her eyes narrowed and drawing the sack close to her breasts, she gave her chin a defiant upward tilt. "I don't know why you thought you had to take it. It's just for my roses."

Kathleen ignored the ridiculous lie and refused to be intimidated. She blocked Margaret's only route to escape. "Will you tell me why, Margaret? Why were you putting arsenic in Reverend Divine's tea? What has he done that would make you want to kill him in such a horrible way?"

"Yes, Margaret, suppose you tell me why."

Startled, Kathleen spun around to find Rachel standing in the open doorway.

Margaret took a step forward and quickly held out the small parcel. "Rachel, thank God you're here. Look what I've discovered in Miss Prescott's room. I've had my suspicions about her all along." She pointed and shook her hand at Kathleen. "She's evil, a killer. She's been putting it in the sugar in Providence's tea cupboard." Margaret glanced at Kathleen and then back at Rachel. "My God, Rachel, she's been poisoning him." She moved another step closer. "Of course she'll try to tell you that she's innocent, that it was me, that I did it, but you know that's not true, you know how much I care for him. It's her, she's the one who's made him so horribly ill."

Rachel Divine stepped farther into the room, tears wetting her cheeks. "Dear God, Margaret, stop the lies. Why? Please, just tell me why you did such a despicable thing." She folded her hands into fists. "I became suspicious when his health improved while we were in Indianapolis." She gestured toward Kathleen. "Besides, you started your unspeakable endeavors against my husband well over a month before Miss Prescott arrived."

"Your husband," Margaret sneered. "Until you came along, he was to be *my* husband. *My* husband. He was courting me for almost six months before you came and spoiled everything!" She slipped the bundle of arsenic into her pocket and then raised her hand to smooth back a straggling lock of hair. "You're ugly, Rachel, a freak. Look at yourself in the mirror, if you can stand it." Her fingers moved down her left cheek. "You've got the devil's mark, not me. What evil thing did you do to make him settle for your damaged goods? He was so easily persuaded." Margaret eased her way across the room toward the door. "I wanted your loving husband to suffer, just like I've been suffering since he chose you." A low, well-modulated laugh fled Margaret's throat, the sound cold and frightening. "Soon you won't have anyone to protect you and your ugly face from the world."

Margaret moved quickly. Delivering a painful blow to Kathleen's ribs, she pushed her against the bureau and knocked her to the floor. Striking out with her left hand, she shoved Rachel against the wall and rushed out the door and down the hall to the stairs.

Kathleen pulled herself to her feet and turned to give chase, but Rachel grabbed her arm. "There's no need. She won't get far. Where can she go without a horse or buggy? It's too far to walk to town and she's afraid of the woods."

"If that's what you want, but we should tell Reverend Divine." Rubbing her bruised elbow, Kathleen glanced around the small simple room, then picked up her bonnet and gloves from the top of the bureau. Her traveling outfit was now complete. Without one last look at the room, she followed Rachel out into the hallway and closed the door.

A shriek, a mixture of frustration and pain, shattered the silence, echoing up the stairwell and into the hall.

"Margaret," Rachel breathed, picking up her skirts and rushing down the stairs.

They found Margaret Lester sprawled on the walkway at the bottom of the porch stairs. A halo of fine powder, glittering in the sun like tiny crystals, scattered on the ground around her.

"Help me, Rachel," Margaret whined. "I've hurt my ankle, it might be broken."

Bending over, Rachel quickly unclasped the cameo brooch on Margaret's blouse and handed it to Kathleen. "I believe this belongs to you."

Stunned, Kathleen took the pin. "Thank you, but how did you know?"

"My sister told everyone that she'd inherited the cameo from a relative." Rachel lifted her shoulders in a slight shrug. "I'm her only relative."

Stunned by what she'd just heard, Kathleen looked down at Margaret. "Your sister?"

Rachel nodded. "Yes, my older sister."

"You're no sister that I want to claim," Margaret railed. "You may have stolen Providence from me, but you never got Elijah, did you?" Her laugh rang cold. "He believed everything I told him about you, Rachel. I told him you could make horrible things happen. I even told the little brat that you made his mother die." Margaret's laughter rose, sounding frenzied. "That's why he never allowed you near him. That's why he's so afraid of you." The gleeful look on her face disappeared, a slyness taking its place. "You didn't know that, did you?" She quickly turned her wrath on Kathleen. "And I bet you told Rachel all about the money Josiah and I have been taking from the school funds." The laugh rose once again. "Don't look so surprised that I know you've discovered another one of my little secrets. You didn't know that Elijah saw you snooping in my desk, did you?"

Kathleen felt something akin to pity for Margaret Lester. "No, you're wrong, I haven't told her a word about the money, but you just did."

Lifting Margaret to her feet, Rachel and Kathleen helped her hobble to the administration building. Climbing the stairs to Providence's office proved difficult, but not as difficult as what Kathleen knew was coming.

Stepping into Providence's office, Kathleen stopped in her tracks. She had expected to find Jesse in the room with

Providence, but she certainly hadn't expected to find him dressed in his beautiful Indian clothes. She drew a quick breath. She'd forgotten how magnificent he looked in them. Everything was in place: the buckskin shirt, the fringed leg gings, the brightly beaded moccasins, and his feathers . . . everything but his glorious long hair. And then she saw the braids, he'd tucked them under his belt and just the wrapped tips hung below the buckskin shirt.

Providence gestured to Kathleen. "Come in, my dear. Your Lakota friend has been telling me a number of appalling and very interesting things." Providence glanced at Jesse, then back at Kathleen. "What has made our conversation even more interesting is his perfect English." His elbows on his desktop, Providence templed his fingers and shook his head. "Sadly, Miss Prescott, I don't believe, as his teacher, that you can take the credit." He turned to Jesse. "You played your part extremely well, Mr. Spotted Horse, and certainly had everyone fooled. I never would have suspected that you were an agent for President Cleveland's Indian programs. Thank God you and Miss Prescott were able to expose Wilks and his men before another child was lost."

Kathleen shot a surprised look at Jesse. Now she'd heard just about everything, and this story was a whopper. Government agent? All he offered her in return was a wide grin, a silly casual shrug, and one of his infamous winks.

"I've sent Mr. Gilbert to town for the sheriff," Providence continued, "and Mr. Felder and Mr. Dobbs have given Wilks and his cohorts a taste of their own medicine. They'll be spending some time in the cold house until they're taken to jail to stand trial." He sobered. "Although, whatever their sentence will be, it won't half pay for that innocent child's life."

Rachel pushed her sister into one of the chairs in front of Providence's desk. "I believe my sister has a few confessions of her own to make."

"I already know about the arsenic, Libby, my darling. Mr. Spotted Horse has told me everything."

Kathleen quickly stepped forward, holding her hand up as though she were a traffic cop. "Please, excuse me, but could you explain something to me?" She looked first at Providence and then pointed to Rachel. "You just called your wife Libby."

"Yes, I did, didn't I?" The smile on Providence's face seemed to dispel the ravages of Margaret's poison. "I believe it's a husband's prerogative to call his wife by her name."

Rachel Divine giggled. "My name is Rachel Elizabeth, but my dear husband prefers to call me Libby. It's his pet name for me." She glanced at her husband and her eyes softened. "He says that Rachel sounds too stiff and over-bearing, as though I were a straitlaced old spinster." Her love for her husband shone in her eyes.

"The very reason that I think someone named Kathleen should be called Katie," Jesse added.

Kathleen knew his teasing was meant to ease the nervousness that had been building all day. The sound of foot-steps pounding up the stairs interrupted her reply.

"Reverend Divine! Reverend!" Basil Dobbs burst into the room.

Jesse took hold of Kathleen's hand and drew her to the door. "Come on, Katie-girl, it's time to go."

She hesitated for a moment, for one last look at her great-great-grandfather, before Jesse pulled her out of the room and down the hall.

Dobbs collapsed against the door frame and struggled to catch his breath. "Fire! There's a fire. Barn!" He wheezed and staggered into the room. "There's a fire in the barn!"

Jesse and Kathleen were at the bottom of the stairs when they heard Libby's cry.

"Oh, my God! Where's Elijah? He was playing with the Indian boys in the barn."

# Chapter 27

*When it comes time to die, be not like those whose hearts are filled with fear. Sing your death song and die like a hero going home.*

—TECUMSEH

"COME ON, KATHLEEN. You've got to run faster." Jesse pulled her across the promenade and onto the parade ground. His grip felt like a steel vise around her left wrist.

"I can't . . . I can't go . . . faster," she gasped, fighting the frenetic swing of her skirts. Grabbing a handful of material, she lifted them up high enough to keep the fabric from twisting around her legs. She had hung the little drawstring purse on her wrist and looped her bonnet over her arm by the grosgrain ties. They swung wildly as she ran, hampering her even more. Keeping up with Jesse was almost impossible.

Her high-buttoned boots were another problem. The heels sank into the dirt with each step and threatened to send her tumbling. Kathleen knew if she fell, she'd never make it to the barn in time. Strands of hair fell loose around her face, and an agonizing stitch bit into her side. Determined to ignore the pain, she pushed herself harder. Dizzy, she soon began to lag behind.

Smoke billowed from between the eaves of the barn and up through the cedar-shake roof, smudging the bright blue sky. The stench of burning wood choked the air, and the crackle of flames reminded Kathleen of the ominous ticking of a clock. Time was running out.

With less than sixty feet to go, they heard the first cries.

Rising high-pitched and filled with terror, they hovered in the air all around them. Another followed, and then another.

"Oh, God, Jesse," she sobbed, her lungs burning, "the boys . . . they're inside!" She wrenched free from his grasp and staggered, almost falling. "Go! Hurry! You . . . you've got to . . ." Another cry rose with the smoke and cut through her words.

"*O'makiyi yo!* Help us! *O'makiyi yo!*"

Jesse shot a quick glance at the barn and then back at Kathleen, his torment clear. "Katie-girl, I can't leave you." He slowed and tried to grab her hand again. "We've got to go through together."

Kathleen veered out of reach. "I'll be there . . . I promise." Her voice became a frantic sob. "Jesse, help the boys!"

Leaving her behind, Jesse quickly reached the barn and disappeared inside. Trails of smoke now slipped over the edge of the doorsill and climbed up the side of the building. Flames spiked through the shingles on the roof, sending sparks into the sky.

In a small corner of her mind she heard the frantic ringing of the school bell and the shouts of Dobbs and Felder and Watson.

"Get the horses out!"

"They're all right. They're out to pasture."

"We're gonna need more buckets!"

"The boys are getting them."

"Is anyone inside?"

Kathleen had no idea how close the men were behind her, but she knew, knew from the archives, that nothing they could do would stop the fire from completely destroying the barn. Gasping for breath, she raced down the slope, almost stumbling before she reached the door. She paused for a moment to catch one last breath of fresh air, and then stepped inside.

Acrid smoke stung her eyes and seared her lungs as she searched for Jesse.

"Katie, stay there, don't move."

Looking up, she found him on the ladder. Above him,

the flames in the loft flared high with each fresh mound of hay they found and consumed.

"Adam!" Jesse stepped up another rung. "Adam, where are you?" Another wail came from behind the wall of fire and smoke. "Weasel, Adam! For God's sake, Isaac, answer me!"

Out of the midst of the screams and the boys' choking coughs, Jesse heard one voice, Adam's voice. "*Letan khigla yo!* Get away, Jesse. Don't come here."

He ignored the boy's warning and moved up another rung on the ladder. "Stay together, you've got to stay together."

"We are each together, but fire all around," Adam choked. "Nowhere we can go."

Jesse climbed to the top of the ladder, but each time he tried to step off, the flames leaped at him, pushing him back. "Adam, talk to me. Tell me where you are so I can find you."

"*O'makiyi ye*, help me!"

"Isaac!" Jesse yelled. "Is that you? Weasel? Can you hear me?"

Terrified, Kathleen stared up and watched as Jesse dodged the blaze and tried time and time again to cross the loft to the boys. Flames, like hungry tongues, licked at him, and he tried to beat them back with the blue chieftain's blanket.

An insidious thought struck Kathleen, the blow almost physical and just as painful. *What if we never were supposed to go back? What if our dying here is how it's supposed to end?*

"Jesse!" Her hand flew to her mouth, holding back the screams that collected in her throat.

The sound, quiet, a stifled cry, barely loud enough to be heard over the spit and crackle of the firestorm, yanked Kathleen's attention away from Jesse and the loft. She turned, looking for what or who had made the sounds.

Huddled against the wall, his face dirty and streaked by tears, Elijah stared up at her. She grabbed his shirt and pulled him into her arms. "Thank God, Elijah. I was so afraid. Are you all right?" He stared at her, wide-eyed and

silent. She shook him. "What happened?" And shook him
again. "Talk to me."

Finally, as if he had suddenly realized she was there,
Elijah began to cry. "We . . . we're going away." He gulped
a breath, and catching a mouthful of smoke, he coughed.
"Adam and Weasel said we'd all go to their home together
so I could see how the real Indians live." Elijah wrapped
his arms around her neck, his body shaking with his sobs.
"I want to go with them."

She glanced up into the loft at Jesse, torn between
Elijah's story and the safety of the man who had become
her entire world. Elijah burrowed into her arms.

The boy shuddered. "Isaac . . . wanted to light the
lantern. Adam told him no, but he did it anyway. He . . .
he . . . lit it and got scared . . . he . . . he dropped it." He
tightened his grip on her. "I came down to get a bucket of
water. I tried to hurry, I really did." He glanced up, then
pressed his face against Kathleen's shoulder. "I didn't hurry
fast enough."

The smoke thickened and flames shot up the walls, over
the eaves, and licked along the rafters. The heat had become stifling, and burning pieces of chaff floated on the hot
currents of air, starting other fires wherever they landed.
Kathleen knew that if Jesse didn't get down now, he'd be
trapped. He'd die.

"Adam!" Jesse yelled again, the smoke choking him,
making him cough, making his voice hoarse. "You've got
to tell me where you are. You've got to try to get out."

"*Ni I'c'ya yo wan. Go, kola. Suŋgleska, wicas'sa iye'cel
mat'in kte.*"

"No, dammit!" Jesse yelled. "Adam, don't you dare tell
me you're going to die." Jesse took a tentative step farther
into the loft. Flames exploded in front of him, the heat blis-
tering, the sound deafening. "Adam! Weasel! Goddammit,
answer me!" He called again and then again. But only the
roar of the fire and the crackle of burning wood answered
him, their message loud and clear.

The cry began deep in Jesse's gut. It tore through his
soul, leaving an unbearable pain in its wake. His voice rose,
high and strong. He raged against the flames and showed

his contempt for death. With a warrior's yell, as old as his people, he cried out and honored the lives of three boys who would never go home again.

Jesse knew he had to get out of the loft now. If he didn't, he'd never get out alive. Quickly backtracking through the smoke, he swung onto the ladder and rapelled down, ignoring the splinters that drove into his hands. The smoke, dark and acrid, rolled after him as though it were alive. It chased after him, spilling over the edge of the loft and down the ladder.

Thoughts flashed through his mind, bombarding his senses. If only he'd taken the boys' stash away from them when Kathleen had found it. If only he'd run faster. If only he'd reached the boys sooner. If only . . . He fought the onslaught of tears, swiping his hand across his eyes. *No, Horse, this is how it was supposed to be. It wasn't for you to change what was or what would be. There's no guilt here for you. This was how* Tokalu Sapa *died. This was why he never came home.*

"Jesse!"

Through the smoke he heard Kathleen. Just knowing she loved him eased his pain. He had lost so much on this trip through time, but he had gained so much more. "Kathleen, where are you?" He found her crouched on the floor, Elijah clinging to her. "Katie, we've got to go, we're out of time."

"I know." She tried to move out of Elijah's grasp, but the boy's arms tightened around her neck. "Elijah, let go. You can't stay here, it's too dangerous. You've got to get out."

"But they promised I could go with them!" the boy cried. "They promised."

"I know." Kathleen glanced up at Jesse, then quickly turned back to Elijah. "Listen to me." She firmly gripped his shoulders. Lifting him to his feet, she steered him toward the open door. "Your father needs you. I promise, he's going to get better. And whether you believe it or not, Libby loves you, too. You've got to go to them, now."

She could hear the men shouting outside, and she heard the first splashes of water as the bucket brigade began their futile work. There wasn't a moment to spare. She pulled away from Elijah.

"No," he wailed, trying to lunge back into her arms. His hand grazed down the side of her face to her neck and his fingers closed around the cameo brooch.

Jesse grabbed Elijah around the waist and pulled him away from Kathleen. She felt a strong tug at her neck as the brooch ripped away from her gown. Frantic, she reached out for Elijah's hand. The boy and the brooch were gone.

"Kathleen, now!" Jesse seized her arm, dragging her toward the middle of the barn, where Tooter had once placed the red tape.

"My cameo!" she cried. "Elijah's got it." She tried to twist away but Jesse's grip tightened as the smoke swirled and danced up around them.

"To hell with your brooch." He pulled her into his arms, drawing her tight against his body, holding her head against his shoulder. "Kathleen, my Katie-girl, listen to me. I love you too much to lose you now. Whether we stay or go home, or spin in oblivion forever, whether that brooch makes a difference or not, whatever happens, we go together." He tipped her chin up. "And I'm going to kiss you till we get there." He settled his mouth over hers, his kiss deepened, and the world around them began to change.

Lifting up and over, around and down, the smoke completely closed around them, embracing them in silence. The sound of the fire was gone. The shouts of the men outside were gone. Only the two of them existed, wrapped in each other's arms.

"JEEZ, FOLKS, ARE you guys all right?" Tooter led Egypt and Arthur Summers toward the front of the barn. "That's the damnedest thing I've ever seen." He handed each of them an iced bottle of water. "I never thought those light bars would explode like that and all that smoke, phew!" He unscrewed the cap on a bottle for himself. "I coulda sworn there were flames shooting up the walls and into the hay, must've been one of them optical illusions from the lights that were still working." He turned to his camera crew. "Hey, guys, see what you can do about getting this smoke outta here. We're gonna get this shot done today and that's that."

Egypt placed her bejeweled fingers on Tooter's arm. "Where'd Kathleen and Jesse get to? I haven't seen them since the horse went nuts."

"You don't have to worry about Jesse." Tooter laughed. "The moment this damned thing hit, I bet he scooted out the back door and took little Miss Kathleen with him."

"I wouldn't be so sure," Arthur Summers replied, pointing toward the back of the barn.

The smoke moved in a slow whorl, dissipating into fine wisps that disappeared before their eyes. In moments it had disappeared, all but a light magical misting around Jesse and Kathleen.

"Well, I'll be," Tooter breathed, unable to take his eyes off the sight before him. "That boy sure does know how to kiss and when to get the action started." He turned to Egypt and winked. "I don't know what the hell is in that smoke, but looking at those two, maybe you and me should get in there and grab us some of it."

Unaware of Tooter, and Egypt and the crew, Jesse held on to Kathleen. He was afraid to let go of her, afraid if he did she'd disappear into the smoke, and be lost to him forever.

"Hey, Horse, give it a rest, man. You're beginning to embarrass me."

Startled, Jesse pulled away from Kathleen. It took him a few moments to get his bearings. Feeling Kathleen's body trembling, he looked down and saw the question in her beautiful gray eyes. He kissed her tears away from her cheeks and drew her into his arms again. "Yes, we made it, Katie-love. We made it home."

"Jesse, look, your hair." She held one of his braids in her hand. "Your hair isn't cut." In the next instant her hand flew to her throat, and her fingers closed around the cameo brooch. "I thought Elijah took it. Your hair, my brooch . . . what happened? I don't understand."

"Time happened, sweetheart." He touched his finger to

her mouth before she could reply. "I have my hair back because that's how it was when we . . . left."

"If that were so, then my cameo . . ."

"Didn't you say that the cameo had been passed down through your family?" He smiled when she nodded. "Your brooch had to stay with Elijah so he could give it to his bride, so it could come to you." He kissed her forehead. "It's back where it belongs." He kissed the curl of her ear and whispered, "And your time machine theory doesn't work. Time passed over there, but here it stood still and waited for us. We're right back where we started from."

Kathleen pressed her body against him, tipping her hips into him. "Oh, no, I think we're far beyond where we started from." Standing on tiptoe and not caring who was watching, Kathleen pulled Jesse's head down and teased his lips with her own.

"You two are acting too weird, Horse. Cut it out, you're spookin' me." Tooter nervously glanced around. "This don't have anything to do with that *waŋagi* or *gigi*, or whatever you called it, that you were talking about, does it?"

A song, high-pitched, yet full-bodied, old and Lakota, rose out of the air and filled the barn with its eerie sound.

A smile slowly settled on Jesse's mouth as he stared up into the loft, the loft where in another time, another barn, three Lakota boys died.

"Jesse," Kathleen whispered, "what's happening?"

"*Tokalu Sapa*," he replied, his voice soft and respectful as the boy's spirit rose in song. "*Ni olowampi ta'*. He is singing his death song."

Tooter walked to the back door and yelled toward Bobby Big Bow's camp. "Hey, Bobby, I thought I told you not to let them kids play their powwow tapes outside."

"Some crazy, 'Skin." Jesse laughed, wrapping his arm around Kathleen's shoulder, taking her out into the sunlight. "That crazy Kiowa doesn't know anything about being Indian."

Kathleen stopped him before they reached the hill to the parade ground. "Look." She pointed at the new gymnasium and the outdoor basketball court. "I liked it the old way a lot better."

Jesse pulled her into his arms. "This will never change."
He kissed the tip of her nose. Before his lips touched hers,
he said the words again. *"Ta'ku kin oyás'in isáηbya cantéciciye."*

"You promised you'd tell me what that means."

"Yeah, Katie-love, I know."

# Chapter 28

If the Great Spirit had desired me to be a white man, he would have made me so in the first place. He put in your heart certain wishes and plans; in my heart he put other and different desires. Each man is good in the sight of the Great Spirit.

—SITTING BULL

"ARE YOU GOING to carry that book around with you for the rest of your life? We've got a TV show to watch, Mrs. Spotted Horse." Jesse settled back on the couch, wrapped his arms around Kathleen, and pulled her back against his chest.

"Isn't it amazing how it just dropped into our laps? You have no idea how long everyone looked for this. We knew the diary had to exist because of the gap in the set of journals. Mid-July through December of 1886 were missing." She caressed the cover, her fingers tracing the embossed date. "My father searched through the school's library, Providence's office and even the apartment, time and time again." Her hand stilled. "The desk drawer never fit properly but we all thought it was because it was warped. We never imagined that the missing journal was tucked behind it." She paused and drew a deep breath. "If we'd only tried to fix the drawer sooner."

"Maybe the book wasn't supposed to be found until now. Fate sometimes plays funny games like that."

"Perhaps you're right," Kathleen said. "I can't believe what Providence wrote, though."

"It answers a lot of questions, doesn't it?"

"And poses a lot, too." Kathleen began to thumb

through the handwritten pages. "If anyone had found it before now, before we did, Providence probably would have been declared insane." She pressed the palm of her hand down on an open page. "How did he know? How did he know who we were? How did he know where we had come from?"

"I don't think he did at the time," Jessie replied, "but he sure figured it out after we left." Jesse covered Kathleen's hand with his. "And, once he'd written everything down, he knew he had to hide it . . . just like you're going to."

"No!" Kathleen brushed Jesse's hand aside, closed the diary, and tightly clutched it against her heart. "It's part of the set. It's part of DuBois history and should be in the archives."

"And how will *you* explain what he wrote?" Jesse gently took the book from her and put it on the table beside the sofa. "It's best that it stay missing."

"But . . ."

"It won't be lost, sweetheart, but it will be safe. You'll know where it is and be able to read it whenever you want."

Her shoulders slumped as a deep sigh fled her lips. She snuggled against him, her resignation clear. "Yes, I know. You're right."

"I love you." Jesse's arms tightened around her and he nuzzled at her ear. "I love cuddling with you, and I love watching you get fat." He lightly rubbed his hand over her well-rounded belly.

Kathleen laughed. "You'd be this big, too, if you'd been pregnant for a hundred and seventeen years and eight and a half months."

"How's my boy doing?"

She shifted against Jesse and tried to get comfortable. "He's practicing his powwow moves right now." She winced as the baby's heel rode the wall of her womb.

"I wish he'd hurry up and dance on out of there so we can start practicing for a new occupant." Jesse placed a trail of tiny nibbles and kisses along the rim of her ear. "What do you say we start our own tribe?"

Kathleen giggled then ducked her head away and

pointed at the TV. "Shh. Watch. Here it comes." She pushed the volume button on the remote. "Jesse, I'm so excited I can't stand it!" She gazed at the screen as the camera scanned the audience. "Oh, look! There's Tooter and Egypt!"

"The boy doesn't look too bad in a tux, does he?"

"Look at Egypt. She's starting to show, too. It's wonderful, isn't it? You two are best friends and our boys will be, too."

A list of the nominees filled the TV screen and Kathleen's nerves drew tight as a bowstring. She grasped Jesse's hand.

"Okay, okay, here we go," Jesse whispered, a slight nervous quiver in his voice. "Mel's reading the nominations." Jesse's arms tightened around Kathleen. "He's passing the envelope to Julia."

Julia Roberts leaned close to the microphone. "Ladies and gentlemen, the Oscar for Best Documentary Feature goes to . . ."

"Oh, Jesse!" Kathleen twisted out of Jesse's arms. "Quick, call Dr. Barnes. My water just broke!"

Berkley Books proudly introduces

# Berkley Sensation

a **brand-new** romance line
featuring today's **best-loved** authors—
and tomorrow's **hottest** up-and-comers!

Every month…
**Four sensational writers**

Every month…
**Four sensational new romances** from
historical to contemporary,
suspense to cozy.

Now that Berkley Sensation is around…

**This summer is going to
be a scorcher!**